Our dad was a larger than life character and a fantastic, happy influence

"Sorry we couldn't get them in print while you were still here!"

Your three boys

About the author

"Allingham" 1936 – 2012

Allingham spent a happy childhood in Halifax the third and youngest child of William, a Welsh born policeman, and Winifred, a local Yorkshire lass.

Apprenticed at 16 to a local iron foundry Allingham's progression to qualified engineer was interrupted by two years of national service, serving as a subaltern in the 1st Guards Brigade. Qualifying as a professional engineer didn't limit his work experiences and over the succeeding decades Allingham travelled to over 65 countries, pursuing careers in public relations, local government, retailing, brewing and innkeeping.

Founding the journal Hong Kong Engineer before his thirtieth birthday and writing all its early leaders demonstrated Allingham's interest in writing, confirmed by a lifetime producing professional technical papers as well as writing, for his own interest, a series of short stories, light verses and other narratives.

In retirement and drawing on a lifetime of rich experience Allingham was at last able to work full time on his final opus: The Grey Haired Knights. This series of four whimsical fantasy novels tells the stories of four 70 year old codgers inspired by the spirit of King Arthur's Merlin to each undertake their own life-affirming Quest.

Published 2017

G2 Entertainment Ltd

ISBN 978-1-782-81-4290

Printed in Europe

The Grey Haired Knights

Four old men, all alike in dignity,
In vile rehab held long incarcerate,
All agree to forget infirmity,
Sense of age, and escape to face their fate.
The four together pledge, as Grey Haired Knights,
To go alone to seek a worthy quest,
A chance for them to put some wrongs to rights,
And then return with stories of their test.
In Avalon, King Arthur restless dreams,
Fearful that his story might be forgot,
He sends Merlin, to make sure the men's schemes
Will add to the legend of Camelot.
What this twelve-line synopsis fails to tell,
My stories of their ventures do full well..

Allingham

Book 2
Tristan's Quest

Prologue

After the Roman Legions left Britain, the dark ages that followed shrouded events from written record. However, during those dark troubled times, the songs and ballads of itinerant minstrels, together with the fireside stories told by father to son, kept alive memories of King Arthur, his Queen Guenivere, and the Knights of Camelot's Round Table. In the eighth century Nennius, a Welsh writer wrote down the mysteries of King Arthur, as historical fact. Two hundred years later, Geoffrey of Monmouth followed with his 'History of the Kingdom of Britain'. In his account, he not only told of Arthur, but also attached to him the ideas of chivalry, courtly behaviour, and justice. He also told of Arthur's magician Merlin. In the second half of the fifteenth century, Sir Thomas Malory set down eight epic tales, in twenty-one books in his more famous 'Le Morte DArthur', to bring together many earlier French and English texts. All this was serious stuff for scholars. In recent times, others have developed the adventures in novels, plays, musicals and film. Thus, for more than a thousand years, stories about King Arthur, the wizard Merlin, and the Knights of the Round Table have inspired men of all ages.

From the time of the great battle that destroyed Camelot, King Arthur lay wounded in Avalon, restless but immortal, waiting for his time to return to restore good governance to a corrupted world.

Preface

If you have not read 'Arthur's Quest', the first of four books in the saga of the 'Grey Haired Knights', I think that for you to understand Tristan it is important that I, tell you as much as you need to know about his life before he took on his quest.

I shall begin before the beginning. That is before King Arthur's magician Merlin inspired Arthur Thomas, Tristan Edward, Percival St. John-Matthews and Geraint Mostyn-Evans, with his idea that each should take on a worthwhile quest to keep alive the spirit of Camelot.

London's East End was not an idyllic setting for Tristan's childhood. He was born when rationing was still in force on bread, potatoes, and some other staples. London was still recovering from the Second Word War.

His mother told him that she had divorced his father, a dockworker, because he was often so drunk that he could not hold down a decent job, or the breakfasts she cooked to sober him up.

During his early teens, Tristan was a loner. He did not mix with any of the local teenage gangs, but he was often in trouble for hacking off school during the day to earn money doing odd jobs for stallholders in the Spitalfields or Brick Lane markets.

He was an un-artful dodger, a chancer. He used the money he earned to go to the greyhound track in the evening where he would get sympathetic grown-ups to place bets for him.

He added to his problems by smoking strong un-tipped cigarettes and drinking Mackeson stout, the easiest drink to con shopkeepers to let him buy, 'For his poor old mum who was sick in bed'.

The man who moved in to live with his mother thought it best not to interfere between Tristan and his mother. His mother agreed. She thought it best not to interfere with her only child.

Tristan's first proper job was as a plonger, a pot washer, in the kitchen of one of London's large hotels. The chefs were so brutal that, aged 17, he sought shelter by joining the army.

The move assured him of food, a bed and laundry. After two years with an infantry regiment, he thought he was lucky when he wangled a transfer to the Catering Corps. It was not a good move.

While working in the kitchen of the Officers Mess, he developed a lifelong love of good food, fine wines and cigars. His Sergeant Cook called them 'Extra rations'. They gave him aspirations he could not afford.

Like many young soldiers, he fell into the trap of a brief relationship with a pretty young woman, unhappy with her home life. She pressurized him into a hastily arranged marriage by claiming to be pregnant, for no other reason than soldiers could get married quarters.

Tristan, who could not accept the idea of a fixed long-term relationship, had a lucky roll up win on the horses. He bought himself out of the army and took jobs on cruise liners to stay away from England.

He never saw or heard from his wife again, nor did he ever again have a roll up win. Because she did not pursue him for paternity benefit, he assumed that she had not been 'Up the duff', the term for pregnancy amongst squaddies in those days.

Feckless by nature, Tristan needed jobs that provided accommodation, clean sheets and prepared meals. His need drove him to work in the 'Hospitality racket', as he referred to it. He had found shelter; in hotels, inns, clubs, pubs, restaurants, and cruise ships. When asked what he did for a living, Tristan always tapped one side of his nose with his forefinger before he would reply, "You name it old boy, been there, done that." A 'Dapper Dan' sort of man, he wore light Prince of Wales check suits and white collared striped shirts with a narrow formal bow tie, instead of a more usual necktie or open collar.

Never once had he worn a clip on tie, or a floppy silk spotted affair favoured by what he called 'Arty-farty types'. He actively disliked men of such ilk. He could carry off the role of a toff with his assumed far back clipped voice.

He deliberately dropped the final 'g' in words such as hunting shooting and fishing, expressed in his affected laconic drawl as, huntin, shootin and fishin. He thought it made him sound rather grand.

During his career, Tristan had held several well-paid posts but he had never accumulated any wealth, because his most serious addiction was to gamble.

He gambled recklessly, on horses mainly, however dogs would do, or spread betting on football if, in his words, "There was not much on."

Unless the risk was high, Tristan did not gamble. Win or lose, it had to affect, significantly, his immediate future. He did not see the point if a punt did not seriously affect his options.

A habitual gambler, Tristan also bet on career moves.

He never stopped looking for the big chance, changing jobs as frequently as many men bought a new pair of socks. Over the years, the cocktail of pills to make him sleep, stimulants to keep him awake, Valium to calm him down, 60 cigarettes and countless cups of strong black coffee every day, had taken its toll.

Stress added further pressure. He had been resident manager of a small hotel unit in Bradford until, during one of his frequent bad tempered outbursts, he had told the hotel directors, who would not let him run the hotel in the way he wanted, to get someone else to do the job, because he was not going to run a hostel for P45 dropouts.

He had been astonished when they did what he asked. They gave him his own P45. It left him homeless.

Aged sixty-two his body gave up; he collapsed while working out his notice. An ambulance took him to a hospital where staff brought him round, but after a few days, they sent him to a drug dependency unit. After assessment, a psychiatrist referred Tristan to the Laurels, a NHS rehabilitation unit where, once again, he had the consolation of a bed, clean sheets and regular meals.

Tristan called the Laurels, 'Ratchet's Retreat', after nurse Ratchet in 'One flew over the Cuckoo's Nest'. Management incompetence had made the Laurels a dreadful place. In a drive for economy, the NHS had combined the rehabilitation unit with a geriatric care home. The overheated, over carpeted combined facility had the inevitable smell of urinary incontinence.

Life amongst the mentally feeble had begun to wear down Tristan's will to live. The failure of the consultants responsible for his rehabilitation to take responsibility for his discharge exacerbated his condition.

Although difficult to approach socially, Arthur Thomas, Percival St.John Matthews and Geraint Mostyn Evans, all long-term patients in the Laurels rehabilitation unit befriended Tristan.

All four men felt a common bond because the Laurels, a truly dreadful place, had incarcerated them, unnecessarily, for far too long. The geriatric female residents of the Laurels had had the most profound effect on the men who for months had sat together at a small round table for their meals and clubbed together in an anti-room to play cards, with a chair lodged against the door to prevent intrusion.

They felt their dignity defiled by the Laurels careless mix of gender and extremes of competence with incontinence, both mental and physical. They feared most, the women they called 'Predators'; the ones who sought them out to ask if they would do little jobs for them. "Would you just fix my television?" or perhaps it was a bedside light, or "Would you fit these batteries to my radio, it's a 'Roberts' you know, my late husband bought it for me."

These petty requests were not real, just a predator's device to get into a one to one situation with any man. It did not matter which of the men a predator approached, it was merely a ruse to make another woman jealous.

Arthur Thomas, the eldest of the four proposed that on Sunday evenings, to stave off mental decline, which seemed to negate any improvement brought about by rehabilitation, instead of playing cards, or watching television, they should tell stories, in the way of Scheherazade, the Decameron, or the Canterbury Tales.

They were never to know, nor did they ever seek to know, that King Arthur, resting in Avalon, from time to time sends Merlin to keep alive in the hearts of ordinary men, the dream of Camelot and its code of chivalry and that Merlin had chosen Arthur Thomas to do his work.

Enthused by Arthur, along with Geraint and Percival, Tristan, 'Escaped' from the Laurels, ready to meet at the Crown Hotel in Scagill for what turned out to be an inaugural dinner of the 'Grey Haired Knights'. Each man pledged to put aside old age and infirmity, ready to go alone to find and follow a worthy quest. By their solemn vow to return, one year hence, they unwittingly changed a whimsical idea into an irrevocable commitment that had fateful consequences.

The stories of Percival's and Geraint's quests will follow, as will the stories of other noble valiant quests yet to come, before the Once and Future King can return to set to rights all that has gone amiss.

Chapter 1

When Tristan Edward woke in a room in the Crown Inn Scagill it was Mid-Summer day, the first time in many months that he had not been in a hospital bed or in a room in an NHS rehabilitation unit.

He had woken uncertain of his future. This strange uncertainty worried him; it was unusual. He had always been a gambler, with a gamblers certainty that his next move would be life changing for the better. Tristan never bet on small odds.

He was confused. He had spent the previous evening in the Crown Inn's old-fashioned dining room, at a round table, eating a superb dinner in good fellowship with Arthur Thomas, a retired police superintendent, Perceval St. John Matthews, a retired schoolmaster and Gareth Mostyn Evans, a retired engineer.

They were all men with a full head of grey hair, in years near to the biblical allotted life span of three score years and ten. They had not met together as a club, an association, or a company.

Their bond was personal. During the afternoon, before they met for dinner, all four men had absconded from the horrors of the 'Laurels, a dread rehabilitation unit incorporated with a geriatric care home full of dementia patients.

Their long tedious incarceration during treatment had reduced their spirits. It had started to erode their will to live. To counter their despondency, by gentle inducement and example, Arthur Thomas had persuaded them to tell stories, on Sunday evenings. Sundays were the worst day of the week, the most boring, because they did not have the five-day week therapists and consultants to engage in banter.

When Arthur's second turn came around, he did not tell a story. He inspired them to believe in the idea of Camelot, not as a lost place of legend, but as a present reality in which they could play their part.

He had dubbed them Grey Haired Knights, charged them, severally, to defy old age, and their present infirmities, to find and follow an honourable quest. They had pledged to adopt the laws of chivalry, known to them as honesty, courtesy and good manners. Fatefully, each man had also vowed to return to the Crown Inn, on the Saturday after the next summer solstice, to tell true tales of their adventures.

In his room, without the company of the other men, Tristan doubted his ability to even part way live up to the ideals he had light heartedly vowed to follow. He even considered returning to the Laurels to ask the consultants for their advice, but quickly scrapped that idea; he had made a wager of his future. He would have to find and follow some sort of quest to see whether it turned out for better, or worse.

Tristan's break out from the Laurels, against the advice of his doctors as well as his therapists, had itself been a leap into the unknown, a risk in itself, without the added pledge to seek adventure.

Determined to break with his drug dependent habits, for which he was receiving treatment, he had neatly piled all his medication on top of his bedside cabinet. His stash included a mug full of co-proximal tablets and two bottles of whisky, previously kept hidden, ready for an alternative exit; an end he had considered more than once. He had left a note under the stack, "Not wanted on voyage, TATA- T.E"

Although captivated by Arthur Thomas's proposal that he should take on the mantle of a Grey Haired Knight, resolved to put aside old age and present infirmities, and make ready to take on a quest, Tristan Edward had no idea about what could, might, or possibly be such a quest.

However, the idea had not just captivated him; it had him wholly enthused. Tristan did not merely want to put off the natural progression of age; he wanted to live his life backwards, to simulate the legendary life of Merlin, the magician of King Arthur's court.

Vague thoughts began to coalesce into the idea that he would use his year long quest to unravel the tangle of his life that had left him stranded, without the three essential 'Fs' needed for a contented worthwhile life; family, friends and funds.

Alone in his room at the Crown Inn, Tristan could not think of any worthwhile cause that he could champion, a cause to fulfil the pledge he had made as a Grey Haired Knight. However, he hoped that during his years left over, if he used his experience of years past, he might be able to put to rights some of his many culpable mistakes, perpetrated wrong doings and misdemeanours.

He reasoned that the gift of hindsight, which only experience brings, would enable him to avoid the past pitfalls that had reduced him to a drug dependent nervous wreck, a loner, committed to a drug dependency clinic, followed by referral to the dread Laurels rehabilitation unit.

Tristan stayed in the comfortable room at the inn because he needed to get the most use of its facilities. Until he left the room, he had comfortable furniture, TV, radio, hot water, bath, shower and clean towels.

He also had provender, tea, coffee, cellophane wrapped packets of biscuits plus the bonus of a sachet of drinking chocolate.

As he sat in the bucket chair, to face the mirror on the dressing table, he reflected that this would be his last chance of comfort for many days, possibly for the whole of the year to come.

He analysed his situation with clarity. With no job, no pension, little money in the bank, less than the equivalent of two days average wage in his wallet, only a few coins in his pocket, by any measure of equity, economic consideration, fiscal, or financial, he declared himself bankrupt, insolvent, bust, skint, in fact, plain broke.

The printed tariff on the dressing table concerned him. With 'Single room occupancy listed at more than half of the money he had with him, he reckoned that when added to his share of the dinner with wine and drinks the night before, he would have little ready cash left.

Although he did not own an overcoat, Tristan felt well prepared for the day in his lightweight grey suite, blue shirt, narrow neatly tied dark blue bow tie with white polka dots. He felt satisfied that the bow tie picked him out as a gentleman.

When he finally decided to leave the sanctuary of the room, he left it three times. After he left for the first time, he went back to the bathroom to comb his hair for the third time since his shower. To build up stores for his journey, he took the last soap still in its fancy wrapper, and a shower cap. His innate honesty meant he could only take consumables, never property.

He returned for the second time to polish his shoes on the paper disposable bath mat.

On his third attempt, he reached the reception desk where he put on his practised lady-killer charm to speak to the young woman receptionist. She turned out to be the only disappointment to mar his high opinion of the Inn. "Good morning my dear, I am Edward, without the 's', leaving room 37 in good order. How little do I owe you?"

"Was your stay OK? Mr. Edwards," she said, with a rising infection on both the K and Edwards. "Edward is without the 's'," Tristan replied, calmly, "Most comfortable, thank you." Tristan looked at the bill the girl had passed to him, folded in a leather case. "Now-now young lady, you have forgotten to charge me for the damn fine dinner as well as for the drinks I had last night." Her reply was arch, "No Sir, there is no mistake. Company policy is to charge our customers no more or no less than they owe. Mr. Thomas paid for your dinner and drinks; he paid for all four at table 12. You owe for your room only, whether or not you had breakfast."

Despite a rise in his temper, he still managed to beam at the girl, "Never do, never have." Without any attempt to be civil the girl snapped, "Card?" Tristan raised his voice to a higher tone, one that carried over all the reception area, "Never had a card, debit or credit, never will. My father said, 'Cash is the only disbursement for a gentleman'. I see no reason to change; the sum is easily settled." From his wallet, Tristan put the notes to match the bill onto the counter.

Without hesitation, he added a tip greater than the usual ten percent. "Please make sure the Chef and plonger get their share. You do operate a tronc I hope. No need for a receipt, good day sweet child of the new ethos." As he passed quickly through the heavy doors, out into the street, his case behind him, Tristan did not hear the girl say, "See you Mr. Edward, without the 's', silly senile sod. There's three to take with you."

To improve his almost prison pallor, brought about by months of incarceration in the Laurels, Tristan sat to face the sun on a bench in a pedestrian precinct centre of town. A confusion of thoughts scrambled through his mind.

They spoke to him, as an outsider might speak. "Well Tristan Edward, I suppose you are only an Edward, without the 's', because your dipso father could not read what he had written when he registered your birth.

That must have been more than sixty years ago, before your mother threw him out. Your mother was useless, the fella she lived with not much better. Fair do's though, he did get you a job in the kitchen of the hotel on the Strand when you were fifteen. You did well to leave there to join the army. You did even better, when the chance came, to transfer from the infantry into the Catering Corps."

Comfortable and warm in the sun, Tristan began a mental argument with himself. "Silly sod, while you were in the Catering Corps you acquired most of your bad habits to add to your unrealistic ideas. Those nights spent in the officer's mess kitchen, when you ate and drank the 'Extra rations' as the cook sergeant called them, they did you no good.

They gave you a taste for good food, vintage wines, mature Stilton, crusty old port, crusty as the colonel. All things you have never been able to afford.

When you left the army, you never stayed in a job for more than two years, not even on the cruise ships, or in the bars of the Costas and Balearics. You always had to go for jobs that provided shelter, beds with clean sheets and free food.

In return, the jobs demanded that you work the so-called un-sociable hours, the great misnomer. The need to be sociable, into the early hours of the next day, day after day, week in, week out, socialising with customers who were not always right, customers who worked a 37-hour week, nine to five.

Your long late night hours were the hours that led to your addictions. That is apart from your addiction to gamble on the gee–gees, the dogs, football, cards, or which of the drunks would be first to fall off his, or indeed in these days of equality, her bar stool.

That addiction is innate. What talent or experience can you possibly call on to fulfil the year to come with a worthy quest? The only thing that you can do well these days is to grow hair."

Despite all his confused memories and self-doubt, Tristan Edward felt, for the first time in months, that he had a future worth living. The thrill of yesterdays imagined 'escape' from the Laurels, that dreadful gulag that had held him incarcerate for too long, followed by the companionship of friends during last night's dinner, had made him resolve to start a new better life. "I shall make my way to London where I will conduct myself in the manner of a courteous knight; Arthur commands no less," he said aloud.

To himself, he made a solemn vow. "I will not fall back into the dark vale of Valium, or stumble on the rocky path of pills, potions, alcohol, caffeine and nicotine. I will not go that way into the anti-room of death."

From his coat pocket, Tristan took a pack half-full of Philip Morris cigarettes. He looked at it for a long time before he dropped it into a council waste bin. "Goodbye for good, silent white habited assassins.

My next smoke will be a Havana cigar, in a year's time, when I shall return to the Crown Inn for the reunion dinner with my fellow knights."

After he carefully considered the alternatives of travelling to London by train or bus, quicker by train, cheaper by bus, he chose neither. He opted to take to the open road, to hitch hike. To hitch hike, he would need to buy the essential kit, a good overcoat, a descent hat, a brief case and a walking stick.

Even if he bought them all from charity shops, he knew they would cost more than the bus fare; nevertheless, as tangible assets they would keep their value for some time, whereas the bus ticket could only be an asset until journey's end.

From the stories that Tristan had read about King Arthur and his Knights of the Round Table, he knew that when every knight started out on a quest, he first met a dark impenetrable forest of thorns.

Tristan realised that, following tradition, he had met his first forest of thorns, 'Closed on Sundays'. None of his usual 'Gentleman's Outfitters' would be open for business. Charity shops do not open on Sundays. It meant that he would have to survive for a day and a night, until business would resume on Monday mid-morning.

He knew, from experience, that street charity does not begin until ten a.m. To survive, he would have to eat. The two digestive biscuits he ate for breakfast, with the other two in his pocket, would not sustain him.

Without a credit or debit card to draw money from a hole in the wall, Tristan had to find somewhere to sleep that would not cost more than his very limited ready cash.

After more than two hours of random thought and speculation, Tristan stood up, stiff in all joints from his ankles through knees, hips and spine to his neck.

He moved because he felt anxious. In the distance, but coming his way, he could see a policeman who might question him since he had already passed him twice.

The second time he had given Tristan a policeman's careful look. He did not want the officer to question him. He feared that he might have him on his list of missing persons.

Tristan worried that he would have a duty, if not the authority, to take him back to the Laurels.

Tristan walked away awkwardly, his case that had supermarket trolley syndrome bumped along behind him. In East Gate, he saw a board that advertised the 'Wheatsheaf's all day Carvery'. Hunger made him decide to chance it.

Unlike his dinner at the Crown Inn, the meal did not please him, though it did fill him, at little cost. The dark interior of the pub, together with the smell of food left too long, turned his stomach. It sent him back out into the June sunshine where he relaxed on one of the many benches provided by the council.

Later, the evening peal of bells from the Parish Church told him that it was still Sunday.

They prompted Tristan to think about religion, even though he had never been to a church service, not even to a funeral, not since church parades during his time in the army.

Although unsure whether or not his parents had had him Christened or baptised, Tristan knew that he had no faith to confirm. He found it odd that he thought about religion. It bothered him, because he remembered that in the Arthurian legends, before a postulate could receive the accolade, he had to spend a vigil night of contemplation in church.

Tristan's quiet thoughts were disturbed when he became aware of a peculiar man, who seemed old, yet somehow ageless, almost skipping, directly, purposely, towards him.

Tristan noticed that his thin black walking stick would not be the choice of an old man. The man, old or ageless, certainly eccentric, embarrassed Tristan, because he sat down close to where he sat, on the same bench, even though nearby benches was unoccupied.

The fellows long limp beard, of extremely fine white hair, under a droopy moustache, marked him out as more peculiar than eccentric.

He had a long nose on which perched an odd pair of spectacles. Each lens had a different shape. Despite the warm summer weather, he wore a full-length dark green cotton smock, a long college scarf round his neck, green duck canvas trousers over worn down trainers. Obviously uncomfortably hot, to fan his face he used the biggest olive green waterproof hat with a stitched brim that Tristan had ever seen.

The old man astonished Tristan when he addressed him as though he had met an old friend, "There you are, sure to be, same for me too by damn, isn't it?"

To Tristan the man's voice seemed to be not much more than a squeak, but it carried the unmistakable tones of the Rhondda. With his head on one side, he peered at Tristan, as though he had to check that he had found the particular person to whom he must speak. "Good to hear the church bells calling to evensong the few too lazy to get out of bed this morning to take communion to absolve them of the sins that they care to admit to, forgetting that God remembers the sins they care to forget. You will go to church will you not, sure to, grand idea. Sanctuary, gives a chap time to think. Often as not, it puts a wanderer on the right path. When the peal stops, the toll starts, then it is five minutes to

25

eyes down and bended knees. You had better hurry, but it won't be a full house."

The familiarity and appearance of the old man made Tristan uncomfortable. Prompted by the urge to get away from the eccentric, and the same policeman approaching again, Tristan thought the church would be somewhere cool to sit undisturbed, to think about his year to come, perhaps a suitable place to spend an hour of the longest day of the year.

The service had started when Tristan slipped into church during the first hymn. He took a seat in a side pew at the back where he sat alone, quietly. He took no part in the service.

None of the few souls who made up the small congregation came near. He leaned forward to put his elbows on the ledge where hymnbooks, prayer books and other elbows had rested for hundreds of years. He felt comfortable with his chin on the thumb pads of his clasped finger-interlocked hands.

Hardly conscious of the service, he did not notice the sparse congregation straining, always failing, to reach the too high notes of the hymns played in a key chosen by the organist who, like many of his kind, played for choirs not congregations. The mid-summer evening sun that streamed through the stained glass west windows caused him to marvel at the patterns made by countless particles of dust caught in the beams of coloured light. The effect drew from him a solemn promise, "Whatever I do, wherever I go, I will try to let a bit of light into people's lives."

"Do you plan an all-night vigil?" the vicar's cheery voice did not awake Tristan from sleep. It recalled him from another place, some other time, part dream, part imagination, part memory, or fantasy. Arthur Thomas, had become Merlin, dressed like a Disneyland wizard in a cloak covered in moons, stars and ciphers.

Except that instead of a conical hat, he wore a green waterproof hat with a stitched brim. In his strange fantasy, Merlin had cast spells that had turned the managers of the Laurels into frogs. The old dementia patients from the geriatric care wing of the

Laurels, morphed into long legged herons, stabbed at the frogs with their beaks.

Brought back to realty by the vicar's question, Tristan's vision faded into his subconscious store of information. His promise to let light into people's lives did not leave him.

"Oh! Sorry vicar, I am afraid that my body and soul were not quite together, that is if I have a soul and not just an overpowered imagination, I am afraid that I have not been in church for many years. I will be off, though it is a strange coincidence that you should ask if I contemplated an all-night vigil. Earlier today I thought about the knights of King Arthur's Round Table, They had to spend a night long vigil in prayer before they could be dubbed a true knight."

The vicar sat down with Tristan, "I think I know who you are. If my imperfect memory has it right, you are one of the four men who went absent without leave from the 'Laurels' on Saturday. I saw you there on more than one occasion."

"Oh dear," Tristan mimicked his old cockney accent, "You have me bang to rights vicar, it's a fair cop." Then he added in a serious in tone, "I hope that you will not try to persuade me to return to that dreadful place. You see, Arthur, he is a retired policeman; he became a sort of leader of the four of us. He has given us hope, coupled with a determination to do something useful with what we have left of our lives, however short they may be. He persuaded us that the Laurels was a place of progressive forgetfulness that fostered slow decline and that the mental degeneration caused by incarceration in that so-called rehabilitation clinic cancelled out any improvement to our physical health. He decided that all four of us, including a nervous chap called Percival, should quit the Laurels. I do not know how he did it. He must be a bit of a wizard. I was half dreaming, half thinking of him when you put me back together. Tomorrow I go to London, but tonight I have a problem. I still have to find a cheap place to rest my head. Perhaps you know of some nearby clean digs. You

27

see, I have some difficulty with my wonky-wheeled suitcase. It seems reluctant to follow me."

Obviously genuinely concerned, the vicar said, "Well, I think that I can help you there. No, I will not grass you up. My wife and I live alone in a large Victorian vicarage that she sarcastically refers to as, 'Heaven on Earth'. It is a mansion with many rooms. They are not too cold at this time of year. Would that suit you?" Tristan replied, "Well yes, of course, however I do not want or need to cadge, I still have some money in my pocket, and some in the bank that I intend to liberate tomorrow."

The vicar cut him short, "My name is Branwell Evans, and you are?" "Tristan, Tristan Edward, Tristan the given name, Edward the surname, without the 's', it confuses people." Tristan replied.

"Well Tristan Edward, I noticed you said given name, not Christian name. Did your parents not have you christened, or is it that you have lost faith?" the vicar asked, but without waiting for Tristan to reply, he stood to offer Tristan his hand. "Come on, enough of my Spanish inquisition, my car is outside. Let's go home. With luck, there might be a cowboy or pirate film on the telly, although I doubt it. It will be the usual cops and robbers, or worse, particularly for you, a hospital drama."

In the car, vicar Branwell talked quietly. "I noticed that throughout this evening's service you did not move, nor did you appear to join in the prayers. You clasped your hands; you did not palm them as Jesus taught us, and the way we teach our children. Am I right?"

To his surprise, Tristan found it easy to answer, "Pretty well, I am so far from good and God that I do not think that I qualify to pray. I did think of God and mortality. For the first time in years, my thoughts were comfortable. The sunlight through the stained glass west windows cast patterns in the dust. It made me think. I thought of it as God's kaleidoscope. Perhaps there is a God, who can count every dancing shining speck. Perhaps he will not overlook me as I try to unravel my ravelled life."

Vicar Branwell said, "Tristan, you did well to come to church this evening. Do not be afraid to pray. If my entire congregation were as honest as you have been, I do not think I should ever hear the crack of knees in our church. I like your idea of the evening sun from our western windows that made God's Kaleidoscope with specks of dust. It will find its way into my sermon next Sunday, I am sure it will. I shall of course take the idea as my own."

"Please do Oscar, please do." Tristan said dryly.

The vicar picked up Tristan's reference to the story about Oscar Wild. "You seem to be well read." "Not really," Tristan replied, "Certainly not educated. My insomnia of recent years has allowed me a fair go at biography, history, a little old fashioned poetry, stuff that has both rhyme and meter. More often, I have read the novels of Nevil Shute and Alistair MacLean. I have struggled with Le Morte Darthur, some of Gibbon, Clark, the elder, not Alan the diarist, most of Churchill and all of John Masters' tales of the several generations of the Savage family in India. Of course, I have read Hornblower, and Flashman.

I confuse historical fiction with fact, but no one seems to notice. My favourite book is 'Wind in the Willows' with White's 'The Once and Future King' a close second. That is why I fell in so well with Arthur's idea that we should all take our leave of the Laurels, take a belated 'Gap Year' as Grey Haired Knights, and find a just cause to champion."

Vicar Branwell's wife turned not a hair at Tristan's unexpected arrival. She soon came in with a trolley set with tea, sandwiches and cakes to make him welcome, as an old expected friend. The three of them talked easily, amiably, until after the ten o'clock news when vicar Branwell showed him to a clean comfortable guest room. Tristan slept soundly, without dreams.

In the morning, his hosts insisted that he have a full breakfast before they let him go. Vicar Branwell came to the garden gate, to bid Tristan a safe journey. He gave Tristan a small sealed envelope; he told him that he must not open it unless his quest led him to the slough of despond.

Tristan carefully put the envelope into a concealed inner pocket of his wallet where he already kept the sprig of white heather Arthur had given him as proof that he had walked that night on Halter Moor. The two men shook hands leaving Tristan free to set off down the hill to Scagill's town centre, towing his recalcitrant suitcase.

Because of the excitement of the change from safe dull monotony of the Laurels, to the raw challenge to survive and prosper, Tristan held his head high, his shoulders back. His tread was determined. Vicar Branwell Evans stayed long at the gate, to watch Tristan's progress. He prayed for Tristan because he knew that he would not pray for himself, not yet, not until he had found his true vocation.

Chapter 2

When he was out of sight of Vicar Branwell Evans, who remained at the vicarage gate, Tristan Edward found his march to Scagill's town centre, trailing his wonky-wheeled suitcase, a trial. It took away his good humour.

It did not take away his determination find and follow some worthwhile quest, although he thought it odd that, as a non-believer, his doubts and fears of the previous day had gone when he thought of God's Kaleidoscope in the parish church.

To follow his quest to London, in his new station in life, Tristan was sure that he must take cash in hand. With this idea in mind, for the first time in many years, Tristan experienced the thrill of freedom. Free of any responsibility, his acerbic old self, not the new Knight Errant, urged him to have some fun with the bank that had often treated him with callous disregard, sometimes stretching to contempt.

He decided to withdraw all bar one pound of his meagre funds. The bank where he had money in a current account had once been the Yorkshire Penny Bank. The building still dominated Scagill's main street with its huge beaten brass panelled double doors big enough to double for St Peters Basilica.

Tristan knew that such doors spoke of an earlier time when local folk founded the bank, as a philanthropic organisation, a time when Yorkshire banks dealt with Yorkshire folk. It dealt in hard bargains when local industry made brass, manufacturing toffee, biscuits, beer, machine tools, cast iron boilers, carpets, worsted textiles, and woollen blankets.

The fallout from over three hundred factory chimneystacks coated the town buildings, the people, and even the grass and trees with black acidic grime. Although the building, newly cleaned, still stood arrogantly proud, the once great bank had gone, almost forgotten, unbelievably subsumed after many mergers into the National Bank of Australia.

After Tristan had queued in the lofty banking hall, for longer than his limited patience could tolerate, he finally stood, supplicant, before the starchy middle-aged woman who presided behind the safety glass counter screen.

She had no words to greet him. Her crow lined unsmiling stone-faced stare rubbed him the wrong way. He saw his opportunity to poke fun at the rigid formality of banking halls the world over.

Putting on his most affected laid-back voice, he spoke loud enough so all around could hear. "Oh Queen in your counting house, before the crows peck off your nose, count out my cash; give it back to me. You have paid it too little interest, both fiduciary and socially. You have kept it far too long. I have need of it for I am off to make my fortune in London town."

"Cheque book," the woman answered, in 'dalek' tones, without a flicker of recognition or humour. Cheekily Tristan said loudly, "Sorry, I do not have such a book, nor have I a passing pig on which to write. I have not used the document for so long that I have no idea where it is, where it might be, or whether it is extant. It has probably biodegraded. If you will just give me my money, I shall say no more about it. My surname is Edward, without the 's', Tristan the single given name."

Without a word of explanation, or change of expression, the woman pulled down the grey screen behind the glass in front of him. It snapped into place, to obscure whatever she might be up to, if she was up to anything at all.

The people in the queue behind Tristan muttered and tut-tutted, quite audibly, because his behaviour and her retaliatory action has reduced the number of counter clerks available to deal with their business.

Un-abashed, Tristan smiled serenely at anyone who caught his eye. Several minutes passed before the screen snapped open again. The image of an Easter Island head used her dalek voice to project past Tristan the one word, "Him," before she addressed the next customer with an equally abrupt, "Next."

From behind Tristan, a conspicuously bald little man who wore a brown suit with ballpoint pens and pencils sticking out chaff from his top pocket said, "Mr. Edwards, please, my name is Mr. Brown; I am the Deputy Assistant Manager with responsibility for customer relations. Please come with me to the 'Discrete room', if you would not mind."

Tristan replied, loud enough for all in the banking hall to hear, "Certainly, Mr. Browns, if by Edwards you mean me; Edward is my surname, without an's'". He continued in the same loud voice, "How long have you used robotic counter clerks Mr. Browns? They are amazing are they not, particularly the one that countered my simple request? I agree that it looked almost human. Of course it's the blankness behind the eyes that gives them away as cyborgs."

Closeted with the manager in the tiny discrete room, Tristan did not give him a chance to open any discussion, "My dear Browns, all that I want is all of my money, save for one pound. You have it; I need it. That can't be too difficult, can it?"

Mr. Brown, who struggled to establish what custom demanded as the correct order of things, finally managed, "Well, it's all most irregular Mr. er Edward is it? We have been trying to contact you for more than a year. Your account has been dormant.

All of our letters have either been unanswered or returned, as not known at the last address you gave us."

"Well, I am here Mr. Brown, in person," Tristan said, "Just try to remember where in your vast emporium you have stashed my cash. If you let me have it, I shall not bother you again for at least another year. That is the way we chaps in my line of business have to work." Tristan meaningfully rubbed the side of his nose with his extended index finger of his right hand. Mr. Brown, who realised that he had lost the initiative, looked most uncomfortable. He asked Tristan to wait.

A little while later, he came back with a chequebook and a printed statement of Tristan's current account; his only account. "You do have a small amount in credit with us Mr. Edward. I hope that you have substantial assets with other reliable institutions; one must always save for a rainy day you know. The Post Office returned this chequebook to us late last year. You see, as far as we knew, you could have been deceased."

"Oh I was I was, well as good as; you will understand that I am not allowed to tell you about that." Tristan, still enjoying himself, winked twice, slowly, again assuming gravitas, he rubbed the side of his nose with the index finger of his right hand.

He made out a cash cheque for all but one pound of the available funds. Keeping a straight face, Tristan said, "That will leave you with a nice round figure to look after. Please keep it secure with my chequebook. I don't want to be tempted to use it to cash in the rest of my savings, not where I have to go."

When Mr. Brown gave him his bank notes and change, Tristan slipped them straight into his pocket before he walked out of the bank, with his case trailed behind him.

Mr. Brown followed, bleating, "Mr. Edward, Mr. Edward, you have not given me your new address, nor have you checked to see if the money I gave you is correct."

Tristan turned to look down on the little bald brown suited man. He raised his voice so that everyone could hear, "Little man, you did not give me the money, it was not yours to give, you merely returned it. It is bank arrogance to think that the money in the vault is theirs to give and take. As to my address, Tristan Edward, guest of the world will do. As to my not counting the money you returned, yours is the job of checking detail, as a deputy assistant branch manager, bracket, customer relations, close bracket, it is what you must do. It is the reason why you must stay here at the branch to balance the daily deposits and disbursements to the penny, a coin that once, together with the County name, gave the bank its name. I have a life to get on with, good day."

Walking back through the banking hall, Mr. Brown blustered, as he tried to regain some authority. He called out to the woman counter clerk who had been unable to deal with Tristan Edward, without the 's', "Thank you Miss Gutteridge; we do have to put up with all sorts of peculiar people these days, don't we just. No respect, no understanding, no manners at all." To himself the branch customer relations manager added, "Toffee nosed, bow tied, bad mannered, pretentious vindictive old git."

However, before he reached the sanctuary of his office, he turned to look again at the counter clerk. Neither her face or body language had changed, nor had her voice. Taken together they registered zero on the personality scale. She did not speak in paragraphs, or sentences, not even in vernacular phrases, just words, spat out in single gobs. "Dull witted, inarticulate, monosyllabic menopausal moron," he thought, "No wonder people use the robot in the wall to draw out cash." Not for the first time he decided to apply for early retirement.

Back in Broad Street, Tristan sat happy in the sunshine; he felt complete.

On his back, his wardrobe, in his pockets the sum of his wealth, bar the one pound still in the bank.

His case contained the rest of his property, two shirts, two ties, a spare pair of slacks, underwear, socks, shaving kit, hairbrush and his old travel alarm clock. He had never felt better. Tristan recognised that what he had was all that he had, and what he had was very little.

The financial and material poverty did not concern him. It sent a charge of energy through his whole being, both physical and mental. He said to himself, "You may be down, but wherever one starts out in this country, one goes up to London, so get up, get on; don't faff about."

The generally run down appearance of Scagill's high streets might have saddened Tristan but the several charity shops that competed with each other to sell clothes, books and tat, cheered him. The charity shops rather than commercial retail shops raised his hopes. From charity shops, he could buy the sort of hitchhiker's kit that had always worked well for him in the past. In the Sue Ryder shop, for three pounds, he purchased an overcoat fit for a funeral director. In 'Help the Aged', the lady assistant said they did not have any hats; however, she offered to bring in one of her late husband's, if he would care to call again. This gave Tristan's vanity a boost, as she appeared to be 'All of a flutter' as she served him. He did not realise that in return, he smoothed back the hair across his temples first with one hand then the other. In 'Cancer Research', he found the marks of upper class status he sought, a soft brown felt Trilby that he thought must have belonged to a racehorse trainer and a black silver topped cane, relict of a gentleman of wealth. As an afterthought, in Oxfam, he bought a white silk scarf, with tassels.

He thought it would remind him of Arthur Thomas who had inspired him to seek a new life. The total expenditure on his four purchases turned out to be less than the bus fare he would have had to pay to go in comfort to London.

In Oxfam, he failed to buy the only brief case that he found in any shop because the fearsome lady in charge would not haggle. Consequently, he settled, at thirty pence, for a green plastic carrier bag printed in gold with the upper crust 'Harrods' logo.

He thought the bag would add a touch of class and hide his suitcase from any driver who might wonder whether, or not, to give him a lift.

By early afternoon, he had completed his preparations to take to the road. Even though the morning had gone Tristan reckoned that the weather looked to stay good, which would give him more than eight hours of daylight to hitchhike to the Capital. To hitchhike he needed to get to the open road clear of Scagill.

To do it he spent more than he could afford on the regular service bus to Wakefield. He had to make a fuss with the driver before he would let him off at a non-designated stop that would make it easy for him to walk to junction 41 of the M1. The driver was not a companionable fellow. He wittered, "It's against company rules. I could lose my job mate." Sheer dramatic nonsense achieved what Tristan wanted. "Not to worry son, I don't want to get you the sack. I shall throw out my case and jump after it. If you slow down a bit, I should be OK. One does not forget the experience of over fifty jumps with second Para. Mind you the moors above Port Stanley and the burning sand of Suez were both a bit softer than abrasive granite dressed tarmac."

After the bus driver stopped the bus to drop Tristan off, where he wanted, he heard the driver shout after him, "Tosser."

Although still buoyant, Tristan thought, "That is the third person I have upset today, the woman counter clerk and the manager in the bank, now the bus driver. All good fun, however not the deeds of an honourable knight. I must curb my acerbic way. On further consideration Tristan adjudged his behaviour with the sharp tongued counter clerk fully justified."

Just short of the slip road to the M1, Tristan let all lorries go past, before he raised his cane, just a foot, at the same time as he gave a practiced shy smile only at oncoming cars with only a male driver. Only two failed to stop when he signalled and mouthed the word 'London' before he got lucky.

The obvious rep in his white shirt and tie took a hard look at him before he pulled over to call out, "Is Northampton any good?" Tristan said, "Oh yes, thank you, that will break the back of my journey. May I put my back breaking case in the boot?" He asked the rep to drop him off at Junction 16, knowing that he would be more likely to get a lift at a junction, than at a service station, because drivers leaving a service station could not afford any further delay.

His second lift turned out to be even better than the first. The car driver, a man about Tristan's age, took him straight into central London. He told him he was a bit tired, as he had driven down from Newcastle and thought that company and conversation would keep him awake.

He explained that he had been an architect and thought that it might be a good way to spend his retirement if he visited art galleries, including Tate Modern, to see if it did make any sense. "I am booked to stay in a Kensington hotel; will Kensington be alright for you?" "Just right," Tristan answered. During the whole journey, the two men chatted like old friends.

The retired architect dropped Tristan off in Kensington High Street in broad daylight, as he had hoped, because he knew that to hitchhike in the dark might not be a safe bet.

For old times' sake he made straight for a pub in Kensington Square where he used to enjoy its friendly atmosphere. He ordered a pint of Young's bitter, half of which he drank in one gulp. When the alcohol hit his empty stomach, his head swam for a second. The unexpected reaction forced him to sit down to plan what to do next. "Steady lad," he said to himself.

He realised that he had not eaten since his excellent breakfast with the vicar, more than twelve hours previously. "Best you get yourself fed and quartered somewhere safe for tonight at least. Kensington Gardens Hotel across the road is out of the question, it's the Cromwell Road for you old lad, back to the early days where you first managed a hotel."

Tristan slowly finished his pint. No one spoke or seemed to notice him. When he picked up his case, ready to walk to Cromwell Road, he smiled. He thought two hundred miles to London, in two lifts, counted as a good start to any quest.

A surly man, aged around forty-five, who wore a tank top that showed his tattooed arms, challenged him. He seemed to have taken offence at Tristan's smile. "What you laughing at pal?" "Oh nothing, I just feel good, I have had a good day, the first for many a long day," Tristan replied. "You watch it pal, you don't show us respect when you shuffled in with an old woman's shopping trolley. We don't like bow tied puffs in here."

When he walked slowly away from the pub, Tristan realised he was back in the city, where life is a challenge, but where the rewards are high if the response is right.

Before he looked for a hotel, Tristan walked the short distance back to Kensington High Street where, in an Italian restaurant, he chose spaghetti Bolognaise with garlic bread, for safety, volume, and economy.

The restaurant full of young people who were happy in each other's company pleased him. He even had a few smiles directed towards him. It saddened him when he realised that the smiles were sympathy for a harmless lonely man, getting on a bit in years.

The thought that anyone might think a knight-errant to be harmless, prompted him to buy a large glass of Barolo that he drank while he ate all the grissini on his table.

When two ladies left an adjacent table, he snitched the packets of grissini they had not touched. He tipped fifteen percent when he paid his bill, although it worried him that, with the tip, the cheap simple meal had cost about two percent of his total capital.

Kensington had always been a part of London favoured by Tristan, because he felt that the people always seemed at ease, happy to jostle and bump along, as they shared the crowded pavements. It did not take long for him to reach the Cromwell

Road, where the ambiance had changed much, all for the worse. On this road, he had to take care not to touch or obstruct any passer-by with his lunatic case that weaved behind him on independently minded wheels. Here the shadows were deeper; people hurried past with down cast eyes, protective of their inviolable space.

The garish green neon sign in the window of 'The Godfrey Hotel' indicated 'vacancies'. He only decided to try the Godfrey because the first five or six hotels he had passed had all displayed 'No Vacancies' notices, that Tristan, with his long experience of hotels, thought might be 'Can't be bothered' notices as most units seemed to be badly managed.

Although the appearance of 'The Godfrey' did not encourage him, he climbed the seven steps from the pavement, struggling with his case, before he could push open the glass door and ring the bell on the small-unmanned reception desk. To the left of the desk Tristan could see a small bar with only two people in it.

The bell alerted one of the two men. After he put down his drink on the bar, he came to the reception desk. "Yes," he said, without thought of a welcome greeting. Putting on his most urbane voice, Tristan said, "Good evening to you sir. How little will you charge me for a cot for one night, a war weary veteran, a pensioner who has come home to the smoke after a long and weary journey from the frozen north?"

The man snapped, "Same as for everyone else pal, young or old, rich or poor, drunk or sober, clean or dirty. Thirty pounds that includes VAT, but excludes service charge, cos there aint any; we don't do service." "Twenty five, nothing said," offered Tristan, opening his wallet that had just two tens and a five clearly showing.

He had already split the rest of his money, amongst an inside pocket in his jacket, a trouser pocket and his case. "Gee us it here then," the man said.

In exchange for the cash that did not go near any cash till, the man handed Tristan two keys attached to a large plastic fob.

"Room 33; third floor; all four floors have four rooms that share one bathroom. The larger key fits the bathroom on every floor, so lock the door, and leave the key in the lock on the inside if you go to the bog or for a wash. Showers don't work, never av. We don't do breakfasts. You can get a good feed across the road in Riejik's caff." "Thank you, Tristan replied, however the imp in him could not resist a tease, "Thank you very much. Pray, when did you attend the Tourist Board 'Welcome Host' course?" The man's quick "What's that pal." cut off any thought that Tristan had of continuing. "Nothing, just my stomach rumbling, I bid you good night, I shall leave early tomorrow morning."

The three flights of stairs depressed Tristan. At each landing, smells common to a cheap boarding house assaulted his sensitive nose. Curry from one room, poor fish and chips on the second floor, on his landing a tart's cheap scent.

In the room, he felt cheated. It did not have TV or radio, towels, soap or facilities to make tea, just a bed and post war utility furniture. He carefully hung his clothes on the wire coat hangers before he sat for a while on the bed, deep in thought.

With nothing else to do, except to think, Tristan got into the bed. He swore quietly when he got out of bed, to turn out the overhead light from the switch by the door. As Tristan stared at the ceiling, he could still clearly see the cracks in the plaster. The unlined curtains let light from the streetlights along with the night noises of the Cromwell Road that punctuated the soft rumble of the city that police car and ambulance sirens more frequently and stridently disturbed.

He thought about the day just spent. It made him aware of the stark difference made by the two-hundred miles that separated Scagill from London.

He had only been back in the smoke for a few hours, yet two men had already called him 'pal', but he had not made a friend of either. In Yorkshire, his friends called him Tristan, never Tris, or Stan or mate. As he drifted near to sleep, he shouted aloud in frustration, "Damn, I have not set my alarm." Once again, he had to get out of bed, to rummage in his case, to find his little red alarm clock.

Tristan set the alarm for seven in the morning before he put it on the cheap table by the narrow bed. Back in bed, he gave out one of his characteristic deep groans "Oh God, thirty-six hours a non-smoker, before he covered his head with the thin synthetic fibre easy wash, easy iron sheet.

Chapter 3

An hour before seven o'clock, the time he had set on his much-travelled alarm clock, Tristan woke to a new day, the third of his yet to be defined quest.

The bright sun of a late June morning, as it streamed through the cheap window curtains, brought in with it the noise of the busy Cromwell Road traffic, itself an alarm call enough to wake all but the dead, or a teenager.

His first thoughts echoed the last words of the previous day. He craved for a cigarette. With no prospect of a bath or a shower, but intent to wash and shave he crossed the landing to the one bathroom that served all four bedrooms on the third floor. He found it occupied. Frustrated, he climbed the stairs to the fourth floor where he found the bathroom unoccupied. However, like the rest of the hotel it lacked the care of a housekeeper. The lavatory seat had lost its attachment to the bowl, the sink retained a ring of scum left by the hard London water, but it had lost its plug. He did not find a nicely wrapped bar of soap, nor any towels. Disconsolate, he went back to his room to get the soap he had taken from the Crown Inn, and the small hand towel he had liberated from the Laurels Rehabilitation unit.

Someone still occupied the third floor bathroom when Tristan set out on his second foray. 'Sods Law' ruled that when he climbed back to the fourth floor, somebody else had occupied the bathroom that he had left empty.

He soon lost patience and had decided to try the bathroom on the second floor, when a woman vacated the room where he waited. She wore a towel wrapped around her head, and a flowered dressing gown pulled tight around her ample figure. As she flounced by him, she piped, "Sorry ducky, I'd leave it a while if I were you.

When Tristan was about to leave his squalid room in the Godfrey, the woman in the dressing gown tapped on the already open door. "Oh ducky, you haven't got a fag have you. I am gasping, not one left. I can't get any until I draw my Giro later this morning." "I am sorry dear lady, Tristan replied, "As of yesterday I gave up the pernicious weed. I took a vow not to smoke for a year. My last half packet of Philip Morris I dropped in a town centre council waste bin, in the far north of our beloved country.

"Ooo, you do talk nice you do." the tart said, "Where did you get the lovely hair, quite a Stewart Grainger you are. How about you come to my room for a quickie, enough for a packet of fags would do it, eh no, for you I would trick for a Woodbine."

"Get on with you scrofulous old tart, it's breakfast I want," Tristan laughed, quite bucked by the Stewart Grainger complement and even more delighted when, without rancour, the woman replied, "Here, who are you calling old," as she bounced back to her room. "Methinks I had it right" Tristan thought, "What I smelt on the third floor landing stairs last night, was only a cheap tart's scent."

He wondered, with the old Woolworths gone, if any shop still sold 'Californian Poppy' or 'Evening in Paris'.

Free of the Godfrey, Tristan bought a Daily Telegraph with money he deemed well spent.

He did not buy the same newspaper every day; he preferred to hone his many prejudices on eclectic opinion. He thought breakfast without a newspaper would be like boiled eggs without soldiers, salt and white pepper.

The sharp tempered manager of the Godfrey had said that he could get a good feed across the road in Riejik's caff. Tristan assumed that the café with the neat fascia sign 'Staples' must be Riejik's, who probably had called his little gold mine Staples because it provided the staple diet for the area's transient population.

The simple chalkboard menu showed him that Staples served a 'Full English Breakfast' with a mug of tea or instant coffee from six in the morning until noon. From noon, every day except Sundays and Christmas day, Riejik's served their 'Daily Special', always roast beef with Yorkshire pudding, roast potato, mashed potato, and peas, flooded with thick rich deep brown gravy, and nothing else.

After the beef ran out, Riejik's offered gammon, egg and chips, sausage egg and chips, or breaded plaice with peas and chips, until the caff closed at eight p.m. For dessert, the menu offered a choice apple pie, cheesecake or ice cream, obviously not homemade. With a transient customer base there was no need to vary the menu. Riejik, who cooked, served, cleared table and washed up seldom smiled.

He was a heavily built man, about sixty years old, with a full head of shiny 'Hammerite' black hair. Tristan thought he might be an Arab, Turk or Lebanese. He wore a grey sleeveless vest over fancy coloured chef's trousers with an elastic waist. Despite Riejik's taciturn nature, Tristan would learn that the local customers thought well of him, though he would also learn, to his cost, of his fiery temper.

While Tristan ate his breakfast, he thought about the small board he had seen in the caff window on which, presumably Riejik had written, 'Cook wanted: afternoons, three until eight, ask Riejik.'

He thought that such a part time job would be useful, as a fallback position, an essential 'Plan B', because if he took it, he would still be free to use the mornings to look for an opportunity more suitable for his age and experience. He thought that it might be useful, as a temporary job, to provide cash to live on, until he could be banker not clerk, bookie not runner.

Although he had long lost the P45, which the hotel in Nottingham gave him when he had one of his temper tantrums, Tristan could legitimately apply for a job because he kept a record of his National Insurance number in his wallet, together with his driving license for identification.

When he left the caff the perfect late June weather still held. It made it necessary for him to find somewhere to leave his suitcase, overcoat and hat, before he could look for work. A quick count of his recently freed up cash showed that in just one day he had spent almost ten percent of his available funds, even so, Tristan still had standards. He could not face another night at the seedy Godfrey, where the Cromwell Road, though not a railway, seemed to run through the middle of the house.

He walked, as steadily as his weak legs and arms trailing his suitcase allowed, until in a small crescent off Old Brompton Road, he reached the double fronted 'Grassington Guest House'. A small card displayed in a window by the door carried the word VACENCY's. That the card had been hand written and was not a neon sign encouraged Tristan, as did the miss-spelt vacancy with its in-appropriate apostrophe.

The card listed the same rate for a single room bed and breakfast that he had paid at the Godfrey. It pleased him more when a woman, not a man, came to greet him, almost at once, in answer to his ring on the door bell.

Tristan laid on the charm, "Good morning madam, could you please tell me how little you would charge to accommodate me, my case, cane, overcoat and hat for one night only, that is to-night, in a single room, to include breakfast tomorrow morning with all Government taxes, impositions and surcharges paid. I am recently come from the derelict north to seek my fortune in burgeoning London Town."

"Go on with you, you soft beggar," the woman replied in flat northern tones, we charge what it says on the card with none of the hidden extras that you were on about. How does that suit." Tristan replied, "It is really more than I can afford, nevertheless because I suspect that you are a Yorkshire lass, who has chosen to call your lovely house 'Grassington', a place I know well, I accept your terms. " Er, sorry ma-am" Tristan added quickly, that is if you will put me up and put up with me?"

Tristan could hardly comprehend the difference between the two different hospitality businesses with the same room rates that were only a fifteen-minute walk from each other. The sour smells of greed that permeated each floor of the ghastly Godfrey Hotel came from a different world to the scent of flowers, furniture polish and fresh air suffused Grassington Guest House.

The room that the lady took Tristan to included a small fully fitted bathroom. The double glazed window that overlooked a small back garden, laid out as neat as the bedroom, in complete contrast to the Godfrey, had heavy lined curtains.

While he unpacked his case, Tristan calculated that if he stayed B&B at the Grassington, skipped lunch, but allowed for laundry, an evening meal and a drink; he would be comfortable but penniless in two to three weeks, unless he found work with an employer who would pay part of his wages in advance.

Before Tristan left the Grassington to go job-hunting, he went to look for the proprietor.

He found her in the kitchen. "What time is 'curfew' tonight?" he asked. "Oh no curfew," She replied cheerily, "Try to be quiet if you come in late. Some of our guests, usually the older ladies, go to bed uncommon early."

Finding her easy to talk to he asked, "How long have you owned the 'Grassington?" Her reply sent him off in high spirits, "Fourteen years, three months, seventeen days, three full breakfasts and a continental this morning. My husband worked underground in the South Yorkshire coalmines until the Coal

Board made him redundant. We took a gamble. We sold our still part mortgaged house, added the money from the sale, to his redundancy money, as a deposit on a massive new mortgage to secure the free hold on the Grassington. John works in a DIY store, I keep house here. Between us, we keep the wolf from the door, however I doubt that we will never get that fortune you told me you had come to make in London Town. We would have been better off in Scarborough."

When Tristan left the Grassington, intent to find temporary paid employment, he walked towards Kensington. After a few hundred meters his back hurt, his knees hurt and his breath came in gasps, as though he had run the distance. The pain forced him to rest. He called himself all sorts of an old fool for not bringing his silver-topped walking cane with him. "You are not fit Tristan old lad," he said to himself, "Good job you have given up smoking. I don't think you will get work as a navy to dig for gold in the streets."

As a betting man, he sat for a while to consider what odds a bookmaker would post against him succeeding with his plan to find, follow and champion a good cause with a long prosperous future. He rated his chances poor, his future short.

When he reached Kensington High Street, he asked a street cleaner where he could find the nearest employment office. "I've no idea where an employment office might be mate," the man replied, "What the government call 'Job Centre Plus' is just down the road, on the right. You have no chance there mate, not at your age, it's all bloody play stations. I can't make head or tail of them. Anyways, all the good jobs have gone, all those on offer are part time and not worth the effort."

In Job Centre Plus, Tristan was not a happy man. Almost all the job vacancies required applicants to submit relevant current C.V.s, addressed to 'The Human Resources Director' of firms or councils of which he had never heard.

Tristan realised that preparation of a C.V. would take too long. He thought it would be a futile effort because any C.V. he prepared would have to be hand written. As such, they would be unlikely to get him an interview. Over the last few years, each time that he sought to improve his job, Tristan had learned that two factors, age and experience, had ruled against him. In the fast moving world of advanced technology, age no longer related to wisdom and experience was always out of date.

Human resources marked him, too old for management appointments and too experienced for menial jobs. After a mind numbing two hours, Tristan left Job Centre Plus in a very negative frame of mind. "His mind and body craved for a cigarette. " If I only smoke a packet a day," he thought, "My present funds won't last a fortnight let alone three weeks."

Back in the High Street, Tristan noticed that, on a single door between two shop windows, a small brass plate indicated that behind the door the 'City Recruitment Agency' lay concealed. Inside the door, a near vertical flight of steps confronted him.

After he struggled to climb the stairs, he reached a first floor landing just big enough for one person to stand, where he faced a small frosted glass window marked 'Reception'.

A plastic notice by a small bell required visitors to, 'Ring for attention'. Tristan duly pushed the bell button. He distinctly heard a satisfactory buzz from deep within the hidden space behind the window. It achieved nothing. A second push on the bell button did not elicit an answer, nor did a longer third.

Frustrated by the lack of response, Arthur had reached the half way point back down the death trap stairs, muttering to himself a bit from, 'The Walrus and the Carpenter', 'But, answer came there none', when a woman called out, "Yes". Tristan climbed wearily back to the small landing to greet the woman who had opened the door. He managed to say, quite affably, "Oh, I see that there is one oyster left." "I was on my lunch," the woman snapped. Tristan could not help himself, "Squashed the sandwiches did you."

The woman ignored the sarcasm. She reacted, as many women often did, to Tristan's good looks. She positively purred. "Oh do please come in. Tell me sir, what are you looking for, management, junior staff, or workers?" It embarrassed Tristan when he had to admit, "Well no, actually, at the moment I am not an employer, in fact I need a job until I can get re-established, don't you see."

Tristan thought her response genuine, if not encouraging, "Good God, I thought a toff like you would be an employer. You should not have to look for work; a gentleman of your age should be able to retire.

Alcoholic are you, released on parole, or has the missus thrown you out?" Tristan, who strove to keep his temper, managed to ask, "Do you have any unfilled job opportunities that might suit me, a respectable, not too old, hotelier who does not smoke?" "Not really," she said, "You are a liar for a start." Tristan still held his temper. "Why do you call me liar, am I also a cut throat dog?"

Pleased with herself the woman coolly replied, "Well look at your nicotine stained fingers." Tristan grinned, "Ah, well observed Homes, but I am a non-smoker, for the first time in more than fifty years I have not smoked for two whole days. "Sorry luv," the woman said, "It has been a bad day, do sit down. I will have a look though the vacancies.

I doubt that we will have much to interest you. You see most jobs these days are either civil service temps, or local government; they will not take anyone of your age."

The woman went to her computer terminal where she scrolled through many pages that were incomprehensible to Tristan. Occasionally she called out unlikely jobs in the far-outer reaches of London. "Dog walker Bethnal Green, magazine distributor Crawley, delivery driver Islington, no that won't do, they want the 'knowledge'. Kitchen porter, lots of those, a lot of pub and restaurant owners don't ask question, they pay cash in hand, below the minimum wage. It distorts the market. Sorry darling" she concluded, "I don't think that you match our criteria. Have you tried Job Centre Plus; they might have something." "Thank you for trying," Tristan said. He could not even raise a wry smile to leaven his despondency.

When he left the office, he thought the death trap stairs might be the staircase to oblivion. His body cried out for a cigarette with more than a silent thought, he blasphemed aloud "Christ I need a cigarette." Shocked by his outcry, Tristan straightened his back, squared his shoulders, and repeated to himself mantras he had often used when he his mood had been black. "Need, you don't need, you want; want does not get. The day is fine, the prospects good.

Man hath no wit that cannot rise and travel forth into the morning. Norman Tebbit's dad got on his bike to seek work. You never failed to give a job to anyone who knocked on your door to ask for work, people with the sense to bypass the bureaucracy that is choking this country. You gave them a chance; someone might give you a chance, get knocking."

Tristan's first attempt at a direct approach led to another of Mallory's dark impenetrable forest of thorns. He tried a tilt at a five star, very large, very grand Kensington hotel. A uniformed concierge in the elegant reception area of the hotel brusquely directed him to the staff entrance at the back of the building.

When he finally found it, he asked one of the attendant security guards where he might apply for a job. The doleful guard escorted him as far as a door marked with the legend 'Human Resources'. The very words spelt out to Tristan that for him, it might be a 'No go area'. Nevertheless, he pressed on. Immediately inside the office, a man behind a reception desk faced him. He looked even more downcast than did the doleful security guard.

Behind him, Tristan could see many clerks who worked at stations topped with computer screens. "Who are you; have you an appointment?" the man asked in dull tones. Tristan answered, "I am Tristan Edward, I have no appointment. I sought out human resources in the hope that you might have a job vacancy to match my resourcefulness. For more years than I care to remember, I have built up cadre of the resources and experience necessary for hotels great and small." "C.V.?" The man had asked the one question that Tristan had hoped to avoid. "I do not possess such a document, I prefer dialog to text." The smug young clerk shrugged, "How do you expect us to know what you can do, if you do not have a C.V." "Could you not arrange an interview?" Tristan asked, hopefully, though he felt the exchange more ping-pong than dialog.

The clerk played a fast return, "No C.V. means no interview; come back when you have one; if you still want to. We always need kitchen porters." "Surly you don't need a C.V. for a K.P." Tristan lobbed his reply. The clerk smashed the every time game, set and match winning shot. "It's company policy, nothing to do with me. Now if you don't mind, I'm busy."

Defeated, Tristan found his way out of the dungeon under the hotel, glad to breathe deeply of what Londoners took to be fresh air. "Any luck sir?" the doleful security guard asked. "No, none at all, Tristan replied, before he went off on a minor rant. " Ye gods, old biddy welfare officer complicated the world of work. Personnel departments with over paid managers made it much worse. Modern human Resource Directorates' by their equality scales choke ambition. Line Managers should be left to manage their budgets and the people only they should employ, to carry out work for a wage that each individual deserves."

The doleful guard said, with some sympathy, "Yer didn't get a job then. Well perhaps you will be better off that way." He went on to sum up Tristan's situation, "If you get your allowances and benefits sorted, you would happen be better off than working here. I don't know why I bother. The difference between the wages they pay me, after deductions, and what I would get on the dole does not pay my bus fare to get here."

Tristan fared no better with his next 'knock on the door' attempt to find work. In a newsagent's window in Kensington

Road, he saw a postcard 'Sales Person, no experience necessary. Apply Ericsson's Book Shop, Craven Crescent, Bayswater.'

Conscious that a walk across the Park would improve his temper, Tristan set off with a will. Because he had worked in the Bayswater area several times, he felt sure that he remembered Ericsson's, an old-fashioned shop that sold a mix of new, remaindered and second hand books.

He thought that it might be just the job to give him some security before he could venture out to further his aim to be self-employed. When he finally reached the shop, to his delight, he saw a card in the window similar in all respects to the one he had seen in the shop in Kensington High Street.

It encouraged him to think that the position might still be vacant. It had taken Tristan much longer to walk across the park than he anticipated. He had needed to rest, twice. Because the condition that the Laurels treaded him for needed no supervised remedial physical exercises, or dietary supervision, the months spent in the rehab unit had wasted him.

Other than the effort to get out of bed to shower and shave, he had only moved from easy chair to dining chair and back to easy chair, three times each dull day, before he retired back to bed. He resolved that whatever job he took, he would walk longer distances each day, until he could jog for ten minutes every day.

Tristan knew that his walk in the park had not been the euphemism for a thing simply done. It had convinced him that if he did not exercise he would become an unemployable good for nothing drop out.

Inside the cool dark of Ericsson's shop, he approached the counter where an elderly man with rimless half spectacles peered myopically towards him to say. "I am afraid we will close in a couple of minute's sir; can I be of any assistance. Is it a special book that you look for?" "Thank you but no," Tristan said politely, "I came in response to your advertisement for a sales assistant." The elderly man replied quietly, "I see, please wait a moment. I will have to ask Mr. Henry if he will see you."

He walked past Tristan, to turn over the notice that hung on the door from 'Open' to 'Closed', before he locked the door with a large key secured by a chain to his belt. "I won't be a moment," he said, as he disappeared through a curtain at the back of the shop, leaving Tristan alone with his thoughts.

Some five minutes later, an even older man, who Tristan took to be 'Mr. Henry', came from behind the curtain. "Good evening Mr. er?" Tristan answered the incomplete question, "Edward sir, Tristan Edward, Edward the surname without the 's'; first name Tristan." "Well Mr. Edward," Mr Henry replied, "Thank you for taking the trouble to come to see us, however, I am afraid we need to find a young person, someone who we can train up to work in our way, a way that I am afraid is not that of most people today. You see my brother and I do not get any younger. We want someone to be here in years to come, someone who will keep to the traditional way we do business, in the same way that we have kept to our father's wishes. You do see our dilemma don't you Mr. er, Edward?"

"Yes, yes indeed, thank you; you have been most courteous," replied Tristan. Mr. Henry seemed to be genuinely sympathetic when he unlocked the door to usher Tristan out into the street, "I am sure that you will find something suitable very soon." He said.

Tristan who had walked slowly back along Craven Crescent had to move like a wraith to cross Bayswater Road to return to the sanctuary of Kensington Gardens, where he sat, for an hour. As he pondered about what he could do to earn an honest crust, he even contemplated ways that he might earn some dishonest dosh, a thing he had never before considered.

All his thoughts, good and bad, drew blank. The good weather that had brought out many nannies and au pair girls with their charges took away his dark thoughts. It pleased Tristan that some of the old ways remained, ducks to feed, balls to chase and catch.

He felt content to watch the new ways where young boys sought to impress the girls by their athletic moves on skateboards. The young couples, who flirted, as they almost danced on roller blades, cheered him most.

Back in the bustle of Kensington High Street, as he had not even had a sandwich for lunch, Tristan chose to eat in the Italian restaurant where he had enjoyed his supper the previous day. However, before he went to the restaurant, he bought a paper back copy of 'Hotel' by Arthur Hailey from the special offer table in the nearby Waterston's bookshop.

Although he had read the book before, he chose it as a long easy read to keep him occupied in his lonesome state. He did not like to eat alone, anywhere, particularly in restaurants. Unless he had a book to read, he felt conspicuously awkward. He considered it unacceptable to read a newspaper in a restaurant at any time and only acceptable in cafés during breakfast.

Tristan dawdled over his meal; he took pleasure in reading the Italian menu names like Zuppa di Vongole e Gamberetti.

Experience had taught him that such a name allowed a restaurant to charge a quid more than for shrimp soup. Throwing caution to the wind, he drank two glasses of red wine. Tristan had long regretted the loss of half bottles of wine that in recent years seemed only to be available in the list of dessert wines.

Altogether, with his generous tip, he reckoned he had blown nearly three percent of his total cash reserve. Any other wealth in his possession he could easily asses. A detailed evaluation would prove that nil, zero or naught would all be within the limits of statistical error. On his way, back to the luxury of the 'Grassington' guesthouse Tristan passed the caff where he had had breakfast earlier in the day. He noticed, still displayed in the window, the card that advertised the job of afternoon cook.

Chapter 4

When he used his key to let himself in quietly through the front door of the Grassington Guesthouse Tristan's spirits were fading faster than the summer twilight.

It was little consolation that his aching back, hips and knees informed him that the day had not been a useless exercise, even though he had failed to secure an interview, let alone the offer of a job.

Before he set out for London, he had known that he would not be able to do heavy manual, kitchen or bar work; he now knew he could only do a supervisory or desk bound job. It added to his frustration that the two brothers, owners of Ericsson's bookshop, clearly his senior by many years, deemed him too old for the job they had advertised.

Alone in his neat little room, he picked up the Arthur Hailey book he had bought, kicked off his shoes to flop exhausted on his bed. Too tired to read, he put the book aside. He hardly had the energy left to think.

Although he craved for a cigarette, he realised that even more than a nicotine fix, he missed the companionship of the friends he had made in the Laurels. It prompted the thought that he would buy a portable radio, an expense he justified because a radio, tuned to the correct station, dependent on the time of day, would be a good companion with few demands.

The next morning, at nine o'clock, a sharp knock on his bedroom door woke Tristan from a deep untroubled sleep. The lady of the house called out, "Come on Whittington, the cat is out of the flap. If you want breakfast you will have to hurry, we finish at nine thirty; I have to go to the shops." "Sorry," Tristan shouted, "I forgot to set my alarm clock."

Anxious not to miss breakfast, he put off both shave and shower. He did not even think about a cigarette. Downstairs, Tristan apologised, most effusively, that he had overslept.

He insisted that he did not need a cooked breakfast, and that cornflakes would do. Mrs. Brassington would not hear of it. She told him that a man seeking a fortune in London needed a good breakfast.

Tristan accepted her compromise of cereal, scrambled eggs on toast with two rashers of bacon, followed by more toast and a pot of tea. A brochure of the Grassington, that Tristan had picked up from a desk in the hall, informed him of his host's name.

"Mrs. Brassington," he asked, "Could you please put up with me for another two nights, until I find a job with a live in position?" Her reply, "Yes, you are alright until Friday morning, but we are fully booked on Friday and Saturday night."

Both relieved and stimulated Tristan said, "Well that is a sharp spur to stimulate my search for success. I will have to do better than yesterday. In these modern times, I have found that employers discount or discard any experience of days of yore. They do not want to engage anyone over the age of thirty. I can't imagine of what they are frightened."

After breakfast, refreshed by his delayed shower and shave, Tristan decided to challenge the Strand. He felt reasonably confident that many of the hotels, restaurants, larger cafés and bars along the badly named road, far from the sea, would require back office workers, administrators and managers.

He chose to start at the Trafalgar Square end, to work his way east until some entrepreneur, business owner, or manager offered him full time gainful employment that provided accommodation with the opportunity for advancement.

To get the start line, he managed to walk as far as Gloucester Road before back pain forced him to take the 'Underground' to Charing Cross.

Tristan did not like to travel on tube trains, particularly when it was the rush hour. Strap hanging hurt his back, because the train rocked him erratically.

With his innate good manners, he could not remain seated if any lady in the coach had to stand. It increased his irritation if any women cold stared him, if he offered her his seat.

He had often caused trouble by his loud apology, "Sorry woman, I thought you were a lady". Travel on the tube had cost him more than the ticket. He had had to buy analgesics tablets from a pharmacist. Without them, he knew that after a tube jolt journey, he would not get far along the Strand. He damned himself, as a fool, that he had left his stash of prescription only pain control tablets at the Laurels.

To start his search, he aimed high. He tried for a job at the Strand's most famous hotel. A genial old fellow, one of the concierge staff, immediately set him back. He told him that an agency in the City handled all recruitment. "The management contracted out recruitment years ago. They use a firm called RRR, just initials, it's the modern way. They used to call it 'Rapid Recruitment Results'. We still call it the 'Retards Recycling Repository'. You will find it in Mark Lane. Get the tube to Tower; it's an easy walk from there." Tristan asked, "Do department heads here have no say in who is recruited these days." The genial concierge shook his head, "Course not old chap, is all mark ups, return on investment, credit control, number crunch and targets for the poor bastards. Customer care is too last year dhaling."

In a large commercial hotel, further along the Strand, Tristan fared no better. The hotel did have a small office where they recruited people for junior posts. They also had a form that gave applicants the opportunity to list their qualifications, work experience and personal details.

He spent three-quarters of an hour to part fill in the form. It proved to be a fruitless exercise. He could not complete the boxes that required an address for correspondence, a telephone number, a fax number, and an email address. When he handed the incomplete form to the clerk, she told him that they would let him know. "How will you let me know?" Tristan asked, "I am not sure where I shall be after Thursday." The clerk's best offer that he should call again next week did not warrant a reply.

Half the day had gone when Tristan walked, downcast, back into the Strand. To brighten his day he bought the 'Sun' newspaper. He did not buy a more expensive more informative paper, as any of the three would deplete his reserves more than a red top and would probably add to his misery.

He stopped for a cup of tea in one of the big store cafeterias, where he treated himself to the luxury of an 'Eccles' cake. After he successfully manoeuvred his tray along the chrome bars of the self-service counter, he tried to fathom the self-service hot drinks dispense machine. Frustrated, he wondered where all the nice girls who used to serve customers had gone. While he sat with his paper, disappointed with the lukewarm tea, not improved by the mini plastic pot of UHT milk, he had unconsciously fumbled in every pocket, to search for a packet of cigarettes. His craving for nicotine had become stronger than any he had previously experienced.

His habit of a lifetime demanded satisfaction. "Best get on with it," his inner self commanded. When he past the girl, almost hidden behind a cash till without keys or numbers, only menu items on a touch screen, he called out, "Thank you my dear," He got no response. He presumed that her till did not have a tab with an appropriate reply.

By Four o'clock, even though the cards in their windows clearly stated, 'Staff wanted', several restaurant, café and bar managers had summarily rejected Tristan's application for work with no more than a "Sorry mate, you don't quite fit" He wondered if the age discrimination act could ever work.

When Tristan reached the end of the Strand, he was at the end of his tether. Despite the many changes in fashion since the war, the famous Keeble Hotel still dominated the scene with Edwardian elegance.

He remembered it when it had been the only place to stay in London for Yorkshire trade, Leeds garment makers, machine tool makers from Scagill, Bradford top merchants, worsted weavers from Huddersfield. Even the well set up shoddy men from Dewsbury and Batley chose the Keeble when business demanded more than a return day trip, first class, on the Harrogate Pullman.

Tristan decided to change his tactics because, thus far, they had been consistently unsuccessful. He planned to find an excuse to ambush one of the managers to bypass the Keeble's recruitment procedures.

He did not go to the Keeble's receptionists, the concierge, or the hall porters to ask where he might find the recruitment office. Instead, in a corridor off from the main entrance lobby, he carefully studied the framed panel of photographs of the hotel's management team, displayed alongside an engraved anodised aluminium plaque from 'Investors in People'. The plaque congratulated the company for 'Best Practice' that included welfare, recruitment and training of staff.

Unable to apply for any job in the hotel's kitchen, Tristan memorised only the names and faces of the front of house managers.

Seeking to confront a manager with some observed irregularity, Tristan went into the cocktail lounge, a room set off to the side of the hotel's reception area. His long experience assured him that bars serving alcoholic drinks breed cheats on both sides of the bar.

After he ordered a tonic, ice and lemon, he took up station at the end of the bar, furthest from the entrance, to give him the best view of the staff as the customers came through the unseen threshold barrier.

He regretted that he had bought the Sun, not a broadsheet newspaper to use as a hide. When he drank alone, in any hotel bar, Tristan always played 'Hotel detective'.

He watched every exchange between each customer and the barman, a man in his mid-sixties who wore a short white jacket, wing collar shirt with a red bow tie. The mandarin slippers he wore, obviously for his bad feet, suggested that he had been a barman for many years.

Tristan felt reasonably certain that he had seen the man somewhere, sometime, a long time ago. His brusque way with some customers that contrasted with the sycophantic deference he paid to those who called him by his first name, marked him out as one of the old rogue school.

A woman blessed with both good looks and deportment that spoke of quiet money, ordered an apple juice as she sat elegantly on a bar stool, alongside a large comfortable man, almost twice her age. "I am on the wagon tonight Charles," she said, "Himself has already shifted a sitz bath full, so I will have to drive the bloody Bentley." The barman spun the bottle in the air, caught it left handed, then using his 'Waiters friend' in his right hand, he half eased the crown cork off the bottle. To complete the trick, in one practiced movement, he used his thumbnail to flick the crown cork in the air and caught it in an empty glass held behind his back.

The trick triggered Tristan's memory. He had seen the man before. He knew him from years before as Charles Lucas Prescott.

He had seen him practice the trick, when they had both worked on the same cruise ship. He knew that in those days Prescott had been as bent as the corkscrew in his waiter's friend.

The ship's purser had dismissed Prescott, and put him ashore, after an astute American blue rinse had proved that he used more than one trick to swindle passengers. Prescott's dismissal had been good for Tristan. The purser had moved him to work the First Class bar that Charles Lucas Prescott had worked. It had proved easier work than Tristan's previous job in the Casino bar, with an added bonus that the customers tipped better than had the punters. Tristan watched carefully.

The cynical manner in which Prescott addressed rather than spoke to customers, as he forced the double and upped the brand, confirmed his suspicion that the old rogue had not changed, just because he had come ashore.

He felt sure that Prescott would supplement his income at the expense of both the hotel's profit and the customer's pocket. Wages, plus a share of the tronc, would not be enough for Charles Lucas Prescott.

It was almost seven o'clock before Tristan spotted Prescott's fiddle. He was impressed; in all his years in the racket, he had never seen theft done with such aplomb.

On the side of the till, managers had secured a small spring clip to hold any proffered five, ten, twenty or the occasional fifty-pound note. This device protected the bar staff; it enabled them to prove to any customer who queried the change, the face value of the note given in payment, before the note joined others in the till drawer.

During the many years spent, first as a barman, afterwards as a manager, Tristan had had many a sharp customer try it on. He had fitted similar clips on tills under his control as a defence for his staff.

Charles Lucas Prescott's theft was beautiful. He had finessed the procedure to his advantage. When customers had proffered cash, that included bank notes to buy drinks, Prescott had given correct change, until a group of young people came into the bar, the men in dinner jackets, the girls in 'Posh frocks'. A fresh faced young man more interested in the girls than the barman, casually handed Prescott two twenty-pound notes to pay for a round of drinks. Prescott performed the distraction as well as any member of the 'Magic Circle' ever had. In what appeared to be a single smooth movement, the clip on the side of the till, previously empty, held a single twenty-pound note, together with a single ten-pound note. Prescott had palmed one of the twenties into a pocket inside his jacket, and replaced it in the clip with a ten-pound note.

The young man, too excited and busy with his friends, did not even check his change; he slipped the coins straight into his pocket. Tristan slipped off his stool; Prescott had given him the excuse he needed for his ambush. By long established habit, he wished the barman a genial, "Goodnight." He immediately regretted it. Charles Lucas Prescott raked him head to foot with cold suspicious eyes.

Tristan realised that if Prescott had recognised him, it would be a real downer. He knew that the man had not changed from the man who years ago had been as vindictive as an anarchist with a lost cause.

Determined to press on with his new tactic, Tristan took up a different station, this time in the hotel reception lobby, inside the main door. He leaned against one of the marble pillars to wait for his chance, a chance that soon came. He spotted the duty manager as he escorted an elderly couple to the door.

Tristan moved to make sure that the manager, on his way back from the door, would have to pass close to where he waited. "Mister Cunningham," Tristan said quietly, "Could I have a word." The use of his name by a stranger pulled the duty manager up short. Tristan knew from experience, that when a customer asked the dread question, "Could I have a word?" it usually preceded a complaint. As he expected, it got him the undivided attention of the manager who dutifully responded. "Yes Sir, can I be of assistance?"

Tristan made sure that his answer did not settle the manager. "Perhaps we can assist each other Mr. Cunningham. My name is Edward, Tristan Edward. My given name is Tristan. Edward, without the 's', is my surname. I have worked in the hospitality racket for many years, more years than you can imagine. I have gained a deal of experience that allows me to spot a fiddle at fifty yards, and I do not mean a violin. I must tell you, that is if you do not already know, your cocktail barman, who I believe is called Charles by too many of your customers, milks them to his advantage, not to the benefit of the hotel or its shareholders." "Are you a shareholder, has he cheated you?" the manager asked, as his face fast lost any colour.

Again, Tristan made sure that his answer did not reassure him, "Whether I am a shareholder, or not, does not affect the issue. What does concern me, and must concern you, is that he is a thief. He has just short-changed, by ten pounds, an unworldly young man who bought drinks for a group of friends, the party with the men in black ties with the girls in posh frocks. He is an artist at it; he also has what looks like a pound coin braised to the gold band on the third finger of his left hand, one of the oldest ways to short change cash known to the trade."

The manager had a minor temper tantrum. "Oh hells bells, if you are not a con-man, and how do I know that might I ask, it's a right bummer. We pay the man enough, on top of which he gets tips galore. Surely, he would not be so stupid. He must net more than I do, with less than half the responsibility or hours I am burdened with."

When he calmed down, he asked Tristan to go with him to his office to tell him more about what he had seen. In the manager's tiny-shared office, Tristan explained the distraction and palming of notes. He did not divulge to the manager that he knew Prescott, or that, years ago, he had worked with him on a cruise ship. "At least you have that right," the manager said, "He is a master conjuror; we occasionally use him at functions. He goes from table to table to entertain the customers with card tricks. He is very popular."

Tristan could not resist an attempt to further discomfort the manager, "Well, I am sure that you can set him up at any time to suit security. They could tape his tricks on video. I suggest that you don't deal with him until you have three or four of his thefts recorded. However, I suggest you first confront him with one incident only, to judge his reaction, before you disclose your other tapes. He may give you, inadvertently or otherwise, evidence of bad practice elsewhere in this acclaimed good practice unit. After that, what you do is up to you."

The manager's reply did not immediately encourage Tristan. "Well Mr. Edward, I don't know what to say. Of course, we will have to act, but it will cost us. He has been with us for years, well before I started here as a trainee, and seems to be well in with some of the senior women managers. When you first spoke to me, you mentioned that we might assist each other. All that you have done so far is to give me a lot of grief. What may I ravel for you in return?"

Confident that his strategy had worked, Tristan replied with a diffident smile, "I noticed that alongside your photograph on the wall that leads to the toilets, there is a plaque that indicates the Keeble is accredited as an 'Investor in People' a fact to which I have already referred.

I would like the Keeble to invest in me. Despite being over sixty, I am a still a people person. To put it in a nutshell, I would like the Keeble to employ me with a job that in addition to reasonable remuneration also provides accommodation."

Mr. Cunningham, unhappy that Tristan had manoeuvred him, took a long time before he replied. "I do not like you Mr. Edward, deficient of an's'. However, we must not kill the messenger, although I am tempted to do just that. I happen to know that we need a night cash controller, one of the few jobs for which the Keeble offers accommodation. We had to let the last one go yesterday; he was letting us down, on the booze and fairy fungus fuel. Such a menial post would suit you. In return for the so-called accommodation, the Keeble reduces the pitiful minimum wage to a pittance. It is more of a slop-out cell really, in a slum on Clerkenwell Road, but it is within walking distance." Tristan replied, "Well thank you, it would get me started again. I have been off work with health problems for a while, but night cash controller I can do." In answer to the raised eyebrow with its unspoken question Tristan said, "No Mr. Cunningham, I have no wife to throw me out. I am not an alcoholic, nor am I a drug user, not as you know it. I just needed help to quit, nicotine, tamazepam, caffeine taken with various other debilitating depressants, and stimulants that stress, but I found the cure worse than the habit, so I gave up both."

The reluctant duty manager shrugged, "Come in tomorrow morning, I am on 'earlies'. I will take you down to personnel. I can't guarantee anything, but I will put in a word for you. The job is so dire that if they take you on, it will be my revenge. Now bugger off, you have right spoilt my day."

With at least partial success in his search for work, Tristan could not face the thought of the Underground. Although he craved for a cigarette, he wanted more than nicotine could give; he wanted a slap up meal. Having worked in London before, on many occasions, he knew that the large hotels that were not flagships, those with three hundred or more bedrooms, had small restaurants, because they could not stop their residents going out in the evening to seek the bright lights.

In their attempt to encourage residents to 'dine in', many hotels served good food at prices far less than most of the glass fronted roadside chain, theme or foreign food restaurants of the West End. Tristan took a taxi to the Kensington Regal, just a short walk from the 'Grassington'.

Before he entered the hotel, he walked to a nearby pub where he drank a swift pint of draught Guinness. He chose Guinness for the double reason that he did not take to London beer and because he knew that the hotel restaurant, would only offer some bottled tasteless over chilled foreign lager with enough preservatives in it to mummify an elephant.

The restaurant of the Regal had ninety covers at most. When the restaurant manager showed him to a table, Tristan could only count eighteen other customers. They were all either Japanese or Arab, all fearful of getting lost, once the green-flagged whistle blowing guides had left them to their own devices.

In common with many London hotels, the waiters were mainly gender deficient, their average age well over fifty. The restaurant menu was of their style and time. He chose Scotch broth, followed by the Roast of the day, which predictably turned out to be rack of lamb; beef being too expensive, pork not an option for many customers, chicken too dangerous on the bone and rack of lamb ideal to cook to order as a single portion.

Tristan chose soup so that he could pocket two bread rolls. He chose the roast so that he could ask for extra roast potatoes. For dessert, he chose cheese. He wrapped the cheddar cheese, together with two little foil wrapped butter portions, in a paper serviette, to add to the previously pocketed bread rolls.

When he checked the drinks list, it pleased him that he had had a Guinness in the pub. The hotel did not serve beer; it only offered several foreign bottled lagers, all at extortionate prices. It pleased him even more that after he called for more roast potatoes, to compensate for the deferred bread rolls, the meal satisfied his hunger, even after his long day with just an Eccles cake between breakfast and late dinner.

With tomorrow's lunch in his pockets, and the bill for dinner and Guinness, less than he had paid for the spag bog and wine he had eaten the night before, Tristan was satisfied that he was learning to live well, using little cash. Even so, it bore down on him that even with frugal days; his funds were fast running out.

After the short walk back to the Grassington, when Tristan unlocked the front door, Mrs. Brassington came out from her sitting room to greet him. "Hello Whittington, any gold in the streets today." Tristan replied with a sweeping bow, "Sadly no ma-am, however I have 'Great Expectations' of the morrow. I hope to get a foothold on the beanstalk where I shall find the goose that lays the right kind of egg."

Mrs. Brassington replied, laughing with him, "You soft happeth, I have never known a man to mix his metaphors with such confusion. It's 'Dick Whittington' you must copy, not 'Jack and the Beanstalk', or 'Mother Goose'. "It is also unlikely that you will have an unknown convict leave you a fortune". She added, seriously, "Would you like to settle-up now to save bother on Friday morning. I have to be off early. Mister Brassington will cook your breakfast; he doesn't have to be at work until ten on Fridays. He is a good cook, but he hates to take any money, he confuses customers with friends and relations."

"Certainly Ma-am, Tristan replied, "I paid you for the first night, Tuesday, so that will be just Sixty pound for Wednesday and Thursday night I believe." Tristan gave her seven ten pound notes adding, "For you kindness dear lady." As an afterthought, he added, "Could you please give me a shout tomorrow morning, at about seven, I usually wake at six, but this morning I slept through my alarm clock, I don't know what happened."

Tristan showered before he turned in. London always made him feel dirty, particularly if he had travelled on the tube. In bed, he did not read, he thought deeply about his prospects, concluding that they did not auger well.

Night cash controller came at the very bottom of front of house duties, on a par with pot washers in the kitchen brigade, although less popular with other members of staff. He had told his fellow Grey Haired Knights in the rehab unit that he would in future be banker or bookmaker, never again clerk or runner.

He knew that night cash controller would not be acceptable in Arthur's new order of chivalry. He also knew that he had made an enemy in Charles Lucas Prescott.

Chapter 5

When Tristan Edward stepped out of the Grassington Guest House, on his way to the job interview at the Keeble, he travelled light. He took with him only the 'Harrods' bag and his black silver topped cane. He had purchased both, second hand, just to give him, as he thought, a touch of class.

After one evening and two long days spent walking the streets of London, the bag was merely functional and he needed the cane for support.

In complete contrast to his normal shopping habit, in an up market gentleman's outfitters, not at a charity shop, Tristan bought a very expensive shirt with sleeves that had double cuffs. The double cuffs necessitated that he purchase a pair of large brightly coloured cuff links to go with the shirt.

After he changed his old shirt for new in the changing room, he asked for one of their smart carrier bags to carry his old shirt. Further along Kensington High Street he bought silk socks, a black bow tie and a pair of lightweight black elastic sided shoes. He regretted that at a quarter of the price advertised for a pair of slip on 'Trickers' they would be still be far beyond his means.

In 'Boots' he bought cosmetics, aftershave, hair gel, sun tan skin cream for his face, and a manicure set. The pleasure to purchase new, not second hand clothes, in proper retail shops, lifted

Tristan's spirits. They reversed the downward drift of his expectations that had been in decline since psychiatrists referred him to the Laurels.

A typical Tristan thought cheered him. "Even if I do go broke in a futile search for work, I might qualify as the best-dressed dosser in town."

He spent a third of his resources before ten o'clock, with no heed to Cunningham, the duty manager at the Keeble, who had warned that he could not guarantee anything. He not only felt justified, he felt the better for it. With his new clothes on his back and feet, the cosmetics in the Harrods' bag, and his old things in the outfitters bag, feeling chipper, Tristan used his cane to hail a taxi.

When he fell back into the seat, he fell back into his old acerbic ways. He called to the cabby, "Have you the knowledge to follow the known way to take me, without delay, regardless of cost, to the 'Keeble'. It is that rather grand hotel at the far end of the Strand, don't you know. They need me there."

The driver, who was as black as his cab, delighted Tristan when he picked up the comedy, to call back, "Sorry barss, this cab don't go east of Trafalgar, but for a toff like you, I could drop you off back at the Burlington where yous belong." Tristan rewarded his good humour with a tip equal to the fare.

Aiming to act part Stuart Grainger, part Leslie Phillips for the interview, Tristan made straight for the Keeble's cloakroom. He washed his hands, carefully trimmed his fingernails with his new manicure set, put sun skin cream on his face, a little of the gel on his hair, before he combed it across his temples, clear of his ears.

The cloakroom attendant brushed his shoulders while Tristan preened in front of the mirror, satisfied that the combined effort had brushed him up well. After he tipped the man a pound, he did not notice the sarcasm in the attendant's voice when he said, "Very smart sir, very trim." The attendant had seeded his tips tray with two five-pound notes, and a ten-dollar bill, held down with several two-pound coins.

Tristan asked at the concierge's desk where he might find Mr. Cunningham. The concierge arranged for a hall porter to show him the way through the hotel underground labyrinth to his office. The porter warned Tristan, "Be careful of this young fella, his first name is Russell. He is twisted; his bite is worse than his bark. He has a temper worse than any Jack Russell terrier I ever owned, and I have had a few."

The porter knocked loudly on the door before he quickly retreated, to leave Tristan to face Cunningham on his own. "Come in, whoever you are," Cunningham called. When Tristan stepped into the carpet-less office he continued, "Oh hell, it's you is it. I had hoped that you might have been run over by a bus, or met with an equally horrible end." To side step the obvious attempt to put him down, Tristan replied sweetly, "Thank you Sir, a very good humoured day to you too. No sugar for your porridge this morning, just salt?"

"Shut it, I don't need any quips from you" Cunningham said sharply, "It has been a bugger all day, and we are not half way through the morning. A full house, three staff no shows, two resignations, three lost suitcases.

The ten o'clock speaker for the conference in the Lancaster Suite is still at Heathrow. However, as you are here, I suppose the least I can do to repay you for fouling my nest last night, is to take you to meet Florence. That should even things up."

It never failed to surprise Tristan just how much of a large hotel lay hidden, like an iceberg, with only a fraction visible to the public. After what seemed to be several changes of level, in long brick built carpet-less corridors and concrete steps, Cunningham barged through an unmarked door. He almost shouted, "Florence, this is Edwards, the deranged man who thinks that he would like to work here. Before you have him certified, will you question him, grill him, or even better spit roast him."

He turned to Tristan to say, abruptly, "Right, that's you and me square, I hope I never see you again." "Push off Russell, go back to your kennel," the woman said. She added, to no one in particular, certainly not to Tristan, "That little rat catcher should be taught some manners. Young managers are all the same these days. They think they know that which they don't know, and that which they do know, ain' necessarily so."

Back from her reverie, Florence snapped at Tristan, "Who are you; why is it that you have come to bother me?" Tristan answered calmly, "Tristan Edward is who I am ma'am, Tristan the given name, Edward, without the 's', the surname, it causes confusion. I am here to take up the position of night cash controller, for which I understand there is a vacancy. I hope that does not bother you.

Florence answered, "If that is what the brat told you, for once he is right, however I have to ask, why is it that you want the job at your age? It pays not much more than we pay the porters, hall or kitchen." To defuse the hostile atmosphere Tristan tried an ironic reply, "Well, dear lady, you may think that I waste your time, or that I am just a waste of time, but if I do not soon get work, I will waste away in quick time for lack of nourishment. You see, the hitherto continuous seam of my blameless bachelor life has become unstitched, the thread quite ravelled. If I can't work with children and for world peace, I must seek adequate remuneration to work in a happy environment, with likeminded people who will encourage my advancement."

Tristan's smooth words did not soften the woman's hard attitude, "Cut the crap Edwards, you are a typical male chauvinist loser, who fails to recognise the obvious. All that I am prepared to offer is a trial period under the cosh of my special friend Ms. Andrews. She is Senior Internal Auditor here at the Keeble. We look out for each other. We do not like sneaks, whistle blowers, grassers or informers. If you don't shape up, she will have you back on the street faster than if a bear was biting your bum."

After Tristan gave the woman Florence his National Insurance number, he signed a standard form that put him on the Keeble pay-role, as Night Cash Controller (Probationary); the woman gave him a key to a room in the company staff quarters. "Edward without the 's', report to Ms. Andrews, who has one, a nice double curved smoothly rounded one. Be there before ten p.m., Friday this week, ready for a busy ten-hour shift."

"Where might I find Mrs. Andrews?" Tristan asked for devilment. "In accounts 'old man', where else," the Florence person of personnel, who had little personality, said sniffily, "Watch your P. C. manners. She is Ms. Andrews." With that, the non-status specific person, referred to only as Florence, waved Tristan away. Tristan understood that she meant her 'Old man' reference to be an insult, not the term of friendship used the world over by men of all ages.

Free for the rest of the day, Tristan had time on his hands. As the job of cash controller, a low wage menial task, required him to be a creature of the night, Tristan felt justified spending his free time shopping for the portable radio he wanted.

In the big stores along Oxford and Regent Street, he enjoyed the buzz of people of all ages who crowded the wide pavements. Although he realised that he had spent money like a drunken sailor, he felt sure he could last until his first payday.

His copy of the Keeble employment form informed him that the Company paid staff engaged on weekly terms, a week in arrears. Tristan noted that the Keeble week did not conform to the Christian canon, it ran from Friday to Thursday, with pay delayed a further day. Tristan calculated that he had fifteen days to wait before his wages would add to his almost exhausted cash in hand.

In the electrical department of one of the big stores, Tristan bought a Japanese portable radio, after he had rejected the salesman's advice that the 'Roberts Radio', although a tad more expensive, was better value. The unctuous young man told him, "Most people of your age choose the Roberts sir." "I am sure that you are right," Tristan replied, "Nevertheless, if I was to buy a radio of that make, it would haunt me like a spectre, coming each day to remind me of the predators who once had me in their thrall."

The long day had tired Tristan. When the stores began to close, he made his way, slowly, towards Soho Square, a favourite haunt of his youth.

In Frith Street, he found what he looked for, a traditional pub with tables and chairs set outside on the pavement. He put the outfitters bag of old clothes on a table to secure a place, before he went inside.

To his delight he bought a pint of 'Bespoke', strong cask conditioned ale, which he had often enjoyed in Yorkshire. His mood bucked up by the beer, and content with his own company, he spent a pleasant three hours, drinking an equal number of pints, while watching the girls go by.

He felt sure he could not have seen more bare flesh, had he been back on that beach in Ipanema. Tristan had twice briefly visited the beach, when the Purser of the cruise ship that employed him, briefly allowed him ashore when the ship called into Rio de Janeiro.

After the warmth of the sun faded, Tristan wandered towards Piccadilly where his pecuniary conscience began to plague him about his rapidly dwindling cash reserves.

In a busy Greek restaurant, he started a damage limitation exercise. He ordered carefully, but enjoyed a very acceptable economic meal. He followed the obligatory Avgolemono soup with a main course of courgettes stuffed with minced lamb, tomato, herbs and rice.

The carafe of Retsina he ordered for congruity with the Greek food did not please his sensitive palate. After he dawdled over the meal, he walked happily back into the swirling mass of evening revellers. Several times the crowd jostled him before he decided he had done enough celebrating for one day.

He took a black cab back to the sanctuary of the Grassington, where he felt sure that his room would afford him his last good night of undisturbed sleep for many nights to come.

Mrs. Brassington came into the hall, while he struggled with his cane and two bulging bags on the stairs. "Good heavens," she said cheerfully, "You look as though you have been to the January sales." Tristan admitted, "Yes, I have celebrated. I have secured a job at the Keeble with a cell to live in. They don' pay well, however it's a start, with the possibility of advancement. Better than the dole, there is no promotion there. To mark the occasion, I have had three pints of good Yorkshire beer, and a tasty Greek supper not quite spoilt by carafe of Retsina."

Mrs. Brassington, obviously pleased for Tristan, said, "Good for you. I hope that you will remember us when you have riches thrust upon you."

When he reached his room, Tristan flopped into the comfortable chair to tune his new radio to BBC Radio 4. He soon retuned his new companion to Classic FM, because Radio 4 broadcast a debate with academics, known only to Oxbridge, who spoke about ethics in human relationships of which they had no experience. "Best do a 'reckon up' lad, you have been a bit profligate," he said quietly to himself.

A moment later, he shot bolt upright, rigid in shock. He could not find his wallet, his treasured Moroccan tooled leather wallet, bought for him by a girl he romanced in Casablanca.

The loss of his wallet meant that he had very little money left. "Bastards, bastards, you bloody thieving bastards," he almost screamed. After his initial natural outburst, he blamed himself almost as vehemently, "You bloody fool."

He quickly checked all his pockets because he always split up his cash to carry it in two or three pockets, as well as his wallet. In two pockets, he found several notes. After he had checked, three times over, he knew that without his wallet he was all but broke.

"Bugger, bugger, bugger," he said, again as criticism of himself, for being so wantonly stupid to carry so much cash in the busy pickpocket infested streets of London. He regretted that he had kept the still unopened letter that the Reverend Branwell Evans had given him, to open in case of emergency, in the inner pocket of the wallet.

He thought of the lucky sprig of white heather that Arthur Thomas had given him to remind him of his friends. That he had paid in advance for this, his last night at the Grassington, gave him little comfort.

The next day, Friday, too ashamed of his crass stupidity, Tristan did not tell Mr. Brassington, who had cooked his breakfast, of his misfortune. Whilst he thanked him for a comfortable stay and for his excellent cooked breakfast, he hoped that he had not noticed he had filched a bag of muesli and two individual portions of Coopers Oxford marmalade from the wicker baskets where the breakfast cereals were set out.

He doubted that John Brassington believed him when he asked if he might take two slices of toast for the ducks in Kensington garden.

Tristan's mood was grim when he left the comfort of the Grassington. It blackened when he accepted that as he could no longer afford taxis, buses or tube trains must be the preferred means to travel across London to his new quarters. With no option other than to wear his heavy coat and drag his worldly-goods behind him, he sweated up even before he reached Gloucester Road from where he took the tube train to Holborn, the nearest station to the Keeble's staff accommodation.

The Keeble staff quarters, arranged on two floors above three shops, were what he expected. Mirror to his mood, the accommodation was grim. His allocated room on the second floor had one window that looked out over the littered back yards of shops, houses, and flats threaded with ginnels, snickets and alleyways fit for a film set remake of 'Jack the Ripper'. Nobody had cleaned the room since the last occupant left.

His taste in décor was the very opposite of Tristan's. He had covered the walls in vile homoerotic posters mixed with dark brooding adverts for heavy metal bands.

Until he had thrown out the carpet, curtains and mattress, given the room a deep clean, and sealed all surfaces with brightly coloured paint Tristan decided not to sleep in the room allocated by the dreadful woman Florence, sans title, sans surname.

He knew that his planned refurbishment had to wait until payday, as after the theft of his wallet, he had to live on the little cash he had found in his pockets.

Tristan reckoned he could manage, provided he could charm the housekeepers to let him live in the hotel and induce the chefs, by return favours, to let him feed off the hotel, until he could make the room fit for habitation.

After he had checked that the door locked securely, Tristan walked to the Keeble, a distance of about a mile, in search of the janitor's stores.

Inside the service corridors of the hotel, Tristan felt that he had walked almost another mile before he found the stores guarded by a formidable keeper.

Without hesitation, Tristan put both hands on the counter, beamed broadly before he said, "Some pratt has just burst a two kilo bag of ground white pepper. It's a right sneeze up. Sous Chef has gone ape, the commis are sneezing, they are, they are, the peppers all over the kitchen floor; Let me have a facemask, a brush and bin bags quick. I will bring the brush back, promise. Come on man, it's my first day, Chef will give me the bloody sack if I don't get back, pronto."

"Yer better ave a dustpan as well as the brush mate," the store man said, before Tristan set off down the corridor, tools in hand, at the best speed he could manage, calling out, "Campbell's the name" "Come back here", the store man shouted after him. "You haven't signed for them, or given me a requisition number." Tristan did not hear the store-man's unkind personal opinion of his mental condition, age and status.

Back in his allocated room, Tristan filled one of the black bags with rubbish that included used needles and a syringe found in the bedside and wardrobe drawers. Under the bed the evidence of several empty bottles of sherry, strong cider, dozens of empty packets of cigarettes of different brands, and an empty wallets of roll up tobacco confirmed that the room's previous occupant had been deeply disturbed.

It was almost six o'clock before Tristan had cleaned, mopped and scrubbed, to make the room at least superficially clean. He was on his last of many trips down to the bins in the back yard when a middle-aged fellow, dressed in the uniform of a hall porter, with the facial expression of an undertaker's mute stopped him.

"You'll never get that room right Gov, it's got a bloody jinks on it. A night cash controller chap had it last, he overdosed he did, a couple of days ago; dead as Pharaoh's father when they found him, poor sod. Before him, a night porter like me had it; he couldn't hack it either. Personnel said they had arranged for him to go to some fancy rehabilitation place in Stepney, the funny farm more like. Before him, the police took a right weirdo away."

Tristan grinned "Thank you cousin for your encouragement. I will get another bottle of Lysol to do the walls and floor again. Surely that will lay the ghosts of people past."

To himself he made a promise, "I'm damned if I will be beat. Many a true knight of King Arthur's court suffered in dungeons dire, more dread than this, I will come through."

At quarter to ten, after he dutifully returned the dustpan and brush to the counter on the wrong side of the grill to the janitor's store, he reported for duty.

He asked for Ms. Andrews, the Senior Internal Auditor. With the experience of fifty odd years of casual flirting, Tristan knew in an instant that he could not possibly divert this one, not unless he had a sex change.

The woman presented a formidable butch appearance, with her thin short cut red hair plastered down with oil. Her Harris Tweed jacket stretched tight round a bosom shaped like the mainsail of a galleon in a fair wind. Under her jacket, she wore a farmer's check shirt with woollen tie. She supported her bulk on stumpy muscular legs stuck into brown leather brogues. "Done cash control before?" She asked, "You look a bit worn at the edges for night work?"

Tristan made sure to be careful with his reply, "Yes, Ms Andrews, a long time ago. Although the technology may have changed, the fiddles will be much the same." Ms. Andrews's reply did not come as the natural assertiveness of a senior to a junior; it was downright hostile.

"Just do your job. If you think you have found a discrepancy, you tell me, nobody else, do you understand. You are not to theorise, you are just here to establish facts, is that clear. I will deal with any irregularities. Mr. Cunningham has already spoken to me about you. We can't afford to lose staff, not unless they are truly out of order, not those who have a customer following, not those who feed the tronc. Be very careful, you don't have much going for you."

Tristan fumed inside. The manner of her reply made him sure that Ms. Andrews knew all about Prescott. He began to wonder where the fiddles stopped, how high the cut went. However, he contented himself with a curt "Certainly Ms. Andrews with the nicely rounded's." "What did you say?" she snapped. Tristan replied quickly, "I only asked if there is a nicety about the round, I mean, is there a fixed time and route to follow for collection of the tills."

Ms. Andrews looked very hard at Tristan before she answered, "Yes, as we are quiet, there are only sixteen tills tonight. I have listed them in the manual. Make sure you get a legible signature for all of them. Bring them back here sealed ready to check and enter the cash and card payments. Now get on with it. I only came in to see whether Florence exaggerated her description of you; she did not. The duty night manager will tell you what you need to know when you get stuck,"

The cocktail bar, domain of Charles Lucas Prescott had two tills. Not sure of the reception he might receive Tristan slid quietly behind the bar, with the two replace till drawers.

He respectfully asked, "Do you mind?" Without waiting for an answer, he started to reset the first till. He slipped the till drawer, full of money, into a self-sealing bag, broke the seal on the replacement drawer with the recorded float, ready to slide it into the till.

"I'll check that," Charles Lucas Prescott's cold voice harboured no goodwill when he continued; "I don't trust company spies. I clocked you as soon as you came in the other night. I have friends here, we watch out for each other. You won't last three days. They will not put me ashore this time. I am worth too much; see how you get on with that, smart arse. In three days, you will be finished."

When Tristan clocked off after his third night on duty, he found a note in the slot that stored his card. It summoned him to report to the personnel office at nine a.m., before he left the building. During the mornings of both the previous days, despite more cleaning, he felt unable to sleep in the staff accommodation provided by the Keeble, that he now called certified 'Infesters of people'.

Tristan had charmed an old biddy chambermaid into letting him sleep in one of the hotels guest rooms which management had marked for emergency use only, due to customer complaints about the noise of the nearby lift motors. After he came off duty at eight a.m. Tristan used the room to sleep for six hours.

Each day he remade the bed with linen the chambermaid had left ready, cleaned the bathroom to make it all fresh, even to folding the end of the toilet paper into a point, to inform the duty housekeeper that he had serviced the room.

Before he arrived at the personnel office to answer the summons, Tristan knew that the Keeble would be 'Letting him go', on some pretext or other, with a handy P45 to help him on his way. Florence simply handed him a pay packet with a curt dismissal, "Your P45 is inside, with little else. You have only done thirty hours. We have taxed you at emergency rate because you did not bring a P45. Accommodation for your three nights in luxury has been deducted."

Tristan said, "Great, marvellous, excellent, what happened?" With a lip-curl smirk the Florence woman replied, "Easy done, we look out for each other. Charles explained that the young man owed him ten pounds from a previous round, when he had no notes to give change. Personnel agreed that it would be wrong for you to check on him. 'Victimisation' he said. Leave the key with security after you have cleared your room. By the way, the company rules state that ex-employees cannot use the hotel facilities until six months after they leave. That won't bother you will it Edwards. You will never be able to afford the Keeble. Leave now, shut the door, and don't come back."

Outside the door, in the corridor, Tristan faced Prescott who had arrived to gloat. "Three days I said, three days it took. Without a reference, you will never get off the dole. You are for the workhouse mate, unless of course you top yourself with your poufs bow tie." Tristan controlled his anger. In a low calm voice he replied, "Prescott, you won't know when I shall visit you again, but be assured that I shall. You are a cheat, a liar, a thief; it is for you to worry now."

Chapter 6

As he walked away from the Keeble, Tristan realised that without a home to go to and with little by way of visible means of support, for the first time in his chequered discontinuous career, the law might deem him a vagrant.

It angered and frustrated him that the dreadful Prescott had contrived to get him sacked from a job that provided quarters, that however sordid, gave him shelter and a contact address. Despite his undeserved misfortune, Tristan did not feel despondent or depressed.

His acerbic forthright nature drove his gamblers optimism that a bad run never lasted. He did not allow despondency or depression. His temper tantrums snapped him out of all forms of melancholy; his 'snap out of it' mechanism never failed.

Already he took delight in one aspect of losing out to Prescott. He had not had to wait another twelve days for his wages. The little cash the Keeble paid him for three nights work, multiplied his meagre reserves several times over.

That Prescott, tipped off by Florence, had waited in the corridor to gloat over his humiliating exit from the Keeble increased Tristan's resolve to prove Prescott a thief, a cheat and a liar. However far the kickbacks, pay offs and fiddles spread up the Keeble management tree, he determined to expose the entire corrupt racket in which Prescott, Ms. Andrews and the woman Florence were obviously involved.

It came to him that to cut down or uproot that particular canker riddled tree would be his just cause, an appropriate quest to follow.

Success would give him a true tale to tell at the reunion dinner of the Grey Haired Knights. It did not occur to him that it might be dangerous, as a loner, to tangle with Prescott who could count on the help of his corrupt colleagues who looked out for each other.

The walk back to the room in Clerkenwell Road, the room that supposedly had been his sleeping quarters for the last three nights, which he had not slept in once, took Tristan half an hour. He went to pick up his worldly-goods; his suitcase, two carrier bags, an overcoat, a hat and cane.

In the corridor, he met the same jaundiced faced hall porter who had told him the room had a jinx on it. The porter said, dolefully, "Leaving us already mate, I don't blame you. At least you leave on two legs, not in a straight jacket, or a body bag."

"Thank you cousin, keep the faith." Tristan could think of no other reply to this obvious Jeremiah.

Outside, in the traffic fumed less than fresh air, Tristan needed time to think. He decided to go down to the Embankment, to watch the river's changing scene, hoping that it might inspire a credible plan B. After a couple of stops for a much-needed rest, he found an unoccupied bench in the Victoria Embankment Gardens where he sat to enjoy the sun while he watched the world go by and the river go on its own way to the sea, with not a ship, tug, or Thames barge to disturb its flow.

The few boats on the move were not working boats with cargo, just tourist boats and the odd river taxi. Tristan thought young Londoners must think of the Thames as 'Old Man River', old hat, like himself, too old for work, pensioned off, retired.

Before Tristan had given a thought to his future, or a possible plan B, a man came unseen from behind, to sit down determinedly close on the bench beside him. His sudden intrusive arrival shocked Tristan out of his reverie.

At first, however unlikely, he thought that it might be the same man who, only a few days earlier, had done the same in Scagill, two hundred miles away. He had quite deliberately chosen to sit close, with other nearby benches unoccupied. Tristan noticed that although he dressed differently, he did have a similar thin black almost useless walking stick and a hat, not unlike the wide stitched brim affair with which the man in Scagill had fanned himself.

He had the same timelessness about him, to which Tristan found it difficult to put an age. However, he satisfied himself that it could not be the same man; his brindle black and grey beard grew thicker, shorter, more Barbarossa than Confucian sage.

After a wheeze, followed by a miners souvenir cough, wiped away with a cloth, the curious chap followed with a thought, so crucial to the moment that it came out in a defiant loud Welsh mining valley singsong voice. "Sod it; things will get better, bound to, worse before better though, sure to by damn, sod em all, it's a bugger, and he coughed again."

He put two plastic Waitrose bags on the floor, by his feet. One full of what appeared to be leftovers from a sale of antique bric-a-brac, the other, for some unfathomable reason, at this time in the morning, smelt of fish and chips. "Got a fag mate?" he asked. "No," Tristan replied, embarrassed. He did not wish to get into a conversation; he needed to think.

After the eccentric had fumbled in several pockets, he pulled out a pack of herbal cigarettes. "Want one?" he wheezed, as he proffered the packet towards Tristan. "No thank you, I have given up smoking." Tristan said, and wondered how long it would be before he would automatically reply, to the same question, "No thank you, I don't smoke."

The reason for the smell of fish and chips became apparent when the eccentric rummaged in the bag without bric-a-brac, to bring out a wrapped bundle of cold chips. "Saved em from last night, always save arf the chips for my breakfast I does. They gives you so many chips where I get em from, too many for us old uns, want one?"

He proffered the package in Tristan's direction. "No, thank you all the same," Tristan replied. He felt a wave of nausea when the man slowly, with difficulty, separated a chip from the cold pulp mass before popping it into his mouth. It came as a genuine shock to Tristan that this obvious genuine grade one listed vagrant, thought him as one of his ilk.

Stung to action by this thought, Tristan stood up to say decisively, to no one in particular, "I can't sit here all day; I have to find work." This prompted the eccentric to stand up, face to face with Tristan. He waved his stick as though to admonish him. Tristan had to look directly into the sun, which transformed the vagrant eccentric into a hazy dark shadow wrapped in golden light.

Although he was never sure, whether the eccentric vagrant spoke the words, or whether it was his own imagination reflecting what he had thought, as he left the Keeble, Tristan never forgot them.

'You must learn what it is to be a despondent, depressed vagrant. It was here on the north bank of the Thames that Arthur turned back the heathen Saxon Oswald; it was here that Whittington turned again, not Highgate Hill. It will be here that your fortune will turn, when the tide turns.'

Blinded by the sun, Tristan turned away. Without a backward glance, he walked up the wide steps to the Strand. The short climb made him realise that if he traipsed around London, in mid-summer, looking for work, wearing his winter overcoat, while trailing his erratic suitcase, he would look as eccentric as the vagrant from whom he had just walked away.

He thought his worn incongruous Harrods carrier bag made him look ridiculous. To have any chance of getting a job, Tristan knew that he would have to be clean, well dressed and of sober appearance. This obvious fact required that he spend money on another night, or perhaps two, in bed and breakfast. All these things considered he took a taxi back to the Grassington Guesthouse.

Abandoning all pretence, Tristan admitted to Mrs. Brassington that his first venture had failed. He asked if he could stay for the night, and possibly the following night, until something turned up. He told her of the racket going on at the Keeble that had led to his losing the job.

Shamefaced, he also asked whether he could stay on a bed only basis, for five pounds a night less than the usual rate for bed and breakfast as, momentarily, he was strapped for cash. Mrs. Brassington would not agree to Tristan's idea of no breakfast, "You daft hapeth," she said, "You'll need a good breakfast to survive, you know that. However, as your request is a last minute dot com, I will agree to the lower charge. We know that you are pinched for cash. John noticed that a packet of muesli had gone to work with you the other day. He thought it odd that you buttered the toast for the ducks."

"Oh dear," Tristan said, "I had hoped that John might not notice. So sorry and all that, I am a bit down at the moment, but one day you will read about me in 'Fortune' magazine, the one that reports the top hundred wealthy people." Mrs. Brassington laughed, "More like in the 'News of the World' the one that reports on scandal." "We are full again after Thursday, so you had better get on with your bother. I'll put your stuff in the same room, but first, pay me for two nights, in case you get yourself mugged or something. You had better give me your laundry; I will put it through with ours."

Tristan knew that he could get a good breakfast at Staples, the Cromwell Road caff, the place where he had breakfasted on his first morning back in the 'Smoke'.

Before he went to Staples, he bought a 'Daily Mail' at the next-door newsagents. He smiled when he walked through the open door of the caff, because the Lebanese owner called out to him, "Back again, nice to see you sir, good for trade when the locals see the gentry dining in a dump like mine. Please take a seat in the window where people who pass by can see you." Tristan responded with a genuine smile; only a couple of hours earlier, an obvious vagrant had judged him as one of his peer group.

He read the paper, enjoyed the greasy high cholesterol all day breakfast, and the mug of strong tea. He absentmindedly fumbled for a packet of cigarettes in all of his pockets, before remembering that he no longer smoked. Once he remembered that, the craving passed.

Tristan thought that the woman who worked behind the counter must be the wife of the sleeveless grey sweat-shirted owner. She spoke to him in what Tristan assumed to be Arabic, occasionally in French, both mostly in monosyllables. He thought her to be a classic Ingres perfect beauty from the seraglio, younger than her husband was by at least fifteen years.

She had a full rounded figure, long shiny black hair, flawless olive skin, huge dark, but very bright eyes. Her appearance clearly showed her to be a healthy woman in the prime of her life. She wore a practical bibbed apron, over a light white cotton shift dress, and transparently not much else, other than high-heeled strappy white shoes. The bright 'Marigold' gloves she wore strangely enhanced her overt sexuality.

Tristan could not help taking covert glances at her as she moved around behind the counter, occasionally putting both hands on her husband's waist when she squeezed past him. Tristan flattered himself that she glanced at him in equal measure. He lingered over his brunch, engrossed in his favourite part of the paper, the letters page, when she came to clear his table. Tristan became acutely aware of her, because she stood unusually close.

When she had come from behind the counter, she had automatically taken off her apron and Marigold gloves. The soft cotton of her dress clung to her body. It accentuated her curves. He felt shrouded in her richly perfumed presence, a perfume so powerful that it even dominated the cooked food smells from the kitchen.

"Can I interest monsieur in a pudding or perhaps a coffee," she said this deliberately in the voice of a French maid in a bedroom farce. He looked up from his newspaper, to answer, "Oh no, nothing thank you." In order to tease Tristan, rather than coming to his left side, to clear away his empty plate, she stretched across the table, quite deliberately to present the décolleté of her superb unsupported bosom at Tristan's eye level.

The front of her dress fell forward, as she knew it would. Tristan could not only see the nipples of her breasts, he could also see her naval and the top of her brief pants. The woman said, "Did you enjoy that?" He did not think her remark innocent. He replied, quite deliberately, "Oh yes, quite lovely." She said with a husky voice, "Don't you mean, or shouldn't you have said, 'very tasty, or perhaps, 'bien-cuit?'"

He was convinced that it was a tease when she raised her curved eyebrows and continued to flirt, "You see, being half Lebanese, half French, I need to improve my English. I am so sorry to have interrupted you."

When he stood up to leave, Tristan could not help it. In a voice that would have done credit on an Indian Army field Officer, as his eyes readily enjoyed her full figure, Tristan said, "Well young lady, if we are to continue your English lesson, you did not interrupt me, you disturbed me." Tristan collected himself sufficiently to ask for his bill. She said, "No bills at Staples; just pay me what you owe." Tristan, who enjoyed flirting, something he had not done for a long time, said, "I doubt I shall ever be able to pay you sufficient tribute. Please take this and keep the appreciation, you deserve much more than a mortal such as I can give."

When Tristan left the caff, he was conscious that the woman's soft beguiling laughter and his response had not pleased Riejik. He had given them both a hard look. He also noticed that the card in the window still advertised the job vacancy for an afternoon cook. "What a difference half a day makes," Tristan thought. "At nine o'clock, Florence, the gorgon woman in personnel sacked me, an hour or so later a vagrant tagged me as one of his kind. By noon, a charming chatelaine took in my washing. Finally, I sparked with a fulsome glamorous exotic creature; all before two in the afternoon."

The brief flirt with Riejik's wife was the high point of Tristan's day. Thereafter, it got steadily worse. He rang bells; knocked on doors, spoke with mangers or proprietors of shops, bars, restaurants, hotels, dubious nightclubs, employment and estate agencies, whom all rejected him in different ways.

However many weasel words they used, when agglomerated, they amounted to just two, 'Too old'. When he had no more strength, or the will to go on, he slowly made his way towards the sanctuary of the Grassington.

On the way, in a small Chinese take away and chip shop that had a few tables, 'to eat in', he bought fish and chips, with the customary pot of tea, bread and butter. He ate nearly all the fish supper, but he could never eat the skin, which forced him to leave half the batter. Although the amount of chips served almost over-faced him, he decided not to save half for the next day. He calculated his total cost of food for the day, that included several cups of dreadful tea, amounted to just less than the hourly rate paid by the Keeble for a Night Cash Controller.

The next day he breakfasted well at the Grassington. At the same time, he talked easily with Mrs. Brassington who listened to his account of his job search, with interest, though Tristan missed out the best part about the Lebanese siren.

When he left to go on his second full day of searching for any job opportunity, he could not find his silver-topped cane that he had left against the hallstand. John Brassington came laughing to the door to wish him good luck. Tristan joined in the laughter when he saw that on the end of his stick, the Brassingtons had tied a cloth holding a packed lunch, pantomime style.

Tristan spent another long day in his search for work. He knocked before he entered through doors that might just as well have been revolving doors, so quickly did he exit back out onto the street. The job centre could not offer anything that did not require a C.V. that demanded a contact phone number, and an address. Three wasted tube journeys, and one taxi ride, left him south of the river in Camberwell with increased temper and diminished physical and cash reserve.

A splendid turbaned Sikh offered him a job as a night sales person, to work in a petrol station in Walworth. However, the Sikh could not provide accommodation. It did not take Tristan long to find out that any job, without accommodation provided, was out of the question. Forty hours at minimum wage, after deductions for tax and National Insurance would only pay for six nights' bed and breakfast at the Grassington.

All local estate agents that handled bed-sits required the prospective tenant to pay, up front, two, or even three months' rent. Up-front money Tristan did not have.

By six o'clock, he began to despair. His search for Plan B had not worked. To secure a live in position would almost certainly mean that it would have to be in the hospitality racket.

The final straw came when a man, half his age, stepped out of a doorway to wave a newspaper in front of him, to whine "Big Issue, Big Issue". Tristan snapped back, "Big Issue, Big Issue, you don't know the meaning of a big issue, you have a comfortable doorway haven't you?"

Because plan B had not materialised, Tristan decided to try for the job of afternoon cook at the caff in Cromwell Road.

Riejik gave Tristan a less than cheery welcome. "Dear god man, you look about as knackered as I feel. What can I get for you that is not too complicated? I'm ready to shut shop. The wife

91

is off spending my money somewhere, and I have been here since six this morning."

"Just tea please boss." Tristan replied, "I really did not come to eat, I came to apply for the job you have advertised in the window. I need to work. I have to find somewhere to live." Riejik grinned, "You don't call this living do you, a toff like you?" Tristan replied, "I'm no toff; in fact I am perilously close to destitute."

Riejik asked. "What makes you think that you can cook?" Tristan answered, "I was fifteen when I began work in the hospitality racket. I qualified as a B2 cook in the Army Catering Corps when I was young." Riejik, who interrupted, "Was that before or after Soyer modernised the Crimea kitchens? Seriously, you are a bit old for the cooking game. Tell me, why are you without funds, has the wife divorced you, are you an ex con, an alcoholic, or is it drugs or gambling perhaps."

Tristan, who felt that he had a chance of a fair hearing, replied, "No, no, no and yes; I haven't heard from my wife for more than forty years. I have never been in clink, I never drink spirits, my regular tipple is cask-conditioned beer, but I prefer good port when other people pay. The drugs that I have used were not the hard stuff of the streets. They were the more insidious prescription stuff, taken with too many cups of coffee and packets of cigarettes. You will have noticed that I asked for tea. I do like to gamble when in funds"

"Well," Riejik replied, "I can't pay enough for you to gamble, but perhaps I will take a chance on you, if only to avert a premature heart attack. I can't go all day, not as I used to. My wife, who flirted with you this morning, lives with me in our small flat round the corner. Upstairs here is our store with a bit of an office. It has a door that connects to a room that could make up to a bed-sit, with a separate bathroom. I occasionally use the office in the evenings, nowhere else. Quite-frankly, it is a bit of a rat hole, although it has a separate entrance, well fire escape really, so you would not have to come and go through the cafe."

Tristan tried not to sound desperate, "Well, why don't we both take a chance? We might make a success of it. I have a P45, courtesy of the Keeble, where I managed three days' work before they got rid of me."

"Why did they do that?" Riejik asked. Tristan gave a straight answer, "Middle management conspired against me because I clocked one of their better scams. They thought it best to brush it under their three-inch thick carpets. Probably two inches of that are all the other fiddles they have swept under them in years gone by."

"I run a straight shop here," Riejik said, "No fiddles, all the take goes through the till. I pay all my bills and taxes by cheque or direct debit. No, I tell a lie, I don't tell the Inland Revenue about the divvy points I get from the Nectar card I use at Sainsbury's and the air miles I get on my petrol. We used to get a few quid by selling used oil from the fryers. These days, with the rigor of health and safety regulation we have to pay someone to take it away, after we ceremoniously exchange waste disposal notices. This bloody government takes too much, and asks for far too much paperwork. I cannot be bothered with fiddles. I have seen too many businesses go bust after a VAT or Inland Revenue inspection. If the Revenue does not get you, it is the environmental health, the fire service, the performing rights, the PPL, and a host of other busy bodies who interfere with the natural flow of business. I don't know why I don't pack it all in. I could go back to Lebanon to chance the troubles, the bombs and bullets breaking out again."

Riejik laughed at his own catalogue of woe before he became serious again. "When can you start?" "Tomorrow, if that is alright with you," Tristan said, "Perhaps, in the morning, I could get started to clean up the rat-hole you so eloquently describe. Is there a cook shop near here, where I can get some chef's whites and cook's trousers?" "Sure," Riejik replied, "Down Cromwell, by Earls Court. You had better get yourself some clogs as well. I'll pay minimum wage, but not deduct for your accommodation for the first month. See how we get on after that."

Five hours a day, thirty hours a week, Sundays off, Tristan thought that he could just about manage. To cook would not be difficult. The American style single-handed cook, serve, clear and clean operation, from the small hot unventilated kitchen would make the job hard, until he got kitchen fit. Another problem for his age and loss of fitness were the refrigeration units. They were all in a shed out in the back yard, to add miles to the distance to be covered each shift.

When Riejik finally closed the cafe, he took Tristan to inspect the upper floor. No one had lived over the cafe for years. The accommodation had deteriorated to dilapidation. The wallpaper seemed anxious to disassociate itself from any past attachment it may have had to the walls. The bath stored long forgotten tins of old paint, brushes and rollers. The toilet bowl had clearly been divorced by the missing seat, on the justifiable grounds that it had grown a furry green beard. The gas heater hung off the wall. It drooped from its connecting pipes like a rotting snowdrop. "At least," Tristan thought, "I don't have to clean the curtains and carpets, there aren't any. No wonder Riejik said I could live rent-free for a month, that way I can't demand that he carry out repairs and redecoration."

Tristan remembered the eccentric Welsh vagrant's statement of fact and repeated it word for word. ""Sod it; things will get better, bound to, worse before better though, sure to by damn, sod em all, it's a bugger." For Tristan it had the same cathartic affect as a tantrum. It reminded him also that his luck would change at the turn of a tide.

Chapter 7

After a good night's sleep in a comfy well-appointed room, followed by a hearty breakfast Tristan felt well prepared to start work at Riejik's cafe.

Both Mr. and Mrs. Brassington came to the door to wish him luck with his new job. Elizabeth Brassington insisted that he must keep in touch and come back again, if things went wrong. She also promised that if she heard of a more suitable job opportunity, John would come to 'That awful Staples place', to tell him.

When she gave him back the money he had left with her, to keep it safe, Tristan had about as much in his pocket as he would get each week on the dole, if he ever lost this job and could not find another. Tristan knew that government handouts to the unemployed were barely enough to live on for a week and not enough if one needed to buy a new coat or a pair of shoes.

To meet the challenge of the new job, Tristan almost marched to the Cromwell Road, even though he had to drag as well as carry his whole estate with him, bags, case, coat, cane and hat. Although the Brassingtons has sent him off in good spirits, he had doubts about whether the job offered security. It worried him that when he had responded to Riejik's wife sensual provocative flirting, he had made a mistake, a mistake that he had not often made. Throughout his working life, he had followed the advice of his elders, 'Never foul thine own nest lad' more-often-expressed in crude terms to do with a doorstep.

He had never flirted with, or befriended, any female member of the firm where he worked, at whatever level, or however attractive, even though, in his youth, his main occupation had been flirting with any half-reasonable bit of skirt, bird, bint, crumpet, or totty. More than once, he had been late for work, after he had followed a well-turned pair of ankles that were not going his way.

As a gambler, he knew that the odds of getting a date with a stranger, by using a blunt approach, were more than twenty-five to one against, yet they were odds he could not resist. Rejection had never caused him to be embarrassed.

When Tristan arrived at Staples, Riejik gave him a key to the first floor room, before he told him not to waste the morning up there, but to be back sharp at three, after he had kitted himself out with kitchen gear, ready for work, because he wanted to go to Cash and Carry.

Of necessity, Tristan spent most of his remaining cash on two pairs of elastic waisted cook's trousers, two chefs white coats, and a pair of kitchen clogs.

Vanity depleted his reserves further when he bought two unnecessary blue neckerchiefs. He spent almost all of what he had left of his cash in a so-called 'ex-army store', on a simple wire frame camp bed and a cheap sleeping bag.

During his leisurely walk back to Riejik's caff; Tristan let his mind range free to consider his opportunities. His first thoughts were to start as a free trader, a sole proprietor, perhaps with a market stall as a platform on which to build to a limited company, before the stock market floated the company as a PLC.

When he recognised that his uncertain future might not allow enough road to make it as an entrepreneur, he dropped the idea. Although he had never even played charades, let alone taken any interest in amateur dramatics, he thought for a moment that an actor's life might be the life for him, to play part Stewart Granger part Leslie Philips characters, in reprise roles, at Ealing Film Studios. Other thoughts that 'Mega Buck Pictures' no longer made such films, only weird fantasy epics, space ship battles, car chase crashes, misery memoirs and pornography put an end to that fantasy.

A better idea came to him, to write a novel, the quick way to riches for those who had the talent and mornings free to write. He felt sure that he had sufficient memories of horror hotels, over the top cruise ship characters, cocktail hour cat fights, brawls in the bars of the Balearics, crimes on the Costas and greed in the Gulf, to cobble together enough best sellers, sequels and prequels to fill both sides of a bookseller's stand in an airport departure lounge.

When he arrived back at the caff in Cromwell Road, it overwhelmed all Tristan's fanciful ideas. Its sheer normality made it clear that, for a while at least, he would have to knuckle down to save enough money to buy essentials.

He planned to buy a pay as you go mobile phone with a number to add to the address of the cafe, on a C.V. he would prepare and have properly typed and printed as a necessary connection to the world of work.

When he let himself into the first floor, from the fire escape, he felt sure that it smelt cleaner. The bath had discharged its cargo, the toilet, though still without a seat, had lost its green beard. Even better, a man dressed in blue overalls had the gas heater in pieces on the floor, with the connecting pipes already secured back to the wall; all points to the good.

On the down side, Riejik's wife, wearing her yellow Marigold gloves, appeared to be cleaning the room. It gave Tristan cause to worry. He thought she must have bought her dress to wear on the beach, not for housework. Her white strappy shoes had four-inch high stiletto heels. She called out, "Good morning Tristan, I may call you that, may I? Wasn't he one of King Arthur's Round Table Knights, I know that Tristan was the sexy young vet from that telly programme. I don't know how Riejik could offer this slum to a gentleman like you."

She had made him so nervous that Tristan stuttered his reply, "P please Mrs. er, Mrs. Riejik, please stop what you are doing, you have enough to do downstairs in Staples. I can manage up here. See, I have bought a bed and a sleeping bag. I shall be quite comfortable. I shall soon have it all ship shape."

He knew, immediately, that he should not have mentioned the bed. "Tristan, you handsome devil, my name is Yvette. What is that silly contraption that you think you can make into a bed? It will be no good, far too narrow even for an under and over double up. I am sure that with your Clark Gable looks, you will soon make friends with lots of lovely London ladies." Again, her eyebrows lifted, her eyes giving Tristan, what he used to know as a 'Come hither look'. Just as flirtatiously, she shrugged, "Well, if Donald Duck is not wanted, I will leave you to exercise your female side. See you at three."

With that, she waved her yellow gloves at him, on her way to the fire escape door. For a second, as she paused in the doorway, the bright sunlight shone through the thin soft white cotton of her summer dress. The sun so revealed her full figures that she might just as well have been naked. Tristan could not help it, he called out after her, "Madam, your slip isn't showing."

He immediately regretted that he had said it. It played to her obvious pleasure in being provocative. She did a quick pirouette, before she called back, "Tristan, the slip you mentioned, could that have been a slip of the tongue?"

The gas fitter grunted, "You watch out for that one mate, she is always at it, she leads fellas on. She does it to provoke poor old Riejik. He gets murderous he does. He almost killed one of his customers who fell for it."

Just before three, Tristan presented himself for duty, immaculate in his new chefs gear, with a blue neckerchief neatly tied. Riejik greeted him with a sarcastic, "Dib dib; where's your woggle?" before he gave him a quick tour of the dry goods store, refrigerators and deep freeze cabinets, to show him where to find the stock.

"Don't worry Mr. Edward; although you may be a well beyond your best before date, all my stock is within the sell by date. I have asked my wife Yvette to keep an eye on you until you get the hang of things. I have cleared the till back to today's float, so we will soon see whether you are worth your keep."

Tristan smiled to himself; He noted that Riejik had not told him the value of the float, so that unless he counted it, he would not be able to argue about any possible discrepancy.

Just as Riejik left the caff, Yvette came in off the street. She hardly spoke to him, although she spoke readily, easily, to every customer, many by name. Yvette's wander through the cafe was not the usual restaurant manager's rush, when each question asked is a closed question, set to discourage anything other than a complimentary or neutral response.

Yvette's greetings were genuine, her enquiries personal; they were sincere. Tristan could tell that Riejik's wife had made the business a popular success. When she finally reached the kitchen, her first words brought colour back to Tristan's face.

"My, who got you ready, bit of an improvement on my old man's grey vest, hairy armpits and tattoos. We shall be able to notch up the prices a peg or two, if you can keep it up. Oh, what am I saying, I am sure you will be able to do that, for me."

Tristan found no difficulty to cope with taking the orders, cooking and taking payment.

The cafe had no automatic till, only a simple old-fashioned cash drawer. He kept the order slips neatly stacked so that Riejik would be able to make sure that the money in the till balanced with the take, plus the float, when he returned to cash up and close up for the day.

For more than the first half of his first shift Yvette sat in a window seat, to read women's magazines and to keep an eye on operations for her husband. Tristan felt that she watched him, in the same way that a cat watches a bird in a bush. Occasionally she helped him when he asked where to find things, or when she described how Riejik cooked his menu items, and when she corrected the portion size that Tristan served if they differed from those served by Riejik.

However, at six o'clock, Riejik's wife called out. "O.K. handsome, I am off home. You seem to have the hang of it. Your not yet mate is about to abandon ship. I leave you without navigation aids until the Captain returns." For the fun she found in embarrassing Tristan, she dropped her voice, to a soft sultry whisper, but loud enough for him to hear, "I am off for a long cool shower, after which I will towel down before I cover myself in scented oil to stretch out on the sun bed for an hour, with only the radio on. It will then be time for me to get dressed to cook old grumpy his supper." Her parting glance raked over Tristan like a cat clawing the curtains."

Tristan had returned everything worth saving to the refrigerator, cleaned down, and made a list of goods to order, before Riejik came to cash up. "You alright for half an hour mate?" Riejik asked. He did not wait for a reply, before he carried on, "Good, let me show you how I like the prep to be done ready for morning. Everything set out on trays ready for a quick start when I get in here at six."

The half hour turned out to be well over an hour before they completed the prep. Tristan was not concerned; he had no money to go anywhere. During a quiet period, just after Yvette had left, he had made himself a splendid three-egg omelette with mushrooms, cheese and tomatoes.

Riejik seemed content after he had checked the cash in the drawer against the order slips. The next two days passed uneasily for Tristan. Yvette's flirtatious behaviour became outrageous. When they were in the caff together, he received several black looks from Riejik. Tristan did not flatter himself that she flirted with him, for his benefit.

He knew that Yvette flirted for fun, and no more. To flirt would always be a game for her, a game she played to the limit, a game for which nature had her superbly equipped.

Although she occasionally pushed at the boundaries, her limit stopped well short of romance or serious engagement. During the afternoon of his third day at Riejik's, when he had been at the counter serving a customer, she squeezed past him. She put her hands on his waist, a habit he had noticed when she squeezed past Riejik.

She alarmed Tristan because she went further. She giggled "Tight buttocks, good boy," after she had pushed her hands down below the elastic waist of his new chef's trousers. Unable to deal with it, Tristan ignored her; he pretended that it had not happened.

The next day she made things worse. She teased him constantly; she probed for answers to very personal questions about his love life, past, present and future. She asked whether he had yet had a friend up to his room, she even asked if he was gay.

Tristan felt trapped; if he responded to her advances, he felt sure Riejik would know. He remembered the grim warning of the gas fitter. If he continued to ignore her, Tristan felt that he might provoke the 'Hell that hath no fury like a woman scorned'.

Under different circumstances, he would have enjoyed the banter. However, although the pay was poor and the accommodation primitive, he needed to keep the job until he could secure a better opportunity.

Even though Tristan had increased, the range of jobs he sought, the mornings he had spent in search for work had been a waste of time.

Lack of money to spend on taxis or tube journeys had reduced the area that he could search. He could only go as far as he could walk before he became too tired, on his return to the café to cook, serve, clear and clean, five hours a day, six days a week. Despite Yvette's best efforts, he continued to keep a straight face. He ignored her double entendres, bottom pinching, and squeezes.

His stoic response had the effect of making her more outrageous, more determined to break down his reserve. Tristan knew
that his job might be at risk.

After six days at the cafe, where he found that he got along well
enough with Riejik, Tristan asked him for a sub from his wages
that were not due until the end of the next week. Lack of cash had
confined him to the bed-sit, still without curtains and carpets."

He wanted to be amongst people in Chelsea, to have a beer
in the 'Grenadier', to go back to the friendly Italian restaurant in
Kensington where he had enjoyed a meal on his first day back in
London.

Riejik readily gave him what he asked for from the till. He
made Tristan sign a slip of paper for what he had received. Riejik
put the signed slip in the till before he made a separate note in a
small cashbook he carried. It was obvious to Tristan, that Riejik
paid great attention to detail, a feature that Tristan admired in
business.

Sometime after eight o'clock, Tristan said goodnight to Riejik
before he climbed the fire escape to his room, intent to freshen
up before a night out on the town. A surge of panic stopped him
when he saw his camp bed in a corner of the un-curtained room.

It was obvious that Riejik's wife, Yvette, the half-Arab, half
French tease, had been up to further mischief. Neatly laid out on
his sleeping bag, she had placed a pair of sunglasses similar to
those she wore.

About twenty centimetres below the glasses, she had arranged
a red silk scarf, tied like his blue neckerchief. Appropriately
spaced below the neckerchief, she had placed a delicate lace bra,
padded out with cotton wool. Lower down still, she had arranged
a small G-string overlaid by a red lace suspender belt attached to
sheer black stockings.

Either side of the arrangement she had carefully placed her
signature yellow Marigold gloves. Yvette had left a note, written
in lipstick, on a piece of card. "Can I be your under and over dou-

ble up? "To complete her 'Brit Art' piece of conceptual art, she had sprayed the arrangement with her peculiar musty perfume.

Tristan froze when Riejik, who held a clipboard, came through the unlocked connecting door from his office, an office he had told him he rarely used. "Tristan, sorry to interrupt mate, can you remember if we have any HP Sauce left in the dry goods store."

The two men stood, side by side. For a long time neither said a word. Riejik broke the silence, his voice an unnatural deep groan, "Oh, bloody hell man, you are old enough to be her father. I'll bloody kill the pair of you."

Tristan was as angry as Riejik. Over the past few days, he had realised that his doubt about his job's security had developed like a Greek tragedy that would lead to an inevitable catastrophic end. "Don't be daft Riejik," Tristan said, "It's not me to blame, and she doesn't mean it; she only does it to get you going." Riejik's reply un-nerved Tristan. "Well maybe you are right, maybe you are wrong, either way it is you that has to go. I want you out of here before I get in at six tomorrow morning. I shall deal with her tonight."

Tristan moved to start clearing up; Riejik hissed, "Don't you dare touch her things." He pushed past Tristan, grabbed the underwear, scarf and sunglasses before he stormed out through his office, down to the kitchen. Tristan heard Riejik unlock the back door, the bin lid crash, and his one shouted expletive, "Bitch." Tristan followed with his own one word quiet expression that summed up how he felt, "Bugger."

Tristan did not go out that evening. He packed, all his possessions, except for his sleeping bag, camp bed and shaving kit. He thought it best to be well clear of 'Staples' before six in the morning.

He did not think that the gas fitter had exaggerated when he had told him that Riejik had almost killed a customer who had fallen for Yvette's flirting. It certainly had a ring of truth to it.

The extra gear he had accumulated since he arrived in London, two weeks ago, would not fit into his case and Harrods bag. He packed the chefs trousers, coats, kitchen clogs, and sleeping bag into a black plastic bin bag. Although he set his alarm clock for five a.m., he woke to switch it off long before he had set it to wake him.

After a quick wash and shave, he dressed, before he let himself out of the bed-sit room, down the fire escape route. When he closed the yard gate behind him, he summarised his situation to say, aloud to early morning London, what had almost become his mantra, "It's a bugger this is." His mood was grim.

Chapter 8

On the street outside Staples caff, Tristan found that once again circumstance beyond his control had left him homeless, short of money, and with no prospect of a job. With the high summer weather neigh perfect, he felt out of place in his heavy winter overcoat and hat that he had to wear because he did not have a spare hand to carry them.

It shamed Tristan that he had had to stuff his sleeping bag, and work clothes into a black plastic bin bag, the mark of a vagrant, not of a Knight Errant, not even as a gentleman of the road.

Like a homing pigeon, he started to walk on his way back to the Grassington Guesthouse in the hope that the money Riejik had advanced against hard earned wages might buy him two nights comfort in what had become his London cote.

He had no doubt that even though the advance had been a quarter of what he had earned for his weeks work, he would get no more from Riejik.

Twice since he had arrived in London, the Brassingtons had made him welcome, but he realised he would most definitely not be welcome so early in the morning.

To kill time, he found a park bench in one of the many small gardens in London to watch the city come alive to a new day.

Tristan thought that Wordsworth's fair city had not shown him a fair hand.

Just after nine o'clock, with his case, carrier bag and black plastic bin bag at his feet, Tristan rang the bell on the front door of the Grassington Guesthouse. John Brassington, who came to the door, gave him his usual genial welcome with an added surprise. "Oh hello Tristan, now what, I was about to set off to find you today, good man, you have saved me a journey." His voice turned to concern, "Are you alright lad?" Only after Tristan gave him his assurance that he was fine, did John turn to shout into the house, "Elizabeth, come see what the cat's brought in."

As he picked up Tristan's case he said, "Come in; bring your stuff with you before the Council's market inspector asks to see your hawker's licence. You look like a bagman peddler. I suppose you will need a bit of breakfast." Mrs. Brassington came out from the kitchen to greet him, "What happened this time, burnt the toast too many times I suppose." Tristan, for once, sounded shy when he replied, "No, I did not burn the toast, the porridge or my fingers, it turned out to be a bit more serious than that. You will not believe this, but old as I am, I had a spot of woman trouble with the boss's wife, a woman half my age.

She is a good-looking Lebanese lass, but a terrible tease.

He got a bit overexcited. He suggested that I go before he served me up as a Middle Eastern mezza, or a Turkish kebab. Thankfully, I got an advance on wages out of him before he flipped his Lebanese lid. Can I, may I, stay tonight, please? Later today, I will set out again on my quest to find a proper job."

Mrs. Brassington replied excitedly, "John would have gone to find you today if you had not turned up. Certainly, you can stay, but listen. I went to visit my sister who works in Kensington Park Road, just off Bayswater. She told me that the 'Whittington Hotel' is advertising for a resident assistant manager. The Whittington, it just has to be a good omen for a man who seeks his fortune in London Town, even if he doesn't have a cat. I wrote down the telephone number for John to give to you. Here it is, give them a call from the phone in the hall while I get you a healthy breakfast. Fruit juice, cereal, with two slices of toast scraped with that less than butter stuff made from olive oil. No fry up for you my boy, not after the greasy spoon all day breakfasts you have eaten."

Two hours later, after he had showered and eaten the healthy breakfast, Tristan felt confident on his way to a genuine interview with a director of a small company that owned several similar commercial hotels in areas of London where there were rows of other small hotels.

In spite of his improved mood, he realised that if he got the job it would hardly be progress, he would be as though he had turned the clock back forty years.

When he thought about the interview, after the Director offered him the post of Assistant Manager of the Whittington Hotel, Tristan had reservations.

The Manager had not been present. The Director, a Mr. Stevenson, had seemed to harp on downside issues, rather than how an assistant manager might help to improve the business. He thought the man had been well enough dressed, but somehow not well turned out. He had admitted to Tristan that it concerned him that the unit, his term for the Whittington Hotel, did not show the bottom line profit expected, nor did it achieve the turnover in bed-lets that other hotels in the group achieved.

Without thinking, Tristan asked whether the company would not be better looking for a general manager, rather than an assistant manager. By reacting as he did, Tristan wondered if he had made a serious error of judgement. There had been a long uncomfortable hiatus before the Mr. Stevenson said, enigmatically, "Let us not cross any bridges before we have to." Tristan wondered why the directors of a small hotel with a poor bottom line would burden it further with the wages of an assistant manager.

The job offered a reasonable salary, with en-suit accommodation, albeit in a garret. It also offered three meals each day, but required payment for all non-soft drinks consumed.

Mr. Stephenson had told him that the Whittington's General Manager, Mr. Damian Morris, who had been in post for two years, did not live in. A condition of the job of Assistant Manager was that he, or she, must be in residence, every night, from 11 p.m. until eight a.m., unless the General Manager had agreed to other arrangements. At the conclusion of the interview, Tristan had agreed to report to Mr. Morris, the next day, at eight in the morning, ready for work.

From his reduced reserves, all that he had left after he paid in advance for bed and breakfast at the Grassington, and taken a taxi to the interview, Tristan happily bought a bunch of flowers for Elizabeth Brassington.

It delighted him when she went through the proper ritual. She blushed, "You shouldn't have, really, aren't they beautiful, it was not necessary." It cheered him equally when John Brassington shouted from their private rooms, over the noise of the television, "She would have poisoned your porridge tomorrow if you hadn't. Good lad."

The next day, Tristan reported for duty at the Whittington Hotel where he met Mr. Morris, the General Manager. Although not much more than fifty years old, he had the appearance of a ruptured cellar man who suffered with a permanent hangover, heartburn, piles and bunions.

He wore a bum-starver black jacket over pin stripe trousers of a style traditionally worn by hotel managers during the middle of the last century. They seemed to be originals from that era, all in need of dry cleaning to remove the accretion of age-old grease. The scuffed brown suede shoes, similarly marked, completed the image of uncared-for neglect.

By way of welcome he said, "For God's sake come outside, I need a fag to sooth my throat. Talking of fags, you are not one are you?

Although Tristan could both see and hear that Morris was a heavy smoker, he could not tell whether flakes of cigarette ash or dandruff had settled on his coat collar. The roll up in his fingers gave him a clue. Nicotine stains reached the second knuckle of his index and middle finger. Stains also spread through one side of his moustache.

"Good God," Morris wheezed, "Do they scout round geriatric care homes to find staff these days. I had looked forward to a bouncy blond bimbo assistant with big boobs. All I get is a pensioner pouf with a bow tie."

Determined that this wreck of a man should not discourage him, Tristan cheerfully replied, "Good morrow Master Morris, what a glorious morning it is to be sure. No Sir, I am not yet a pensioner, nor am I gay by proclivity. However, my mood is occasionally joyfully gay. Where would you like me to start?"

Morris blew smoke directly at Tristan before he answered. "Well, you will have to meet chef; he's a Polack, but he does speak English. He won't be in the kitchen yet, so go to say hello to Helga the housekeeper from hell. She does the rooms with Beaka; I call Beaka a mug, for putting up with Helga. Beaka is on her day off today. Both are Estonian, or Latvian or some other such Baltic barbarian breed.

After Helga, you can make a start in the office. There is a backlog of cash reconciliations to do. The cashbook balance has not been right for days; you could take a stab at that. Marian, the group's accountant will be in later today. She is a right tyrant; she will run you through the drill. Right now, I need a snifter before I go to lunch with the directors. George the barman will put me right. You can meet him later. He is gay, a veritable old queen. Oh, I forgot Wendy our receptionist. I suppose you met her on the way in. She works seven until twelve in the mornings, when she has not rung in to take her statutory PMT leave, welcome to 'Broken Down Towers.'"

Despite Morris's crude welcome, Tristan felt that he had done him a great favour. He had made his decision to give up cigarettes a cause for celebration, not a trial.

At every level from cellar to roof space, where Tristan inspected the Whittington, every part of the business disappointed.

A perceptible air of decay permeated all four floors. After he had established which bedrooms the receptionist Wendy had let, he upset both her and her arrangements.

He re-allocated rooms to leave all the rooms on the top floor vacant. Wendy, born an immediate post war Londoner got in a huff. Her accent suggested her 'East End' childhood when the docks still worked cargo, off and onto merchant ships. The years had not blunted its sharp edge. "We don't do it like that Mr. Edwards; we have systems here at the Whittington. I should know; I have worked here twenty years. We let the 25 rooms on the front first, we always have."

Tristan answered her, "Miss Wendy, my family name is Edward, not Edwards. Today is a new start for us all. Please follow the revised arrangements."

He left Wendy bleating, "I don't know what Mr. Morris will say, we have always done it his way. It had always been the way with managers before he came."

Tristan left Wendy on his way to find Helga the housekeeper. After he introduced himself, he gave her clear instructions. "Today, the top floor is to have every door, window and drawer left wide open, with all the curtains drawn to let fresh air into every corner, every cupboard, every wardrobe. Tomorrow, with Beaka's help, you must strip all beds to bare mattress, which you must turn over, side to side, followed by top to bottom.

Helga told him that she could not possibly open the windows because it would let all the heat out. She added, forcibly, that Mr. Morris had said the fuel bills were too high anyway. Tristan replied genially, "It is high summer; the central heating is switched off. Let in a little fresh London air, if that is not an oxymoron, it might blow away stale smell of confined habitation."

He left Helga in tears after he asked her to polish every bit of visible wood with wax polish, proper polish, not polish from an aerosol tin. Before he went to meet Marian, the group's peripatetic accountant, he collected every tin of spray polish he could find and dumped them into the big wheelie bin in the yard.

Tristan found Marian seated at the only desk in the office. He tried his usually successful urbane approach to women. With his most practiced gentle intonation he drawled, "Good morning, I see that she who controls the cash flow has taken post. Miss Marion isn't it?"

He could not cajole the woman into a smile, or any pleasant welcome. She did not look up from the desk, but said coldly "'She', is the cat's mother; 'It' has no gender, I am neither Miss nor Mrs. I am Marion to my friends, Ms. Maude to you. Finally, she condescended to look up at Tristan, as though she had only just noticed him. "Who might you be?" she asked. Tristan again tried his charm offensive, "Tristan Edward ma'am, the brand new still in the box Assistant Manager.

Tristan the given name, Edward without the s the surname, causes confusion, always does." Ms. Maude, still determined not to have any small talk, cut Tristan short, "Well Mr. confused Edward, short on plurality, have you brought with you your UB 40 record of the unemployable, or the more unlikely P45 record of when you last employer had the sense to let you go, the euphemism for the sack."

Tristan, still hopeful, risked a shot at humour, "No P45, sorry, I left my previous employer because of his rather pointed insistence that I should move on. He had a kris and he was cross. It would not do any good to go back to ask for the wages he owes me or my P45. He would prefer to issue me with a death certificate. I do have my National Insurance Number." Tristan realised that there was no humour in the woman who snapped at him, "Just remember, you are on probation for a month, so don't get uppity with me."

The peripatetic accountant who seemed to be determined to discourage Tristan said, "It will not be worth my while to tell the tax people you are here, you won't last five minutes. If you last a week, I shall be surprised, if you are still here at the end of the month, I shall be astonished. When you don't last until the month end, I will pay you out of petty cash, pro-rata, less accommodation, tax and insurance. For the duration of the economic crisis that besets the Whittington I am required to come in at ten until two, three days each week, the rest of the week I spend better time in our other units. If you will pay attention, I will show you how we do the cash reconciliations." Tristan put on a silly French accent to say, "I suppose you vill only tell me vonce".

What the very Ms. Maude had to tell Tristan he found familiar stuff. He quickly realised that both Mr. Morris, the General Manger and Wendy the receptionist had undercharged, or completely missed items on customer accounts, and cash shortages in the tills had not been unaccounted for. At two o'clock Ms. Maude left, after she told Tristan, "The day after tomorrow I shall be in at ten. If you are still here, try to get the cash right for once." She stimulated Tristan with a barb as she left, "You can do decimals can you, or are you so old that you are still on pounds shillings and pence," It sealed the nature of their relationship. He called after her, "Farewell Marion, virago maid." adding under his breath, "Nothing will give me more pleasure than to call you to my account."

After he spent the afternoon getting the hang of the Whittington's procedures Tristan went to the kitchen looking for the chef. Although small and ill equipped for a commercial kitchen he could however see that the chef had left the floor and surfaces clean.

When he did the standard environmental health officers trick of running his index finger along the under edges of the tables they too were clean, clear of congealed matter. A quick look into the refrigerators and freezers pleased him. The chef had neatly arranged and covered all the food items and day dated them.

However, he found no trace of the Polish Chef or of any prep for evening meals, or any ingredients visible that the chef could use to prepare meals, other than breakfast or sandwiches.

When he found the ingredients to prepare a three-egg omelette with cheese, for immediate personal consumption, Tristan set to work, but a deep bass voice behind him interrupted his happy mood. "Who do you imagine you are; one of the too many flash-in-the-pans, TV celebrity chefs I suppose? I cook in my kitchen, no one else, understand."

Tristan turned to see who had interrupted the preparation of his supper. He blinked a bit, because the man who wore chef's whites filled the doorway. He was not just huge; he was massive.

Fat men can be huge; it takes height, a thick neck, big hands, big feet and muscle to be massive. The man who filled the doorway had them all. The tightly curled hair that peaked at his forehead was almost white. Across his temples, it still showed some of the grizzled red hair of his youth. It gave him the appearance of a prize Hereford bull. His dark bright eyes showed a depth of understanding. As he wished to exert authority, despite the chef's size, Tristan risked a sharp enough rejoinder.

"Right Chef, I want a good dinner; I want it right away. My terms of engagement allow me three good meals a day. As you have just stated, emphatically, that in this kitchen you cook and no one else, please take over. I shall sit here to watch. However, you might occasionally prefer to let another fully trained talented chef into your kitchen to cook breakfast on a quiet morning, to give you a lie in; savvy?"

"Sorry," the massive bulk replied, "Are you the new bloke they told me about. George said you were a pouf. You don't look like one to me."

"Yes, I am the new straight Assistant Manager, straight in all ways," Tristan said, "My name is Tristan Edward, Edward without an 's', you are?" "Stan, Stan Kay if that will do," the chef replied, "Formally, as in polite, as well as formally, as in previous, I am Stanislause Klaginskaieski. As no one west of Gdansk can manage that, I answer to Stan."

"Pleased to meet you Stan," Tristan said, "Nice tidy kitchen you have here; friends?" Tristan offered his hand. He received a bone-crushing grip in response. The chef smiled when he said, "Przyjaciele, that's friends in my language. Put the pan down boss, we can do better than the scratch food of the weary, the time saving, stomach salving, although bowel binding, colon clogging, three-egg omelette."

Stan took a bunch of keys from his pocket to open a small locked larder room. Inside, Tristan saw a small fridge, a separate freezer, and shelves packed with a cornucopia of food, most of Polish origin.

An hour later, he sat with Stan, at a small table in the kitchen, feasting on a rich meal of Eastern European origin. In the time it took to prepare and share the meal, the two men, as different in physique, origin and experience as possible, formed a friendship that both men knew would stand the test of time.

Tristan asked, "Do you ever get customers, residents, guests, anyone who wants to have an evening meal." Stan shrugged his huge shoulders, "Very rare, usually only those residents who have young children. It's steak and chips for him, plain omelette for her, burgers for the kids. For such small beer it is really not worth the trouble."

Because he found his company convivial, Tristan, enthused by Stan's cooking, wanted to know more about him. Excited, he mixed his opinion, with a question, "Stan, you are a wonderful cook, are you married?" Stan roared with laughter. "No, is that a proposal Angol?" Tristan, replied, seriously, "No you daft Pollack, I just wanted to know the demands of your home life. With your skill, surely you would like to work more hours as a chef, with a breakfast cook to leave you free to do proper meals. I will have to have a serious think about this; together we could change the dining room to a restaurant."

Supper finished and cleared, Tristan thought it time to meet the 'Old Queen' in the bar. None of the several owners had altered the bar since the Nineteen Sixties when developers combined five large Victorian terrace houses to create the Whittington Hotel.

The bright lights, mirrors, beech wood furniture with sharp edged 'Formica' topped tables, made it difficult for any barman, or barmaid, however talented or attractive, to keep customers long enough to order a second drink.

Tristan waited until there were no customers in the bar before he went to meet George. He did not want a drink; he did need to get a measure of the wet trade. George, the barman, appeared to be engrossed with the Evening Standard. When he looked up to greet whoever had come into his domain, he said, automatically, "Good evening sir." His demeanour changed when he realised that he had greeted the new Assistant Manager.

"Oh it's you is it. I heard that we have been burdened with more aggravation." His voice that had a definite 'Brummy' accent tinged with gay overtones. He made Tristan's flesh creep with his next remark, "Mmm, quite the matinee idol aren't you, lovely hair, I must tell my friend."

Tristan ignored the remarks. Determined to assert his authority, he asked for the stock book and stock transfer account. "Oh don't you bother about those, Mr. Morris doesn't. Leaves it all to me, always has, anyway they are not ere they are at ome." Tristan stiffened, "My surname is Edward without the 's'. It sometimes causes confusion. You must get it straight, because that is what I am, in all respects. I want two things from you, your surname name will do for the moment; the books can wait until you come in tomorrow morning."

George bristled, "Now just a minute Mr. bloody Edwards, you can't talk to me like that ....." Before he had chance to go on, Tristan stopped him. He said curtly, "I can, I have, the books, tomorrow morning at the latest, I want your name this instant." The barman, who had become uncertain but still bellicose, replied, "Colliss, Colliss with two bloody s's, so stick the spare one up your arse." "Thank you Mr. Colliss," Tristan replied, as he left the bar. He stopped just outside, to hear Colliss's unsolicited but not unexpected remark, "Dick head."

To get an idea of the state of things, Tristan spent the rest of the evening in the small office. The management accounts that he found, still sealed in an envelope, showed the Whittington to be in a parlous financial state. Addressed for the attention of Mr. Morris, the accounts were already three months out of date when the postmark showed they had arrived two weeks previously.

His experienced opinion of the main figures, as presented, showed that all margins and ratios were well out of kilter with those required of a hotel the size of the Whittington, in a location ideal for a business hotel.

The figures did not depress Tristan. They showed that given half a chance, if Mr Morris would keep out of his way, he had an opportunity to make significant improvements. It did not concern Tristan that the company would not pay him until the end of the month.

He was confident that with the changes he would make, there would be enough work to keep him fully occupied throughout the day and evenings, seven days a week. He felt sure that with Stan to talk to and his food to enjoy he would not go short of sustenance or entertainment. He also reconciled himself to a few weeks abstinence from alcohol.

Tristan realised that it would take time to get the revenue from accommodation to an acceptable level, although he thought that if he rang round the tourist information offices each morning, and co-operated with other hotels in Bayswater, he might make some improvement.

To improve the restaurant income both Tristan and Stan worked hard. In the basement, they found an old 'A' frame board with a box of waterproof chalk. On the board Tristan wrote, 'Genuine Polish dishes prepared by our award winning Polish chef.' before he put it outside, on the hotel steps.

They worked together to introduce new lunchtime and evening menus, at realistic inclusive prices. During the first week, when they offered the new menus, the food take doubled over the same period of the previous two years. They were even more encouraged when some of the resident business guests stayed in the hotel for their evening meal and a few booked ahead for accommodation, a thing that Stan told Tristan had never happened before.

However, some things were not good. Each day, when Tristan checked the money in the tills he found one or other of them short by twenty to thirty pounds, without reason or explanation.

The discrepancies worried him. The explanation came when Mr. Morris, in front of Colliss, opened the un-reconciled till, from which he took out some notes. He put the currency notes into his top pocket without putting into the till a written note to record the amount or the reason for the withdrawal. As he did this, he gave Tristan a very hard look before he said the one word "Expenses. "The explanation did not stop Tristan's worries.

It did not take Tristan long to find that George Colliss, the barman, amongst many other fiddles, operated one of the oldest rackets in the book.

Colliss suggested that customers run a tab. When the customer offered to pay, Colliss tapped the till screen twice for the spirit, for each mixed drink ordered, such as a whisky and dry ginger. This enabled Colliss to steal a full bottle of spirit after he had entered 20 doubles, when he had served single measure, without the stock take revealing a discrepancy.

Tristan made a note of all the discrepancies in all departments. To bypass Mr. Morris he planned to send, direct to the Directors, a full confidential report, to include a detailed business plan that if fully implemented would put the Whittington back into profit. He had told Stan that he would complete the report after an accurate stock take, first thing in the morning, on the first day of August.

Tristan knew that all business class hotels, similar to the Whittington, were quiet at the weekend. This gave him an idea for an opportunity to increase revenue. He persuaded Stan to go to his Polish club, 'Dom Polski', to offer its members a traditional Polish dinner party, with the club members required to pay only five pounds per head for the meal with their children's meals free.

They decided to host the Polish dinner on the last Sunday in July, the following day being Monday 1st August, stock take and pay day.

Both Tristan and Stan worked hard to make the evening a success. They thought Mr. Morris's reaction to the Polish promotion to be peculiar. He made no comment about Tristan's idea, nor did he question Stan about his unusual requisitions for Polish staples.

Almost every day he claimed that the Directors wanted him for important discussions at Head Office. The rest of the staff, except for Colliss, the old queen, caught the excitement of change.

They began to enjoy their work. Evan Helga, the head housekeeper smiled when she spoke to guests, a thing previously thought to be beyond her. She had even volunteered to cook, as well as to serve breakfast on quiet mornings, a task that she had well in hand.

The Polish club dinner justified all their efforts. It proved to be a both a happy occasion and a financial success. The last of the customers had left by eleven thirty, after the club's secretary had called for three cheers for the chef with the promise that they, like Whittington, would return.

Tristan had given Colliss the night off, so that he could run the bar himself. During the evening, he took more cash over the bar than Colliss had put in the till during the previous 31 days. The profit on the soft drinks easily covered the cost of the children's free meals.

Mr. Morris, who Tristan and Stan called the absentee-landlord, made an unexpected appearance just as Tristan, with Stan's help, had finished cashing up both tills. "It's the first of the month tomorrow," he said, "The Directors have asked me to bring all the cash to Head Office, except one till float, first thing tomorrow. It is the usual security check; no need to fuss. I will take it now, to save time in the morning.

When Morris had gone, Tristan sat with Stan in the bar, both of them happy to discuss the success of the evening and to plan future events. Helga and Beaka had agreed to work and each had brought a friend to help, but they had gone home after they had finished work. Suddenly Tristan jumped to his feet, "Damn it, why not," he said, "I have been teetotal long enough, I have just enough money left in this world to have one drink. What the hell tomorrow is payday. Even bled by the Government's twin leeches of income tax and national insurance, I shall pocket more than I set out with from Scagill six weeks ago. I shall honour your country with a toast of straight Polish vodka. It will leave me with just one pound, exactly. I remember a sergeant cook told me that if I kept a pound note somewhere about my person, the police could not arrest me as a vagrant without visible means of support"

Stan's great hand pushed enough cash across the table to match Tristan's, "I have a better idea, to seal a good friendship, you buy me a vodka with your money and I will buy you a vodka with my money."

Tristan set two glasses on the bar, took out a bottle of Polish Vodka from the icebox of the under counter fridge from which he measured out the two vodkas, before he rang both his and Stan's cash into the till. The two friends stood to face each other.

119

When the clock struck midnight, Tristan raised his glass, and said "Rule Britannia" before swallowed the ice-cold neat spirit in one gulp. In response, Stan called "'Za Zd Rowie Ojczyzny'. Which to you my unlearned friend means 'Good faith Poland', before he too tossed back his neat vodka."

The two friends shook hands and were about to leave the bar when one middle aged man, two young men and one woman, walked in. "Excuse us gentleman" said a man who seemed to be in charge, "We are from Thompson, Williams and Proudfoot, we are the appointed receivers in the bankruptcy of the Whittington Hotel Limited. Where, or which one of you, is Mr. Morris the General Manager?"

Tristan had gone pale with shock, but he managed a response "Oh hell, Morris has gone; done a runner if I am not mistaken. He has taken the cash with him. I am Tristan Edward, the Assistant Manager, what now?

The senior man said calmly, "I want your full co-operation. Perhaps we could start with the keys to all safes, tills, PDQ codes, all the security details. Here is my card of identification." A quick telephone call to the number on the card satisfied Tristan that the team were not deceivers but genuine receivers.

The efficient practiced way they went about their business impressed Tristan. The woman put the money from the one till drawer with a float and sealed it in a strong black bag. Tristan winced when she clicked the bag shut as it included the money Stan and he had used to pay for the vodka. She found nothing in the safe. The two young men did the fastest stock take Tristan had ever seen. "Do you live in?" the senior man asked Tristan, "Yes, upstairs in the garret," "Well you can stay tonight, however you must be cleared out before eight tomorrow morning, if you don't mind. Take only your personal affects with you when you go, do not take things that belongs to the hotel. Tristan sighed, "I do mind; do not be rude to me young man, I am the one sinned against, not the sinner. What about my wages, the well-earned wages that I was due to be paid in the morning?"

"Sorry old chap" the man said, "As of midnight, all funds were frozen. I am sure we will pay you, eventually, once we have sorted out the mess. The real estate here will fetch a tidy sum. To get change of use to convert it to luxury apartments the owners will probably persuade the planners that it was impossible to make a profit as a hotel business. From the change of use, they will make a fortune. You see the limited company in receivership was only the business. The bricks and mortar belong to the group. It has probably been their intention since they bought the hotel. You must have been the last thing they wanted, an efficient manager".

The receivers left before two in the morning. Their immediate work complete, they left a security guard on duty.

With nothing left to say or do, Tristan went to his room. Just before he fell asleep, he said to the darkness, "This has been a triple bugger experience this has. It seems as though some external force has worked against me. Through no fault of my own, by events unconnected, I have lost out to fraud at the Whittington, jealousy at Staples and to the thief Charles Lucas Prescott at the Keeble. If I do nothing else, I will find a way to bring down Prescott. He had been asleep and dreaming for an hour before he said aloud, "But I have no idea how."

Chapter 9

The financial collapse of the Whittington Hotel, signalled by the midnight arrival of the receivers, hit Tristan harder than an unexpected punch in the solar plexus. It made him cash broke; it almost broke his spirit.

He thought his treatment unfair, unwarranted. He had followed the code of the Grey Haired Knights. He had put aside all thoughts of age and infirmity, except that he now used his cane for support.

He had stood on his own two feet. He had walked the streets of London to knock on doors in his search for work. He had made new friends who had helped him. He had received no help from old friends, state or charity. He felt dumped, discarded, as though he had inadvertently passed an unseen, undeclared 'Use by' date.

Well before 8 o'clock, the hour when the receivers had told him to leave the building, after a short fitful night's sleep, he took the lift down to ground floor. The noise of what he thought might be more than a bit of a row between Stan, the massive Polish chef and the small slightly built security guard, called for his immediate intervention.

Stan's great fist that gripped together the lapels of the poor chap's uniform jacket held him against the wall. This would not have alarmed Tristan too much, except that the security guard still wore his boots that were six inches from the ground. "Put him down Stan," Tristan demanded, in a light tone near to laughter, "What has he done to upset you?"

Turning effortlessly, while he still pinned the guard to the wall, Stan began to explain his grievance. "This lesser sardine, this sprat, this anchovy this matter of no use, he don't know about food. He tells me that I can't take with me my own special private stock of Polish sausage, spek, quark, pirogi and kvass, all bought and paid for by me."

Tristan said calmly, "Why don't you offer to cook him some breakfast instead of sticking him to the wall like a white hunter's trophy. I am sure he will be less bellicose with a bellyful of bigos."

Tristan's counsel prevailed. Thirty minutes later Stan had cooked a meal for them all that would last them all day. Earlier, he had packed all the perishable goods, together with his personal kitchen tools, into two coffin-sized boxes that he put outside the kitchen door, ready to carry away.

Tristan had a different problem. He needed to spend the day unencumbered by personal effects to allow him to search for a job. However, he decided to take his silver-topped cane with him, because he expected to spend the day walking.

In addition to the essential support it gave him, he felt that the cane gave him a dignified air of respectability.

The security guard told Tristan he had enough to do without the bother of acting as his storekeeper. After one meaningful look from Stan, he nervously agreed 'to see what he could do'.

He explained that his twelve-hour shift starting at nine in the evening, which meant that Tristan must pick up his things during those hours, as no one else would know where to find them.

He gave Tristan his mobile phone number so that he could call him to arrange to collect his stuff.

Stan gave Tristan a scrap of paper with the address of Dom Polski, his Polish club. He told Tristan, that if he needed to get in touch, he could leave a note with the club stewards, because he usually spent a couple of evenings there each week to read the Polish newspapers. He added, a bit subdued, that it might be a while before he found a job with somewhere decent to live.

He gave Tristan another bone-crusher handshake, before he marched off with one of the huge boxes under each arm, secured by a rope over his broad shoulders. The little security guard, who stood with Tristan to watch Stan leave whispered, "My God mate; he's a bloody pedestrian pantechnicon."

"He is more than that," Tristan said, "He is a big man in every way. Look at him, he reminds me of the magnificent drum horses at the Trooping of the Colour. He has told me something of his early life. During his young days, he had a hairy escape from the Russians. They never cared from where they recruited their athletes, provided they were from their side of the iron curtain. Apparently, when he worked in the shipyards near Gdansk, he had won a reputation as a weight lifter. The Reds took him to Russia to train for the 1964 Tokyo Olympics, in the heaviest of the ten classes. His girl did not wait for him, making the young lad very bitter against the communist regime. During a competition held in East Berlin, he took a midnight swim, in his underpants, across the Wannsee, to freedom in the West. You would not be wise to get him started about the 'Bloody boss eyed Bolsheviks', which is what he calls them. They shot at him, as he swam across the lake, forcing him to swim zigzag, mostly under water, until he reached a point well inside the freedom side of the rope. Despite his size, they missed him."

A fruitless hour spent at the Job Centre Plus, the so-called access to the world of work, irritated Tristan. He could not find a job or a plus.

He could see little use for lessons in how to prepare a CV, or how to improve interview technique. He needed a job with a firm that provided accommodation that also offered a cash inducement to join it, a 'Golden hello'.

124

By late afternoon, he had exhausted all possible opportunities to find work of any kind. His response to job vacancy cards displayed in shop windows and pub doorways had all led to disappointment; too old, not the right experience, company policy.

The rejections, usually the polite 'So sorry', occasionally the curse 'Sod off' did not improve his temper. He felt angry with himself because he had foolishly kept in his wallet, the letter from Branwell Evans, the supportive Scagill vicar.

Tristan understood that when the pickpockets stole his wallet, with the letter, they deprived him of a link to security that was better than any Bank of England's promise to pay whatever its denomination.

By six o'clock in the evening, with all the offices shut, Tristan knew that he had nowhere to go. He finally admitted, to himself, because he had no one else to talk to, that his attempt to quest, as a Grey Haired Knight had failed.

He had not achieved any of the things that he had set out to achieve. He had failed to become self-employed, he had failed to have people work for him, and he had not managed to be a banker or bookmaker. He had even failed to find work as a clerk, or a bookies runner. Although he had left Scagill with the equivalent of an average months' pay in his pocket, in three weeks he had no money left. Pickpockets had taken most of it; Riejik had not paid him in full, and the receivers of the Whittington would not pay him for months.

He was bust, broke, bankrupt; he was without visible means of support, he was destitute.

The word destitute reminded him that he had laughed with Stan, the massive Polish chcf, about the odd fact that if one had a pound in one's pocket, the police could not arrest you as vagrant. Even in his distressed state, he managed a wry smile when he wondered if inflation had affected the statutory pound.

Although Tristan had been a lifelong chronic serious gambler, since the dinner with his friends, when he had joined in with

Arthur's idea that they should seek adventure, as Grey Haired Knights, Tristan had not bet on a horse, a greyhound, a football match, or two flies on a window.

Having failed in everything else, his parlous state caused his gamblers certainty to flood back. In his mind, his one remaining pound coin became a talisman. It was clear to him that if he invested the coin in the Lotto Lucky Chance he could restore his fortune if he bet what he won, even if it were only the smallest possible win, on a long odds accumulator bet on the dog races at Wimbledon.

It only took Tristan a few minutes only to find a newsagent that displayed the familiar 'Lotto' sign. The shop was as tired as the Pakistani proprietor who took his money.

After he checked the card, he gave a grim, although somehow very sympathetic smile before he said, "Sorry, no good mate, better luck next time."

It had taken Tristan less than a minute to lose the pound coin, the very last of his liquid assets. It concerned him that all his tangible assets were all in the care of the guard in the Whittington Hotel, on the other side of London Town.

Tristan left the shop, head down, disconsolate. He blamed his bad luck on the pickpockets who not only took his wallet but also his lucky sprig of white heather.

He wandered aimlessly, for hours, until he reached the Thames Victoria Embankment Gardens, below the Savoy Hotel where he sat on the same park bench where a few weeks earlier the oddly dressed bearded eccentric had offered him cold day old chips.

He remembered, though he did not know why, the strange words the old man had said when he had rambled on, about King Arthur defeating the Saxon heathens and Dick Whittington who tuned again here on the riverbank, not on Highgate Hill. 'It will be here that your fortune will turn, when the tide turns.'

He sat staring at the river, with his palmed hands between his knees. He did not see its progress, or the water-born traffic.

He did not see the people on the embankment. He only saw his memories. Most of them of misadventure or lost opportunity, brought about by lack of self-confidence. Several times, when young, he had lost in love because he would not commit to a stable future. He had sought to find solutions in the excitement of exotic distant places and reckless gambles.

This night, Tristan could not bring himself to think, as he had often done in bad times, 'What the hell, it was worth it'. He could only think that some dark force had worked against him since he took a vow to be a Grey Haired Knight.

The rain started after Tristan fell asleep. He had curled up with his feet on the bench, his head on the crook of his arm, but not before he murmured "Nowhere to go, no one to go home to, no family, friends or funds."

While Tristan slept, a figure dressed in the ancient magician's robes of King Arthur's court at Camelot formed in from the shadows. For a while, he stood silently as he watched over Tristan, before he nodded, smiled and said, "Enough; it is done."

The small boats at anchor on the river swung on their mooring ropes to face the changing tide. The dream, hallucination or manifestation of Merlin faded away.

When Tristan woke, he did not wake with a start. From a deep dream troubled sleep, he came slowly back to the present. A young uniformed policeman had rocked him awake by a hand on his shoulder. "Come on granddad, you can't sleep here. My Sergeant uses this bench to have his snap on nights when it does not rain, however even though it is mid-summer, it has rained this last hour. You will catch your death."

Although at first confused, when his brain cleared, Tristan understood that, as he had become a vagrant, the policeman had every right to move him on. With his innate good manners he had the good sense, first to apologise, then to thank the officer, "Oh sorry young man, er, constable, I must have dozed off, thank you, yes that's it, thank you."

The Constable stopped Tristan as he started to walk away. "Excuse me sir, do you have anywhere to go?" Unconsciously, Tristan used the same words he had uttered as he fell asleep. He turned to quietly respond, "Nowhere to go, no one to go home to, no family, friends or funds. Awfully sorry and all that, apologies all round, most reprehensible, not good form. The name is Edward, Tristan Edward, surname Edward without the 's', my father must have lost it somewhere."

The young policeman said, "Well sir, my name is Tom, Constable Tom Warwick. You had better come with me. We can get a good cup of tea at the station."

The two men walked slowly up the wide stone stairs to the Strand with the policeman's hand under Tristan's elbow, to support him. On the Strand, PC Tom Warwick flagged down a patrol car.

He asked the two patrol officers to give them a lift to the Islington Police Station. "I should be grateful," he said to his colleagues, "Granddad here is clean, just tired. We don't want a worn out old soul to wander the mean streets at this time of night. He is not one of our regulars, I am sure Sergeant Robbins will be able to sort him out."

The elderly sergeant who sat comfortably at ease behind a counter at the police station gave the Constable and Tristan a genial greeting. "Hello Warwick, who have you brought in to keep me company?"

"Hello Sergeant," Tom Warwick replied, "I wondered if you could sort out this gentleman, he appears to be one of Peter Pan's lost boys. I found him where he had dozed off in the gardens below the Savoy. The rain had come on a bit heavy so he is a bit wet. He did not have a coat, so I presumed he must have wandered off from some care home, as some of them do. By the way, I promised him a cup of tea."

The Sergeant, who had an easy manner, even with young constables, said, "Well you had better make a pot quick, then toddle off before the Inspector fails to find you on your patch and calls in the River Police to drag the Thames; milk with two sugars for me; what about you sir?"

The tea brought the colour back to Tristan's face. The sergeant made him comfortable in an old oak swivel armchair with a threadbare cushion.

Tristan watched while the sergeant dealt efficiently with phone calls as well as queries from his uniformed colleagues. He also dealt amiably with some very rough bare sleeved tattooed characters who wore tank tops tucked into camouflage trousers tucked into high-lace up boots. Tristan assumed that they were plain-clothes policemen.

When Tristan was not dozing, or deep asleep, in between his many other duties, the sergeant gently quizzed him about his circumstances. For the way the police treated him, with genuine courtesy, that night, Tristan would always be grateful. Of all the parts of Tristan's tale, the Sergeant seemed to attach most interest to the theft of his wallet.

Tristan told him it had been a bit special, Moroccan tooled leather. He added that it had not contained any credit or debit cards, only some money, a letter from the Vicar of Scagill Parish Church and a sprig of lucky white heather.

The Sergeant pressed Tristan for details of where and when he thought that the pickpockets might have taken the wallet. He also wanted to know whether the vicar had put Tristan's name on the letter. Although he had dozed, on and off, missing many telephone calls, Tristan woke to see the Sergeant take an incoming call, beam a great smile, and give thumbs up with his free hand.

"Well that can't be bad," said the Sergeant, "I think we might have your wallet. Scotland Yard, no less, will send a car round with it. You see, we collect lost and discarded wallets. It's a new initiative to do with what my Superintendent calls 'Modus operandi'. The hope is that we can get DNA or dabs from them. The dips never keep them more than a minute at most. Once they

129

have the cash and all the cards they dump the wallet. They often get handed in, or our lads on the beat find them."

"Good Lord" Tristan said, "I never even thought to ask at the police station." The Sergeant shook his head, "People seldom do these days, they have forgotten Dixon of Dock Green, and PC 49. Most of us in the force believe that we still work as they did. Unfortunately, the television has conditioned the public to think of us as those mad, bad desperadoes, Starsky and Hutch, the originators of police bad manners. They started a trend; rude police brutes who knock folk about, the Sweeney, Dalziel and Pascoe, or worse, Taggart, the completely out of order Scottish knock about detective. The TV women police are as bad."

Half an hour later, two plain-clothes officers drifted into the charge room. After a quick word with the station sergeant, they brought a wallet for Tristan to look at. "Is this yours old chap?"

Tristan managed a grin, "Could I have a look inside please, it surely looks the same. Like me, it is a bit thinner since I last saw it. The letter I want should be inside." Tristan opened the concealed inner pocket where he found the folded envelope on which the vicar had written 'For Tristan Edward'.

Although Tristan's eyes misted with tears of relief, he managed to say, "Yes that is me, Tristan Edward. It is my wallet, thank you; I could not be better pleased. This will help put me right, I know it will." The policemen were obviously pleased with their success. One put on his best PC Plod voice to say, "That's alright sir, just doing our job." They all laughed, the first time Tristan had laughed all that long day and night.

Before he opened the envelope, Tristan found, folded with it, the sprig of lucky white heather Arthur had given him, heather a strange old man on Halter Moor had given to Arthur. Tristan showed it to the policemen, "Perhaps this will change my luck for the better. It is a bit special; it reminds me of three good friends".

Inside the envelope, Tristan found a bank note sufficient to buy a good meal and a letter from Vicar Branwell Evans, written using black ink and an elegant italic script.

'Dear Tristan.

Here is a groat from the parish discretionary fund. When you read this, if you are rich, please put it in St. Martins in the Field offertory box. If you are in reduced circumstances, use the groat to buy yourself a good breakfast. After which I suggest that you make your way to 'Retreads' at number 2 Chapel Street, opposite Rising Hill behind King's Cross railway station. Show this letter to the old chap in charge. You will find it easily; it is an old Methodist hall no longer in use for their services. My brother Harry, brother not just in Christ, he is also my eldest sibling, is Master of Retreads. He aims to retread tired old souls. It is a terrible pun but he does God's work. Please remember the lovely thought you had in our parish church, I believe that God does know each dancing shining speck as they move in his colourful kaleidoscope, and that God knows you and will protect you.

Yours very sincerely
Branwell.
The Vicarage
Wood lane
Scagill
SC2 3EH 01423 298434

Tristan passed the letter to the Station Sergeant, who read it quietly. He asked, "What is that bit about God's kaleidoscope?"

Tristan replied shyly, "Oh, just a thought I had in his church, where I had gone into rest. Sunlight shone like a beam from a torch through a stained glass window. The dust turned to dancing jewels, it made me think."

The sergeant smiled when he said, "Well, if you decide to find this 'Retread' place, you had better stay here until about eight, before you set off. You don't want to get there too early. There are plenty of good cafés near the railway stations. It's not that far, do you think you can manage it. I will ask the day sergeant to wake you about eight, if you are asleep. I am off to my cot at six. I am too old for night shifts; however, I have only two more years until I clock my thirty-year pension. I did fourteen in the Navy before I joined the force."

The kindness of the young uniformed constable, the desk sergeant and the detectives encouraged Tristan. They gave him cause to believe that the new day would bring a new beginning.

He felt able to think that at least some of his life had been worth the living. At that moment, he remembered that the young Constable had the same name as that of the boy who King Arthur sent to safety, before the battle that destroyed Camelot, Tom Warwick. The boy he ordered to live to tell the story of his court at Camelot so that the idea of chivalry would live on.

This coincidence, in addition to the Police sense of duty as they cared for him, a vagrant, renewed Tristan's confidence. He quietly reaffirmed his promise to find a cause; a quest to champion. His recent experience made him realise that such a cause might not be the pursuit of wealth, or a chance to set a wrong to right. Perhaps, as he had promised in the church in Scagill, it might be to let some light into the dark fate-ravelled lives of other men.

Tristan found the old Methodist hall without difficulty. On a rather worn sign, fixed somewhat askew to a wooden side door, someone had painted, 'Retreads – Fitted free to willing souls'.

The main hall doors, a few yards further along the road, looked as though no one had used them for many years. Alongside the small door, an electric bell push with a neatly engraved sign invited callers to ring three times'. Under the bell push a crudely carved piece of wood, stained with ink where the knife had scored it, read, "No answer means I'm not in. Come back after six o'clock. – Harry."

Tristan rang the bell and waited. After he had rung a third time, he had decided to come back later when he heard the sound of slow shuffling footsteps approaching the door from the inside. It seemed to Tristan like someone in carpet slippers that were too large. A deep baritone voice sang out, "Just a minute, I have my hands full."

Tristan heard the noise of a strong bolt drawn back before the door opened to reveal the very image of Mr. Badger, as illustrated by Shepard, in Kenneth Grahame's book 'The Wind in the Willows'.

He had a long solemn wise old face, framed by a head of hair, with a wide silver grey streak that ran along the crown. Curiously, contrary to normal, his temples were still almost black. He had close trimmed his bristled silver white beard, so that it only barbed the underside of his chin. Over a home knitted brown cardigan, he wore a full-length unbelted golden brown Paisley dressing gown that trailed the floor. The cardigan dropped to mid-calf, below which, just visible, old brown cords stopped short of worn down at heel carpet slippers. Tristan saw that the carpet slippers were, as he had thought, too large for the bare feet that dragged them, unorganised, along the carpet-less floor. In his left hand, he carried a torch; his right hand pulled a huge galvanized coalscuttle behind him.

"Hello Boyo" he boomed, "Just on my way to dig out some coal from the cellar when you rang. You must be Tristan, isn't it? Come you on in. Don't stand on ceremony. This place used to be an old chapel; however, we don't do ceremony. I am Harry Evans, Evans the elder. The Reverend Branwell Evans, my very much younger brother, rang about an hour ago. The police rang him to say you might come along."

Harry's unconditional welcome completely overcame Tristan. He could only muster a quiet "Good Lord." "Yes he is and ever will be," Harry Evans sang out, "Be a good lad will you; get the coal for me, the steps do my back in. It's just down there at the end of the corridor. I will go to put the kettle on. The shovel is in the bucket."

He shuffled away, still with the torch in his hand, leaving the scuttle to Tristan. He also left the door wide open. Tristan thought that Harry Evans had deliberately left the door wide open to give him the chance to change his mind about Retreads.

Carefully, quietly, thoughtfully, Tristan closed the old wooden door. When he shot the old iron bolt, he felt secure but unsure. He wondered if he had shot his own bolt and once again faced some form of institutional incarceration.

Chapter 10

The task that Harry Evans had set Tristan turned out to be a bit of a handful. The coalscuttle turned out to be an old-fashioned galvanized thing, in size, half way between a milk churn and an oil drum. Behind a door, at the end of the corridor, down ten steps, Tristan found the cellar.

When the door closed behind him, he could not see, because Harry had absentmindedly taken the torch with him. However, when Tristan had groped his way back to the top of the steps, he fitted a wedge someone had made to keep the door open. This gave him enough light to fill the scuttle, with coke, the only fuel in the cellar. With difficulty he lifted the scuttle, one-step at a time, as far as the corridor.

After he put it onto the coconut doormat, he managed to drag it along the wooden floor, following the direction taken by Evans the elder, the look alike of Mr. Badger.

"Through by here, Tristan," the incumbent Master in charge of Retreads called out, through an open door that gave access to a kitchen, a kitchen dominated by an huge cast iron range with an open hearth between two ovens. The hearth glowed with burning coke. Harry Evans, who could see that the range intrigued Tristan, said, "It's an old baker's oven; I got it, years ago, off a bombsite. It's so old it probably started the fire in Pudding Lane.

I admit that it is too hot in summer, but in winter, it is as comfy as any Rayburn, or the sainted AGA. Now that you have been kind enough to bring in the coal, I will boil a kettle so that we can have a cup of tea and a chat."

Harry, it's coke not coal," Tristan explained, "I'm sorry, I could not find any coal." "So it is, but for a Welsh valley man like me, if it burns, it's coal, whether coke, breeze anthracite, steam or wood, so it is. As for the chat I mentioned, you can tell me as much as you want to, or need to, about your good self. In return, I will tell you all about me, in no time at all, because there is nothing at all to tell."

Harry Evans held Tristan's attention with one of the most engaging smiles he had ever seen. Either side of the hearth he had drawn up two armchairs, each with curiously high backs. Hessian sacks, worn smooth by years of use, completely covered the chairs. Shrouded, as they were, Tristan thought that they must be relict of the old chapel, except that they were comfortable enough for elderly bishops; not at all suited to non-conformist principals or principles. When Harry eased himself down into one, he indicated that Tristan should do the same in the other.

As Harry put a black iron kettle onto a trivet that he pushed over the fire with his slippered foot, he gave Tristan a smile that would put a prisoner about to hear a jury verdict at ease. "Tristan," he said, Sergeant Robbins whom you met at the police station, told me that he learned from brother Branwell that after a long rough passage in some dread place in Scagill, you set out to make your fortune in this city of dreams and disappointment.

It seems, as Prime Minster Macmillan said, 'events dear boy, events, have gone against you.' I think that it might be a good idea, only if you want to mind, if you tell me about the events that brought you to sleep in the rain on a park bench in the Savoy Gardens, instead of in one of the comfortable warm dry beds in a suite at the Savoy Hotel."

Harry proved to be such a good listener and prompt, that he drew from Tristan an account, not just of the events since his recent return to London, but also of the trials, tribulations and only occasional triumphs of all his adult life.

After he had talked to the wise old elder brother of Vicar Branwell, Tristan realised that although he had lost all his money, he had had good fortune; he had made some good friends. Hardly moving from his chair, Harry had effortlessly warmed the pot, scalded the tea and arranged cups, saucers, spoons, sugar and milk on a tray. Before pouring the tea, he had taken up an old-fashioned biscuit barrel from a handy shelf, to offer, "Chocolate or plain?"

Harry, who always spoke in a deep baritone voice that carried absolute sincerity said, "Well boyo, I have a feeling that the 'Good Lord', as you called him when you arrived this morning, might have been working his purpose to lead you to Retreads by the rocky path you have taken. What we do here is to try to help the not so young homeless men who allow us to help them. Perhaps you might help us to do that, for a while at least, before you have another go at the Dick Whittington bit. To tell you the truth, I am glad that you have come. For the first time in my long life, I sense the clock ticking down. I have begun to show the first signs of age, sometimes grumpy, occasionally weary, often forgetful, most of the time anxious about the future, all the time no longer fit for purpose. Like me, Retreads needs a bit of a scrub up. Together, with God's help, I am sure that we can make some improvements.

What do you say to my idea that you spend a bit of time with a leftover like me, to give Retreads a 'Makeover', as the TV programme has it? Before you answer, let me show you around the whole estate. The grand conducted tour only takes two-minutes; even so, it will give you an idea of the true nature of what you would take on. From what you have told me, you seem to be a dab hand at cooking. That is all to the good. I find that the better the grub, the better our old boys do. Another truth that I must tell you is that there is no money in the kitty. Nevertheless, here at Retreads, we know that God will provide. That is, he will provide if we clock all the clues to the opportunities he sends our way."

Harry's charm, backed by his obvious sincerity, so impressed Tristan that he agreed to stay at Retreads, for a while at least, Harry solved Tristan's worry about accommodation with a suggestion.

"You had better use the spare bedroom in my flat in the balcony. It is my refuge, a space of my own that I have not previously shared. It is not a bad set up, two bedrooms, a kitchen, a bathroom and my box room study. If you will help me in all matters to do with Retreads, with particular duties in the kitchen, your board and lodging will be a fair exchange, isn't it, to be sure it is, don't you think. We will have to see about pocket money when you are settled. I would like you to take charge of breakfast and supper for the old boys; we don't do midday dinner. Retreads is run as a selective old age youth hostel, a place with an address our guests can use when they have to fill in the silly CVs that seem to be essential in their search for work. We don't use Retreads on the letterhead paper we give them, we call it Cloisters Executive Apartments. Entry is restricted to men over the age of fifty-five who are fit enough to help with the daily chores. Ageist, elitist, sexist I am sure, although I have not yet had any complaints from the Equal Opportunities Commission, or the Commission for Racial Equality. Mind you, the 'Michelin Guide' has been a bit sniffy." Tristan said, "Good idea that, to give the men an address for correspondence, I ran up against that difficulty when I looked for work here in London."

Harry explained that Retreads operated as a registered charity with a board of governors, helpers and volunteer fund-raisers. The helpers had cleared most of the old chapel furniture, to build eight cubicles down each side of the main hall. Each cubicle had a single bed, a bedside locker and a curtain to screen it from the hall. Although the cubicles had no ceiling, they were under the balcony that ran across the back and round two sides of the hall so no one could overlook their space.

This arrangement left room in the centre of the hall for a large communal table made from two large sheets of thick plywood. Each sheet still had the tell-tale marks that showed builders had previously used it on a construction site. The table legs were old lemonade crates. None of the assorted chairs set around the table remained part of a set, or even one of a pair. Books occupied all available wall space.

Harry had arranged the books in subjects, set on shelves made of builder's planks, spaced by old bricks or breezeblocks. The toilets were barely adequate for a full house of sixteen. When Harry apologized, Tristan said, "Better than those we had as boy soldiers. More often than not, we had no hot water and we had broken most of the windows. It made the lats icy cold in winter; it caused a lot of constipation that did.

" Harry agreed. "Oh yes, no different from me in the navy. I just missed the main event. I did see a bit in Korea. The cold-water shave made many of the lads seek permission to grow. Mind you, I hardly shaved in those days."

The barely adequate toilets were five star rated compared to the less than adequate kitchen. Winter and summer, the open coke fired oven range, a double gas ring on a wooden board supported on old bricks, and an electric kettle that supplemented the iron kettle completed the inventory of cooking equipment.

A single small fridge-freezer took care of any perishable food. A large table covered with a sheet of galvanised iron folded down over the edges served as the worktop. Two white porcelain sinks, both heavily chipped, one with a wooden draining board acted as the stillroom.

All the pots, pans and plates, together with an array of ill matched cups and saucers were set out on a huge elaborately carved green painted wooden dresser set against the wall. After the conducted tour Harry, who stood alongside Tristan, mumbled, "Not quite up to 'NAFFI' standards is it, or the requirements of the Environmental Health Officer?"

Tristan did not know where it came from, or why he said it, he just blurted it out. "Listen Harry; buy me a Baby Belling, throw in a Bunsen burner and I will prepare, cook and serve a banquet fit for an army victory feast. I shall soon have this galley turned into a field kitchen fit to feed the troops. You sailor chaps need a bit of military discipline with some of Alexis Soyer's imagination". Tristan, shoulders slumped when he had to admit to reality.

"Sorry Harry as usual with my ideas, there is a snag. I shall need a couple of quid from your beleaguered funds. I left my cooks gear with a security guard who is on nights at the Whittington Hotel in Bayswater; the one I told you has just gone belly up and where the receivers have frozen my wages until the end of time. I can't get it until after nine o'clock. I can get there by bus, but I will need a taxi to get back. There is too much for me to carry. I spent almost half of the money your brother gave me on breakfast, and a newspaper, before I got here. First things first though, how many do I have to feed tonight, and with what."

Harry pulled a grim face before he replied, "Well, we only have seven, so far that is. I am afraid that we are a bit low in the larder. We have some onions and a few potatoes that have sprouted better than purple broccoli. I suppose we will have to rely on our fall-back position. That is when we have to use some of the tinned corned beef from the cupboard." For the first time in many months, Tristan gave a cheery response.

"Leave it with me Harry, I will have a wander round to see what I can come up with, a bit like 'Ready Steady Cook' that programme that upsets all real chefs. It is as daft as if they put on a programme with gardeners having to garden at the gallop'. What time is supper?" Harry replied with a shrug, "I usually leave it late on these light evenings. If we eat too early, the lads get restive before they feel it's time to turn in."

Tristan's mind flicked back to the stupid staff convenient 'Lights out at ten' that used to make him so angry when in the care of the Laurels rehabilitation unit.

The modernisation of the hotels and the arrival of supermarkets, chain stores and coffee shops had altered the Kings Cross area from that of his memory when he had worked as a barman at the Skinners Arms in Judd Street, before he first joined a cruise ship. However, he recognised that in the area, there were still many small family businesses, run by good people; people he needed to involve with ideas he had in mind.

He had taken notice of Harry's comments "The better the grub, the better our old boys do," and, "God will provide; provided that we pick up on all the clues to the opportunities he sends our way."

Confident that fresh meat would give him the best chance to provide good food, Tristan hoped to find a real, not a white box butcher's shop, where there would be cheap forequarter meat and offal, not just prime cuts.

He walked on past two national chain stores that only sold pre-packed or frozen meat, all well beyond Retread funds, but further on, an ultra-modern butcher's shop, full of stainless steel and glass with bright overhead lights that gave it an almost surgical appearance attracted Tristan's attention. The small man who served behind the counter wore a black turban, a spotlessly clean white warehouseman's coat protected by the traditional blue and white striped apron of a British butcher.

Tristan hoped to find rich picking's in this shop, if he timed it right, as a small queue wound out of the shop. He went close enough to read a notice displayed by the door. On a neat white board engraved with figures filled in red, in what he took to be Arabic script it also gave details in English. 'Open every day when not closed: 8 a.m. to 6 p.m. Not open Fridays or Sundays.

Tristan calculated that if he could master the old coke fired oven range he would have just enough time to have a meat and potato casserole ready for supper by half past eight.

His next discovery, an old cracked white enamel sign with blue letters, at the junction of a main road with a minor road of once fashionable houses pleased him just as much as the butchers shop. It clearly indicated, by a broad arrow, that somewhere along the minor road lay allotments of the 'LMS & LNER Railwaymen's Growers Association.'

A second smaller sign indicated the minor road as a 'No through road'. At the end of the minor road, over a fence, Tristan found the hallowed ground. It had forty or more allotments, each marked out with narrow cinder paths, either side of a wider cinder path that ran parallel to a railway embankment.

Tristan knew that he could play the vanity card, a card that trumps all resistance to giving. As he opened the gate, he could see that nature had reclaimed a few abandoned plots, however most were showpieces.

A sign on the gate warned, 'Trespassers will be prosecuted,' to which some wag had drawn a line through 'prosecuted' to change it to 'Dug in and forked over'. Only one man worked his plot, an elderly fellow of slim build with weather browned skin and silver hair. He wore brown cord trousers, heavy boots and an open necked long sleeved check shirt with the sleeves held clear of his wrists by chrome spring armbands.

The man patiently hoed between rows of neatly planted vegetables as Tristan approached, with both hands raised, to call, "I come in peace, as ambassador plenipotentiary from Retreads, a refuge for clean, not dirty old men. Please don't render me for use as blood and bone meal." The gardener put both hands round the top of his hoe, rested his chin on his hands, before he replied with a smile, "What do you want you silly sod." Tristan replied, "Well, a bit of help as well as information. My! Your carrots do look good, no black fly even though I don't see the old trick of inter-planted garlic. You will put them into the autumn show I am sure; no doubt, they will get a medal. Mind you I prefer their pale cousins the parsnip for a roast."

As Tristan expected it was as easy as shelling peas, in ten minutes he had a carrier bag filled carrots and lettuce that the gardener had thinned out, parsnips that had split yet were suitable for a stew, and two head of well-hearted spring cabbage that had crowded others in their row. In his wallet, he had the name and address of the person to whom he could apply for tenancy of one of the plots, should one become available.

Tristan knew that he had also made a friend when the gardener said, "Come back anytime, I am here most days. Since I retired, my wife likes me out of the house before ten. It has been quiet today; usually there are others here if it does not rain. I am sure they will want to help, we all admire Harry for what he does."

Tristan still had to face up to his most difficult task. He had to get a continuous supply of the dry goods that all cooks need in the larder, flour, milk, salt, butter, eggs, all things that did not need thinning out, goods that he could not cajole from kind neighbours. To set up such a supply, Tristan had a plan. Almost half a century in the hospitality racket had taught him that his best hope lay in worry; the worry that all chefs carry with them, on duty or off duty.

Worry that salmonella, listeria, or a dreaded botulism might just conceivably break down their defences, to cause vomiting, diarrhoea, dehydration, sometime even death. Worry about prosecution by the authorities.

Worry that the people affected might claim damages. Tristan knew that in all top hotels, their risk averse culture demand that once chefs had drawn food ingredients from store, that which they had not used must be safely disposed of before the end of the that working day. His hope was that he could persuade the Sous Chef of the great railway hotel, where the kitchen entrance was only a few hundred yards from Retreads, to let them have a daily 'Goody box' of leftovers to stock Retreads' larder with goods that otherwise would go to waste.

A regular supply of bread rolls, butter pats, milk, cream, all leftovers collected after the breakfast buffet and lunchtime service would be food safe to use at Retreads for the evening meal the same day, or for breakfast the next day.

On his way to the hotel, Tristan noticed that the halal butchers had no customers. He took a deep breath before he walked quietly into the shop. The man behind the glass and stainless steel counter did not speak. He did not greet Tristan; he met him with a calm stare, while he quietly sharpened a bayonet long stiff backed butcher's knife on steel.

Slightly built, he had a dark close trimmed beard, very deep-set dark eyes, part shielded by small rectangular gold-rimmed spectacles. Tristan decided that a direct approach would be his best option.

"Good afternoon, my name is Edward, Tristan Edward," he said nervously. Because the man's expression did not yield, he tried his most ingratiating smile before he continued with his usual patter, "Tristan the given name, Edward without the 's', the family name, causes confusion, always does."

After a further long pause the butcher spoke. "Really, my name is Raul, is that easy enough for you? May I ask what you want, or worse, why you are here? Not sent by the government to help, are you, Allah forbid."

The droll Oxbridge manner, plus the cultured voice surprised Tristan, however when he realised that the man teased, he recovered quickly enough to stutter, "W w, well I am here to ask for your help. I, that is, we, well my friend Harry Evans runs a shelter for destitute men who are without family, friends and funds, who find it difficult to get work. We would give them some meat for tonight's dinner, save for a current currency crisis. From today, I have taken on the responsibility of feeding a dozen or so guest with dinner tonight and breakfast and dinner in the days to come. I hoped that you may have some clean off cuts and soup bones in the scrap bin that you might let us have." Tristan's voice faulted, "I, I thought I might do a savoury casserole. Harry already has onions and potatoes. A man in the railway allotments has given me these." Tristan opened his carrier bag for inspection.

Again, the man who wore the black turban took a long time to reply. Tristan felt as though a combined team of psychiatrists and psychologists had examined in depth before the impassive faced butcher finally broke the silence, "Well let me see, the Council charge us enough to take away our trade waste, so perhaps we might be able to help each other. The housewives of today, even those of my faith, don't cook as they used to. Much of our forequarter meat, along with most of the fat, goes for pet food or scrap. For a casserole, you will need dumplings. For dumplings, you will need suet".

The man changed his long knife for a boning knife. From two sheep carcases that hung from a rail, he expertly cut away both kidneys, complete with the suet. He cracked open the suet to release the four kidneys which he arranged on a small stainless tray in his glass counter unit. He put the suet into a bag and went on to say. "The twelve not quite senior citizens will require one hundred and seventy grams of meat each. You will need just over two kilos in total. That should not be too difficult at this time of day."

In minutes, he had picked out from a blue plastic bin several off cuts, from which he trimmed most of the fat. On the scales, the trimmed meat yielded the required amount. He added the lean meat to the bag with the suet. He also added some fat. "You will need fat to render. Anything else old chap." "No" Tristan, added, in a nervous voice he did not recognise. "Except my, I mean our thanks, you have been very generous. May we, I mean me, come to scrounge again." Raul replied in his Oxford drawl, "Go with God and by all means, come again. I know of Harry

145

Evans, he does God's work. Oh, before you go, you had better take the kidneys with some bones. A casserole is not worth a bean unless it has a kidney or two for flavour, with soup bones to stiffen it."

Before he headed off to brave the far more difficult task to put his idea of a daily goody box to the Sous Chef at one of the largest traditional hotels that served both Kings Cross and Euston railway stations, Tristan dropped off the carrier bag of fresh vegetables and the bag of meat in Retreads kitchen.

To follow the technique that he had used successfully, when he got a job at the Keeble, Tristan first went to the front entrance of the three hundred plus room hotel, a four star unit with four star facilities. Akin to all hotels of its class, it had the 'Investors in people plaque', prominently displayed alongside photographs of senior managers.

Once he had committed to memory, not only the name of the two top men in the kitchen, the head Chef and the Sous Chef, Tristan also memorised the name of the front of house manager on duty, a Mr. William Brownlow. His lowly station in the hotel only allowed a small label to display his name on the reception desk.

One of the girl receptionist, all tight skirt, tight Botox forehead, stiletto heels, gloss lipstick, varnished fingernails and hard lacquered hair gave him a smile as genuine as the rest of her presentation. In estuary English, she asked, archly, "Are you lost sir?" "No, no" replied Tristan, however he could not resist a return to his acerbic ways. He added, loud enough for all to hear, "When I saw you, I found the way." He turned quickly on his heel towards the door that an elderly hall porter opened for him. He said softly, as Tristan passed, "Silly tart, the young uns are all that way these days. They make anyone not of their peer group feel as welcome as a slug in a salad sandwich."

It took Tristan some time to find the office of Pasqualle Mazzerella, the Sous Chef. He had his name on an open door that had a clear sight line to the factory sized main kitchen. Inside the office, sat at an untidy desk, Tristan could see a small dark swarthy man, in his early sixties, dressed in immaculate cook's whites. He seemed to be determined to add to the deep worry lines that had riven his face as he shouted into a telephone, "I've told you, two commis and a chef de partie, not turned in, a K. P. drunk already. So how in the name of Gordon bloody Blue not Bennett, do you expect me to run a kitchen." His voice went up a few decibels to scream, "Get onto the agency, now," before he slammed the phone down. When he saw Tristan he shouted, "Who the hell are you. What brings you to my kitchen in your spotty bow tie?"

Tristan grinned before he replied sweetly, "Afternoon Chef, I am Tristan; you don't want to be bothered with the rest. Mr. Brownlow, the stiff shirt over pin stripes out front suggested I call on you. I see that it is situation normal. Captain not on the bridge, ship on the rocks, crew split between deserters and drunks with you left in charge. Me, well at least I am not the pirates or worse an EHO. In exchange for the help I can provide with your staffing problems, I just want to take away some of your out of date dry goods and leftovers, on a daily basis." The chef resumed in a more normal tone, "You seem to speak like a man familiar with kitchen routine. What is it that you really want?"

It took very little time for Tristan to explain Retreads needs before Pasqualle ordered one of his commis to fill a good-sized sturdy box, which had contained bought in chips, with useful goods. For his part, Tristan promised to deliver Stan, his friend from the Whittington Hotel, for interview, on the next day, after he had assured the Sous Chef of his friend's talent, strength and good sober nature.

The provisions that Tristan had garnered in one afternoon, overwhelmed Harry Evans, Master of Retreads. He greeted him with a mixture of joy and concern. "Look old man," he said "why don't you let me cook tonight, you look about done in, just sit you down there boyo. You can tell me what to do with this boun-tiful harvest."

He flashed a look at Tristan, "You haven't nicked any of it have you?" Tristan replied happily, "No Harry, in all ways it is all ko-sher, in fact, the meat is halal, the vegetable are from the allot-ments at the end of that cul-de-sac off the main road, just passed the butchers. The dry goods, even the salt, would you believe, are out of date, although safe for us to use They come courtesy of the biggest of the station hotels. By the way, before we go to pick up my gear tonight, I have to find a friend of mine. I want to get him embedded in their kitchen to secure our future supplies."

"Right on boyo, Harry said, "Where do I start?" He called through the door into the main dormitory, "John, come, give me a hand in here; we have a feast to prepare."

Chapter 11

Ordered to rest by Harry Evans, the Master of Retreads, Tristan relaxed in the worn cushioned high backed hessian covered kitchen chair by the fire. He watched Harry and John prepare the evening meal. John, who Harry had called in to help, proved to be a neat, small, competent cook.

Tristan guessed that he would be seventy, or thereabouts. Later, Tristan learned that John had passed through Retreads many years before. Twice, every week of the year, he came back to help Harry prepare, serve and supervise the evening meal. The two old men worked easily together, to serve up ten plated meals prepared from the produce Tristan had garnered that day.

All the Retread guests ate quietly, with none of the usual banter of men at the office or seated together in clubs or pubs. When they had finished the meal, John set out pots of tea, cups, saucers, milk and sugar on the rough plywood table, before he returned to the sanctuary of the kitchen. Only then did Harry, John and Tristan eat their fill of the same meal, seated together at the galvanized iron topped kitchen worktop.

Before half past nine, Tristan left Retreads, with Harry in support. John stayed on to supervise the residents, who after every meal, were required to wash up, clean down and tidy away before making up their beds for the night.

Although Tristan needed to retrieve his worldly-goods from the defunct Whittington Hotel, he knew that he must first find the massive Polish chef Stan Kay, who used to be Stanislause Klaginskaieski.

After he had dismissed Tristan's idea to borrow a handcart to push his luggage across town Harry insisted that he should accompany Tristan to fund the necessary taxi fares from his own pocket money.

The two men called at Dom Polski, the Polish club where Stan had told Tristan that the club stewards would know where to contact him. When they asked for Stan Kay, they only received a blank stare.

They fared no better when Tristan tried to pronounce Stan's Polish name, Stanislause Klaginskaieski. To make them understand, Tristan in charade mode mimicked weight lifting, but cheated to say aloud the clue words 'Haystack' 'Colossus' 'Man Mountain'. He even tried walking pantechnicon, but without success. Finally, he tried the only word, other than Coca-Cola, that is understood, all over the world, in any language, 'Olympic'. Immediately there was recognition and laughter.

One of the men told Tristan that, if he hurried, he would probably find his friend at the 'Old Swan', in Kensington Church Street, Notting Hill Gate.

When they arrived at the Old Swan, Stan's great bulk was easy to see in the thick of a busy crowd of men who watched as he took on all comers at arm wrestling. Stan beat off all challengers without fuss; his easy smile did not once turn into a grimace. One of the bar staff told Tristan that it was a regular event when the big man came in for a drink. Stan finally noticed Tristan.

He called to him, "Hey Angol, you thin sliver of a man, fancy I twist your arm?" Tristan replied, "I do, although not in the way you want to, you great beached Pollack. I will allow you twist my arm into letting you buy me, and Harry my friend, a pint a piece.

That is if the landlord will serve you after you have mangled the drinking arm of half his respectable customers."

True to form, Stan would not buy either man a beer; he insisted that they drink genuine under the counter Polish Vodka, but as he had not yet secured a job, he did agree to meet the sous chef who needed sober reliable staff. They agreed to meet at four o'clock the next day, outside the front entrance of the hotel where Tristan wanted to implant Stan to secure a daily goody box of comestibles for Retreads.

After a short taxi ride to the Whittington Hotel, it took a long time to get the attention of the security guard, before Tristan could collect the things that he had left in his care.

While he had waited for the guard, Tristan read the statutory change of use notices pinned to the front door of the already boarded up hotel. The notice detailed plans to turn the building into, 'Luxury executive apartments'. It confirmed Tristan's belief that he had been conned. The Receiver's opinion had been correct; the company had never intended to make the Whittington a viable hotel.

He had only been engaged to increase the operational cost on the profit and loss account. He wondered just how much money the so-called managers had siphoned off before the receivers arrived and when, if ever, the receivers might pay him his due wages.

Although it was late before Tristan's long day was over, he lay awake in the small second bedroom of Harry's little flat, deep in thought.

He knew that on this soft summer night, men who were alone in the world occupied just over half of Retreads cubicles. They were men adrift who, by not conforming to the majority opinion of normality, had fallen through the safety net of society.

He thought of the many others, of similar kind, those who would sleep rough, in doorways, or under arches, in this city of dreams and broken promises. It had surprised Tristan that there had been so little conversation amongst the guests when they sat together at the rough plywood table, to eat the evening meal prepared from the staples the Butcher, the Gardener and the Sous Chef had willingly given to Retreads.

Each man at the table seemed only to look inwards. They took little heed of Harry's patient attempts to learn how they had spent their day. Unknown to Tristan, his thoughts and concern for other people, a rare event in his life, changed him. Sleep came, deep untroubled natural sleep, a sleep better than he had had in many years.

For the second time in two days, a hand on his shoulder rocked Tristan awake. This time, Harry Evans, Master of Retreads, not a young policeman woke him.

Angry with himself, that on his first morning on duty he had overslept, Tristan blustered, "Oh fiddle and drumsticks, what time is it. I am so sorry Harry; my alarm clock hasn't gone off. As he fumbled for his bedside table, he rambled, "Where is the damn thing. I am sure that I set it for 6 o'clock."

Harry said quietly, "Calm down boyo, I took it away last night, you were about done in. I have need of you for more than help with a breakfast or two. I wanted you to sleep, to rest. Don't you worry; John came in to help me. Years ago, he was a Circuit Judge, day after day required to deal with London low life. It depressed him. He sought solace in whisky. He was one of the unfortunate few for whom alcohol is an addictive drug. He resigned when he realised that he had made mistakes that affected people's lives. When he came to Retreads he needed help, but by helping other guests with legal problems, he recovered. Like many of our leavers, he is a great help to our Retread's network of old boys who have done well, some professional, some artisan. You can have a bath now that the water is hot. Come down when you are ready."

As Tristan bathed in the small bathroom in Harry's flat, for the first time in his life, he felt curiously weepy, near to tears. They were unlike the tears he had shed on a few occasions during his life; they had been tears of frustration.

Harry's influence had made him aware that since leaving the rehab unit in Scagill, he had received more acts of genuine kindness than he could remember during any other period of his irregular life.

The Vicar of Scagill's Parish Church, the Brassingtons, Stan the chef at the Whittington, young P.C. Tom Warwick, Sergeant Robbins, the allotment gardener and the halal butcher who had filled his bag with good food. They had all been kind to him, a stranger. He remembered that once he had counted that he had had at least thirty jobs since he left the army. None of them had amounted to much. He had only worked with colleagues; he had never made true friends. He had never had a home of his own.

His onetime only love had been Hoopey, his black Labrador. He reflected, sadly, that he could not recall that he had ever been genuinely kind to anyone. It led him to wonder if people had been kind to him due to his age, as he no longer posed a threat to anyone, not for a job, not for recognition, not for a place in the sun, not even for the love of a good woman."

Harry's rest cure had worked. Refreshed, Tristan came into the kitchen, shaved, hair combed, at least twice, neatly dressed in a pair of slacks and an open necked shirt. Harry greeted him cheerfully, "Cup of tea on the table boyo. What are your plans for today?" Tristan used his reply to clarify his plans, "Well, I have to be at King's Cross at four this afternoon to meet Stan the man. I have promised to introduce him to the Sous chef from whom I scrounged some of yesterday's food. I will use what is left of the morning to seek further provender. How many do you think will join us for supper tonight?"

Harry scratched his beard, as though it were an aid to forecast events, "About the same as last night I should think, unless the weather turns nasty, or there is a good football match on our telly."

Tentatively, Tristan said, "Harry, I have had an idea about how we might be able to refit the kitchen. After I have collected some meat, before I meet up with Stan, I want to do something about it." "Steady on Tristan," Harry cautioned, "It's early days yet. I admit the monthly cheque came through from the Trust this morning however, I don't think it would cover the cost of that Baby Belling, or even the Bunsen burner you were on about, let alone a new kitchen. The Trusts cheque barely covers our routine running costs, if at all."

Tristan excitedly replied, "Who said it would cost you a groat. Just you make sure that we have a registered plumber as well as an accredited electrician amongst the present guests or amongst the Retreads' network of volunteer helpers you mentioned".

When Tristan reached the halal meat butchers shop, it only had one customer, a woman dressed in a burqa. He waited until she left the shop before he went in, confident that he would be able to pick up some off cuts. A much older man than Raul stood behind the counter. The man, who wore a similar black turban to that worn by Raul, tilted his head forward to peer over his thick bottle bottom glasses before he raised his hand with an extended forefinger and spoke just one word, "Retreads?"

Tristan's confidence had waned. He replied lamely, "Er, yes I am sir, I'm Tristan, their newest drop in. Er, um, did Raul mention our problem of mouths to feed with no money to spend? The butcher took some time before he agreed, "Yes, Raul did mention that he gave you meat we could not sell. However, now we have had time to consider the matter, he has told me that we must insist that you pay us for what we sell to you."

Tristan shoulders slumped. He turned toward the door, all his earlier spirit of the day quite knocked out of him. He managed to mumble, "Oh dear, that's that I suppose; thank you anyway, yesterday was good."

A deep magnificent voice that called him back sent shivers down his spine, "Tristan, you man of little faith in your Christian God, why do you go, where do you go to? It is true that we have decided that Retreads must pay for that which we sell to you, but surely, you can afford a penny, if I put it on your account. Raul, who is my son, who today is back at work, asked me to put up a parcel of fine well-trimmed pieces before they reached the blue bin." Tristan, confused, said, "I'm sorry, I don't understand,"

"Well, that is not a surprise," the turbaned butcher said, "Few, if any, can understand the numerous petty regulations that our successive equally ludicrous governments of no practical experience impose on us. If I explain, you may comprehend the intricacies of my trade that lie beyond the slaughter, cleaving, cutting and sale of meat to our customers. If I were to pass waste to you, regulations require that I must give to you a signed and dated waste transfer certificate. The tricky bit is that you will have to have a licence to receive it. If I sell it to you, there is no need for all that fuss."

"Good Lord," Tristan said. "Who's mine or yours," the old man laughed. "I have opened a special account for you. Look here." He showed Tristan a neat dated entry in a new receipt book. He went on to explain.

"Raul is not a butcher; he is a special sort of doctor, a doctor to cure the sick mind, not the body corporal. You see, because he did not inherit my butcher skills, he had to go to Oxford. Now the poor chap is a clinical psychologist at Bart's. He took yesterday, as a holiday, because I had to go to see an eye specialist at Moorfield's, to see if they can stop my sight from further failure. That is why Raul cut meat yesterday. That is why we had so much waste in the bin; Ayee Kids these days."

When Tristan left the shop with his parcel of meat, the old man with the bottle glasses called after him, "Tristan, go with God, I should not have teased you. He is a loving god, the one God, the God of all people, of all faiths, monotheist or pluralist, of atheists and agnostics. He is the God of all creation."

Tristan went straight back to Retreads to make a start with the evening meal, an eclectic meat loaf. He had no need to collect further vegetables or salad stuff because he had sufficient. The gardener from the Loco men's allotment had given him three small thinned out 'Webs Wonderful' lettuces.

The Goodie box from the hotel contained boiled new potatoes, tomatoes, already cut in quarters, cucumber slices, red onion in slices, together with two bags of bought in salad leaves that had just passed their sell by date.

Tristan worked quickly to prepare a meat loaf, which he left for Harry to cook, ready to serve cold. Because of the high summer weather, he thought that the guests might enjoy a slice of well-seasoned cold meat loaf with a salad, provided he also served some buttered new potatoes.

Before noon, Tristan had finished his preparation for the evening meal. He had four clear hours before he had arranged to meet Stan the man, however he had distances to travel to test his idea for refitting the kitchen. He put his head round the door of the upstairs flat to call out, "Have you got such a thing as a bike hidden away anywhere. The Bentley's in for service and I need more than Shank's pony."

Harry emerged from his little study, "Sorry boyo, I left mine outside the front door one day years ago, chained and padlocked. Some rascal kindly left me the chain, although he took both the bike and the lock, but I knows of a lady who might lend you one of hers, if we ask her."

Ten minutes later, after Harry had introduced him to the lady who owned a nearby newsagents, Tristan selected from several bikes in a shed, a very sturdy ladies upright and beg Rudge, with a Sturmey Archer three speed gear in the back wheel. Best of all, it had a frame over the front wheel designed to carry a large basket.

The affable lady newsagent said, "Keep it as long as you need it. It's no longer of any use to me; it just takes up space. We can't get paperboys anymore. They would lose their street cred, whatever that is, if their mates saw them on a ladies bike. They would not peddle to save their lives; they will not settle for less than a motorbike or at a pinch a moped."

As Tristan took his leave, the Lady called after him "Just a minute duck, you will need these. She thrust into his hands a pair of bicycle clips for his trousers. She laughed, when she also offered Tristan one of the new style streamline helmets worn by keen young eco warrior cyclists. "I don't, suppose you would be seen dead in on one of these. It would be such a shame to hide your lovely silver hair."

Tristan vindicated her supposition when he declined the helmet. He did however thank her for the loan of the bicycle and afterthought trouser clips.

Tristan, who had not ridden a bike for more than forty years, muttered a silent prayer, to whom he had no idea. He asked for the accepted wisdom that, 'One never forgets how to ride a bike', to be the truth of all faiths.

Tristan did not worry about street cred. The ladies bike pleased him because he did not have to cock his leg over the saddle to mount his new charge, or as he imagined it, his spirited charger.

To give himself a chance, he turned towards his known way, towards the allotments, to get in some practice. At first, he wobbled like a five-year-old beginner just free of stabilisers, but he soon got the hang of things, ready to face the challenge of London's city traffic.

At first sight, the dresser in Retreads kitchen had inspired in Tristan the idea that it might be the solution to providing a new kitchen. He felt sure that a thing of beauty lay hidden under the tatty cheap domestic ware and chattels that cluttered its drab shroud of thick green paint.

The overall size, shape, balance, and every detail of the dresser somehow spoke to Tristan to tell him that it was as much a prisoner as he had been when incarcerated in the Laurels rehab unit.

He thought it to be a classic piece of furniture of style. He felt sure that it did not come from a tenant farm, or city institution.

Despite its present condition it spoke of the opulence of a grand country house, or city mansion, where it would have smelt of beeswax and displayed silver, not aluminium, cut glass not plastic, bone china, not earthenware pots.

Tristan realised that it would probably cost a few hundreds of pound to restore it, however once restored, he believed that it would command several times the cost of restoration, with the possibility of a good profit, if the trustees would agree to sell it at the right auction.

He needed the bike in order to get to St. James's, where he might get advice about the dresser from a reputable dealer in antique furniture, and to get back to Kings Cross in time to take Stan to meet the Pasquale the Sous Chef.

It took Tristan far longer than he thought to get to St James's where he knew there were top class shops that dealt in antiques and fine art. He thought that such shops would need to be genuine, as experts in valuation and provenance would look in on their way to and from Christies and Bonhams, the world famous auction houses.

Although he had never bought any artwork, fine or not, or any antique furniture, he felt he would get a better deal from the shops in St. James's, rather than from the smart shops that crowded around Church Street, off Kensington High.

Although Tristan had set out in high spirits to seek advice, he regretted that he had borrowed the bike. Age had severely affected his knees, hips and elbows. More than sixty years of smoking had diminished the capacity of his lungs and reduced his muscle power. It had alarmed him how little regard the motorised traffic had to peddle power. He shouted at one particularly inconsiderate driver, "Give way to pedal power you top gear petrol headed road hog."

The reply the driver gave described his mental capacity, sexual proclivity, technical ability, use to society and geriatric incompetence with swear words interposed between every noun and adjective. Several times, to rest his weary limbs, he had had to push the bike, not pedal it.

In Duke Street, he found what he had come to look for, a shop with a few elegant pieces of furniture on display. To Tristan's relief, the man in the shop looked respectfully middle aged, also a bit shabby. The name of the shop, worked in gold leaf, arching across the top of the window, 'Beeswax and Tung-oil' revived Tristan's hopes.

Two nearby antique shops he had already visited had part crushed the optimism with which he had set out. The sales assistant in the first, a woman sitting unoccupied behind an antique desk, had driven him out with an unforgiving rhetorical question, "You do know that we are trade only."

In the second, an old man, dressed in velvet cords and velvet jacket, who simpered, "Mmm, I do like your hair, are you looking for something a bit different?" caused Tristan to flee.

The faintly shabby man restored Tristan's hopes. "Can I help you old chap," the man said, "You look a bit antique, on the dilapidation down side of possible realistic restoration, however we can achieve wonders, if not miracles. If that is your bike outside, the Rudge without a lock on it, you had better bring it in. It won't last two minutes out there."

The man's recognition that the bike was a Rudge pleased Tristan. He said, "Surely, no one would nick an old thing like that."

The antique dealer, obviously an enthusiast about all things collectable, explained, "Don't you see, it's a classic, it's a Rudge dear boy, circa 1925 I'd say, not the Sturmey Archer hub of course, that's a later addition." With that, the shop owner went out, wheeled the bike inside his shop where he leant it against an elegant polished mahogany side table. "Now that the Rudge is safe, what might I be able to do for you," he asked brightly, "My guess is that you wish to sell, not buy. My best customers arrive in a chauffeur driven Rolls Royce; the worst turn up in flash Ferraris. You are my first customer to ride up on a bicycle, with bicycle clips round your trousers. It sets you apart. Unique is what a dealer like me looks for; you are more than welcome."

Fussed because he had forgotten about the trouser clips, Tristan mumbled an apology. "Don't bother yourself man, just sit down to catch your breath. When rested you can tell me about the treasure you have found."

Recognising that no assistant would have dared to wheel a bike in amongst the high value furniture Tristan knew, for certain, that the man must be the owner of the business, if not the property.

Tristan started, "I have to get back to King's Cross by four, so I have very little time, however I have very little to tell, so here goes. I am Tristan. You are right, I cannot buy; I am flat broke. I have been broke on previous occasions. This time I went a bit further. The police removed me from the streets of London as a destitute vagrant. However, thanks to a charity called Retreads, I am no longer homeless. The charity tries to retread old souls like me who, for one reason or another, have had their thread pulled out from the normal fabric of life. The idea is to get the old boys back in the weft and warp of society. Please understand that I have no knowledge of antique furniture. At Retreads, which the trustees of the charity have housed in an old Methodist Chapel, there is a large green painted piece of furniture. I think it is the sort of thing that you chaps call a dresser. We use it to store all the stuff used in what we euphemistically call the kitchen. Well, this dresser thing cries out to me for recognition as relict of an aristocrat's country house, or a city mansion, not a common kitchen cupboard. I am probably completely wrong about the dresser, but please believe me, I am not wrong about Retreads. It is in desperate need of improvement, particularly the kitchen. I am sure that if the local Environmental Health Officer should ever pop his head round the door, he or she would close us down. It would be a shame."

He paused for breath then continued, "A chap called Harry Evans runs it. His brother, a Vicar I met in Scagill in Yorkshire, believes that Harry does God's work. I could get a second hand half-descent kitchen for just a few hundred pounds. Could you come to look at it for us? We can't pay you a valuation fee, and you will probably think it rubbish. I don't know why, yet it seems to call out to me to set it free. Oh, I am sorry, I have faffed for too long; I must start back soon. I shall have to push the bike; I am as saddle sore as if I had ridden a bony camel across the Sahara. All my joints from ankle to neck need a shot of Redex followed by a massage with WD 40. You see, I have not ridden a bike for almost half a century. Could you, would you, can you help us?"

The antique dealer looked at Tristan with a wry smile, before he said, "I wish that I had recorded that soliloquy of truth, worthy of record in the world of half-truths, and suggestions shrouded by innuendo where I work."

He picked up a telephone, pressed a pre-set button, and spoke easily to the person who answered. "Charles, get the van out, no the small one, it's big enough for an old Rudge bike, bring it round straight away, I have work to do in King's Cross. You can look after the shop until I get back, or you can lock up if I am late."

When he put the phone down, he smiled at Tristan, "How about we have a cup of tea, it will take Charles at least ten minutes. We must be ready to go as soon as he gets here. The dreaded traffic wardens will get us, unless we are nippy."

Tristan drank the tea gratefully. At the same time he wittered, "I do hope that you will not find that I have wasted your time, or made a fool of myself." The owner of Beeswax and Tung oil said, seriously, "That is not the issue about which you should worry dear boy. You have admitted that you are not expert in matters of antique furniture. It follows from that, that what should bother you now, is whether I can be trusted. You have not yet even asked my name. The Antiques business is not all truth, honesty or reasonable trade. Leave the cups; Charles is here, bring the bike."

With the bike safely stowed in the back of a very highly polished van that had 'Beeswax and Tung oil' in discrete letters in gold on the side, the antique dealer said, "Tristan isn't it? My surname is Bentley, my parents baptised me Ralf Oliver Lincoln Leonard Stuart, to give me the initials R. O. L. L S. to mark me as a Rolls Bentley. My father had a passion for classic cars; mother thought it sounded posh. Of course, it misfired. At school, my chums called me Figgy after the fig roll biscuit. It stuck; it stays with me still. I have not yet managed to afford a car better than a Ford. Perhaps one day I will buy myself a Birkin Blower Bentley, with a strap over the bonnet and a wicker basket on the back. They are about the same age as your bike. Today I feel lucky, so please direct me to this Retreads place of yours where we can find out whether or not you are a 'divvy.'"

Chapter 12

The affable owner of Beeswax and Tung Oil, dealer in antique fine furniture, directed by an anxious Tristan, found a parking spot within yards of Retreads door. Before he locked the van, he took off his jacket to put on a brown warehouse coat. This simple act encouraged Tristan as it showed him to be a hands on dealer, a practical man.

The bell rang four times before Harry opened the door. He first greeted Tristan, with an exclamation, followed by a question. "Oh it's you boyo, back so soon," followed by, "You have not lost the bike have you?"

Tristan ignored the question to say quickly, "Harry, please say hello to Mr. Bentley. He has kindly given up his time to see whether he can provide us with a new state of the art kitchen. "Well, Dieu Dieu; how do Mr. Bentley," Harry chirped, "Come you on in, the pair of you. Come through to our state of the ark galley. Are you a 'Lead beater' a 'Chippy', or 'Sparks, the clever one'? I think you would need to be a bit of all three to tidy up what we have here." Tristan broke in, "Mr. Bentley, this is Harry Evans, the Master of Retreads I told you about. Harry, Mr. Bentley is a dealer in antique fine furniture. He has a shop just a street away from Christies. He is not a kitchen makeover merchant. I have asked him to come here to advise me about an idea I have."

Harry pretended to be chastened "Oh, sorry butty, no offence meant".

"That's the dresser that talks to you, isn't it?" Mr. Bentley asked, as he looked towards the very large green painted, kitchen utensil encrusted piece of furniture set against the sidewall. "Yes, that's the one" Tristan acknowledged, his expression glum, his voice morose. "Problem is though, now that you are here, I have either gone deaf, or it has lost its voice." The dealer slapped Tristan on the back, "Don't despair just yet old chap. All cars lose their annoying squeak when they are taken to the garage to have it seen to, and an aching tooth heals itself on the way to the dentist" "Let me see if your treasure will sing for me if I use the plectrum of my thumbnail to pluck at its peeling paint".

He did pick at the paint, before he ran his hand along each shelf. He went on hands and knees to poke his head inside the cupboards. Back on his feet, he emptied one drawer of its contents onto the galvanized iron table top. He looked carefully at the neat dovetail joints before giving the underside of the drawer a clout with the soft side of his closed fist.

He surprised Tristan when he turned his back to the dresser, to go on hand and knees again, this time to stick his head under both of the hessian covered high backed fireside chairs. Lying on his back, he wriggled under the table, where he grunted and snorted, in between muttering to himself. Once again on his feet, he pulled up a corner of the galvanized iron that covered the table top to peer under it, intently, while letting out an uncertain sort of thoughtful drawn out 'mmm', followed by, to Tristan's horror, a 'tch-tch' or two, while shaking his head.

Mr. Bentley brushed his coat free of dust and cobwebs before he intoned in a voice serious enough for a graveside committal, "Tristan, I will not buy your kitchen cupboard, but after a short pause, he joyfully sang out, "But I know a man who might. He is a genius at restoration; it is what he does. The only bad news is that it is very big, so the market is limited to people rich enough to own big houses. The good news is that those who own big houses can afford to pay lots of money. Because the market is limited, it may hang a bit before my restorer chap can get the right price. That will affect what he will be prepared to pay me up front. If you let me deal for you, I shall of course take a percentage, however I think I could negotiate with him to get enough to leave you with around eight hundred pounds."

Because his whole body ached from the unusual exercise of the bike ride, Tristan had eased himself, painfully, into one of the hessian covered high backed chairs. He punched the air as he cried aloud, "I knew it; for once in my life an outside chance came in a winner. That's wonderful news isn't it Harry? I told you a new kitchen would not cost you a groat. Eight hundred pounds is a grand start."

He asked Mr Bentley, "Does that make me a 'Divvy'? Am I like that chap on the telly, the one with the ability to sense a genuine antique, however dilapidated dirty, disguised, neglected or misused it might be."

Mr Bentley shook his head, "You were right about the kitchen cupboard. It is what we chaps call a dresser. It is of considerable age, it has classic lines with authentic grandeur. Sadly, in general terms, you are no divvy. You see Tristan, a true divvy, if there ever has been, is, or ever will be, a divvy could not sit still, not on that chair."

With a flourish like a stage magician, with both hands, he grabbed the top of the hessian sack covering the back of the chair where Tristan sat. He pulled it clean away. His theatrical gesture shocked Tristan.

It surprised Harry even more when he saw revealed, a deeply carved oak panel back to a chair he had used for more than thirty years.

Mr. Bentley announced to his audience of two, "If you put this pair of Tudor carved oak conversation chairs up for auction at Christies, or Bonhams, you will be able to afford to have Harrods do a full kitchen re-fit with new bedroom furniture for your guests thrown in. I know of a similar pair of chairs on display at Hampton Court. I shall have to check, but I think that the heraldic arms carved into the back of your chairs are those of an historically famous Tudor family. If, as I suspect, the table under the galvanised iron cover is of the same period, you will be able to do a bit more."

Harry had jumped up from his chair, excited as a teenager who has just passed his driving test. Tristan froze, hardly daring to move, in case he caused the chair he sat in some damage. "A new toilet block, that's what we need" Harry's voice sounded like a distant prayer. "Better still, how about a loo for each cubicle," Tristan whooped.

"Yes, that's it, that's what we want," Harry agreed, "The old boys would not risk a fall, or wake the others, when the old man's curse makes them get up in the middle of the night. Even prison cells have their own lavatories these days. We could be more BUPA than the NHS."

As he had to be serious, Mr. Bentley said firmly, "Hold on you two, it's not the Lottery you have won, it will all take time. First, we must have a contract. Tristan has told me that Retreads is a registered charity, therefore the trustees must be involved. I hope that they will not want to keep the table or the chairs, because they were a gift, or some restrictive codicil that governs the sale of any of the charities assets."

The colour drained from Harry's face that had been flushed with excitement, while he lovingly stroked one of the chairs. "Oh damn a darro," he said, in the voice of the South Wales valley where he had spent his youth, "I had not thought about that. I will talk to God tonight. Tomorrow I will call the Trust's solicitors. I could not bear it if the chaps could not benefit. Thank you Mr. Bentley, thank you very much, who would have thought it? I have been sitting on a crock of gold these thirty years. Look you here, we can't go on calling each other by surnames Mr. Bentley, what do your friends call you.

"Please call me Figgy, he replied, "I am comfortable with that. Tristan will explain. May I suggest that we get a move on to get the pieces away from here, kitchens are dangerous places, their fires are all consuming. You cannot possibly afford to insure them for their antique value. In my warehouse, they will come under my stock insurance, however you will have title to them, until the fall of the auctioneers hammer. I shall come back tomorrow with a draft contract, if that is convenient. Please let your trustees' solicitor have sight of it. Make sure that they do a reference check on me. I am the sole proprietor of Beeswax and Tung Oil; it should not take long. Once the contract is agreed, I shall come with Charles, in the big van, to pick up the Retreads treasures. Please be aware that most antiques have little or no intrinsic value. In the main, they only have value because someone, somewhere, has a desire to own them. The provenance of unique pieces of pot, porcelain, metalwork or woodwork that has survived, intact, for over a hundred years is the draw. Your functional table and chairs will afford you a new kitchen when they morph into some unused curiosity in America, or they will circulate for years within the trade, sold or exchanged by one dealer to another who will display them in their shop window, or picture them in auction sale catalogues, always with an increased guide price. Whatever their future, they will never again be usefully employed, as they have been in your comfortable old kitchen."

After formal handshakes, he left a Beeswax and Tung Oil business card on the galvanised worktop.

Tristan went with Figgy to take the bike out of the back of the van. When he returned to the Kitchen, he and Harry stared at each other. For a long time they said not a word.

Harry broke the silence to say, "When you first came to Retreads, I said that the Good Lord may have sent you here for a purpose. It seems that he has revealed his purpose. Tristan, do you trust Mr. Bentley?

Tristan replied with confidence, "Yes I do; Figgy is genuine. He comes with good provenance, assayed, hallmarked also copper-bottomed. He must be the sole owner of the business. When he brought the bike into the shop, he lent it against a lovely antique polished mahogany side table. No manager or assistant would have dared to do that. Sorry Harry I must rush or I shall miss Stan who waits for me at King's Cross. I am five minutes late already."

To save time, Tristan ignored his aches and pains, to ride the Rudge ladies bicycle the short distance from Retreads to the front entrance of the hotel where he had arranged to meet Stan. "You are late Angol," Stan said without rancour, "Nevertheless I am thankful that you have come to my rescue. It does not do for a slender innocent young chap like me to hang around street corners in King's Cross. I have already turned down several offers, one from a girl who offered me a good time, one tried to sell me coke, and I do not mean cola or coal with the gas taken out. A trendy transvestite told me I had a beautiful body and a flashily dressed old bloke with blond curly hair offered me a job as a bouncer at 'Stringfellows'. I like the wheels Angol; not quite a 'Ferrari', nevertheless it is a start. Nah then, where is this Sous chef who is in want of a cooking chef?"

Tristan remembered the way to the Sous Chef's office where they waited because neither man dared to knock on his door.

Pasquale, or whoever he had in the office with him, had closed the door, but Pasquale's temper was the same as it had been on Tristan's first visit. He shouted at someone, to ask in the name of St. Martha, why he could not raise the wages of the commis chefs to enable him to keep a brigade together for more than two days at a time.

Both Tristan and the towering hulk Stan winced when some solid heavy object crashed with force against the inside of the door. When the door burst open, they both quickly stood aside to allow a bespectacled patterned pullover wearing youth to flee

Pasquale's office, in full retreat, shouting over his shoulder, "But you are already over budget."

"Budget, fudge it" Pasquale shouted after him, "Don't you understand, its ratios that rule, not fixed sums, you worse than useless number crunching goggle-eyed auditor. If I can manage accounts, why can't you cook the books?"

When the florid colour left Pasquale's face to resume its Sicilian brown deeply riven patina, he smiled at Tristan, "I remember you; you are the professional scrounger." Bending to recover his white leather wooden soled kitchen clog that they had heard hitting the door, he continued, "Missed the dimly lit twit."

He looked up to speak to Stan, "You must be the bribe. Come in, sit down, tell me why you would risk having to dodge burning pans, scalding stock and flying cold steel to work for me. Are you a deranged delinquent divorced dipsomaniac, or is it dementia that brings you here?" Stan replied, "I keep myself fit. I have not seen a doctor in years. I have had it a bit easy of late, but last month this Angol here got me to cook real Polish food again. I realised that I can still do it, or cook French, Italian, German, even Russian, though it is hardly worth the bother, and I still enjoy it."

Pasquale addressed his next remark to Tristan, "You go pick up your goodie box. Leave us proper men, who do real work, to see if we can come to an arrangement."

After he had waited at the hotel's staff entrance for his friend, for no more than fifteen minutes, two ham-sized hands around Tristan's waist lifted him two feet clear of the ground. Before gently setting him down Stan said, "Thanks Angol, I got the job, good pay, start tomorrow, three until finish."

With the goodie box already in the bike's basket frame, Tristan said, "Good, we can celebrate; come with me to Retreads, so that you will know where I live. As a special treat, I will let you plate up the evening meal. I made a sort of eclectic meat loaf this morning, which I left in Harry's care, but right now, I feel like a punctured soufflé. I am a yard or two on the wrong side of spring in the step youthful athleticism to take up travelling by pedal power. I have found muscles that I forgot about years ago. They urge me to get into a hot bath."

Stan responded earnestly, "Nonsense you wimp, if you follow my training regime and diet, you will soon be as fit as an Olympic champion." Tristan mocked, "Oh yes, pray tell, what regime is that; what Olympics, 1936 Berlin or 1948 London? None of those champions are world class anymore, not even those that are still with us."

Stan did not allow Tristan to have the last word, "Good Polish food, sausage, spek, sauerkraut, borscht, ragu, pirogi, zurek and baklava and Polish vodka, that's all you need Angol. If you follow my diet, you will soon start chasing after women again. It's a fact."

It only took Figgy just over two weeks to come up with the money for the dresser. He came early one Friday evening to the door of Retreads, with a cheque made out for nine hundred and fifty pounds. He had left the top line 'Pay' for Harry to fill in the correct name of the Retreads charity.

The cheque delighted Tristan who felt vindicated, "Thank you Figgy that is even better than you expected." Figgy, a modest man, apologised, "I am sorry it is not a nice round thousand. I did try for the other fifty, however the chap who bought it is a thoroughbred third generation dealer. He had to haggle, even though I told him about the work that you do, it's in him, both by nature and nurture. By the way, I have not charged any commission on this sale. I will get my reward when the auctioneers do their work with the Retreads treasure. I have had the right man from Bonham's look at the three pieces. He has told me that they will put them up as two lots, one to follow immediately after the other. He confirmed my opinion that the chairs are of the same period as the table, although they are not part of a set. They will not do any restoration; they will only tidy them up for the sale by taking off the chewing gum clogged with hessian. Their first estimate is for a reserve of something in the order of a sum-total of fifteen thousand pounds for the two lots. Please do not get too excited, it is not yet confirmed." Tristan said, "Half of that will do for what we want, a quarter for what we need."

During the weeks that followed, Tristan fell into a routine. Up early, to cook breakfast. After breakfast, every morning, except Sunday, he had to act like a seaside landlady to shoo the old boys out of the door, rain or shine, at half past eight.

Harry made it a strict rule. Daily he justified the routine with a mantra, "If they do not have a routine, a rhythm, they will quickly get out of kilter with what the media choose to call the 'world of work'. They will become good for nothing. It is all one, the same world, the only world we have, God given, entire, indivisible."

After the guests had left for the day, Tristan usually cooked breakfast for Harry and himself, and for Stan, when Stan did not work an early shift. Stan arrived sometime during every day, always with a cool box under his arm that contained so-called 'waste' from the kitchens of the busy commercial rather than prestige hotel where he worked. With the food, Pasquale, the sous chef, always included a stock transfer invoice for variable small amounts. He assured Stan that the accounts office recorded it in odd multiples, as miscellaneous revenue, they would write off each quarter, as an unrecoverable debt. Over breakfast, which they took at a leisurely pace, they planned the rest of the day's activity.

The Retreads trustees had authorised Harry to use the money received from the sale of the dresser to buy kitchen equipment. Harry had automatically passed the responsibility onto Tristan. By a stroke of good fortune, he bought all the necessary kitchen equipment second hand, from one source.

To improve his stamina, every day he rode the Rudge bicycle, with a plastic box in the frame, taking different routes to collect meat from the butcher, vegetables from the allotment gardeners and to look for other opportunities.

One morning, he noticed that children no longer played in the local school playground. Contractor's lorries, vans, excavators and a crane with a wrecking ball had moved in to develop the site. A sign on a new security fence that enclosed the whole school area stated, 'Danger - Construction Site - Keep Out.' A second larger more colourful sign carried the message, 'The Joseph Atkinson School demolition - Making way for road realignment - Part of the Borough of Islington's regeneration programme - Providing for a better future'.

For small cash in hand sums in ten, or twenty-pound notes, Tristan took the trouble of disposal of the schools kitchen equipment off the hands of the contractors.

In one hour, he bought all that he needed to re-equip the Kitchen at Retreads. He calculated that with the old cast iron range removed, all the commercial quality items that were larger than required to for prepare meals for no more than twenty men, who no longer had the appetite of youth, would fit into the kitchen at Retreads. He tipped twenty pounds each to two of the contractor's men, to disconnect, take out and move the equipment, on their lorry, to Retreads.

Harry arranged that the Retreads network sorted out all necessary adjustments to the kitchen to accommodate the new equipment. The Salvation Army heavy gang broke up and took away the old cast iron range. A firm owned by one of the Trustees fitted safety flooring. Stan, with Tristan's help, made good the walls and gave them a fresh coat of white gloss paint. The completed project was good enough to cater for a hundred. It had however changed the ambiance from that of a dilapidated yet comfortable farmhouse kitchen, to that normal for a modern works canteen.

Tristan developed confidence due to his achievements at Retreads. However, he began to feel restless. The routine cooking he had to do was simple; it lacked any sense of challenge. Occasionally his thoughts turned again to his promise to follow a quest that would satisfy the other Grey Haired Knights with true tales of his adventures, when they were to meet again on the Saturday after the next summer solstice.

He had also not forgotten the promise he made to Charles Lucas Prescott, the barman thief, that one day he would visit him again and that it was for Prescott to worry about the consequence.

Tristan Edward and Harry Evans were comfortable in each other's company. When eating breakfast, they were in the habit of each having half of the morning paper to read, with a change over every fifteen minutes between outside and inside pages. They tossed a coin each day to decide who started with the letters page.

One quiet morning, when he noticed that Tristan had stopped reading, Harry brought him back to earth with a simple statement.

"Tristan, I have come to know you well since the good Lord brought you to help me here at Retreads. I sense that you think of leaving our shelter to take on another challenge. Your work here has restored you to good health. I believe that it has given you a sense of purpose to achieve more than is available for you here. You can be proud of your achievements; they are remarkable. You have created a grand new kitchen. Of more importance, you have given the guests a much-improved diet. You have also made a good friend with Stan. You have improved your strength, stamina and general health. I have not seen you smoke. Your knee has stopped trembling when you are sitting at ease. You have been patient and kind to our guests; also with me. You have not complained about being short of money, even though I have only given you pocket money to spend on yourself. I knew that the change in you would come about, so I did not tell you that you have been on the charities official pay roll since you came to us. The trustees were so pleased with what you have achieved, and the way you have gone about things, that they put you on the payroll, back dated to the day when you first brought the coal up. With the minimum wage, even if you were to walk out today, you will have a little over eight hundred and thirty pounds to put into the bank; there would be more if this rapacious government of ours had not taken more than a tithe."

Tristan involuntarily rose to his feet "Good Lord" he exclaimed, "that is as much as I set out with from Scagill." He sat back onto his seat, regretting that he could not slump into it, as he used to in the old high backed hessian covered fireside chairs. "I can't leave" Tristan wittered, "Who will do the cooking, what about the new en-suit cubicles, what about the allotment?

Harry replied with a serine smile, "That is for me to worry about, not you. I have faith that the Lord is good, as you yourself have just said, as you said when you first came to us. Besides, I have inside information. Stan the man has agreed to take under his wing the thin as a stick Polish chap who came in off the street a few days ago. You know, Bartoz who does not yet speak much English. He will teach him to cook. He had been a farmer in Poland; farmers know about food. After a while, who knows, he may get a job with Stan. To get people back on track is what we do. Retreads is all about giving deserving men, those who are willing to be helped, a sure tread with a firm grip, to travel safely on whatever road they choose to follow what about it Boyo; what about a new start?"

That night, stimulated by Harry's challenge, Tristan lay in bed, unable to sleep, his mind too full of memories and ideas for the future.

He remembered the awful thought he had had before he had fallen asleep on a bench in the Embankment Gardens. He had been sure that some unexplained force had worked against him to leave him with "Nowhere to go, no one to go home to, no family, friends or funds."

He felt sure that whatever force it might have been, it had tested his worth as a Grey Haired Knight. He felt that the same force had directed him to Retreads not the Good Lord as Harry suggested. Retreads had given him strength in mind and body. He determined to resume his quest to put to rights the corruption at the Keeble and to bring down Charles Lucas Prescott, whatever the cost, whatever the risk.

Chapter 13

To rest in Retreads refurbished kitchen, Tristan had to take careful aim to lower, slowly, his slim backend onto one of the two new modern chrome and plastic chairs that Harry had arranged along the wall where the range had been. Tristan missed the old solid fuelled cast iron double oven range, with is central open fire that had previously dominated the kitchen. Undeniably, the chairs looked stylish. They fitted in well with the stainless steel table and the nearly new kitchen equipment, although they afforded little comfort. They were not suited even for Tristan's slender frame.

"Damn it Harry," he said, "I am about bushed, but these modern Fosteresque, or is it Rogeresque, presumably ergonomically architect designed chairs are no help. They lack the comforting sackcloth and ashes of your old friendly fireside chairs. You could flop into those without fear of missing them, or that they might skid away from under you. They really did provide succour to the weary. One can only perch on these clinical supports. The designer must have had a brief to discourage even the briefest respite. They are kin to the seats in McDonalds, Burger King, KFC, railway station coffee shops, or those in London bus-shelters."

Harry laughed, "You've had a good day then." At the same time, he handed Tristan a cup and saucer of freshly brewed tea.

Harry always brewed tea in a warmed pot. He never used mugs for tea. He would gently scold any guest who he caught with a cup of tea without a saucer; "Mugs are for cocoa, not tea," he would call out.

"No! I have not had a good day, nor have I had a good week for that matter," Tristan replied, wearily. "The world of work, the world that you state does not exist, as a separate entity, has manifested itself in reality. It has closed its doors against me."

"Well Boyo," Harry said to encourage him, "It is early days yet; who knows what the morrow might bring. Come, have another cup into which I shall put two spoons of sugar to sweeten that sour temper of yours. I am not surprised that you have not been successful. Top to bottom you need a spruce up. From the top, your hair needs a proper cut, not just a trim. The middle bit is in want of a new suit. Your bottom, I mean your shoes, they too are in need of attention. I have never understood why we name the top of the leg the bottom. Good quality well polished shoes are the definitive mark of a gentleman. Tomorrow, take the day off. Give up on your job hunt for a day. Go to 'Billy the Barbers' in Calshot Street where you can read his pornographic magazines. Billy buys them in special, though it hurts him a bit. You see he is a preacher at the Bethesda Baptist in Camden Town. He says his customers will not come to his barbers shop if he does not keep up with the times; he does not mean Rupert Murdoch's rag. I go to Billy's because I can't abide the obversely named 'Unisex' salons, where chits of girls use cheap combs to fiddle with what little hair I have left, before they snip at it in the way that a timid but knowing mouse nibbles cheese from a set trap."

The next morning, after he had cooked breakfast, Tristan took Harry's advice in part only. He did have his haircut, however not at Billy the Barber's premises. One look through the window of the dull dark old-fashioned shop persuaded him that Billy would give him a short back and sides whatever he asked for. In Euston Road, he found a brightly lit hairdressers salon with a notice in the window that showed that someone had a sense of humour: 'Men only - Haircuts, while you wait'.

Although the salon claimed to be men only, all the trouser-wearing hairdressers were women. When Tristan entered the shop, an odd-looking old man, wearing a long coat, despite the summer weather, brushed past him on his way out. As he did so, he knocked over a pile of magazines set on the reception desk. Muttering, in a language Tristan did not recognise, he rapidly shuffled them back into some sort of order, before he put them back on the counter and left the shop without an apology.

Tristan took a seat amongst several men who patiently waited their turn in the first come first served queue. All were staring vacantly before them. Not one of them read a newspaper or magazine. Without looking at the title, Tristan had taken the top magazine from the pile that the old man had put back on the counter. For a while, Tristan's gambler instinct let his eye wander, trying to guess which women hairdresser, in a men only salon, would cut his hair. When he glanced down at the magazine in his hand, he saw that he had picked up a copy of 'The Lady', but could not be bothered to leave his seat to find a better read.

For several minutes, he idly turned the pages. Although he found no interest in the articles or the many adverts for idyllic rural cottages for holiday let, he did become seriously interested in the pages that advertised job opportunities.

They did not seem to Tristan to deal with the world of work, or type of jobs that the 'Job Centre Plus's computers catalogued. Jobs that for the past two weeks, Monday through Friday, had black balled him. A small advert, with a strap-line 'Gentleman's gentleman', in a bold font, caught his attention. The lines under the strap-line were in very small print. 'Mature male to be modern 'Jeeves' to single old fashioned stickler for detail. Resident permanent position. Good remuneration, excellent accommodation. Ex-service man preferred. It gave no address only a London telephone number. When Tristan read that the edition was only two weeks old, it raised his hopes. He thought that the job, though not ideal, would give him time to find a business opportunity that he could develop to become employer not employee.

A second sharp call of "Next" from the woman at a vacant chair broke his reverie. "You go mate," whispered a man sitting beside him, "She's rubbish, I'll wait for the young one with the boobs." Tristan took the magazine with him. "How do you want it Granddad," the woman asked in a voice loud enough for all to hear. Tristan fell for it, "Who are you calling granddad". The woman smirked when she said, again for all to hear, "Good, you won't ask for the pensioners' discount then."

Tristan tried to get back on even terms, "No, Mrs. Lovett, just a nice Stewart Granger please, 'Prisoner of Zenda', 'Bhowani Junction' you remember. No macassar oil, or Brylcreem the stuff gentlemen used in your apprentice years, no modern gel or blow-dry either, just give me a proper haircut, if you can remember how you used to cut hair before the invention of cutters graded one to four. I need a neat trim; I have a photo-shoot tomorrow."

The woman said, "Don't you get sarky with me old man. I know your sort. Men who read the 'Lady' are all the same; pathetic divorcees, past their sell by date, who seek to trap some rich old lady in some scam. Or are you a perverts looking for a nanny's job."

Through the mirror, Tristan gave her his most charming practiced smile "No, not a nanny's job, quite the opposite. If you don't mind, I would like to take a page from your magazine with me. There is an opportunity advertised that might suit me for a while. From the cover title of the magazine, I assume that it is yours to give in this gender confused salon."

After the woman finally stopped faffing with his hair, she posed behind him with the double-handed mirror. When Tristan saw that she had given him a good trim, he laid on his practiced charm. "Thank you dear Lady, I shall recommend you to the rest

of the cast; it's damned difficult to get a decent cut these days."
He did not hear the coarse remark she made as he left the shop.

After failing twice, Tristan found an un-vandalised telephone box from which he rang the telephone number given in the advert that sought a 'Gentleman's gentleman'. It only took a few rings before a woman answered his call. Her voice had a lively bell like tone that had the air of quiet money upper class authority.

It gave Tristan the impression that she might be older than he was, although clearly not elderly.

After she asked Tristan for his name, she told him that the Major had offered the position to one of several men interviewed during the past week, but went on to say, "Do you know, the wretched man has rung this very morning to say that he will not take up the post as he has been appointed butler to an American? Could you please come to meet the Major, the day after tomorrow, at ten a.m.? I am anxious that he is settled, as soon as possible; he is my favourite cousin."

Tristan had difficulty in sounding calm when he wrote down, on a scrap of paper, the name and address of the Major who had advertised the post. The prospect of an interview, un-apposed, in less than forty-eight hours' time, excited Tristan.

Conscious that a major with a Mayfair address must be wealthy, he decided to brush up on how the other half lived. In W. H. Smiths, he bought a copy of 'Tatler' that he took with him to a nearby café where he treated himself to a pot of tea and a toasted teacake, before he settled down to read about 'Upper-class goings on'.

The photographs in the magazine made Tristan realise that Harry had been right. To get a new job, he needed a new suit, as well as a haircut. It fixed his itinerary for the rest of the day.

Revived by the cups of tea, Tristan had started on his way back to Retreads when he noticed, on the other side of the wide busy road, the same peculiarly dressed old man who had knocked over the pile of magazines in the hairdressers shop. His appearance was even more eccentric.

Despite the sunshine, as well as his long overcoat, he wore a peculiar wide stitch brim green waterproof hat. It bothered Tristan that the old man waved his stick at him as though in recognition. Tristan thought it a sign that he must be getting old; in his youth, he attracted pretty girls, in his prime, he attracted good-looking women. It seemed that he now only attracted peculiar old men.

The old man in Scagill for one; the man who had suggested that he go to the parish church where he had meet the vicar, Harry's younger brother. Then there had been the vagrant who had taken him as one of his kind, offered him cold day old chips, and tried to influence him with talk of King Arthur, Dick Whittington and who had told him that his fortune would change at the turn of the tide. This eccentric, by waving his stick toward him, seemed to want to draw his attention to something he had not noticed. He was so engrossed as he looked at the old man, wondering if he had met him previously, that he tripped over a small wooden 'A' frame board.

It was only after he had made sure to put the board back on its feet that he noticed that it advertised, 'Rose, for Second Hand Clothes'. The sign also had an arrow, that when he put the A frame back on its feet, pointed to a black brick lined entry. The coincidence made Tristan wonder if he had had simply been clumsy, or whether, somehow, the peculiar old man, who he could no longer see, had tried to prevent him from tripping over the sign, or whether he had deliberately distracted him to cause him to trip over it, to bring it to his attention.

Twenty yards into the alley, Tristan found the shop. Its size amazed him, as did the racks full of clothes, all good quality suits or jackets for gentlemen. At the far end of the shop, like a scene from a fairy tale, an old man sat cross-legged, on a cushion set on the floor. A spotlight, arranged to shine over his shoulder, enabled him, with the help of gold-rimmed spectacles, to use needle and thread to stitch the collar of a dark blue worsted pin striped jacket.

To confirm his faith he wore, on his head, a traditional kippah. The picture formed by the bright light cast over the old man seated in the almost forgotten posture of a traditional bespoke tailor pleased Tristan, the more so, when the old man looked up with a twinkle in his eye, to ask, "Vot do you vont." Tristan laughed when he realised that the tailor teased him because he had read his thoughts. He replied, "Well, I think I might want a suit," The old tailor persisted with his tease. "Vot do you mean a suit. Vot kind of an answer is that."

He called aloud, "Simon, we have a goy who thinks he vonts a chalifah; come help the poor chap vill you."

A young man came out of a small office. He said, "Granddad, behave, or I will tell Grandma Veasey." "Vell," persisted the old man, "Vot kind of suit do you think you might vont. Is it for a vedding, a funeral, to be presented at court or in front of a judge, a city suit, a country suit, a summer suit or one for winter?

Everyone is different, except your birthday suit. Even old Veasey the tailor cannot supply you with one of those."

Tristan felt that his accident with the A frame advert had been fortuitous. He volunteered, "Well a suit to wear for a job interview." "Ayee, a suit to wear for a job interview, no kind of an answer at all," the old man said this in a well-rehearsed comedy act. He went on, "Accountant, bookmaker, undertaker, black no stripes, BBC TV presenter; just a jacket, no trousers, stable lad, actor, hotel manager, pimp, magistrate, butler."

The young man tried to rescue Tristan, "Really Grandpa, give the gentleman a chance." Tristan took the chance to cut in, "Actually a suit for a butler is close to what I need. I have applied for a job as a gentleman's gentleman, a sort of Jeeves."

The old tailor beamed "So, at last we have it, Simon third row rack seventeen the gentleman will be about forty long." In a moment, Simon, the grandson, came back with two coats on hangers; the shoulders covered by protectors.

Neatly pressed pin stripped trousers hung from each hanger rail. The old man looked first at Tristan, then at the two coats. He pointed to the one held in Simon's left hand, "That one; please sir, do try it on." In the changing room, Tristan realised that he had never worn material of such quality. When he saw his reflection in the full-length mirror, Tristan thought it a near perfect fit.

However, when he came out, Simon waited with a tape measure round his neck. Under the scrutiny of his grandfather, Simon tugged, pulled, smoothed and stuck long large headed pins into the cloth at the same time as he made bold marks with his tailor's triangular chalk. Mr. Veasey declaimed, "That will make it a suit fit for purpose. How much would you like to pay?"

Tristan had no idea how much second hand high quality clothes from a bespoke tailor cost. He had always bought new from chain stores or second hand from charity shops. As he did not want to commit himself to a price, he said defensively, "Well, as I have not got the job yet, perhaps the question should be how little, not how much."

Mr. Veasey picked up a black fat notebook from the floor alongside him to flip through the pages before he said, "We had to pay for quality, moreover it does need to be adjusted and pressed. Does one hundred and thirty pounds sound little enough for you? If you don't get the job we will buy it back for eighty."

Tristan felt quite euphoric, "I'll take it, if you can have it ready for nine a.m. the day after tomorrow; my interview is at eleven in Mayfair. Simon, the tailors grandson, said that such short notice would not give them chance for a second fitting. Nevertheless, he promised to have it ready for Tristan to wear, when the shop opened at nine, the day after tomorrow.

Anxious to tell Harry of his good news, Tristan walked briskly back to Retreads. When he found no one at home, he moped about the kitchen until he had an idea that cheered him. He decided he would search the bookshelves to see if he could find a copy of one of P G Wodehouse's books about 'Jeeves', the archetype gentleman's gentleman of the Twenties. He soon realised that Harry had indexed his vast collection of books, both hardback and paperback that lined the walls of the main hall in an idiosyncratic manner.

He did not find any Wodehouse in the fiction shelves under W or any Jeeves under J. Moments later he shouted 'Eureka' when he found the best of all the Jeeves books, 'The Inimitable Jeeves', safely tucked away in the two shelves marked 'Historical Biography'.

Harry's voice rang out, his face broken with a great smile, "What book is it boyo that you have found to bring you back to sunny uplands after your dark days in the valley of despond. Sorry I was out; I had to pop along to the quack to get a stash of the rat poison he gives me to give my old ticker an easy time. I would have been back ages except that he will talk. Every time I go to see the sybaritic, whisky drinking, chain-smoking old rascal, he insists that I listen to his diatribe on what he calls a healthy 'Life style'. I have heard it so often, that I know it by heart; word for word I know it. It is so drear that one day I shall set it to music, as a requiem."

When Harry mentioned his heart condition, it took the joy out of Tristan's moment. He asked of his friend and mentor, "Harry, I did not know you had a dickey heart, how long has it been a bother?" Harry's reply brushed aside Tristan's concern. "No bother at all, not since they fitted me with a by-pass. It felt, for the first few days at least, as big as the one round Swindon, the old railway town, roundabouts and all. Marvellous what they can do these days, isn't it? Tell me what you have found in our library that has so pleased you." "Jeeves Harry, 'The Inimitable Jeeves'," Tristan almost shouted. "I must commit it to memory before breakfast the day after tomorrow. I have an interview for a job as a gentleman's gentleman, for a major in Mayfair."

"Dieu Dieu, I told you that all you needed was a haircut," Harry said, "Who is this fellow who needs someone to be gentle with him".

Tristan took out his scrap of paper to read out 'Major the Honourable Humphrey Redvers Erskin-Powell MFH MC (Retired) Erskin House, Lee's Crescent, Mayfair."

Despite Tristan's exuberance Harry's demeanour became serious, "Tristan, you may need more than Wodehouse for tips. I have a tape of Hopkins in 'Remains of the day'. We could watch that in my study tonight; perhaps we should get a six pack to help our concentration." To get Harry to celebrate with him Tristan clicked his heels and said, with a supercilious voice, "Certainly sir; would one care for a cucumber sandwich with a cup of Darjeeling's finest for Tiffin."

Harry joined in the fun, "Good show Edward, without the s; that will do very nicely, set it in the orangery if you please. I expect my friend Archie at any moment." The door burst open, but Archie turned out to be Stan with a cool box of goodies under his arm.

On the morning of the interview, Harry excused Tristan from his breakfast duty and fussed over him. He brought down from his study his tan leather briefcase.

"You must carry this, with today's Daily Telegraph inside. Don't forget to take your black cane; the two together will look well. By the way, I had a quiet word with Sergeant Robbins at the station. I also took a squint in 'Who's Who'. Your Major, the Hon. Humphrey Redvers Erskin-Powell MFH MC, is a proper gent. He won his MC as a squadron commander with the Blues in Korea. He never married, however he is very well connected. In addition to his house in Mayfair, he has estates in Scotland, South Africa and Brazil. Perhaps you may get to travel. Before you go; have you got money?"

Tristan replied cheekily, "Yes Dad, I am properly prepared; I have a penny for the toilet, two-pence for the telephone and a clean hanky. I have also washed my neck and polished my shoes."

Tristan's mood suddenly changed. He took Harry's right hand in both of his to say, "Harry, I won't go if you feel that you need me here." Harry equally serious with his reply said, "Get on with your bother, who knows what adventures it might lead to. I feel sure that you will prosper. Perhaps one day you may take your place in the Retreads old boys support network, or even make a fortune and become one of our trustees. Truly I believe that the 'Good Lord', you often mention, who is also mine, will bind you to Retreads."

After he changed, at Rose for Second Hand Clothes, into his second hand re-tailored jacket with pin stripe trousers, because Tristan had never worn materials of such quality, he felt good, although disappointed that Mr. Veasey could not be in the shop to wish him well. His grandson Simon, who Mr. Veasey had left to look after Tristan, brushed the jacket, before he offered Tristan a formal silver necktie.

"Grandpa Veasey asked me to tell you that the bowtie just won't do sir. He has asked that you take the tie with our complements. I believe that it belonged to a hereditary Peer of the Realm, not one of the politically placed parasites. Most of our good stuff comes from deceased aristocracy, county or quiet money. The family usually gives the better clothes to their staff. On their first day off, they bring them to us in exchange for cash. Talking of which, I have a lovely pair of black slip on 'Trickers', size nine, if you have as little as a twenty pound note to take them off our stock. Your light browns just won't do, although they are of good quality."

Tristan could hardly believe his luck. "That's a done deal," he said, "I had a pair, years ago, when I had backed a good outside chance and was in funds, I ask one more favour, may I please leave my old stuff here until this afternoon." "Certainly sir" Simon answered, "My Grandfather and I will look forward to celebrate with you when you return."

After he had waited across the road from Erskin House, for almost three quarters of an hour, Tristan straightened up, pulled his shoulders back before he marched across the road to the white painted double fronted Georgian four-story house, the centre of the crescent row of attached smaller but equally elegant houses.

It had become obvious to Tristan, from the number of bell pushes by all the doors along the crescent that developers had converted the houses, either side of Erskin House, into apartments.

Erskin House had only one bell push on a more elaborate entrance than the rest of the houses, set back some six feet from the wide York stone pavement. The architect had arranged the ground floor to be about three feet above the level of the Lee's Crescent, with access to the huge canopied door by six shallow steps of Portland stone.

Tristan pressed the single large round brass bell push on the right hand jamb of the most beautiful double doors he had ever seen, each a dark oiled oak eight-panelled affair. Tristan assumed that the Major's antecedents had had the two top panels deep carved with what he thought might be his family crest.

Tristan thought that the woman who opened the door could not be the lady Tristan had talked to on the phone. After he gave his name she barked abruptly, "Follow me," in a voice that before the First World War, Billingsgate fish wives would have considered coarse. She led him through a wide deep spacious entrance lobby, with inner glass doors. After that, they crossed the marble floor of a magnificent, almost circular, hall. A wide central staircase, directly opposite the door dominated the hall. It divided, at a mezzanine, into two flights that lead to a first floor balcony supported on marble Doric columns.

Tristan presumed that each of the several double doors around the hall led to a reception room. He thought the woman who escorted him to be an out of place old trot box. She smelt like an early morning pub taproom, before the cleaner arrived. Without another word to Tristan, she knocked on one of the double doors. She did not wait for an answer, but pushed open one side to announce, "The man my Lady." She indicated that Tristan should go through and closed the door behind him.

The lady, who the trot box had referred to as 'My Lady' faced the door through which Tristan had entered. He thought her appearance fit to inspire a court artist. She had perched on a chair, big enough to accommodate her twice over with enough space left for a cat. She did not rise, or speak.

With her bright grey blue eyes, she looked Tristan over, very steadily. Her posture was erect, her head held almost imperiously high. She had had her hair, the colour of a pedigree red setter, swept back into a small bun clasped in a neat gold cage, secured by a jewelled pin. Like King George the fifth's Queen Mary, she had shielded her neck with a quadruple choker string of large equally sized pearls. Wearing a dark blue long sleeved silk dress, she carried her beauty with style.

The room the Lady had chosen for the interview was the most magnificently appointed library Tristan had ever seen. Floor to ceiling, the room had shelves full of beautifully bound books. It even had a sliding ladder that Tristan thought were joke ladders in old black and white comedy films.

Dressed for the part, in a setting appropriate for the part, Tristan melded into the role of servant. "Tristan Edward Ma'am," he volunteered, because the lady had not yet spoken. Without realising it, he gave a slight bow from the waist. At the same time, his left hand swept back the hair on the side of his head. "Tristan the given name, Edward the family name, without the 's', causes confusion, always does."

The moment that he said this, one of the panels of library shelves full of books revolved to discharge into the room the master of the house, Major the Hon. Humphrey, Redvers –Erskin-Powell MFH MC. His eyes that twinkled behind gold-rimmed circular glasses, matched his genial smile. They immediately put Tristan at ease.

188

The Major had a large forehead, backed by a large almost bald-head that at his temples, had evidence that it had once supported ginger hair. His clothes were of the country, not the city. Though they were of the finest quality, he managed to appear faintly untidy.

The lady spoke at last, "Copper, this is Mr. Edward who has kindly given up his time to be interviewed for the position we had offered to Mr, er, oh, I can never remember names, no matter, the man who let us down." In a voice, with an up-market British intonation, the equal of an Indian Army cavalry officer, the Major asked, "Well young man, what makes you think that you could put up with an old soldier like me eh? Tell me that sir, tell me that."

Tristan found it easy to reply, "Well Major, I have worked for hotels and restaurants, both private and corporate, on cruise ships and in bars around the world. I have always found that market traders, artisans and gentlemen are the ones with whom it is easy to get along. It is the pretentious professionals, the social climbers of the middle class who are difficult."

"Army?" the Major barked. Tristan replied, "Yes sir, not a distinguished career. Boy soldier, briefly with the Ox and Bucks, transferred to the Cater Corps. Having learnt the trade I bought myself out."

"Army do you any good?" the Major asked. "No sir," admitted Tristan, "On the contrary it ruined me. The extra rations after the officers mess nights, when I worked in their kitchen, gave me a taste for habits I could never afford."

"What habits? Eh," the Major wanted to know. Tristan paused before he gave his reply, "Smoked salmon, caviar, prime cuts, great mature cheeses, fine wines, vintage port, V.S.O.P. brandy and Cuban cigars for a start."

"Good God Margaret," the Major spluttered, "We will have to lock and bolt the cellars. Now sir, a serious question; What if I found out that you had read my paper in the morning. What

189

would you have read first?" "Why 'Matt' of course sir," Tristan had made the reply that the Major wanted to hear. It sealed the deal.

"Good man, I have waited years to here that; not the fools answer, 'Scanned the headlines before reading the leader'. No further questions, the job is yours, if you think you can put up with this old-fashioned house infested by an old-fashioned buffer like me. What do you say to that eh? What do you say to that?"

Tristan grinned; a memory had come to mind. He assumed a cockney voice, to reply, "Take the bill down. I'm let to a single gentleman."

The Major picked up the reference immediately, "Good God, the very same words that Sam Weller's said when Pickwick offered him the job, they are, or I will cut out my tongue. Am I so like Pickwick, as people often remark, that you noticed, or had that cheeky girl, my cousin Lady Margaret, put you up to it?"

"No Copper darling," the Lady laughed, "It's just you. It will always be so, until you change your tailor, hairdresser shoemaker, spectacles and club."

"I told you she is a cheeky young thing," the Major addressed this remark to Tristan, before he continued, "Lady Margaret will explain what to do in the meantime. I hope to see you tomorrow at eleven hundred hours, if that is convenient?"

"Of course sir; I shall he here tomorrow, at eleven hundred." Tristan could not help clicking his heels. With that, the Major pushed at the panel of books to exit the room in good order and military style.

"Well done Edward, You got that just right." Lady Margaret handed Tristan a card with the name and address of a firm of solicitors in Greys Inn.

"Please call there at two o'clock this afternoon, Mr. Maxwell Erskin-Powell, our second cousin, who acts for the family, will explain your terms and conditions. I understand they are a little better than normal for such positions."

Tristan automatically gave that short stiff bow from the waist, as he said, "Thank you Ma'am." The Lady Margaret pulled on a silk bell pull by her side. Without a word said, the woman who had let him in escorted him to the front door.

Outside, Tristan walked steadily to the end of Lee's Crescent, before he turned into Brook Street, where he startled nearby people when he punched the air and let out one great joyous shout; Yes!

Chapter 14

Maxwell Erskin-Powell, the solicitor who acted for Tristan's new employer, had some of the characteristics of the Major. Figured like his cousin, his frame had not made him quite, as round as he was long. He had the family trait of a baldpate, although he had more traces of ginger in the hair at the back of his head, as well as in his neat clipped moustache.

After a vigorous inquisition into Tristan's past career, the solicitor explained Tristan's entitlement to salary, days off and annual leave entitlement. When he listed Tristan's duties, he gave him a clear brief, in a voice more military than legal.

"Your duties are simple, in fact less than arduous. The only downside is that the insurance company's underwriters require that there must be an approved designated resident in the house at all times, otherwise, it is impossible for me to arrange insurance. Failure to comply would invalidate the insurance. Furthermore, it would lead to your dismissal without notice. You will be the principal approved designated resident. It will be up to you to arrange how you share this duty with Mrs. Edna Spitewinter, the cook-housekeeper, who I have also approved as a designated resident. If you have to get a substitute, you must get my authorisation in advance, after you have let me have details of who will be resident in charge if you leave Erskin House."

Erskin-Powell's manner changed from a factual brief to that of a concerned relative of the Major when he said, "Your responsibilities are more difficult to define than your duties. The Major, as his record shows, has great courage, but frankly, he is a simple naive man. He needs protection from devious men, and duplicitous women. I cannot ask you to be his guardian however, please watch out for him. As you will become aware, the Major has great personal wealth. His income comes mainly from property around Westminster and Piccadilly. His estates in South Africa and South America add to his income. The estate in Scotland does the opposite. Every year since Fortune magazine first published its vulgar list, they have included the Major in their top one hundred. The trouble is he is sublimely unconscious of his wealth. With men, he is very clubbable; he finds women difficult to understand. That he takes everyone on face value makes him vulnerable. If you have any concerns on his behalf, you must contact me directly."

Erskin-Powell's manner changed again. He became a little diffident when he asked Tristan to take over the household's day-to-day expenditure, routine purchases and ledgers from Mrs. Spitewinter.

"She will be as mad about this as a baboon with a boil on its bottom, but I have become increasingly unhappy with her stewardship. I will write to advise her of your appointment. I shall also explain the new arrangements. It will be hand delivered today, to ensure that she has sight of it before you take up your duties. I am sure that you will find the right way to deal with the Spitewinter woman. The only other members of your staff are Barbara and Caroline, the cleaning ladies. Their hours are nine until noon, every day except Sunday. I have put the maintenance of the small garden out to contract. I shall be grateful if you will make sure that they do their job to specification. I am sure that with your hotel experience you will find your duties easy to manage. The household has an account with Coutts. I will arrange for

193

you to have control of the five hundred pounds petty cash float with authorisation to write cheques for sundry purchases and maintenance. I manage the Major's bank accounts. I also write his personal cheques. I think that is all. Oh! I almost forgot; there are two cars in the garage, both are Bentleys, one is a Mulliner 4 door Continental Saloon, the other is a four and a half litre, two-seat tourer. The family have owned them since new. Please ensure that you drive both cars once every week, far enough at least to ease the springs and warm the engine up to temperature. It seems that even mechanical devices develop necrosis if not regularly used. My only real concern is that you will be able to find worthwhile tasks to occupy your mind for the next six months, while the Major is away in South Africa. I would not like you to catch cabin fever."

Astonished, Tristan forgot his manners. He blurted out, "What? Erskin-Powel looked puzzled, before he responded with an apology, "Sorry Edward, didn't Lady Margaret tell you? Since the ban on hunting, the Major has given up on the English winter. He chooses to go to his estate in South Africa. He leaves next week. His Indian bearer looks after him over there. After Indian independence, Copper spent three years with the Deccan Horse playing polo and pig sticking." Tristan asked, "Why employ anyone now, why not wait until he comes home."

Erskin-Powel explained, "Tried it once; no good at all. We learned that lesson when he went to Brazil for six months. A house not lived in dies; pipes burst, the boiler fails, mice, bats and two legged rats get in. It develops a sort of pneumonia. It gives up the will to live. It took us two months after he returned to make it habitable. Copper took a suite at Brown's, although he spent most days at the Cavalry and Guards club. It did not suit him."

When Erskin-Powell stood up, obviously to end the interview, he escorted Tristan to the front door of his chambers where he handed Tristan his card, "My private mobile number is on the card. Ring me, day or night, if you have any problem to do with the welfare of the Major with which you do not feel comfortable. If I am not available, your call will divert to someone who knows the situation. They will be able to help. By the way, you may get a couple of odd calls within the next day or two from the Met's Special Branch."

Tristan took a bus back to 'Rose for Second Hand Clothes' to collect his ordinary clothes. Both Veasey grandpa and grandson seemed genuinely pleased that Tristan had secured the job, wearing the clothes that they had recommended.

The old tailor put on his music hall Jewish comedian voice to tease his grandson, "I told you my boy, manners may maketh the man, but the Veasey tailored suit gets you the job. Vot do these upstart trouser makers, Matalan, Next, or Gap know about clothes for a gentleman, or even a gentleman's gentleman."

When Tristan told Harry Evans his news, he could not understand how anybody could afford to pay to have their home lived in for six months, just to keep it aired. "You tell me" Harry said, "That there is a woman to cook for you, cleaners to mop around your feet and dust under your elbows, with nothing for you to do until next spring when, God willing, the Major is due to follow the swallows home from South Africa. Dieu, what will you do all day Boyo. You will go lock up loony."

Tristan replied, "Don't you see Harry, it's perfect, I will be able to come here to do any odd jobs or even spend some time at the allotment. One thing that I would like to do is the shopping. Not on the Rudge bicycle, I shall be able to do it in style. I have to drive both cars at least once a week."

Harry slowly shook his head, "I suppose they are Rolls Royces isn't it?" Tristan's replied with schoolboy enthusiasm, "Oh no, nothing so common, the family solicitor told me that both are Bentleys, proper cars, not the square fronted things that make the driver look pretentious, unless he is the chauffeur." Harry said, "Well Tristan, I think Retreads has given you more than a new sole on your boot, to get a grip on life's slippery slope. More like a pair of those blades that the South African runner Pistorius uses on the end of his legs."

During most of the last night that Tristan spent in the small bedroom in Harry's flat, he could not sleep. He worried that he might have made a bad decision. He thought that six months of an idle life, spent not just in apparent but actual luxury, would not be acceptable to his fellow Grey Haired Knights. He realised that he would have to find some worthwhile task to fill time between breakfast and bedtime, if only to stop him from becoming unemployable. He found no answer until the following morning. When he woke, after a short fitful sleep, the distillation of thoughts that occur during sleep had made up his mind. He would take the job as gentleman's gentleman; it would be his disguise, a velvet glove over his mailed fist. Chivalry demanded that he reverse that bleak encounter when he had tilted in the lists with Charles Lucas Prescott, the barman at the Keeble, the corrupt character who had brast him, the first in a series of calamitous ventures that had left him destitute.

Ready to take up his new job, Tristan arrived at Erskin House by taxi, five minutes before eleven o'clock. After he rang the bell, he realised that the woman who opened the door must be Mrs. Spitewinter, the cook-housekeeper, from whom he was to take over some of her duties.

Her body language told Tristan that she had already read the hand delivered letter from Erskin-Powell. Her verbal language confirmed it. The few words she uttered were full of aggression. "It's you is it," she said, before she indicated that he should follow her. In those few words, she gave full expression of her disapproval of Tristan's appointment. She made it clear that she would not let an upstart male intrude into her space. When they came to the door to the library, she indicated that he was to go in. She shortened her vocabulary, to the one word, "Wait."

It was difficult for Tristan to comprehend the wealth that surrounded the Major. His life experience had given him no benchmark for comparison. The library, with its beautifully bound books, sliding ladder, elegant antique furniture, the Tsin Sin carpets and exquisite Persian rugs demonstrated wealth in abundance.

On his way through the hall, he had noticed the colourful oil paint portraits of high-ranking service officers in their be-medalled glorious dress uniforms, mounted in massive gilt frames. He saw them as a record of the family's courage.

The darker portraits of men dressed in the robes of bishops, judges and government ministers, were testimony to the family's public service.

The few portraits of their wives demonstrated how powerful men, however physically unattractive, have always attracted beautiful women.

A silver framed photograph, set on a reading desk, intrigued Tristan. It was a studio portrait of the Major when a young officer. It showed him with a wild shock of ginger hair, mutton chop whiskers that framed an almost handlebar moustache.

For the photograph he had worn the most glorious officers mess kit Tristan had ever seen; a cut away dark blue jacket with French grey facing trimmed with gold, worn over a dark blue cummerbund, tight britches and spurred mess Wellingtons.

Tristan stepped back a pace when the Major popped out from the revolving bookcase, wearing a 'Loyd' dressing gown and slippers. "What have you got there eh? Tell me that sir, tell me that," he said, as he walked over to pick up the photograph. "Good God, what a wreck half a century makes of a fella. Would you believe it! I was that young fella, in India, after the war. We chaps had fun when we played polo or hunted; bit of a bore the rest of the time. We spent most days escorting trains, at walking pace. Even in those far off days, they were faster than British Bloody Rail. Sorry shouldn't swear; not a Methodist are you, eh, or Seventh Day whatever they are, eh?"

Tristan replied, "No sir, non-sectarian, not committed. Your cousin the solicitor tells me that you were with the Deccan Horse. Is that their mess kit?" "Yes indeed it is," the Major said, "Indeed it is. Still have it somewhere in a trunk. We were a set of dandy's were we not? I don't think it would let out; do you?"

Anxious to establish the correct way for a gentleman's gentleman to address his employer, Tristan asked, "Major, Sir, I know that you are the Honourable Major Erskin-Powell MFH MC. It begs the question, how do you wish me to address you. Is it to be 'Master', as you are Master of Hounds, or 'Major' as a retired field officer, or formally as 'Major Erskin-Powell', or simply as 'Sir'?"

The Major replied, "Good question Edward, certainly not formally. Good God, the way that you said it made it sound like the opening line of an obituary. My chums call me 'Copper' because of my hair, sadly though, most of my hair has gone, as have most of my chums, the war saw to that. Senior officers at the Guards Club pointedly call me 'Major', to rub it in that I did not make the grade. The family, except for my favourite cousin, the little rascal Lady Margaret, call me the 'Old fart'. Sir will do nicely. I shall call you Sam; that is if you do not mind. I have always fancied a Sam Weller to help, ever since I first read the Pickwick Papers. Will that be alright with you Sam?"

Tristan felt greatly relieved to find the old gentleman to be just that, a gentleman, and genial with it. He replied, "That will do for me, as the Under-Butler said to a passing footman, when he took a large brandy off the tray. Do I get two suits and a striped waistcoat every year?"

The next few days for Tristan were hectic, filled with hours of pressing and packing. He also chauffeured the Mulliner Bentley on a dozen short errands to complete the Major's preparations to fly out to South Africa.

When the preparations were complete, the Major told Tristan, sadly, "Used to go Union Castle in the old days. Always had a good bridge school and a not half-bad cellar, if one can have a cellar on a boat, never thought of that before. They kept good cigars too, in the humidifier. These days I have to travel in a damned cigar tube. I would not mind if before take-off, like a good cigar, I could be rolled on the inside of the thigh of a nubile dusky Cuban maiden." However old were the Majors jokes, they delighted Tristan. They confirmed an amiable association with his new boss.

After he had seen the Major safely into the hands of the VIP attendants at Heathrow, in addition to ensuring that the airline staff had tagged his luggage correctly, Tristan waited until the flight had departed before he left the airport.

Back at Erskin House, he found himself at a loss, with nothing to do. Of Mrs. Spitewinter, the cook-housekeeper, there was no sign, or sign of any supper.

Tristan had been too busy with the Major's departure, to give any thought to his relationship with the woman. He sensed the hostility that radiated from her every time he asked her to do some small job for the Major. He had never asked her to do things for himself.

By eight in the evening, boredom, combined with hunger, encouraged Tristan to seek out the woman. He knew that she had accommodation similar to his own, a sitting room, pantry, bedroom and bathroom, arrangement on the fourth floor. After knocking on her door, several times, he finally got an answer that did not surprise him. Mrs. Spitewinter shouted through the closed door, in a slurred dull tone that spoke of alcohol excess, "Sod off, I've finished for the day,"

Her gross response made Tristan so cross that he positively barked, "Madam, I require you to come to my office at ten tomorrow morning. If you do not do so, I shall take it as your resignation. Furthermore, I shall require you to leave the house before noon, after you have cleared your quarters. Do you understand?" Tristan thought that she sincerely meant her reply, "Go to hell."

Before World War Two, when the Major's Grandfather had kept a compliment of staff appropriate for the London house of a wealthy family, the office that Tristan referred to had been the butler's pantry.

Although small and dark, with a single small window, Tristan found it cosy and practical. The architect had arranged it just beside the top of the internal stairs to the kitchen, opposite to the dumb waiter. The small well-furnished room had a leather-topped desk, a comfortable chair, a splendid antique side table and a lockable cupboard. The electric kettle along with an up to date computer appeared to be anachronisms.

His spat with the old trot-box had quite cheered Tristan. It brought back many memories of similar encounters with recalcitrant staff when he had managed bars and hotels.

Tristan could already tell that, during the months when the Major would be away in South Africa, his new job would be not much different to managing a small bed and breakfast unit, other than he would have no customers to foul his arrangements.

His only worry was that Erskin-Powell, the Major's solicitor, might not back him when he had the inevitable show down with the Spitewinter woman.

The architects had designed Lee's Crescent during the mid-Georgian era, when style and custom put the reception rooms well above the effluvia of the street, and the kitchens in the basement, below street level.

When Tristan went to look around the kitchen, although he found it dirty and untidy, he could see that at some time in the recent history of the Erskin House, someone had entertained on a lavish scale.

After a not too successful foray through the refrigerators, cold room, and wine cellar, Tristan fell back on the three-egg omelette. He went for luxury. He stuffed it with chopped smoked salmon, before he dressed it with the contents of a small tin of Segruva caviar. A small bottle of Worthington White Shield, bottle conditioned beer, that he found left upright on one of the cold larder stone shelves, though years beyond its sell by date, poured out in top condition. It pleased him that he found Worthington glass from which to drink it.

It amazed him that he found, amongst a stock of glassware in boxes, at least six dozen of every type of glass he could remember; glasses for cocktails, spirits, wines, white, red and sherry, liqueurs, water, beer jugs for cask ale, flutes and Worthintons for bottled beer. After he cleared up, he put the used pots in the dishwasher.

When he put the Worthington glass in a separate glass-washer, he began to understand the wealth of the Major, the Gentleman, for whom he would be gentleman, on the Gentleman's return.

He rated the kitchen as good as any commercial kitchen he had ever seen, more than suitable for a competent chef to prepare a banquet for fifty or a buffet for a hundred.

As Tristan started on the long climb to his room, he had the happy thought that he might invite his friend Stan to come to Erskin House to cook a four-course dinner for Harry Evans, Figgy Bentley, and himself.

He knew that Stan would not believe his description of the kitchen until he allowed him free range of the ranges.

The next morning, as Tristan expected, Mrs. Spitewinter did not come to his office at ten o'clock as he had instructed. He left it until half past ten before he rang the old trot box. He used the neat telephone system that was identical to the system installed in the hotel he had managed in Nottingham, his last real job. After the phone had rung about twelve times, Spitewinter finally deigned to answer with the single word, "What?" Tristan ignored her hostility.

He spoke quietly, in a soft voice, "Mrs. Spitewinter, either you come down to my office straight away or, as I promised, I will take it as your resignation. Furthermore, I shall have you removed from Erskin House as a security risk. I do mean now, savvy."

Ten minutes later he heard the cook-housekeeper's rubber trainers squeak as they crossed the hall, coming towards his office. No timid knock or delay followed. Edna Spitewinter burst open the office door. Without pause, she stepped right up to Tristan's desk. With both her hands spread wide, she gripped firmly onto the edge of the desk to support her body weight. She leant over the desk to come face to face with Tristan. She opened the discussion with an angry broadside and a spray of saliva.

"Get this straight you bony bow tied faggot. I am the house-keeper; I am in charge of Erskin House. I am not here to run round after you. You can stuff that where you may."

Tristan sighed, however he managed one of his sweetest smiles, as though to greet her as a friend, before he spoke. "Good morning Mrs. Spitewinter, please sit down for a moment."

He took from his wallet Erskin-Powell's business card, which he put on the desk in front of the woman so that she could be in no doubt of its provenance. Without a further word, he reached for the telephone, obviously intent to call Erskin-Powell. Spitewinter's hand shot across the desk, to cut off the call. "What the hell do you think you are up to," she asked, now more concerned than aggressive.

"Dear lady," Tristan replied urbanely, "I thought that would be obvious, even to your whiskey pickled brain. I intend to call Mr. Erskin-Powell to confirm that I have just sacked you for gross misconduct. It will be of no surprise; he expects my call."

Spitewinter almost spat at him, "Sack me would you; oh no, it's you who will get the sack. The Major relies on me. If I chose to leave, until he gets back from South Africa, I will use the time to wreak a savage revenge on you, you washed out wanker. I know people who will cut you for a drink, break your legs for a joint, or better still, your neck for a line."

Tristan still kept his urbane manner to reply, "Unlike you madam, losing this job would not indispose me. I have a home to go to. If you will take your hand off the telephone, perhaps we will be able to test your hypothesis. On the other hand, shall we resume our discussion the day after tomorrow, at ten a.m. sharp, without me having to wake you from your stupor? I expect that you will have taken the two days of your leave entitlement to consider your position. However, before you go, you must bring me the stock books, the supplier order books, invoices and statements, and leave all your keys to the house with me."

Spitewinter did not hand over the books; nevertheless, she left Erskin House with the cleaners, when they finished their shift at noon. Using a passkey, Tristan entered Spitewinter's room. It shocked him how untidy she had left it. In a desk, he found the stock records, order books, delivery notes, and invoices.

After a further more careful search, hidden in a bedside table, he found two nuggets of pure gold in the form of two 'Red and Black' notebooks.

From Spitewinter's notes in these books, it did not take him long to establish that she had more than one racket on the go. The main one was that by arrangement with a dodgy catering supplier, they invoiced at prices higher than their list prices, for meat, vegetables, dry goods, wines and spirits. The supplier had, on a regular monthly basis, paid her, not to the estate, the difference in retrospective discounts. In one of the Black and Red books Spitewinter had recorded details of the retrospective discounts due and received. In the other, details of the goods off loaded to, and cash received from, a French restaurant not five minutes' walk from the Major's home.

The restaurant had paid cash to Spitewinter at fifty percent of the invoiced value of the goods they received and had done so for more than two years. Double benefit, retrospective discount plus fifty percent cash back on the stolen items.

Tristan felt confident that when Spitewinter realised that he had taken her Red and Black notebooks, she would make haste to leave, never to return. Later on that day, as he sat behind the closed door of his office, he listened to the cleaners help Spitewinter to do a daylight flit. As soon as all three women had gone, he again let himself into her quarters to find that she had left them bare. She had not left her set of the house keys.

The next morning Tristan rang Erskin-Powell to tell him that he had flushed out the cause of the stock losses. When he told him that Spitewinter had gone and had not left a contact address, or the house keys, Erskin-Powel agreed that Tristan should arrange for a locksmith to change all the locks for which she had keys.

Tristan assured the Solicitor that Spitewinter had operated the racket for more than two years. The news delighted Erskin-Powell who said, "By golly, that didn't take you long. Are you sure of your ground; we don't want any claim for unfair dismissal."

Tristan replied, "She must have built up a tidy nest egg, so you don't have to fear for her future. I have written evidence of her theft, so she won't be back, unless it is to exact a terrible vengeance on me, which the old trot box has promised to do."

Tristan took the opportunity to ask, "May I recruit a replacement, I must have someone to talk to if I am not to go stir crazy." Erskin-Powell immediately said, "Of course, go ahead. Make sure that you let me have her full details so that I can check her out."

Tristan who had already planned to bring Harry Evans into the recruitment procedure replied, "That I will do, although the replacement may not be another woman, he will probably be another old wreck of a man like me; I will call you."

After he put the phone down, Tristan realised that, for the next few days at least, he had stymied himself. He had consumed almost all that had been edible in the kitchen, but in accordance with his terms of employment, he could not leave the house.

He decided that he could not ring through any orders to the suppliers Spitewinter had used, because they had been equally corrupt to agree to give her retrospective discounts. He decided that it would be a better idea to ring Harry to ask him to come over with some provender and to ask him to find a replacement cook-housekeeper."

Harry marvelled at the luxury and clear signs of wealth after Tristan had given him a short tour of the house. As Tristan had no food to cook, and as Harry had brought nothing, (he would never take anything from Retreads,) after he found the 'Yellow Pages' phone book Tristan rang through an order to a Chinese take away in Victoria. He ordered fish and chips twice, two buttered teacakes and a pot of mushy peas.

Harry could not get his mind round the difference between Retreads, where they sometimes housed sixteen men in a bleak converted chapel, and the much bigger, grander, better-equipped and furnished Erskin House, the Mayfair home of a single bachelor.

Harry Evans, of the old school, fretted about the 'take-a-way' supper Tristan had ordered. He said, in a hushed voice, "Dieu Tristan, this will most certainly be a first, a take-a-way fish supper delivered to Lee's Crescent. I wonder what the neighbours will say. I hope you have got some vinegar in this far too posh palace."

As Tristan hoped, when he asked Harry whether he might be able to source a replacement cook-housekeeper, Harry felt sure that one of his recent Retread old boys would be ideal as a competent live in cook, if not cook-housekeeper for Erskin House.

He explained, "Ideal he is boyo, not yet sixty; for years he cooked lunch for the main board directors of a major bank in the City and their special guests. In a fit of democratic revisionism, they brought in a contract caterer, a scheme that made him redundant. He passed through Retreads about a year ago. After some time he proved to be a first class cook, even though earlier events had brought him to a state of nervous collapse. After the bank let him go, he had worked in Michelin starred madhouse kitchens that broke his spirit. At present, he is working in a school canteen. It is no life for a man of his talent. Only trouble is, he's French."

Tristan said, "He will do nicely Harry, it seems that the old boiler, who had been cook housekeeper here, until today, did very little of either. I am sure that with the two cleaners we can manage to keep the house tidy until the swallow comes home."

"Well Tristan," Harry said, "that takes care of the domestic detail. Have you yet decided what you might do, to stop you from going barmy with boredom?"

Tristan replied, "Yes Harry, I have. You will probably think that I am living a fantasy. Before I left Scagill to come to London to seek my fortune, I had been a long-term patient in the Laurels, a foul NHS rehabilitation unit, where they were supposed to get me clear of my reliance on prescription drugs, as well as caffeine and nicotine. I had used them to excess. They had sapped all strength from my body; I had almost stopped eating. They had blanked my mind, because I had no interest in the future. The dreadful place had also trapped three other chaps, patients they were there for different reasons. Over many awful weeks, they put up with my bad temper. We became good friends. Arthur Thomas had the idea that on Sunday evenings we should take turns to tell stories to stop us being bored to an early death. For all of us Sunday had become the dullest day of every week. The stories led Arthur to a better idea. He proposed a whimsical idea that we form ourselves into a sort of new order of chivalry, the Grey Haired Knights of a present Camelot, determined to escape from the Laurels, each one to go alone to seek an adventure. Driven by frustration and inspired by Arthur's enthusiasm, we made too much of it. We each made a vow, as Grey Haired Knights, to return to Scagill on the first Saturday after the next summer solstice, to tell the true story of our chosen quest. That vow, for me at least, turned the whimsical idea into a firm commitment. Harry, I have a chance to set a wrong to rights. I have a score to settle with a low life corrupt thief who got me the sack from the Keeble Hotel. He is a barman there. The incident brought me very low. I am sure that the hotel's Night Manager, and probably many others, are in cahoots with him."

Harry gave a considered response, "So be it Tristan, fantasy seems to be the rage in books, film and particularly in video games these days. It is not wrong to take inspiration from the Arthurian legend. Just remember you live in the real world. Make sure that whatever you do is for a good reason, not just for vengeance; for vengeance is an ugly weapon; its recoil can be powerful."

Harry Evans's sixty-plus some year old protégé Marie Antonin Ratier jumped at the chance to become chef at Erskin House. With the approval of Erskin-Powell, Tristan offered him the job of chef, coupled with the duties of resident house occupier when needed. Tristan felt that with Antonin to share his house sitting duties, he would be able to start his quest to bring down the corrupt barman Charles Lucas Prescott.

However, one unexpected telephone call changed everything and unknown to Tristan, it made sense of everything. Tristan had been in his office when the phone rang. A voice, which he felt sure that he had heard before asked, "Sam, is that you?"

"Er, no sorry," he replied, "Perhaps you have the wrong number. This is the residence of Major the Honourable Erskin-Powel, Tristan Edward speaking, Tristan the given." He got no further before the bell toned voice cut in. "Good, it is you that I want to speak to, the man my cousin Copper likes to call Sam; Sam Weller. I am Lady Margaret; we met a while ago, when you came for interview. He has agreed that I can borrow you, for special occasions, however only if you will agree. May I call tomorrow morning, at about eleven, please?"

"Certainly Ma'am," Tristan replied, "I shall have coffee ready." Lady Margaret, who Tristan remembered the Major refer to as a 'cheeky young thing' said, "I would prefer tea if that is possible. I think that you will find some of the right type of Yorkshire tea in the pantry, the blend we must use in London to accommodate our hard-recycled water. I like a good cup."

As the phone went dead Tristan could not help thinking that the Lady sounded quite coquettish.

Chapter 15

On the morning that followed the telephone call from Lady Margaret, his employer's cousin, Tristan made sure that he rose early to prepare for her visit. He was intrigued because she had told him that, if he agreed, she had the Major's permission to borrow him.

With nervousness taking over from interest, he combed his hair in front of every mirror he passed and for the first time he chivvied the morning cleaners.

He made a fuss about their attention to the library, the room he thought most appropriate to meet the woman who he only knew by name as Lady Margaret.

To find out more about the Lady he took the trouble to find a copy of 'Who's Who', but it did not serve him well, because he did not know the Lady's full name, or whether she was married, widowed or spinster.

Before eleven o'clock, Tristan had set a tea tray for one, using the Georgian silver tea service and a fine Spode china cup and saucer. At eleven o'clock, precisely, he heard light footsteps as they crossed the marble-floored hall before Lady Margaret called out in bell like tones, "Good morning Sam, I let myself in. I am so glad that you had unbolted the door. I do not like to stand on the steps like a socially outcast smoker, or a Piccadilly whore.

Copper gave me the keys years ago. He thinks of me as one of his chums, even though I have never been in the army, or a camp follower for that matter."

Rather more stiffly than he intended, Tristan greeted her formally, "Good morning my Lady, if you will go through to the library, I will follow with your tea. I did manage to find the Yorkshire Tea, but I am afraid I am short on biscuits."

It did not surprise him when Lady Margaret said, "No, no, that won't do at all, find another cup, we can take tea in your pantry, without ceremony. That is if you allow anyone to encroach on your holy of holies. As I mentioned on the phone yesterday, I have a proposition, not a proposal, to put to you."

Tristan managed to say, with what he thought due deference, "I am intrigued ma'am to know how a humble servant to your absent cousin, could possibly be of assistance to a Lady."

Lady Margaret frowned before saying, "Oh, don't be so formal Sam, I am not going to abduct you, I only want to get back into the swing of things, just like I used to be. Five years is long enough to be a weeping widow. I want you to escort me to 'Annabel's', for dinner, this coming Friday. I need a new start. I am out of practice. I cannot ask any of my generation of relations. They all think that they are too old to go to a nightclub, even though most of them are younger than I am. I understand that escort agencies are unsuitable as few if any have a man on their books over forty. I have been a recluse since my husband Geoffrey died only one week after he retired. He died too young. He had been Principal Secretary at the Ministry of Defence. I met him at the Café Royal when I came out. We used to go together to the Ivy, the Caprice, Wheelers, L' Ecu de France and Ketner's, in addition to the coming out balls given by the parents of our friends. The all night hunt balls in the country were the most fun. We both had an interest in horses. Geoffrey was a thoroughbred, by Eaton out of Sandhurst. I was out of Cheltenham Ladies College by good fortune. He commissioned as a cornet of the Blues. He was lovely. I loved him; he loved me for more than forty years, until he died, still my only ever will be lovely man."

Tristan, on the defensive, began to stutter, "M, mu, ma'am, you may be out of practice, but I have never been to such a place as Annabel's. I do not know the rules, or the codes. I did not rank as officer class. I would embarrass you by being not only out of my depth, but also out of date. I have only read about such places in magazines or the tabloid papers. If I rang them, they would not let me have a table, not on a Friday night, not on any night. I think it might be a club for members only. You have to be known to get into such places."

Lady Margaret gave him a smile that would convince an on course bookie to accept a cheque. "Oh, Sam," she said, "Stop being an Eeyore; such a fuss. I want to make a start by going to Annabel's because one of my best friends will be there. She has been a widow for less than a year, yet she has persuaded someone to take her there, this coming Friday. She has bragged about it for weeks."

She mimicked, in a shrill Hampstead hostess voice that would curdle granite, "You never get out dhaling, you really must or you will wither on the vine. I want to see her face when I come in on the arm of a tall handsome man. When I heard how well you responded to dear old Copper's eccentric behaviour, I observed that you have a quick wit able to cope with events. You will be my escort for the evening, won't you Sam? It will of course be my treat."

In a voice that he hardly recognised, Tristan replied, "If you are sure, I shall of course be honoured, although terrified. However, I must also respectfully ask you, whom it is that I shall have the honour to escort? You see ma'am, your uncle did not properly introduce us." Lady Margaret contrived a contrite manner to say, "Oh Sam, how awful, I am truly sorry." With a smile that would melt a misogynist's mind set, she gave Tristan an embossed calling card from a gold card case that she took from her small clutch bag.

Lady Margaret went on to say, as though they were already old friends, "Shall we have that tea you promised me, before it gets cold?"

Her bright chatter, taken together with the difference in their station, overwhelmed Tristan. He found it impossible to respond with the practiced banter that usually came easily when any female smiled in response to his opening bant.

Un-interrupted, Lady Margaret went on gaily, "You will not know the name on the card, it is my married name, however as we are about of an age, you may remember my maiden name. The press created such a lot of fuss during my debutante season, in those far off far better days. Before Geoffrey and I married, I had the honorary title, Lady Margaret Elizabeth de-Vere Erskin Tempest Powell. We pronounced the last name Pole, though we spelt it Powell, with a w and a double l."

As she said this, she cocked her head on one side with a shy grin; she quite definitely blushed. Tristan could not help himself because he did remember. Lady Margaret had been the talk of the tabloids. A response came unbidden; unstoppable, "I say; upper crust crumpet."

It turned out to be just the right thing to say. Obviously delighted, Lady Margaret replied, "Oh super! You do remember. You see Sam; it is not too late for you to make your debut, or for me to make a comeback."

Without waiting for a reply, let alone an agreement, she chirruped like a little songbird. "Book a table for two for nine o'clock. Use my name; pick me up in the Bentley in good time. I understand that they always start late at Annabel's. Wear what you like; it does not seem to matter anymore. Well now, that is all settled then, isn't it? I must go; I will let myself out," and go she did.

For a long time after she had gone, Tristan stared at the door before he made another more positive response, saying aloud to the empty room, "Ding dong." He thought next to ring Annabel's, to see if he could reserve a table for two. When he turned over the card that Lady Margaret had given him, he saw that she had written the number of Annabel's on the back, in green ink. She had also printed her full five-barrelled maiden name, with an added scrawl, 'Just in case, cut to Midge'.

It brought back memories that the tabloids had used the sobriquet 'Midge' to report on the activities of one of the leading, well connected, pretty, petite and vivacious debutantes of the season. Tristan's first attempt to book a table for two, using Lady Margaret's married name, elicited the expected response from a suave male receptionist who politely said, "Very sorry sir, Annabel's are fully committed for that evening, in fact for most evenings. I am sure that you will understand."

Tristan was proud of his reply, "I understand perfectly well, however perhaps you have missed the connection." Reading from her card he said, "Lady Margaret's had the title The Honourable Lady Margaret Elizabeth de-Vere Erskin Tempest Pole spelt Powell." He added, "Her friends call her Midge." With a respectful tone the receptionist responded, "Of course sir, I misheard the name, what time would you prefer?"

"Is nine o'clock too early?" Tristan asked. "No sir that will be just fine, we look forward to Lady Margaret, Midge, being with us on Friday at nine."

After he put down the phone, Tristan punched the air. Even though the Lady had asked to borrow him, as though he were a commodity, it would still be a 'date', of sorts, his first for many years.

He decided to ask Mr. Veasey for advice about what he should wear for the occasion. He thought smart casual would probably be the fashion. He considered that his one grey suit would not suit. Before going to See Mr. Veasey, Tristan rang Harry at Retreads to tell him his news.

"Harry, you won't believe it. I have a date. I am to take Lady Margaret, the Major's cousin, to Annabel's. What is more, she has asked me to pick her up in the Bentley."

"For goodness sake Tristan," Harry voice expressed genuine concern, "Do you know what you are getting into boyo? It will cost you a month's wages at least; it is a different world." Undismayed, Tristan laughed, "Harry, you have always preached that we live in, 'One world, God given, entire, indivisible.'" Harry, not to be put about replied sharply, "Don't you be cheeky to your elders, and don't be daft. What good is a Bentley without a chauffeur, with nowhere to park at all? I shall ask Jack Drummond. He is one of ours. We got him a five-day week as a chauffeur for Shell executives. He is tops; he had been an international class rally driver when young. Retreads paid for his training in security. He will love the opportunity to drive a Bentley; Shell only has Jaguars. I'll bring him round at about seven on the day."

Tristan began to understand about Harry's function at Retreads. In addition to providing shelter for needy men, until they found work to make themselves self-sufficient, he used Retreads graduates as an effective support network.

Erskin Powell had arranged that one of his junior clerks stand in as 'House Resident' for Friday, to enable Tristan to shop for the right sort of clothes to wear as escort to Lady Margaret. When Mr. Veasey saw Tristan come through the door, he shouted aloud, in mock horror, even though there were other customers in the shop, "Simon, Simon, lock the door; close the shop, the gentleman's gentleman vants to ruin us. He vants his shekels back on that morning suit, the one vee almost gave him."

Simon came out from the back office to give Tristan a genuine welcome. Hello Sir, what can we try to find for you this time?" Tristan said, "Professional advice for a start. I need something to wear when I escort a 'Lady', who is about my age, to dinner at Annabel's this coming Friday night." The elder Mr. Veasey sighed, "Ayee, 'The princess and the pauper', my favourite fairy tale; more tricky than our last commission. Simon, this is your field of expertise. I'm too old, I don't do young anymore."

"Well Granddad," the grandson said, "It's not a suit place these days, not many ties either, not so much smart casual, more smart statement, even smart arrogant; slacks, loafers, impeccable plain dark shirt, open at the neck. May I suggest that you take the black leather retro James Dean jacket, to carry, not to wear? It will get anyone past the doormen." Granddad Veasey groaned, "We are ruined, every day a dress down day."

When Tristan arrived back at Erskin House, he had spent a week's wages on the pale cream heavy cotton un-pressed slacks, a deep terracotta coloured raw silk shirt and a pair of Italian soft brown leather shoes that were almost slippers. The leather jacket had such exquisite quality that even second hand he could not afford to buy it.

However, Simon said, "Take it on hire for the weekend. If you do not lose it and bring it back undamaged, it will cost you a tenner. Whatever you do, do not wear it. It is only a poser's accessory.

Prompt at seven, on the Friday evening of Tristan's escort duty, Harry Evans arrived at Erskin House. He brought with him, Jack Drummond, the chauffeur for the evening.

Harry fussed around Tristan, like a much-elder brother, giving him old-fashioned advice about manners, and tips about behaviour on a first date. Tristan tried to calm him down by insisting that his escort duty would definitely not be of the romantic dating kind. He added forcibly, "Harry, Lady Margaret made her position perfectly clear with an expression that no one will ever think or say about me. I thought it wonderful. She said that her late husband Geoffrey was 'Still her only ever will be lovely man.' Being her escort is just part of my employment with the Major."

Harry replied, "Alright Tristan, a fair point that you must honour. Is she so out of sorts that she cannot get one of her own kind to take her to this ultra-posh pub?"

Tristan's reply was enthusiastic, "No, actually, she has kept her good looks. From what I have seen, her energy is very much the same as when her parents arranged for her to be presented to her Majesty at the Queen at the Queen Alexandra's Ball as "The Honourable Lady Margaret Elizabeth de-Vere Erskin Tempest Powell. I understand that the last name is pronounced Pole, even though it is spelt with a w in the middle ending with a double l at the end."

Harry had just started to say "Who in the name of," when he gasped, "No, not that lass, who in the fifties was one of the top debutantes, when the term really meant something, the one the papers called 'Midge'. Dieu man she may be small, but you will have your hands full with that one. By the way, dressed as you are, it appears that you have abandoned the gentleman's gentleman role for your escort duty. You look like an Italian gigolo on the make."

Tristan raised his nose to say, snootily, "I have it, on the best authority, that my outfit is de-rigueur for the occasion." With an exaggerated movement, he swept the folded leather jacket over his shoulder.

As escort to Lady Margaret at Annabel's, Tristan's evening went well. Harry's inspired idea to provide a chauffeur impressed Lady Margaret. During the short journey to Annabel's, she used her little girl voice, "Sam, I will call you Sam, because I want to. It seems right, like Copper said. I know your given name is Tristan; a noble name, however I am no Isolde. Tonight, and in future, I would like you to call me Midge, for my old times sake." She treated Tristan to one of her smiles that brooked no refusal before she concluded, "You will do that for me Sam, won't you? Despite his best efforts, Tristan could only manage in chivalrous response, "Oh - er - mmm - yes milady; Midge it shall be, - mi-Lady, oh lumme!"

Jack Drummond expertly drove the Bentley to stop, as near to the entrance as possible. He had the car door open before the club's uniformed doorman had deigned to move.

Drummond performed his chauffeur's duties smoothly, professionally. He handed Lady Margaret out, with a quiet word that

Tristan did not catch, before he put her hand on Tristan's arm. Near to the entrance to Annabel's, a small clutch of paparazzi waited for any opportunity to take pictures that the tabloids or magazines that live of celebrities might buy. One of them, who noticed the Bentley and the chauffeur who took great care of the attractive lady, took a flash photograph that startled Tristan. To his surprise, Midge paused, leant on his arm to put her head closer to his shoulder before she shone a smile brighter than the camera flash.

The second longer burst of camera flashes came from the other three or four scruffy jean wearing professional hunters of saleable pictures. Tristan noted that they all wore black leather jackets, similar to the one he had slung over his shoulder, his index finger through the little brass chain hanger loop.

Inside Annabel's, the restaurant manager, who made a fuss of Lady Margaret, almost ignored Tristan, while he went through the ritual of greeting and seating them at their table. Once seated, Tristan relaxed, a little. He mused aloud, a not quite direct question to the Lady who had borrowed him for the evening, "I wonder who those chaps with the flash cameras mistook us for. They must be expecting someone famous."

He did not notice her amused expression before he asked, "Have you seen your hated best friend yet?" "Oh Yes," Midge replied, "Did you not notice. When the Maitre'd showed us to our table, we passed right by her and her escort. You might have heard me say to her, 'Hello darling isn't it a bit passed your cocoa time?' I was unkind but she deserved a put-down comeuppance if that is not an oxymoron. I will call her tomorrow to make friends again."

The service, though smooth, was slow. The first course was pure artistry with little substance. The main course did not have enough on the plate to support a healthy appetite. The over fussy wine waiter interrupted their conversation more than once, as he tried to force the second bottle.

Nevertheless, despite his interruptions, they talked easily until quite late. On the short journey back to Lady Margaret's home in St. John's Wood, Tristan said how much he had enjoyed her company, even though the food and service had disappointed him. He told her about the Crown Inn in Scagill where people go for no other reason than to be with friends, to be comfortable, to enjoy discretely served good honest food, and where no one goes to show off. "Bye the way," he asked, "Were there any famous celebrities there tonight. I did not see any one that I recognised."

Lady Margaret puzzled Tristan with an enigmatic smile before she answered, "Sam, I don't know, I told you that I am out of touch. Perhaps if you look in the Sunday rags you may find out. They often include photographs of people going into or leaving places like Annabel's, the Ivy, more recently 'Stringfellows or Bijous, even the latest restaurant opened by a TV celebrity chef, if they cotton on to it before their short commons forces closure."

When they arrived at Lady Margaret's home, Tristan walked her to the door. She gave him a smile that would convince the three judges of a Court of Appeal, to commute a life sentence, to a day of community service.

As she stepped inside, she called to the chauffeur, "Thank you Drummond," before quietly saying to Tristan, "Thank you Sam that was fun; quite like old times. We have made a start, you the new man on the block, Midge on the comeback trail; what next I wonder."

The next day, day, all day long, Tristan felt very flat. Although he wanted to ring Lady Margaret, Midge, he felt unsure of the form, the etiquette. After all, he said to himself, "I am merely a servant borrowed for the evening, just like I borrowed the black leather jacket." He found it confusing.

Just a day later, Sunday, things were very different. At about half past eight, the insistent telephone by his bedside woke Tristan from deep sleep, long before he had planned to get up.

Barbara and Caroline, the house cleaners, had the morning off every Sunday; the only time that he had the chance of a 'Lie in'.

An excited Harry Evans shouted down his end of the phone connection. "Have you seen them Tristan; it's fantastic. What have you been up to that you should not have?"

Tristan answered, his tone a bit sharp, "Harry, you have just got me out of bed. I was fast asleep. Calm down, so that you can tell me what have I got to see that is fantastic?" Harry, still excited, said, "The papers man, the papers - 'News of the World', 'Sunday Express', 'The Mail on Sunday', the 'Mirror', even a modest piece in the 'Sunday Telegraph.'" "What's it about?" Tristan asked, trying to make some sense of the call. Harry calmed down enough to explain,

"You: it's about you, you daft hapeth; you with Midge. It's fantastic, splashed all over; you known only as Midge's mystery escort."

"Oh it can't be," Tristan moaned; "she will be very cross. I had rather hoped that I might be able to invite her out, in return for the other night, when it was her treat. Not at Annabel's or the Ivy or any place like that mind." Harry broke in, "Put the kettle on. I am on my way round. I have rung Stan. He has a day off today, so you can expect him anytime."

The three of them, closeted in Tristan's pantry, read the papers, while drinking tea and eating Sunday special bacon sandwiches. Tristan, who wore a newly acquired dressing gown, stood to allow his guests the use of the only two chairs. They did not hear the front door open, or the light stocking footsteps cross the marble hall. Nor did they notice the petite figure, who stood, shoes in hand, just outside the open pantry door, listening.

Both Stan and Harry were unmercifully teasing Tristan. Tristan, who had a face as long as a saxophone, complained, "It's not fair, I enjoyed the night, I mean evening," he made the change quickly when he saw Harry raise his eyebrows.

"The press have ruined it. She will never come here again; I am sure that she will never speak to me again. She will probably ask the Major to sack me." Startled, they all jumped to their feet, when, with a wicked chuckle, rather than a laugh, the Lady they were discussing said imperiously, "She, to whom I believe you refer, does not wish to be known as a third person singular.

May I remind you that my full name takes up three lines in Debrett's? The old-fashioned mode of address, 'The Lady Margaret', used in Who's Who, is used more often for small fishing smacks. I am 'Lady Margaret Howard' on my passport, driving license and chequebook, but Midge to my friends.

You gentlemen should not tease the gallant Sam. The fault, if any fault there is, must be down to me. Sam, are you going to stand there looking like Noel Coward who has lost an epigram, or are you going to introduce me to these rude men, before you put the kettle on. By the way, I hope you have a pair of big scissors and a pot of 'Gloy', the only suitable paste for a scrapbook. I have dug out my old ones because I want to start a new chapter. I bet that we will be in both 'Hello' and 'OK' before long."

Chapter 16

Three days after the excitement of the Sunday newspaper, Lady Margaret rang Tristan to ask whether he would be 'At home', at eleven o'clock the next morning.

Unsure of where the boundaries of their relationship were drawn he replied, a little nervously, "Good Morning Ma'am." He saw her as his vicarious employer, who acted for her cousin, the Honourable Major Erskin-Powell MFH MC, whom she called Copper, or darling, who he referred to as Sir or Major.

Inevitably, the evening they had spent together in the Bentley and at Annabel's, although not in the least intimate, it had not been purely that of employer with employee. However, Tristan had always found it easy to talk to women on the phone.

He rambled on; "You will be more than welcome, just to have you in the house will brighten it more than all the flowers at the Royal Horticultural Society Chelsea Show. As far as my being 'At home', you can be certain of it. At home, is what I do, seven days a week, morning, noon and night. Until Antonin takes up his post, or the Major returns, it is the totality of my job. I am here to prevent the unlawful entry of burglars, thieves, robbers, and squatters. I also have to deter all vagabonds, rouges, hawkers, street traders, double-glazing sales representatives, Avon ladies, Jehovah's Witnesses, fortune-tellers, canvassing politicians of all parties, and any other persistent doorknockers not listed. Should I ever come face to face with any such miscreants I fear that I would be useless. I shall have a tray of tea ready." "Thank you Sam, a pretty speech." He was pleased to hear her delightful chuckle before she switched off her phone.

The next day, when Tristan came down from his quarters with fifteen minutes to spare, she was already in his pantry, arranging cups and saucers either side of a plate of fancy chocolate biscuits taken from a Fortnum and Mason tin.

"Good morning lie a bed. I found our new chef in the dungeon. I have taught him how to make tea. The French have never understood how important it is to bring to a full boil, water freshly drawn from the cold tap, and the need to warm the pot. Is he any good, this Frenchman, or does he feed you on moules en frites with a mayonnaise dip for breakfast, lunch, tea and dinner? These days, it is all that they seem to offer in France and Belgium." "Ouch! Who burnt your toast this morning; I would have you know that I have been on dawn patrol betimes, since when I have yellow stoned and white stoned the steps. Antonin our new chef is old enough to have withstood all the passing fads of food fashion. He makes a true Lancashire hot pot, his Yorkshire puddings defy gravity, and his Eccles cakes win prizes. His traditional Cornish pasties are meet for all occasions, one end of meat the other of apple. Good morning Ma'am."

"Midge, if you please, I thought that we had an agreement. Now, tell me about your friends that I met last Sunday. The big man, did I hear you correctly that he too is a chef? The older one, who has the voice of a Welsh Bard is very kind, is he not. He reminds me of someone I know well, although I can't remember who, I am sure it will come to me."

When he heard the muted bell, Tristan collected the tea tray from the dumb waiter. "Well Ma'am," he began stiffly, unable to use the name Midge when he talked to or about the very attractive, bright, undoubted Lady in every sense.

"About my friends; the big man, the one built like a Martello tower, he is Stanislause, known as Stan. He is a great chef, also a good friend. In his youth, he had been a weight lifter on the Russian Olympic team, although in fact he was a misplaced Pole, as you were a miss-spelt Pole before you married. A chap I knew described him best. He likened him to a walking pantechnicon. The other man, the one that you think you may recognise, is Harry Evans. He does God's work, hands on. He is Master of 'Retreads' a small charity that retreads old soles like me, to make them fit for work after adverse circumstances have worn them down. He is very good at it. I already know of whom he reminds you, however I will leave it for you to remember. When you do, you will know all about Harry."

Midge went straight to her idea, about which she seemed to be very excited. "Last Friday night, we enjoyed ourselves when we ate at one of London's most famous dining rooms. However, I have to agree with you, we were both a tad disappointed. It set me thinking. However hard restaurant chefs try, they can never achieve results that equal that of a good cook who works in his or her own domestic kitchen. Circumstances force restaurant chefs to attempt the nigh impossible. They have to cater for the disparate tastes and foibles of their customers, without any control of order or reason. Competition with other chefs leads them to create dishes to appeal to the Food Guides and food writers, not what they would prefer to cook for themselves or their friends. At home, whoever is in the kitchen knows how many meals to prepare. They also know the time to have them ready. They have no need to offer a huge choice. When they go to the shops, they can choose whatever they find to be best at a price they can afford. When people dine in private, either at home or with a good host, they can relax, without worrying that people on other tables may ear wig, or gawp. What is needed, is a private place for simple people of like mind, or for complex confident people of different opinion, willing to meet and share a single table. Could we create such a place for people who would like to eat out, but cannot face the miserable experience of dining alone in a hotel or commercial restaurant? Do you think we could do it Sam?"

"Well ma'am, technically I suppose that it is possible, but where?" Midge, her eyes wide open, gesticulated to encompass the whole house, "Why here Sam, here. I know that I sound like a sixties film musical, nevertheless I think that Erskin House would be ideal. It is amongst the best addresses in London. It used to be a happy crowded family home, where Copper's family held parties and dances. My parents gave my coming out ball here. I am sure that the house is sad while it lies idle, while cousin Copper plays the absentee landlord thousands of miles away in Paarl. Anyway, for a trial run only mind, I have invited several singletons to a single table dinner party, a week on Saturday. They will make up a table of two dozen if we are included. We must give Antonin things to do, otherwise he will lose interest and leave. Cooking must be in his blood. With his given names, his parents must have named him after Carême. May I take it that you will help Sam?"

"Well it looks as though I have no choice, although don't you think it would be better if I were to act as a sort of butler, however inadequate I would be. I would prefer such an arrangement."

"Oh tush, I thought that you might say that. It means that I shall have to get another male. I do not want anyone to get the wrong idea. I do not look for another man; I never will. I could not put up with any of that malarkey. If I agree to your role as 'Jeeves' for the occasion, instead of Sam, you must promise me that after the guests have gone, you will sit with me to disclose all the scandal that butlers seem tuned to hear. You see Sam, deep down I am a real scandalmonger, just like my mother. Despite chronic ill health, she refused to die until she had received the telegram from the queen. Her interest in other people and their affairs kept her alive; she wanted to know what happened next. I read 'Private Eye', 'Tatler', OK' and 'Hello', all from cover to cover.

Of course, it will mean a lot of extra work for which I think that it is only fair that you make an extra penny or two, or even three. We must not use Copper's larder or cellar. I will pay for all that we need for the trial run. You must help Antonin with the purchase of victuals. If it is a success, as it will be, you could make such events into a legitimate business." As he looked glumly at the biscuit tin, Tristan muttered, "If I help with the buying, we will not be shopping at Fortnum's, or Harrods; it will be at the Cash and Carry or the Boro Market." Midge pretended not to hear.

The suggestion of a business prompted Tristan's interest. "How will you let people know about your idea. You can hardly put an advert in the 'Evening Standard' or the 'Metro'. Otherwise, I agree it is a good idea. If there is an opportunity to earn a little extra, it might give me a chance to restart my quest."

"What quest is that?" Tristan paused before he replied, "One day I may tell you ma'am, not today; we have work to do. How about I persuade Harry Evans to act as 'Twelfth man', he is a wonderful raconteur. He can tell tales all dinner long, from aperitif to coffee, without anyone wanting to get a word in. He is an even better listener. He could get the Savoy's wooden dog to talk. The one they use as the fourteenth guest, when they have a table of thirteen."

"Could you do that Sam, could you really, that would be so kind. The party will be black tie of course. I want to dress up. I want everyone to feel a sense of occasion about our first event, as we used to when I did my first season. Did you see that silly woman at Annabel's, who wore jeans? I am sure that their house rules do not allow them. I do not care whether they cost hundreds of pound from some fashionable boutique; I think that they are awful. I agree with what my mother used to say, 'Girls should only wear jeans to muck out the horses, even then, never on Sundays.' I do not care how couturiers tailor or decorate them; women who wear jeans look like misshapen leftovers. Men who wear jeans look like incontinent bin-men."

It took Tristan a deal of persuasion to get Harry to agree to be 'Twelfth man'. "Dieu man, can't you see, I am an old wreck. I haven't dined formally for years. I sit below the salt in a Sally Al's soup kitchen. I am not, nor ever have been, high table. I know that with table cutlery, course by course, one must start at the outside and work to the middle. I would start to talk or listen; either way I would forget. More than likely, I would eat every course with a soup spoon. Anyway, from where would I get a dinner jacket? As usual, I don't have a bean to spare. I can't even afford a visit to Billy the Barbers."

"Harry," pleaded Tristan, "I need you to do this for me. It could be my way forward. In any case, it is about time that you let someone spend a bit of money on you for a change. I am sure that my boss will cover the cost to hire a dinner jacket. I have found the best place in London to buy or hire tailored second hand clothes that are better than any new suit that you or I could ever afford."

"Alright, boyo, however there are conditions, I must be back at Retreads, before the witching hour, there will be old Charles Freeman to see to. I will accept the invitation, not for you mind. I rather fancy the chance of a chat with that lively girl who seems to be having a bad influence on you. I remember that years ago the papers featured her as a bit of a goer."

Tristan enjoyed the activity that came to Erskin House with the preparation for the dinner party. Antonin became all over Gallic; hunched shoulders, arms stretched out with upturned hands when he insisted on being in complete charge of the shopping. "Ow do you expect Marie Antonin Ratier to prepare a decent meal if you bring me a surprise bag of ingredients. You must not treat me like one of those animated cardboard cut-out commis chefs on TV 's 'Ready Steady Cook'. That programme is as useful for cooks, as would be a programme of 'Gardening at the gallop' for expert horticulturalists; you ave no soul."

Lady Margaret made frequent visits to the house, to make sure that the table arrangement and place settings in the dining room were to her liking. She also made sure that the furniture in the anteroom, where the guests would gather before dinner, had been arranged 'Just so'.

When Antonin showed Tristan the menu, which had seven courses, in the style of a great celebration dinner from the period before the First World War, it did not surprise him. As a sop to present day food faddism, the menu listed alternatives for most dishes. Tristan doubted that any of the guests would have the capacity to do it justice. Antonin seemed relaxed about the choice.

"Of course, it is all her idea; obviously not what I had in mind. I found that I had no answer to her discussion closer, 'Well that's all settled then isn't it'. There will be much waste. Nevertheless, I feel challenged for the first time in years. I know now how your Mrs. Thatcher got her own way with our President Giscard d'Estangne. Don't worry, you under-nourished specimen; a nice ripe pear is the correct shape for a butler, not the vanilla pod thin under footman that you resemble. We will eat well for the whole week after the party."

On the day of the trial dinner, Lady Margaret came to Erskin House, during the early afternoon, accompanied by the woman who had opened the door when Tristan had taken her back to her home, after their evening at Annabel's. Tristan could see that even though she called her employer Ma'am, their relationship had become that of companion and friend. They took possession of two bedrooms on the same floor as the Major's master bedroom. The house had been modernised to provide, in addition to the Major's bedroom, eleven bedrooms, each with en suit facilities.

Tristan thought that the Major must have employed professional interior decorators to furnish most of the rooms in the style of an English country house, although he had had one room furnished to remind him of the last days of the Indian Raj. It had ceiling fans, fabulous silk curtains, cane furniture, and a tiger skin rug.

At ten minutes to seven, Midge came down to make one last check that Tristan and Antonin had arranged and prepared every detail exactly as she wanted. She introduced the woman who came with her as Mary, her treasure.

She told Tristan that Mary would assist him with table service. Mary told him that she would answer the door when the guests arrived. "Will that be alright with you Sam?" Midge asked, without giving him a chance to reply. She followed with one of her compelling smiles that left him with no alternative other than to say "Yes Ma'am."

Dressed in a Balmain peach chiffon high-necked long sleeved dress that flared round her mid-calf, Lady Margaret smiled when she caught Tristan's look of admiration. "Do you approve of my confection Sam? I last wore it to Fiona Campbell-Luards coming out party in Yorkshire, and I wore these shoes that night. I knew that they would come back into fashion one day; that is if posh frocks ever do go out of fashion."

Tristan failed to think of a gallant answer, however a smile beamed by Harry Evans, dressed in a beautifully tailored dinner jacket, courtesy of Rose for Second hand clothes came to his rescue. Mr. Veasey had insisted that under the jacket he must wear a patterned gold brocade waistcoat over a light blue cummerbund. They had also provided him with patent leather dance shoes. Harry immediately took hold of his hostess's gloved left hand, to twirl her under his arm. With his rich baritone voice he almost sang, "You must be the almost full sized incarnation of the ballerina from my music box. The first and last dances are mine, Harry Evans; no good boyo, of nowhere at all, at your service." He turned to declaim, in exaggerated Rhonda Welsh, "Tristan, bach, the Lady does not have a drink, a poor state of affairs." As Harry had broken the ice, Tristan gained confidence.

"What may I get for you ma'am that will free you from this lecherous old man." Charmed by Harry, Lady Margaret whispered, "He is no such thing. I know of whom he reminds me. You

227

were quite right; he lives in the wild wood does he not. You are very lucky to have him as a friend. Tonight you must remember our agreement; while the guests are here, you may call me Ma'am but remember, when they have gone, Midge wants all the gossip."

When the first guest rang the doorbell, Mary went quickly to answer it. Harry sang out, "Right on, we are under starters orders, let the black dog see the rabbit."

The whole evening went as smoothly as a palace reception. When the first person arrived, a single man, Mary surprised Tristan when she formally announced him by his full name and title, as she did for all the guests as they arrived. Including the host who flitted amongst her guests making introductions, they were twenty-four, all talking, all relaxed. Although they all came alone, Tristan quickly understood that all the guests knew their host, though not one of them seemed to know anyone else.

They ranged in age from the mid-forties to late sixties. They were all of a type, well spoken, up to date with affairs, economic, political and social. Tristan rated them all in the top tier of his scale of wealth.

All seven courses that Antonin sent up from his basement kitchen, excelled anything that any restaurant in London or Paris, or any fashionable country house hotel, could produce, however many Michelin stars it rated. Service of each course taxed Tristan, although Mary coped with apparent ease.

Throughout the meal, Harry Evans captivated those guests, who sat at his end of the table. He hardly spoke; he just smiled, prompted and listened. It seemed as though they were anxious to tell Harry the story of their life so far, followed by their plans for the future. Tristan thought it uncanny until he realised that his own relationship with this remarkable man was much the same.

He had not been able to find out about Harry's history or early life. He remembered that Harry had said, when they first met, "You can tell me as much as you want to about your good self, then I will tell you all about me, in no time at all, because there is nothing at all to tell."

At eleven thirty, the guests retired to the library, where port, brandy and liqueurs waited and where Midge was able to introduce those who the long table had kept apart. Tristan noted that she had made no effort to separate the ladies from the men, a move that would have been customary for a hostess when she had been a debutant.

Tristan saw Harry make his excuse to leave. It did not surprise him when he kissed her hand, nor when she, on tiptoe, gently kissed him on the cheek with a proper kiss of friendship. She did not insult him with a false 'moi' air kiss.

When Harry left, it had the same effect as a window left open to let in a draft of cold air, the time served trick that pub landlords use to encourage their late night customers to go home.

When the guests did leave, they did not all leave alone, as they had arrived. Several ladies shared taxis; two men went off in one car. Two guests left together, as a couple. They were delighted to explain that they had found out that for years they had lived almost next door to each other, in Belgravia, but had never met.

After the last guests had gone, Midge, still full of energy called, "Come on Sam, we can rustle up a pot of fresh tea in your pantry. Mary has gone to help Antonin wash up. I have told them just to make things safe. You must get Barbara to help Caroline to do a thorough clean on Monday. I want to review this evening's event, in detail, while they are still fresh in our minds."

Chapter 17

Before she started her late night review of the evening's single table dinner party, Midge had kicked off her shoes to curl her legs back into her chair. Her idea of a review surprised Tristan. She had no interest in the timing, service, food, drink or table arrangements. Her questions were only about the guests, most of them personal.

Tristan had no need to emulate the perfect butler, who would be circumspect with his answers in such circumstances, because he had nothing to report that would be of interest. All the guests had behaved impeccably.

They had been polite to each other, considerate to him as well as to the excellent Mary, appreciative of the chef, and grateful to their hostess.

Obviously disappointed, she declaimed imperiously, "Tush, how terribly dull. We shall have to do better next time. I had hoped for a few sparks, a few indiscretions. It seems that we all held your friend Harry Evans, who I believe to be Mr. Badger from 'Wind in the Willows', in such awe that we took our cue from the young hedgehogs; we had to behave respectfully." That his aristocratic employer thought of Harry Evans, as the kindly Mr. Badger delighted Tristan. He almost crowed, "I told you that I knew of whom he reminded you; I was right."

Not to be put down Midge thought aloud, "Next time, we must invite a 'Mr Toad', a boogle of weasels, and a trip of stoats. They will be more fun."

"Oh, you do intend to have another dinner party." Only his eyebrows visibly curled, his curled toes remained discreetly hidden in his highly polished shoes. His obvious pessimism made no affect.

We shall not have any more formal dinner parties, we shall arrange lots of informal suppers, soirées, dances, all sorts of social events; all on a fee basis of course. If we do not charge, our guests will fail to value our efforts. They will go hungry and sober, as they will not wish to appear greedy. Worse, they might feel under an obligation to return the hospitality. That would never do. I already have someone in mind for Mr. Toad. He is a minister, or shadow minister, I can never remember which. We can easily get a weasel from one of the broadsheets, and stoats, in their winter ermine, from the Lords. We need a good bit of juicy scandal if we are to build a solid client base. That is how the celebrity magazines prosper. However, we must keep it as our private scandal, with never a breath of it in the 'Tabloids' or the 'Glossies'. Now Sam, you must not keep me up any longer with your chatter. I need my five hours sleep."

Midge almost sprang from the elegant chair from which she had held her court of one. She crossed the corridor, opened the hatch door to the dumb waiter, stuck her head inside the shaft to call down, "Come along Mary, we are being sent home."

Two days later, Tristan sat in his pantry with Antonin. He had asked him to calculate the cost of the food and wine bought for the 'Trial Run' dinner. Although he had enjoyed the challenge of preparing and cooking a seven course dinner Antonin remained sceptical about the whole idea, "It's not Cordon Blue, it's Sacre Blue." He made his declaration with a pronounced Gallic shrug. "Just to cover the cost, we would have had to charge about a hundred pound a head. If we add a reasonable charge for the hours worked, to include Mary and the cleaners, a reasonable profit would require three hundred pounds a head, without accounting for the hire of Erskin House. It's not a goer; it will never work. Who has that sort of money to splash around in these days of high taxation?"

Slumped deep into his chair, with his eyes closed, Tristan groaned, "I dread to think. I can't imagine that they will be the quiet money people who came on Saturday. They will be the sort of people who watch Arsenal or Chelsea from hospitality boxes, or those who dine at Annabel's, the Ivy, or midlife crisis folk who party at Stringfellow's; rich bored people who sulk in suits in Claridge's, the Grosvenor and the Dorchester, or worse politicians not daring to go home to their constituencies. If not them, dear God, there are the celebs, the Notting Hill nabobs, the Chelsea charioteers, the Hampstead thinkers, the frightful Dockland wannabes. If she casts her nets in those muddy waters, we could become notorious, perhaps raided by the vice squad. News would get to the Major in South Africa. He would fire me for sure."

Antonin gave Tristan some cause for hope, "I don't think that we have any need to worry. How could she promote, let alone market, or advertise her idea? I tell you, it's a non-starter; she cannot possibly go on inviting old friends. Who, outside her circle, are to know about my cuisine or Erskin House?"

"I wouldn't be too sure about that Antonin. We forget just how many people there are in our country who live in their own world, quietly, comfortably, unconscious of their wealth. Our mentor wants to put the clocks back to a happier time. You admitted that she got you to agree to the menu, with her set phrase, 'Well then, that's all settled then isn't it. 'My Lady' gets me to accept I know not what, when, or how. I find myself committed before she asks me for an opinion, let alone my agreement."

The next day, Tristan drove the saloon Bentley to Retreads, anxious to get his friend's reaction to the dinner party. He took unconcerned delight to drive either Bentley. As it was a specified requirement of his job, he felt cost and conscious free. He was concerned when he did not find Harry in the kitchen, or anywhere downstairs.

After he called aloud, with no answer, he found him upstairs in his flat, resting on his bed, eyes shut. "You alright old chap?"

Harry replied, his eyes still shut, "Oh yes, yes, fine boyo, I am sure I have no time to be otherwise. I am only having a Churchill moment. Now that the kitchen is altogether modern, I take my afternoon nap up here. I just cannot get comfortable down there. I miss the old range. I know it is not possible; nevertheless, I am sure that the water boiled in the old cauldron kettle, over the trivet, made a much better cup of tea than the new-fangled urn that you bought. That square stainless steel tank may be all right to make coffee, a drink that stimulates but does not satisfy, however it does not do the trick for tea. In time of need, if properly brewed, mashed or drawn, tea can restore a broken spirit. Come on through to my study, it's time I was up to see to things."

Concerned for the man who had given him more than shelter Tristan asked, "Do I detect that the late night plus rich food on Saturday broke the rhythm of your ordered day?" "Well perhaps; it did give me indigestion, however I was able to observe how the other half live. While we ate like Victorian sybarites, our old boys had cottage pie with cabbage. Stan brought some excellent cold beef that the Sous chef had thrown out. We have a new guest who is a mad keen gardener. With the help of one or two of the other chaps, he works the allotment well, as both plantsman, and scavenger. That allotment idea of yours is a boon."

To bring the subject back to the dinner party Tristan said, "Harry, despite your worries about top table etiquette, you seemed to cope very well. You held the whole group at your end of the table in thrall. I also noticed the kiss that Lady Margaret gave you."

Harry smiled at the memory before he admitted, "Well, that must have been the first kiss I have had for many years. It had to be a bit special for an old wreck like me. Midge is a charming woman, with more energy than many half her age and most teenagers, however you must take great care boyo. It is not in her nature to preside over sober dinner parties. Midge is a get together festive girl, not a Hampstead hostess."

"You are spot on there, Harry. We sat up late after the guests had gone. She did admit that next time she intends to liven things up."

"There is to be a next time is there?"

"Funny you should say that," Tristan grinned, "Not my exact words but the same rhetorical question to her."

"Go on, what did Midge say?" Harry, obviously keenly interested, sat upright, moving forward on his chair, while Tristan tried to look innocent.

"It was some nonsense about weasels, stoats, Mr. Toad and The House of Lords; I can't think what she was on about."

"Well Boyo, whatever she meant, just think on. I can see complications ahead. I don't want you back onto 'Extra Rations', after these Saturday night soirées that she has in mind. It will be cards next, after that a full-blown casino, Fridays as well as Saturdays. What do the kids have these days, 'Sleepovers', isn't it? Just be careful, I cannot see that running a night club, however upper class, is why your 'Good Lord', brought you to Retreads. I hope that you remember that you mentioned him when you first came to us."

A great bellow from downstairs announced that Stan had arrived. "Are you up there Angol? I have just had to put the nice lady traffic warden right. I told her that your car is 'Diplomatic'. I fibbed a bit. I told her that I saw two little scruffs run off with the CD badge. To sweeten her bile, I gave her a piece of gateaux that I had hoped to have with my tea. Come down; tell Harry we won't need him tonight. Lewis and I have it in hand."

Harry smiled, "He's a tower of strength is that one, he has already taken on one of our difficult guests to do veg prep at the hotel, four hours a day seven days a week. It seems to work. You go to see to the car; if I am not needed downstairs, I can get on with my monthly report for the Trustees."

When Tristan joined his massive Polish friend in the kitchen, he asked, "Is Harry alright?" Stan reassured him, "Probably a bit tired; nothing that a bowl of good Polish borscht won't put to rights." As always, when he talked about food, he went lyrical.

"Polish borscht is so much better than Russian, even their Poltava with dumplings, all bloody beetroot and tomato, only a smidgen of goose grease, dipped in like a tea bag; no kvass, no smoked sausage, no wonder the cross eyed Reds could not shoot straight."

Tristan was not surprised to find a parking ticket on the Bentley, to which the 'Nice lady traffic warden' had added her own endearing note, 'Tosser'.

On Sunday morning, a few days later, the telephone rang early, before Tristan had finished his breakfast. Without preliminaries, the bright cheery voice surprised him.

"Sam, it's a lovely autumn day; the Bentley needs a run. Can you please pick me up at about ten, or are you still under the covers." Aping an Edwardian Butler of a great country house, Tristan replied, "No Ma'am, I have already inspected the staff, checked the wine cellar and issued all necessary house orders for the day. I personally ironed 'The Times'. I have enjoyed a full English breakfast; however, I have yet to adjust the handkerchief in my top pocket. Any particular Bentley you require today"

"Another pretty speech, you should write them down to use in a history of the Old Sloan's Club. The two-seater of course, I told you it is a fine autumn day. Do not bother about food; Mary will make us up a picnic. I will not take up all your day because I must be back home by six for 'Evensong'. Is that all right with you Sam?"

235

When he replied, "Of course Ma'am, it will be a pleasure," he did mean it, however he did not understand what she meant by 'Old Sloan's Club'.

Tristan enjoyed driving the open Bentley with an engine that growled and roared rather than purred, except that he found it needed more than a flexed ankle to depress the clutch. He had to brace his back into the seat to push down with his foot, with the same force that he used to double-dig the allotment with a rusty shovel.

He felt pleased that he had not forgotten the knack he had learned in the army, when it had been part of his job to drive a Bedford truck fitted out as a cook's wagon.

When she skipped down to the gate of her grand house in St. John's Wood, where he had just parked the Bentley, Tristan thought that he might be required to take his vicarious boss to the heather moors to join a shooting party for late grouse. The beautiful carved leather boots, heavy tweed skirt and jacket with a cloak and a small deerstalker hat, of the same tweed, that topped off her ensemble turned out to be a false clue.

Mary, who had followed with a picnic basket, asked Tristan to stow it carefully in the trunk.

"Good morning Sam, if we are not to be late you will have to drive like Stirling Moss dicing with Mike Hawthorne. First chukka usually starts around mid-day. Do you like polo? Today is the last match of the season. It always takes place the week after the Autumn Cup. It should be lots of fun. You will have to drive, I can't reach the pedals." All this, she said at speed, while Tristan held the door for her to clamber over the running board into the passenger seat.

"I am unable to answer your question ma'am. I do not yet know whether I like polo. I have never been to a polo match, not as rider, groom, spectator, bookmaker or punter. In fact, I have never ridden a horse of any kind. I fear that because of my height, if I were to be astride a polo pony, my feet would be so near to the ground that I would appear as though mounted on a Lambretta motor scooter. Pray tell me where this event you wish to attend is to take place."

"Why, Cowdray Park of course, I think it will be the 'Lawns' today. I do not think that any of the Royals will be there. It is amateurs only, if you count the military as amateurs, so lots more fun, lots more tumbles, you see the season really finished last week. It will be sign posted from Midhurst."

After a couple of short stops, Tristan began to enjoy the journey. The first stop was to get travel rugs for the comfort of his passenger, the second for his comfort. In the big wicker basket strapped to the back of the car, he found soft leather driving-gloves that covered his forearm and a leather helmet to cover his ears.

Most of the modern cars on the road could go faster than the Bentley could, however many of their drivers waved him though when an open stretch of road appeared. Once they had shaken off London's suburbs, Tristan could tell that his navigator had begun to enjoy herself as whenever he dropped speed, she mocked, "Come on Sam, I could go faster than this in my 'Mini'."

He followed her directions to drive unchecked into the official car park. A marshal directed them to a reserved space, nose up to a rope that gave them a good view of the lawn.

"How did you arrange that?" Tristan asked. "Oh, I called yesterday to tell them. Sam, I am sorry but I must leave you to your own devices for a while. I have friends to meet. I will be back in an hour when we can see what Mary has put up for our picnic."

Away from the field of play, Tristan wandered around the horseboxes, and tents, where men who looked like on course bookies talked to rather brusque women who sold things related to horses, from bronze statuettes, through jodhpurs, saddles, horse rugs, 'Ifor Williams' trailers and 'Oakley' horseboxes. Coming closer to the field, he eavesdropped on the conversations of groups all who seemed to belong to an Edwardian period comedy performed by a West Sussex amateur dramatic group.

The male voices sounded studiedly laconic; the female responses were clear and confident. 'This really is Jilly Cooper country,' Tristan thought. 'I am out of my depth here.'

He watched fascinated, as Midge darted from group to group, as a little bird might flit from bush to bush in search of seed. He could see that she was in her element. Everyone she met made a fuss of her.

However, it puzzled him that she appeared to hand out to the older people in each group, what appeared to be oversized calling cards. All of those given a card glanced at it, and smiled, before they put it into a pocket or handbag. One card fell un-noticed onto the grass. When the first two teams moved out onto the field of play, a pony trod on the card. When the commentator began to announce the teams and riders, most groups moved to the small stand or nearer to the edge of the lawn.

This gave Tristan the opportunity to recover the fallen mud covered card. After he scraped off the mud, he managed to read the embossed script. The shock of what he read caused the hair on the back of his head to bristle. His right hand involuntarily smoothed back the hair on the side of his head.

'Bored with London at the weekend.
Why not join a club where talk of
golf, cars, diets and fashion is forbidden,
where it is fun to talk of
Money, Sex, politics and religion.
Membership exclusively for singles, widows and widowers
born before 1960'
PTO

A second shock reached his toes when he turned the card over to read the reverse. It made clear the meaning of the unfamiliar words 'Old Sloans'.

Old Sloanes Re-united
Patron: (Midge.)
Erskin House, Lee's Crescent, Mayfair, London.
Secretary; Sam Weller
Call 020 356 975 743 weekdays 10 am to Noon

Long after two o'clock, Midge returned to the car where Tristan had laid out the picnic on a small table that he found in the boot of the Bentley together with two small collapsible chairs. The food from the hamper packed by Mary proved to be Fortnum and Mason's best. It included a bottle of Gewurztraminer in a plastic cooler sleeve.

Flushed with excitement, her apologies were profuse, "Oh poor Sam, I am so sorry to keep you near to starvation. My feeble excuse is that I had to talk to so many old friends. I see Mary has packed pepper wine as I call it. I often use it for picnics. To be acceptable, it does not have to be ice cold like champagne. For goodness sake Sam, sit down. Please try not to look like a judge about to commit a poor woman to a public execution."

Without comment, Tristan poured her a glass of wine before he sat down, but not before he put the recovered card in front of her.

"Oh! Now I see what has bothered you, but I do not understand why are you not pleased? Mind you, I do not know if we are right to call it, Sloane's Re-United. I think Sloane's Re-Incarnated might have been better. Some of my chums have let themselves go so far that they look old, dare I say decrepit, even though Sloane's came along much later than when I did my first season."

"Ma'am" Tristan managed in a steady voice, "Don't you think that you might have gone a bit over the top with this? I really must protest; 'Secretary' indeed."

"Well protest away if you must. However, you should be pleased, as you gave me the idea." "I gave you the idea; good grief woman, what convoluted course of unfounded defective reason gave you that idea?"

Midge used one of her temper defusing smiles. She put her hand across the table onto his arm, "Don't be cross with a woman who is frightened of old age. We will have such fun. Do not worry about the secretary bit. I will get a social secretary from one of the agencies to do all the stuffy stuff. All that we have to do is to think of good ideas for our events. It was your idea to begin with; your idea to play Sam Weller to Copper's Pickwick. Pickwick had a club; they had lots of fun. He had already retired when they set off on their adventures." Tristan replied dryly, "If I remember the story correctly ma'am, Pickwick ended up in a debtor's prison."

There was an embarrassed hiatus before Tristan asked, "Where else have you distributed your upper crust flyers?"

"Oh dear you are cross. Well, one of my chums has put them into all of the mailboxes of the over fifties in the House of Lords. He has asked one of his chums, the cabinet minister who looks like Mr. Toad, I told you about him, to use his discretion when he canvasses the commons. We want all those of our kind, even if they are not one of us. Cousin Copper's cousin is doing the Cavalry and Guards club, the Athenaeum and the Carlton. I have just contacted the polo clique and the Lord's Taverners are covered. I shall have to write to the far-flung friends in Yorkshire and Scotland."

Without conscious thought Tristan reached out to take a smoked salmon pin wheel from the table." Immediately Midge relaxed; She said in her usual disarming way, "Well then, that's all settled then, isn't it?"

Chapter 18

Well before nine o'clock in the morning, only a few days after the visit to the polo grounds at Cowdray Park, the front door of Erskin House opened and closed. The lighter click of high heels, as they crossed the hall, alerted Tristan to the arrival of the Lady who had borrowed him from his employer, during the Major's absence in South Africa.

Somehow, Tristan had agreed, or perhaps not disagreed, that he would help her to organize events to recall the social habits and happier times when she had been a debutant.

"Morning Sam," she called out, when she had not yet reached half way across the hall. Without a further breath, she continued when she arrived in Tristan's pantry, "I expect a certain Jennifer Johnson-Jackson at any moment. The 'Greycoats' Agency has sent her to see if we think that she will be suitable as the Old Sloan's social secretary. I have suggested nine-thirty until twelve-thirty for her hours, Monday to Thursday. Twelve hours should cover what we need. The girl must have enough free time to do whatever nice young things do these days. You will be pleased to know that clever Mary has arranged for someone to fit an answer phone in the Major's study. It is the phone with the number I have used on my 'Sloans Re-united' announcement, the card that you vulgarly called a flyover. The number is ex-di-

241

rectory. It is not the listed number for Erskin House. He had the second line installed so that, on race days, he could always get through to his bookmaker. He likes to make a last minute bet, when the horses are on their way down to the start. He will not need it until he gets home from Paarl, where he will probably use the bush telegraph to bet on ostrich racing. The gel, if we appoint her, will be able to record a message to state that she will only accept calls, ten 'til noon, Monday to Thursday. As I told you, you will not be bothered with stuffy stuff. We shall be scot-free to arrange events."

All this said before Tristan had time to say good morning, and before the front door bell rang. "That will be the gel," her equally bell like voice chimed, "A good start to arrive early. I will let her in. Please set a tray of tea with biscuits, for three. We must appraise her looks, deportment, dress sense and voice modulation. It is most important that she enunciate both the consonants s and t. These days, most young people seem unable or unwilling to articulate either one; they seem to prefer the glottal stop. To be our social secretary she must be socially acceptable to folk of an earlier generation. We will meet her in the library."

It only took a few minutes for Tristan to set a tray, and arrange a plate of biscuits from the Fortnum & Mason tin, before he took it through to the Library.

Lady Margaret had affected a rigidly formal pose in one of the high backed Regency chairs, her hands folded on her lap, her neck stretched, and her head half turned. Tristan could see that 'milady' intended to test the nerve of the young woman. To improve her advantage she had asked the girl to sit on a low upholstered leather pouffe, set in front of, although slightly to one side of her chair.

It delighted Tristan that the young woman showed few, if any, signs of nerves. Hardly seated, she perched on the edge of the pouffe, her long legs folded back to one side, her ankles touching, not crossed. She had inter-linked the fingers of her long thin hands to hold her pleated skirt over her knees. Tristan thought that she had dressed with care for the interview. He deemed her twin set, single row of pearls, and court shoes, a statement of class, rather than fashion.

He guessed that she would not yet be twenty. Something about her made him hope that she would be acceptable to the high expectations of the Patron and sole arbiter of Old Sloan's Re-united. Without regard to academic qualification, political correctness or prejudice, she high-handedly dropped the C.V. the young woman offered, onto the carpet, unopened.

The shrill sharp voiced expression of her first question shocked Tristan. It demanded an answer. "Are you married, engaged or do you co-habit with a partner as you young people tend to do these days?" The girl blushed, before she replied in a soft voice, unmarked by accent or dialect, "No; none of those relationships ma'am."

"Lady Margaret preferred," her interlocutor said haughtily. "Not a lesbian are you?"

"Good heavens no," the girl blushed again, "I like boys; it's just that I have not met many. I only left Cheltenham last year when I went out to my parents in Hong Kong. All the boys of my age were back in UK at UNI, or back packing round Australia during their gap year."

To his relief, Lady Margaret reverted to her usual gentle bell like tones, "Sam, do sit down please, you make we girls nervous when you stand around in your pin stripes, a doppelganger of a Harrods floor walker."

She turned her attention back to the girl, "Will you please pour the tea and pass the biscuits miss. I am so old that I am incompetent to do such things, however I do have to be careful how I pronounce incompetent." With a radiant smile the girl relaxed, "That is what my Grandpapa says. Oh good, the biscuits are Fortnum's, they are scrummy aren't they."

The girl rose so elegantly from the low pouffe that she reminded Tristan of a time-lapse film of an unfolding flower. Before attending to the tea tray, she crossed the room to pick up side tables to place them beside both Lady Margaret's and Tristan's chairs. Only then did she ask whether they took milk and sugar. After she served the tea, the girl passed round the biscuits, first to Lady Margaret, then to Tristan, before she took the biggest biscuit with the fanciest foil wrapper.

Clearly satisfied that the Greycoats' Agency candidate would serve the Old Sloans well, the familiar phrase rang out, "Well then, that's all settled isn't it? The job is yours if you can put up with a crowd of gad about geriatrics. You see, you did not need a C.V. You cannot express personality in print. Please call on my cousin Mr. Erskin-Powell, at Greys Inn. He acts for the family. He will give you written conditions of your employment, that our paper bound government regulations require. He will also arrange to pay your remittance into your bank account. Sam will reimburse any expense that you may incur from petty cash. Please take my card. I have written Erskin-Powell's address with his telephone number on the back." That done, she left the room through the revolving bookcase.

"Gosh, isn't she wonderful," the girl gushed with the enthusiasm of a teenage fan for a pop star. "My grandpapa told me all about the summer when she had been leader of the pack that he went about with, to parties, summer balls, Wimbledon, Henley, Ascot and the Polo at Cowdray; It must have been wonderful. I think that he must have been a bit in love with her, but the army took him off to Cyprus where there seemed to be a bit of a squabble at the time."

Despite the obvious difference in their age, education and experience, Tristan felt comfortable in the company of Jennifer Johnson-Jackson. He asked, "Miss, is it all right if I call you Jennifer, or would you prefer Miss or Miss Jackson-Johnson?"

The girl had an immediately friendly reply ready, "I think Jenny would be best. If you insist on formalities, the family name is Johnson-Jackson. That issue aside, what am I to call you? The

Greycoats agency did not give your full name, just your Christian names, Tristan Edward. Lady Margaret called you Sam; how is that? "

The girl was so young, with such charm that Tristan felt protective. Like an elderly uncle he replied, "Well Jenny, Lady Margaret calls me Sam, because she believes me to be an incarnation of Sam Weller from Dickens's 'Pickwick Papers', so you had better join in the charade. I shall be Sam to your Jenny." Jenny, wide eyed, said, "Cool, I do hope that I will be allowed to help during the parties, in addition to the secretarial bit."

"So do I Jenny, so do I." Tristan said with affected weariness, "To tell you the truth, I am out of my depth with the goings on of the upper crust, past or present." Jenny had the ease of the wealthy well-educated young, able to engage with people of all ages and status without discrimination or prejudice.

"Sam, don't worry, I will get my Grandpapa to give me ideas for suitable events. I will dig out Mummy's old copies of Tatler and London Illustrated. She kept all those that had photographs of her along with some that had photographs of her boyfriends. I will let you have her copy of the 'Sloane Rangers Handbook'. It is a bit late seventies early eighties, nevertheless it will keep you right with the fashion and popular places of the old days." Tristan teased, "I thank you truly young lady. Even though you are the cruel heartless child, who dismissed the recent prime of my life, the time I think of as only yesterday, as 'The old days'. You had better pop off to Greys Inn to meet Mr. Erskin-Powell. However before you do, try 'Super' instead of 'Cool'. If it really is, 'Utmost cool', 'Spiffing' is the word they used to use. I hope that you can start fairly soon."

Jenny positively bubbled with excitement, "If tomorrow is not too soon for you, I shall be here at 9.30, sharp. By the way Sam, 'Spiffing' might not be the right word. A spiff is a marijuana cigarette, a joint. Spiffing is the gerund, the future progressive of spiff."

When Tristan replied, with an old-fashioned politically incorrect, "Until tomorrow my dear," her single word response, 'Super', cheered him.

A few moments later, a glimpse of the back of a middle-aged woman reversed, revoked, and cut short Tristan's good humour. It blighted his day. It happened when he went down stairs to the kitchen, to tell Antonin about Jenny, the new girl, the Old Sloans social secretary.

Although he only had a glimpse of the back of someone as they shuffled down the long corridor that led to the back door, he felt sure it could only be Edna Spitewinter.

Edna the dreadful housekeeper he had forced out of her job at Erskin House, a job that she had used to create several lucrative kick back fiddles. Tristan rated her as truly evil, a creature about whom he had reason to worry. He felt that the only redeeming fact might be that she had not seen him.

Tristan found Antonin in his little cubbyhole that passed for an office. Unsure of his position, he cautiously asked who had just left from the back door. It worried him when Antonin told him that he did not know her name, but that he had seen her before, always when she had been talking to one or other of the morning cleaners. He said that she had twice asked him if the butcher, the grocer or the wine merchant had left an envelope for her. He added that she had accused him of theft when he told her they had not left anything for her and that they no longer supplied the house.

"Antonin be careful. That one is trouble, twenty-two carat hall marked everlasting fixed in the weave double dyed back to back inevitable trouble."

"You don't fancy her then." Antonin laughed. Tristan felt it quite the opposite of a laughing matter.

He said, grimly, "Antonin, it could be serious. Frankly, she scares me. I am sure that she is a vindictive harpy who will work hard to get her revenge on me because I forced her to leave Erskin House. She had more rackets going than the Soprano family. When she left the Major's employment, without notice, and without a forwarding address, she not only lost wages due, she forfeited holiday pay and she lost a lucrative, corrupt, tax-free fiddled income."

Later that day, alone in his pantry, Tristan sat forbidding as an unmarked slate tombstone in a rain swept closed graveyard, but his mind raced in a tangle of thoughts. He could not decide whether to deal with the Spitewinter woman himself; to bar her from entering the house and to require the cleaning ladies to keep her out, or whether to tell the police about her corrupt activities, or let Erskin-Powell the family solicitor know about his worries.

After an hour spent in consideration of his options, without a resolution, he called Antonin on the internal phone. He asked him to stand cover in the house for the rest of the day and night, because he needed to ask Harry Evans for advice. "Ok Tristan," Antonin said, "I assume it is about that old hag housekeeper that you worry. No need, I Marie Antonin Ratier, great chef to this small house, will take on the duty that the crabby old chatelaine disgraced. I will keep the safe keys safe."

Antonin's self-mocking, but assured reply calmed Tristan, however Edna Spitewinter had more than upset him, she had rattled him. He had become so distracted that, he polished his 'Trickers', put on his best suit, a clean shirt with his most suitable tie, just to visit Harry Evans, who would, most likely be wearing his dressing gown and his worn down carpet slippers.

Talking with Harry Evans, while they drank tea, confirmed Tristan's opinion that the old man was the best listener he had ever known. He could draw out a man's inner thoughts without causing him to be embarrassed, uncertain, discomforted or foolish.

After an hour together, Harry's mood changed from receptive to instructive, "Right Oh boyo, there are three things that you must do. First, you must try to split the three witches. Talk to the two cleaners separately. Tell each one that you are taking her into your confidence. Do not let either of them know that you have talked with the other. Make out to each one that she is your favourite. Ask her not to tell the other that you have talked to her. Ask each one to tell their good friend Mrs. Spitewinter that you want to meet with her privately, to discuss a proposal. The Spitewinter spinster of no good parish will not be able to resist. Those of a criminal mind believe that the rest of us are of the same mind. She will think that you want to restart some, if not all, of her old fiddles. She will want a cut. If she does come to see you, keep it simple. Tell her she is not to come inside the house, no more than that. If she does not come to talk to you and you find out from Antonin that she still comes to the house, or if you see her yourself, you will know that the corrupt old trot box intends to bring you down. You will also know that both cleaners are in league with her."

"Second thing that you must do is to tell Erskin-Powell about Spitewinter's visits to the house. The family pay him far more than they pay you to worry about the Major's affairs. It is for him, not you, to decide whether to inform the police about Spitewinter's wicked ways. There is no need to tell Midge. It is not for her to worry."

"What is the third thing that I must do," Tristan asked. Harry had sprung from his chair like a man half his age when he answered, "Call a taxi to take us to find Stan. He told me he would spend an hour or four at his pub tonight, to play dominoes. A pint or two, over an hour or two, spent with vulgar friends in low places will do you the world of good. You have mixed of late with highborn aristocrats; you need to get back to basics boyo, back to basics."

The evening Tristan spent with Harry and Stan worked in the way Harry knew it would. He had drunk little, but had laughed a lot. After the pub closed, the three friends went back to Retreads where Stan cooked supper using ingredients from his private stash of Polish staples to improve a part prepared stew.

He quickly raised it to a goulash with the addition of red cabbage, apple, and pork-sausage with a suggestion of garlic, finished with slices of spek, fired up with paprika. The three men talked so late, as they put the world to rights, as men do, that Harry insisted that his visitors stay for the little that was left of the rest of the night, at Retreads in two unoccupied cubicles in the main hall.

At seven a.m. precisely, Harry brought Tristan a cup of tea, with two oatmeal biscuits in the saucer. He told him that Stan had left early for his morning shift. He added that Tristan must be out before nine; otherwise, he would be breaking house rules that would set a bad example to the decent folk properly entitled to use the hall facilities.

When he let himself into Erskin House, just before nine o'clock, Tristan heard the familiar female voice sing out, "Good afternoon you miscreant stop out."

With her characteristic fluency she went on without a pause, "I came in early to ensure that Miss Jennifer gets a good idea of what we want her to do. By the way, the man is here to fit the automatic answer phone thing. I have set Miss Jennifer to work in the Major's study for the present, because that is where the phone lives. Before he comes home, we will have to find her an office of her own, where she can work unhindered. Miss Jennifer can arrange to have a new phone installed for Copper's hot line to the bookies. However, that is mere detail. The important news is that I have the theme for our first proper party, 'Monte Carlo and Bust'"

"Don't you mean Monte Carlo or bust?" Tristan said, pleased that, for once, he could safely correct the Lady who always led their conversations. It was not to be. Once again, she put him down with a laugh. "On the contrary my dear Eeyore, the men will be in white tie and tails, the ladies décolleté. I have arranged with 'Park Tower' for the loan of a real roulette wheel complete with one of their croupiers. There will also be tables for Bezique and Vingt-en-Un. We will not gamble with money; we will only play for the chip things they use. I will give a small prize for the most successful lady and gentleman gambler. Now, we must get Antonin up from his dungeon to discuss then decide on my idea of a Mediterranean menu. I thought that we might have caviar and foie gras on blini to start with, followed by a choice of two salads, cold lobster mayonnaise with asparagus, or cold roast fillet steak with jellied consommé. No choice for dessert, Crêpe Suzette, everybody likes posh pancakes. Only three courses, our trial run showed us that none of we creaking gates can do full justice to six or seven courses, not in the way that we used to. Oh, before I forget, clever Miss Jennifer has told me we must open a bank account. I will ask my man at Coutts to arrange it."

Tristan assumed his best possible lady's gentleman demeanour. "Good morning ma'am. I beg my Lady's pardon, however I did not quite catch what you have just said, Could you please repeat it, 'Words twice, slowly' as my army signals sergeant used to say?"

"Sorry Sam, I am as excited, as when I first went to Monte Carlo, I am sure you understood every word, so that's all settled then, isn't it."

"Yes ma'am of course. How many customers may Antonin and I expect."

"I told Miss Jennifer to close the list at forty. Instead of a formal dinner, it will be a sit down, five table, knife and fork buffet before we go to the casino that will be set up in the ballroom. When we had the single table for twenty-four, I found that we no longer had the full set of Minton. We are also a few knives and forks short from the Asprey. I am sure they go out in the bin bags. We will have to use the Spode and you will have to dig out the 'Oneida.'"

"When is this event to take place ma'am?"

"A week on Saturday, That gives us ten days, plenty of time to get it all set up. Are you alright with that Sam?" As he replied, almost automatically, "Yes of course, Ma'am," he could not stop himself from asking, "but ma'am, will anyone want to, or be able to come to your gambling den at such short notice. You only put out your flyer, I mean elegant card, a few days ago."

"Oh don't be such a patch of mildew Sam. We are already over-subscribed. To be fair, I have had to draw names out of a hat, although I admit, I did cheat a bit to get the balance right."

The 'Monte Carlo and Bust' event went well. To Tristan's surprise, he enjoyed the evening as it proved to be full of laughter and good humour.

He worked smoothly with the invaluable Mary and Jennifer Johnson-Jackson, who had begged to come to help, also to learn.

The ladies, none of whom was younger than their early fifties had surpassed themselves, some wore empire style dresses, others with cut away cleavage, all seemingly determined to at least match, or possibly outdo the busty young film stars they had seen in magazines and on the television.

The Guests called for the chef and gave Antonin an ovation, to compliment him on his choice of menu in addition to the superbly presented meal. Unlike the previous dinner, the ladies retired after the meal, to leave the men to their Port, Madeira and cigars. However, when they were all together again in the ball room, an elegant man, who must have been the oldest guest, gave a witty toast to their hostess.

He thanked her for her sublime idea to bring back, for them all, a style, a Joie de Vivre that many around the table had thought gone forever. Tristan later learned that he was a retired Air Marshal with a distinguished war-record.

The gambling on the casino games had been fun. Because it did not involve any money, most of the guests made reckless bets which soon lost them all their chips, leaving them to follow the fortunes of the few diehards with serious intent. Tristan guessed that those still in the game had real money side bets that rested on the outcome. Midge, as Patron of Old Sloane's Re-united presented a silver framed photograph of the white dressed debutants at the Queen Charlottes Ball held in 1927 as the prize for the most successful lady. She gave as the prize for the most successful gentleman gambler, a dance card from the same ball. On the back of the card, many young gentlemen had put their name. Her choice of prizes caused general excitement because some of the guests were able to point out mothers or aunts in the photograph as well as the signature of fathers, uncles and cousins on the dance card. It also caused a moment's sadness when the Air Marshall, and some of the older guests, pointed out the names of those young men who died, while on active service, during the Second World War.

Just before two in the morning, the shadow minister, he who Lady Margaret had called Mr. Toad, called the evening to a close with a short speech.

"Members of the Old Sloans Club, it is time to go home. I must remind you that your invitations clearly stated, 'Mobility scooters at two.' For those of you who are about my age, Matron will be wondering how you got out. For the younger ones amongst us, your grown up children, still at home, will lie in bed worrying until they hear you fumble with the front door keys. If we linger, the magic dust might blow away, the dust that Midge used to take us to Monte Carlo, and back in time, to when men were gentle and women were ladies. Away with you, until Midge finds for us another idea, another way to turn back the clocks."

By the time the last guest departed, after the thanks, fair wells, handshakes, and exchange of cards had finished, the clock had past three a.m. Tristan did not feel tired, nor in need of a drink, or cigarette.

Midge began to clear glasses before Mary, her companion maid, rebuked her. "Madam' it's home time for us. You have promised the vicar to read the lesson tomorrow. Do not forget it is the Remembrance Service. I have kept Mr. Drummond in the kitchen with bribes of left over lobsters. His pumpkin Daimler awaits. If we go on keeping late hours, people will think that we are no better than we ought to be."

Settled, comfortable in his bed, in his cosy room in Erskin House, Mayfair, London, Tristan knew that he was not only well looked after, he had met people who accepted him as a friend. He promised himself that he would take flowers to Elizabeth and John at the Grassington, a haven during his early troubled weeks back in the smoke. He would have to admit that although not yet Lord Mayor of London, he was at least a citizen with a fixed abode and a good address. He wanted to show them the photograph he had cut from one of the Sunday papers, the one that showed Lady Margaret on his arm, with Mr. Drummond beside the Bentley in the background. He thought of Arthur, Percival and Geraint. He remembered the pledge they made as Grey Haired Knights to put aside old age, and to seek and find adventure, before returning to Scagill on the Saturday after the next summer solstice to tell true tales of their quest. For the first time in his life, Tristan's thoughts turned to prayer.

He prayed, not knowing to whom, that they would all return safe in both mind and body. He thought of the Reverend Branwell Evans, Harry's younger brother and wondered if Branwell's prayers had brought him to Retreads and to all that had followed.

That night Tristan dreamt that he felt safe as he swam in a warm tropic sea, until a cold-eyed great white shark circled round him. Terror gripped him when it turned and swam deep under him, ready to rise vertically to shred his body with its many rows of teeth.

His dream changed to the strange man who had directed him to Branwell's church and of the equally strange man who had prophesized that his fortune would turn only when he had become destitute. His dream changed again to the weird stranger who had knocked over and rearranged the magazines in the barbers shop and later distracted him to cause him to trip over the A frame that advertised Rose for second hand clothes.

He woke with a start, covered in cold sweat, when the three strange men fused into one blinding light in the shape of a sword.

Awake early, Tristan decided that his role as a Gentleman's gentleman, or Lady's gentleman, as he had become, would not be enough of a tale to tell at the reunion of the Grey Haired Knights. He made a decision that from this day forward, he would begin his quest in earnest, to bring down the grey complexioned, cold-eyed, corrupt barman at the Keeble Hotel, one he knew as Charles Lucas Prescott.

Chapter 19

Tristan had no doubt that his decision to bring Charles Lucas Prescott to justice would be difficult. He knew Prescott to be a liar, a cheat, a confidence trickster, a practised professional deceiver who used both sleight of hand and flattery to rob innocent people.

He also knew that the management of the Keeble Hotel, at senior level, protected and favoured him because he had a loyal following of gullible customers. They had even named the bar where he worked as 'Charles's Bar'.

Throughout the morning, Tristan worried that he had no idea of how, when or where to start on his chosen quest.

When prompted by Arthur Thomas to seek a worthy quest, he had thought about the legends of the Knights of King Arthur's Round Table. Most legends told of a thick forest of thorns that an errant knight had to penetrate before they could challenge a false knight, or rescue a fair maiden.

He realised that the managers of the Keeble Hotel were the thorns that would make it difficult to bring down Prescott. Whether they took a percentage of Prescott's thefts, or simply ignored his thieving to have a quiet life, he did not know. One minor obstacle came to mind straight away. Florence from Human Resources had been more than pleased to tell him that company rules excluded sacked employees from the hotel for a period of six months. However, he assumed that the ban would not be a major problem, as few Keeble staff had met him, except for the bad tempered Russell Cunningham, to whom he had reported Prescott's theft, Ms. Andrews the Night Manager and the cold-blooded Prescott.

They were the razor wire, the modern thorns through which he would have to cut. He felt stymied.

He had no evidence to take to the police, nor could he approach the hotel's security force. He did not know how far the web of corruption spread. His only certainty was that to make progress with his quest he needed help.

Once again, Tristan decided to visit his mentor, Harry Evans, to ask him for ideas.

Antonin, whom Erskin-Powell had cleared as a routine substitute for Erskin House insurance cover, agreed to be resident for the rest of the day.

Tristan took the opportunity to exercise the Mulliner Bentley. Every time he drove the car, it pleased him that many drivers paid it due deference, when they gave way courteously, or waived him through, just as they had when he drove the open tourer to Cowdray Park.

On his way to Retreads, just because he could, Tristan stopped at a delicatessen to buy a large tin of chocolate biscuits for the Retreads guests. He also bought a packet of fig rolls for Harry, and two jars of Sauerkraut for Stan.

Harry Evans, Master of Retreads, who had insisted that Tristan keep a key to the little side door of the converted chapel, put the kettle on when he heard Tristan call out, "It's only me."

"Now Tristan," Harry sang out in his exaggerated Welsh valley voice from his flat on the balcony, "How many times do I have to remind you never to say 'Only me'? Be up-front, open hearted, call out 'It's me'. Sing it out, it cheers people no end. That dull word 'Only' takes everyone down a peg or two. It is as bad as when I ask people how they are, when and they reply, 'Not too bad'. Even if their bunions have burst or their piles pop out like grapeshot, their reply should be 'Champion marvellous'. Like my old dad used to, though he was crippled with arthritis and he had the coal on his lungs."

When Tristan gave Harry the biscuits, he became effusive with his thanks, "Oh, thank you Butty Bach, the fig roles cheer me, because they remind me of Figgy Bentley, bless his heart and wallet. He brought me the auction catalogue the other day; the one lists our chairs with the table as the next lot. They must expect some interest because they have included a picture of the chairs. We will be rated five stars for accommodation when we get the job done. Sit down before you tell me why you are here, bearing gifts. You have not gone Greek on me have you?"

Tristan admitted, "Well the biscuits could be construed as a bribe. I want the help of your polymath brain with a plan I do not have. You know that I do not have enough to do at Erskin House to keep a lead toy soldier occupied. Lady Margaret, with Jenny's help, organises the parties, Antonin cooks, the cleaners clean. I twiddle my thumbs."

"I have already told you how I am committed to do at least one good deed to justify my place at the round table with my friends, Arthur, Percival and Geraint, the 'Grey Haired Knights' of Scagill. I must do this before our reunion. It will be enough if I can bring to justice the thieving magpie Prescott. The dyed black haired, white coated, red bow tied, baggy trousered, mandarin slippered barman, who conspired to get me sacked from the Keeble. That Harry is my Bowlderised description of Prescott. I use a cruder lexicon when thinking about him, even though, after various further trials, together with many tiresome tribulations it brought me to Retreads. You have warned me that revenge is an ugly weapon; nevertheless, I think that someone should bring Prescott to the attention of the law. I want more than his collar felt. I want him arrested, handcuffed, locked up, tried, condemned and incarcered for a long time. I do not want him to have a stash of cash ready for him when he gets out. In Arthurian questing terms, I want him cast into a dark damp dungeon. I am sure that he will have other scams, in addition to his penchant to short change and over charge. I don't know how, when, or where to start. I do know of three reasons that make it difficult. One; as an ex-employee, I am banned from the Keeble, two, Prescott would recognise me even if I disguised myself in Arab clothes or dressed in drag, three, I do not know who else is involved in his racket, or how far up the management tree the poison ivy climbs."

As Harry Evans, shuffled round the tiny kitchen of his quarters he said, "Well Tristan, my kitchen is too small to dance, so if you will sit down, as I asked, I will be able to finish that pot of tea I started when I heard your welcome, though down beat call. If you are good, you may have a biscuit from the big tin. What you hope to do, without any idea how to do it, sounds to me like a job for the Retread's Old Boys Association. The task requires espionage, followed by action. Espionage has three phases, observation, penetration, and recognition. Only when we have completed all three phases will we be able to plan what action to take. However, to help us, we can call on all sorts of skills, capabilities and experience. Retreads' Old Boys Association is a network of men who help us or who have helped us in the past, or who have been guests of Retreads. They are a useful mix, clerics, artists, artistes, artisans, authors, politicians, professionals, and technicians. Age dictates that the manual labourers are few, however our friends at the Sally Al can usually find for us men who will to do any heavy work that we may require."

After Harry settled himself comfortably in his best chair and dunked a second biscuit in his tea, he sat brooding, quietly. Tristan hoped that he might be hatching a plan. Suddenly, in a voice like a Welsh mining valley Baptist Minister, full of pulpit fervour, Harry declaimed, "First things first Sir Tristan; we must establish that your earlier intervention in Prescott's affairs has not made him repent of his evil deeds. We must find out if he is still practicing his sleight of hand to rob the rich, not to give to the poor, but to build up his pension pot."

He calmed down to add ruefully, "We will need a fist full of ready cash to solve that one boyo. Perhaps Midge will include the Keeble in one of her madcap ventures. Motorcar treasure hunts were popular in the old days with the clues scattered around the fashionable watering holes of the day. If she can arrange such a treasure hunt, with the treasure at the Keeble, it should do the trick. In my office next door, I keep a card index system that helps me find the right man for almost any job. I will run through it this afternoon. We will need someone to fill any vacancy that may come up in the Keeble's cash control department. With the high staff turnover in the hotel industry, we should not have long to wait."

Tristan recognised Harry Evens as a tactical, practical, pragmatic and tactful thinker. Throughout his well thought out response to Tristan's request for help, he had never used the word 'you', only 'we'.

"Thank you Harry, why did I not think about a treasure hunt, or to infiltrate a mole to dig in that heap of iniquity? For hours, I searched my mind for ideas, however I found nothing; obviously, there is nothing there to find. You came up with good ideas, instantly, as though your profession has been, or perhaps still is, 'Spy Master'. One day I will get your life story out of you, even if I have to tie you to a chair, play loud pop music, and use bright lights followed by the truth drug. However, right now, I had better get back to Erskin House to resume my toy lead soldier duties. I shall call Lady Margaret to put your idea to her. Thank you again Harry, you are a wonder."

Soon after he got back, Tristan rang to speak to Lady Margaret. After an exchange of pleasantries with Mary, her maid companion, Midge answered from another extension. "Good afternoon Sam, have you burnt the house down, crashed the Bentley, or have you called to tell me you have repelled boarders with a round of grapeshot."

"Sadly no ma'am," Tristan replied, "However, I wonder if perhaps you might come round next time Jenny is here, to consider an idea Harry Evans has given me." Immediately the reply came, "Oh no, that won't do at all, not if it is an idea Harry Evans has given you, it can't wait that long. I will pick Jenny up on my way. Put the kettle on, this sounds fun." She switched off her phone without a chance for Tristan to reply.

Forty minutes later, two pairs of high heels tapped across the hall on the way to his pantry. The two ladies, one young, the other old enough to be her grandmother, were both beautiful in the expectation of their generation. They were also obviously happy in each other's company.

Before Tristan could welcome them, Lady Margaret took charge, "Have you not brewed the tea yet, do we girls have to do everything in this house. Jenny, tell the man to sit down to watch how we girls do the job properly. Good afternoon Sam, I am sorry to have taken so long. When I called to pick up Jenny she had just returned from the modern day sweatshop; she calls it the gym. She looked a sight in what they call tracksuit and trainers. I shall have to get her membership of the Sloan Gardens Riding Stables. Riding is the only suitable exercise for a girl. Hard-hat, jacket jodhpurs from Dege and Skinner with riding boots from James Taylor, so much more attractive, don't you think? Now Sam what is this idea that Harry has given you?"

Tristan decided that he must first tell the ladies that it was all a plan to catch a thief.

He explained how he had seen Charles Lucas Prescott palm a Twenty-Pound note to short change a customer and that when he had reported the theft to the hotel management; they had sacked him not Prescott. He asked them to help to collect evidence to give to the police, so that they could charge Prescott with theft and any other connected misdemeanour, together with any Keeble staff involved. Only then, did Tristan tell them about Harry's idea of a treasure hunt around what remained of the fashionable watering holes of the days of debutants and their 'delights' to finish in Charles's bar at the Keeble.

As always enthusiastic, Jenny said, "I think that I have seen a sheet of treasure hunt clues in Grandpapa's scrap book. It might be a bit more difficult than in the old days when cars were easier to park and when there were no controlled zones or drink drive laws. We will have to make the competition a quiz with clues hidden in each place we visit. A clue solved will score one point. There will be a bonus point for the first team to solve all clues in each destination. The last clue at each stop must be the most difficult, as it will reveal the next venue. The other teams will have to follow immediately, even if they have not solved all the clues. That will allow us use a coach to take a planned route. It will keep us all together. If I get on the phone tomorrow, I am sure I can fill a twenty-four seat luxury coach for next Thursday evening."

Lady Margaret picked up Jenny's enthusiasm.

"We can start here with stirrup cups and hors d'œuvres. When someone solves the first destination clue, we can all set off on a peripatetic supper with successive courses at four different old venue favourites, before we finish at the Keeble for coffee, liqueurs and the presentation of prizes. Including the start, here at Erskin House that will make six venues in all. We must include 'the Ivy because the destination clue could be 'A phonetic American after an early Italian four'. If we have four clues in each of the six places, if we add the five points for the venue clues, it will give us a maximum twenty-nine points. It should be enough to find a clear winner. It will be fun. I will help Jenny to arrange the venues and menus. Sam you can arrange the coach. Well that's all settled, isn't it?"

Tristan could not resist asking, "How does 'A phonetic American after an early Italian four' lead us to the Ivy." Jenny gave him the answer almost immediately, "Simple, Y is Yankee in the phonetic alphabet and IV is four in Roman numerals."

Tristan wished he had not asked. He pressed on, because he wanted to make sure that the main purpose of the event would be to catch a thief.

"I think that all the ideas are sound ma'am, except that we must not assume too much. You see, Harry thinks that the first thing we must do is to make sure that Prescott is still on the fiddle. That will mean someone will have to pay using twenty pound notes, not their debit card, though as I think about it, debit or credit cards probably provide a way for him to leach out more money than he should from customer's bank accounts."

Midge noticed that Tristan's reply had been unusually thoughtful. "Sam, do you really know the man that well?"

"No, I do not ma'am, although I knew him well enough, a long time ago. I was a barman on a Caribbean Cruise liner when the Chief Purser put him ashore for the same sort of theft. He is an insidious deceiver, who uses prestidigitation in evil ways. The Magic Circle would not let him through the door. Because the Purser promoted me to take his place, he vowed to hold his grudge against me, for however long it took to get back at me."

Tristan also had in mind, that he had another threat of revenge against him, still pending. A threat issued more recently by the Spitewinter woman. She had promised to wreck a savage revenge on him, through her friends who, 'Would cut you for a drink, break your legs for a joint, or better still, your neck for a line'.

"This is what we shall do," Midge decided, "Tomorrow we shall be ladies who lunch. We shall take our custom to Charles bar for pre-lunch drinks before we move on to lunch at the Savoy Grill. I shall take my mother's old stick to play the part of an absent-minded old lady. I shall pay for the drinks using my debit card to find out if he fiddles with people's plastic as well as their pocket money. Jenny, who is good with figures, must verify the bill. Marys will be observer to watch your Mr. Prescott. She will see if he has any other tricks up his sleeve. We will soon have him checked out. After our lunch we will ring Coutts when we get home, to determine whether or not he has added a little earner to my card."

Tristan forgot himself; he felt so pleased that he flustered, "I am sorry to cause you so much trouble Midge, I beg your pardon ma'am, sorry Lady Margaret, but I really am most grateful." Intrigued with the idea of being a real private detective Midge said, "Don't be obsequious Sam, I have told you before, I am not a small fishing smack. I shall be Detective Inspector Midge. Harry's idea could not be more exciting. Tomorrow afternoon we will come back here, with our dossier, that is what detectives build up, is it not? Come along Jenny, bye Sam." The ladies left, arm in arm.

The next day, while he waited for the return of the lady detectives, Tristan could not settle to read any of the books in the library, an occupation he had come to enjoy during his quiet days spent as guardian of the house. He felt a rush of colour to his face when he heard the three ladies come into the house.

The noise resembled a crowd of women charging through the doors on the first day of a Harrods sale. Even before they came into the library, Midge piped out, "We got him; he is a scoundrel." Finally, they came to rest, Lady Margaret in her favourite chair, Mary stood behind her, with Jenny on the floor, at her feet, curled like a faithful Labrador.

"You were right Sam," Midge said, "Do you know he swindled me out of almost five pounds! Clever detective Jenny, with her eye for figures, spotted that he had charged for olives that we did not have. Clever Chief Detective Inspector Midge found three unaccounted for pounds taken on my debit card. He is truly bad, a corrupt unctuous ingrate. He has prison pallor; his fingers are nicotine stained." She shot her neck up to full extension, to add triumphantly, "That is not all, our even better Detective Superintendent Mary, the observer, is sure that my card transaction did not go to the Keeble Hotel's bank account."

Taken aback, Tristan asked, "How did he do that?" Mary explained, "Prescott is clever, he is ahead of the game. He has his own 'Blue Tooth' credit/debit card terminal. He used it twice, both times for small amounts, once when he took a card payment from an elderly man who was busy attending to his even older wife in a wheelchair, the second time, when he took payment from Lady Margaret. He has a poacher's pocket in his barman's coat. All the time we were there, he ingratiated himself with gullible customers; it sickened me to have to watch him. I would not have done so, if Lady Margaret had not nominated me as 'Observer', because I won an 'Observer' badge when I was a Girl Guide. He has his own what they call a Blue Tooth P.D.Q. card-reading machine. I am sure that my sister uses one of the same make in her restaurant. It is blue coloured and smaller than the larger black Keeble Hotel machine. He only used his P.D.Q. machine to take money from the old man and Lady Margaret. He used the Keeble machine for all other transactions. The receipt printed out from that hand held card gizmo that he used to take money from Lady Margaret was headed, 'Keebel's'. I managed to pick up a discarded receipt from the black gizmo. It was headed 'The Keeble Hotel'. I don't think that one in ten thousand of the people who bother to check their bank statements would notice that their payment went to 'Keebel's' not to the 'The Keeble Hotel'. Lady Margaret said, "My man at Coutts has confirmed that the bank has debited my account with the full amount shown on my receipt. He hopes that, despite the data protection act, he will be able to verify that the money did not go to the Keeble Hotel's bank account."

Tristan felt elated, although at the same time frustrated, "Oh! Well done you clever ladies, you have exceeded all expectations, but I feel left out of it. You three have done it all, while I have been stuck here utterly useless." Jenny said, "Sam, you must not think like that. Think of yourself in the role of 'M' top spy controller. We girls just do the leg work in your master plan."

Midge returned to the Old Sloan's part in the business, to bring Prescott to book. It delighted her that she could to tell Tristan that Jenny had taken less than an hour to fill the coach that she hoped he had remembered to order.

She said, "The pickup point is here. We will come back here with the key players, to debrief, after I have presented the prizes at in Charles's bar. The Air Marshall and Mr. Cooper, my financial advisor from Coutts, will each pay half of the bill. It will be more than a hundred pounds. They will both pay with used twenty-pound notes, the numbers of which they will keep on record. They will bring back the bill, together with whatever change they get, for forensic examination. My man at Coutts thinks that the change may well contain forged notes. The Mint, Scotland Yard, and the Treasury people believe that criminal gangs use London Hotels to get forged notes into circulation because hotel guests disperse so rapidly across the counties with many leaving the country within hours of paying their bill. Bureau de Change on both sides of the Atlantic and at ferry terminals on both sides of the channel have recently found more than the usual number of forged notes. He has told me that some people who work in currency exchanges in the Euro Zone would not know the difference between our debased British Twenty-Pound note or a soap coupon."

On the day after the lady detectives' triumph, Tristan went to see Harry at Retreads to tell him about their success. He planned to drive the Mulliner Bentley, to arrive middle morning, when all the Retread chores would be done. When he let himself in to the old hall, he found Harry in his little upstairs office, huddled over an electric fire, wrapped in his Paisley dressing gown, his hands wrapped around a cup of tea.

"What time do you have to be back?" were Tristan's first words. "Back from where you cheeky ill-mannered boy, am I so old that I don't get a polite, 'Good morning'." Harry replied, a bit grumpily. Tristan felt excited by what he said next, "Back from wherever you would like to go today, in the nice big motor car. You never seem to get out of these four walls. A breath of fresh air would do you no harm at all. Stan has agreed to look after the guests this evening. He comes off shift at three. I have the house covered; Antonin needs a quiet night in, so no excuses."

"I can't possibly, how can I it's," then Harry's face broke into one of his Sunday best smiles. He resumed happily, "Give me five minutes Boyo, then I will be ready. I'm sorry I can't go halves on the petrol, I am right out of pocket money."

It took a little more than the promised five minutes before Harry managed to be ready because he had to write many notes to Stan; however, the two were in the car at eleven, heading, at Harry's suggestion, to Eastbourne and Beachy Head. On the way, Tristan told Harry about the lady detectives' success in exposing Prescott as an even bigger scoundrel than he had thought him to be.

When he told Harry about the private Blue Tooth P.D.Q. card reader, it surprised him that he did not react, as he would have expected. He went very quiet, with his eyes closed. After several minutes Tristan asked, "What is it Harry? I can tell that you are not just taking one of your Churchill moments."

"Quite right," Harry replied, "I have been thinking, now I have thought, moreover, as you would expect, I Harry Evans, mystic of Merthyr, have a plan, both cunning and credible. The newspapers tell us that asset recovery from convicted criminal masterminds is hopelessly inefficient. The cunning bit of my plan is that we must strip this man Prescott, this evil piece of callous selfishness, bare of all his assets before we alert the police. The credible bit is that I know a man who can do it. How about I ask him to hack into his funny little gizmo card reader, what you called a 'Blue Tooth'. Our man can drill into the root canal, to draw out all that lies behind it. By that, I mean transfer all the money in his account to the account of Her Majesties Treasury. It will not return the money he stole from the Keeble Hotel or the customers he overcharged, but he will never be able to get it back. Even credited to our profligate government, it will do more good in the Treasury than it would if left with him. Whichever bank he has used to stash his nest egg; it will not try to recover the money from the Treasury. If they did, they might well be prosecuted under the laws that prevent them from dealing with money launderers or those who deal in stolen goods."

"Harry, you are worth pound notes you are." Tristan said, "Dammed right I am," Harry said with emphasis, "Except they don't print pound notes anymore, not since 1988, so by implication you have just told me that I am both out of date, and worthless. However, I have just remembered there is a nice pub on the Pantiles in Tunbridge Wells. To absolve your sins, you may take me there and buy me a pork pie and a pint; Foot down boyo, we are clear of the smoke."

On the road home, after the two friends had spent a happy day together, Harry had a broader smile than ever. "A great idea you had boyo, even better than the fig roll biscuits you gave me the other day, though they were nice. I have written rude messages in the beach pebbles with my stick, paddled in the sea with my trousers rolled up to frighten the old ladies with my knotted varicose veins. I have eaten an ice cream cornet. Like fish and chips, they taste better, al fresco, by the sea. Like blind Gloucester, I stood high on a cliff top. I heard both the sea and the lark ascending. Up there, the sweet smell of seaweed super charged the breeze with ozone. It made it all so much more beneficial than the air that stales in the canyon streets of London." Before they reached East Grinstead Harry was asleep, still with a smile across his deep lined face.

Because he could not take part, Tristan had been anxious during all of the day of the peripatetic quiz. Antonin provided trays of excellent hors d'œuvres for the early guests to eat, while they waited for the party to be complete.

Jenny made sure that she separated the guests into six teams of four, so that no one would feel embarrassed if they did not know the answer to some or all of the questions set by her Grandpapa.

A few of the guests were particularly excited because they had never been on a bus or a motor coach, let alone a coach trip. Tristan, had he not given up even the odd bet, would have put pounds to win on the team with Lady Margaret, Mary her companion maid, the Air Marshall and the Manager from Coutts.

As Jenny called on the guests to embark on the mystery tour, she gave each team a note pad, a pencil and each team member a coloured wristband to wear as their team colours. As she understood Tristan's concern, Midge put a hand on his arm to say, "Be patient Sam, we will bring you back the evidence you need, together with a piece of cake and a balloon from the party."

It was after midnight when the five key players arrived back at Erskin House. The other guests had left the party after Lady Margaret had presented the prizes at the Keeble. "We won," trilled Lady Margaret "I had to ask the Air Marshall to auction my prize, so to be fair, we all put our prizes up for auction in aid of Retreads. Do you know, we got over five hundred pounds. The white beaded purse bag I had at my coming out ball went for over two hundred.

Now, while Jenny gets any drinks you may want, we will ask Mr. Cooper to have a look at what that barman, Charles Lucas Prescott gave us as change from our bill. As arranged, he and the Air-Marshal each paid half the cost in used twenty-pound notes."

As expected of a banker, Mr. Cooper proved to be very business-like. "Well the rogue, for rogue he is, had itemised the bill. The addition was correct. It did however include an un-announced fifteen percent service charge. When I checked it against the drinks that our guests ordered, there were twenty-eight drinks on the list. Jenny assures me that she did not order a drink. She also confirmed that no one bought one for her. I checked with everyone before they left. Only two guests had a second drink. That made only twenty-six drinks ordered. Clearly, he had charged for two drinks that our party did not have. In my opinion, all drinks in that bar are overpriced. He only has a minimum number of drink prices on display, all in very small print. They are sufficient to satisfy the regulations required by Trading Standards, but no more. It is not possible to argue against what he charges for drinks that are not on the list, or for any mixed drinks such as cocktails. I shall continue to use my golf club bar as my watering hole."

Now the result; we are ten pound exactly down in the change given to the Air Marshall. Sorry Sir, you must have looked the most gullible." This jibe got a good laugh at the Air Marshall's expense; however, Mr. Cooper had engineered a bigger laugh against himself. To finish his debrief, he said with a flourish. "However, he chose me as the Charlie on whom to stick a forged ten-pound note."

Chapter 20

The evidence found by the lady detectives that proved that Charles Lucas Prescott had not given up his thieving ways cleared the way for Tristan's revenge, the resumption of his quest to put a wrong to rights.

A tale he could tell at the Grey Haired Knights reunion. It did not occur to him that to tangle with Prescott might put him in danger. He did not want to bring him before the courts merely on charges of theft that would get him no more than minor retribution; perhaps not even dismissal from his well paid job.

He determined to press Harry to call in a favour from the expert computer hacker to make Prescott penniless. Tristan realised that the man would have to do it before the Police, the Crown Prosecution Service, or the moribund Asset Recovery Agency, all ham strung by European human rights legislation, could frustrate his efforts.

To help him find out whether Prescott acted alone, or whether senior managers at the Keeble were involved Tristan persuade Mr. Cooper to ignore his Banker's duty to disclose that Prescott had included a forged ten-pound note with his change. Mr. Cooper also agreed that Tristan could keep the forged note.

The condition of the note intrigued Tristan. It did not feel in mint condition, or look quite new; it was limp, worn out. A numismatist would hardly give face value for it, because it appeared to have been in circulation for a long time. The feel of the note made Tristan think that Prescott might only be engaged to fence confiscated forged notes that some felonious gang had stolen from the Bank of England, before the Bank had burnt them as scrap.

However, he felt it to be more likely that the forged notes had been artificially aged, in the way that forgers fake their paintings to match the natural aging of old masters they copy, or counterfeit. Tristan realised that such apparently old notes would not be scrutinised, as people would be confident that age gave them provenance. He also thought that if Ms. Andrews, the Keeble's Night Manager, could not put any forged notes into circulation through Prescott's till, she could easily bank them.

Dispersed within counted bundles of genuine bank notes, the cashiers at the hotel's bank would fail to spot the notes as forgeries, although the automatic machine counters might reject the notes as too old and mark them for destruction. Once destroyed any trace back to the forgers would be lost.

Because Lady Margaret and Jenny were busy with plans for a February event, to compensate for the ladies challenged by the 'Monte Carlo and Bust' party, Tristan had time on his hands.

"No thank you Sam, this is girl fun," the ladies told him, whenever he asked if he could help. "No, not until you have put that horrid barman where he belongs, behind prison bars, not cocktail bars."

Not wanted at Erskin House, Tristan chose to retreat to Retreads. He arrived just after ten, in time to disturb Harry and Stan, who shared the newspaper, while they eat breakfast.

Harry's grin of welcome was broad. "Pull up a chair Sir Tristan, Knight Errant. Find for yourself a cup with a saucer to match. In the pot, there is tea that gruntles the disgruntled, in the jug, there is milk to restore the weary body, in the bowl there is sugar to sweeten the sour temper. Stan takes his time over breakfast, porridge, half a dozen eggs, a pound of bacon, and two full slices of fried bread with tomatoes.

That is before he starts on his 'Continental' with cheese, polony, spek, black bread, cold toast and croissants. It is a good job he brings his own, if he didn't, I could not keep him for a week, let alone a fortnight."

Stan pushed his chair before he thumped his huge fist on the table. "Hello Angol; that might last me until elevenses."

Holding the forged note between his thumb and forefinger Tristan waved it in front of Harry. "Lady Margaret's treasure hunt did the job. The purse and pocket picker prestidigitator Prescott not only charged for drinks we did not have, he also short-changed the Air Vice-Marshall. Not content with that, he passed this dud ten-pound note in the change he gave to Mr. Cooper, the banker from Coutts."

After Harry took the note from Tristan, he carefully put it on the table, before he pulled out his wallet, to lay a good note alongside it, for comparison.

When he showed his open empty wallet to Tristan, his expression would have melted Pharaoh's hardened heart. He followed two short coughs with a "hum" a "ha," and again a "hum", before he asked meekly, "You don't happen to have a ready on you do you Tristan. I forgot, I had to sub a couple of the guests this morning, you know how it is; they are run down, as well as worn out by bad habits, however too young for free prescriptions. Tristan boyo, do you think you could find for us a pharmacy, one that might let us have pills, potions, laxatives, creams, liniments, cold cures, cough mixtures, expectorants, knee bandages and trusses on the same terms that you arranged with the butcher, the allotment holder and the sous chef of that great hotel where you found a job for Stan?"

"You forgot corn plasters," Tristan said, as he laid a clean ten-pound note alongside the forgery. "What do you think Harry; a bit clever of them to age them isn't it? I would never have thought of it."

Harry answered, "No, you wouldn't Tristan. You are an amateur in these things. The people that we must bring to heel are professionals. Nevertheless, sometimes a good amateur can best a professional. That is if he has a good coach and boxes clever. The man I mentioned who might be able to do the root canal work on Prescott's ATM card reader is due to call on me this afternoon. He is a good lad, a genuine supporter of Retreads. He did do 'time'. He hacked into government computers, not to steal money, but to make a good income by selling advance copies of No 10's confidential reports and Number 11's budgets to lazy journalists. The government became so fed up with him that they employ him to advise them on the latest breaches in their security. Retreads looked after him for some months when he first came out of prison: it had done him great harm."

With his motivation to bring Prescott to book equal to Tristan's, Harry Evans spoke in full flow. In such a mood, his Welsh tones rang out as an oration rather than conversation, or discussion.

"Tristan," he said, "Do you remember the three pillars of espionage I told you about. First is observation, next penetration, followed by recognition of fact. We must complete all three before we take any action. You have been successful with the first, observation, however there is much still to do before we will be able to formulate our plan of action. If we are to succeed, the second stage, penetration, is vital. With this part of our plan, we come up against some little local difficulties. You cannot go in Tristan, not even in disguise. Stan is too busy, besides he is too conspicuous. I might get in once or twice, if I did nothing, however I would become nosy. Their security people would rumble me. They would evict me as a dosser, without recourse to arbitration. I have noticed recently that some of our new arrivals are in better condition and are better dressed than I am. "

"My card index has not come up with anyone from the Retreads Old Boy fraternity who might take on the job of Night

Cash Controller at the Keeble, when it becomes vacant, as it surely will. Even if do put someone in place, his inside information will only tell us about the cash fiddles. Unless we get lucky, we will have to 'Turn' one of Prescott's partners in crime to find out about the forged notes. I cannot think of how we might apply sufficient torque to turn any of those who are involved. Both MI5 and MI6 use money, shed loads of it, or they employ men or women with deviant sexual proclivity. We do not have any or either of those, so maybe that is a non-starter. However, in the case of Charles Lucas Prescott, before we take any overt action, I recommend we should plan for sequestration before incarceration. Sequestration has such a fine ring to it. Observation has revealed that there is rampant unlawful activity at the Keeble. Such wicked ways must be rooted out."

Both Tristan and Stan loved to listen to the old man when he declaimed like a Welsh non-conformist minister preaching from his pulpit in a Welsh coal mining village chapel. His sermons were never drear.

They were always an Easter Sunday morning sermon, full of hope. Tristan mimicked Harry's accent, "Well butty, if the Welsh Bard who daily dresses like the last druid does not have a plan, I had better get back to my abode to ring Lady Margaret; she will want to be involved. Moreover, she has a way of twisting the arm of the right people to get what she wants; she does not need to turn them."

Stan who also wanted to be involved put both of his massive hands on the stainless steel table to push himself to his feet. It groaned under his weight. "I'll come with you," he said, "I want a word with Antonin about a bigos I have in hand."

When Tristan phoned Lady Margaret to tell her about Harry's idea to send someone to penetrate the Keeble's accounts department, she understood how important it would be to find out how far the creeping vine of corruption spread into the canopy of the management tree.

Before she ended the call she asked, "Sam, will you be at home to callers this evening? If you are, I shall come round for supper; seven thirty for eight, it will give Antonin something useful to do. Please ask him to prepare a light super, not dinner, for four, you, me, plus two guests. For goodness sake Sam, don't wear your pinstripes."

Later that day, Lady Margaret, accompanied by Jenny, arrived with a young man he did not recognize. Lady Margaret, who had used her key, started to talk as soon as she was inside the door.

"Sam, this young man is William Erskin-Powell, my great nephew. I introduced them to each other on the way here, since when Jenny has become silent pale and interesting. William has gone the other way. He has become garrulous, and developed a nervous tick. However, unlike many young men of his age, he has not wasted his early years. He has just come down from Cambridge with a double first, Economics with Divinity. It should set him on course to become Governor of the Bank of England or the Archbishop of Canterbury. Nevertheless, he has decided on the Army. At present, he twiddles his thumbs until he goes to Sandhurst with the September intake. While we have supper, you can tell William about the dreadful people who work at the Keeble. When the opportunity comes, if he can get appointed to do that dreadful night job you did, he will be our spy, it will only take a couple of weeks for a young man of his talent to add a full chapter to our detective dossier."

Tristan told his story, as best he could, despite many interruptions from the others. When William said that he would like to have a go at espionage, Jenny spoke for the first time that evening, just the one word, "Super," but her eyes, blushes and shy glances at William spoke volumes.

Only seven days later, William Erskin-Powell arrived at Erskin House with an appointment card that required him to attend for interview at eight p.m., that evening, to see Ms. Andrews, the Keeble's Night Manager. William told Tristan that he had called at the Employment Office nearest to the Keeble each weekday since the supper party. This day, the computer displayed a vacancy for the job that Tristan had held briefly. William asked excitedly, "Sam, I am sure to get the job, aren't I? Do you know, every time I have been to the employment office, I have seen similar night jobs offered by, oh, it must be a dozen hotels. What is the matter with the industry? I am not surprised there are so many vacancies. The pay is awful; the hours are even worse."

"You won't get the job if you act, speak or dress as you are at present. The woman that you are going to see," Tristan paused before he went on, "Well, put it this way, she is not quite wired up right; she is all DC. I am sure that she would much prefer a woman for the job. You must dress down; jeans, tee shirt, scruffy shoes. Whatever she asks, do not mention Cambridge, or admit to your degrees. You must act as though you don't care whether you get the job or not, however you must ask about staff accommodation. Tell her that you worked for a building society, but that you have had a row with your folks at home. Tell her that you need to get away. Tell Florence, the dreadful woman in the personnel department, that you will take the room, but do not tell her that you will not occupy it."

Tristan's advice astonished William, who said, "Well that is just about the dead opposite to what our careers master at school recommended when he told us how we should dress and conduct ourselves at interview. All he wanted us to apply for were estate management posts, if our parents were rich, the army for the well off, and teaching for those whose parents struggled with the fees. The church was his mandate for all junior siblings, rich or poor."

Later the same day, when the doorbell rang at about 10 pm, Tristan guessed it would be William. It pleased him that Jenny was with him. There was no need to ask; Jenny burst out, "Isn't William wonderful; he starts work tomorrow night. He is the new James Bond, although he is much better looking than Connery or Brosnan. No we won't come in; we just wanted you to know."

William finally got his word in, "Sam, please may I call tomorrow morning, about ten?" "Tristan happy for them both replied, "Yes William, well done lad, I will take you to meet a friend of mine who you will find a great help."

When Tristan waved, as he watched the couple almost skip back to William's racing green Morgan Roadster, his smile became serene, almost as good as Harry Evans's Sunday best.

Harry suggested that while William worked nights at the Keeble, he should use the bike Tristan had used, so that straight after work he could cycle to Retreads, to give his report, while he had breakfast. He also suggested that Tristan should be there to give advice on hotel procedure, organisation and hierarchy.

After his first shift, when William gave his report at Retreads, his description of the Night Manager, Ms. Andrews, matched Tristan's opinion perfectly.

He began, "That Andrews Woman is a tartar is she not. When I introduced myself, her opening remarks, that lacked a few aspirates, were a bit daunting, He mimicked her estuary accent, 'Where the ell ave you come from, some junior nick I suppose. The fings I av to put up wiv; I don't know why Florence agreed that I take you on. I shall be surprised if you last more than two nights.' She gave me a list of the tills to collect, in what order. She told me how to reconcile the money in the till with the till record. When I asked her what I should do if I found any discrepancies she almost bit off my head. She told me that I must only fill in the standard check sheets. She stressed that any errors or discrepancies were none of my business. The ratty woman told me, with some force, that the company had employed me to record, not to interpret, information. She threatened me with the sack if I spoke one word to anyone about such matters. Still, I should be grateful. If I can survive a fortnight with Ms. Andrews, I won't be frightened by the drill pigs at Sandhurst."

Harry, who had been most attentive, raised his great bushy eyebrows, "Well Tristan, I think that confirms your suspicion.

Ms. Misery Andrews is in on the rackets for sure, maybe even the boss, although we can't be sure yet." Tristan asked the inevitable question, "How did you get on with Prescott? William replied, "Oh, just as rude as Ms. Andrews. When I checked, both his tills were correct to the penny."

Tristan nodded, "They would be, it will be the same every night. It is a sure sign that he is on the fiddle."

Harry, who had been drilling soldiers round a boiled egg, looked up to say, "Stan will drive me to an early grave with his yield from the hotel kitchen. I am not supposed to eat eggs. Doc says they block up my arteries, but I believe breakfast starts the day properly. Anyway, doctors do not understand men of good conscience. I pray that my God will call me up while I sleep. A stroke will do. I don't want to suffer a painful heart attack or to go through the long trauma of Alzheimer's, the newly named although ancient disease."

Harry put the upturned empty eggshell back in the eggcup before he continued, "I have had a thought that it might be good idea to unsettle the villains while we have William on the inside. If we can disturb their equilibrium, they may start to make mistakes. I wonder what you think of my idea. We ask Lady Margaret to lend William some old ten-pound notes. He could keep his eye open to collect all the counterfeit notes he finds, and replace them with Lady Margaret's good ones. When he has collected ten or a dozen forgeries, he could report his find to Ms. Andrews. He could pretend that he had checked Prescott's till early, when Prescott was on a break, and found them in one of his tills. If Prescott is not immediately dismissed, we will know for certain that she is complicit in the forgery racket."

William asked, "How will I be able to spot the forged notes, if indeed there are any? Harry produced the forged note Tristan had left with him.

"Yesterday, I asked one of our old boys with a special interest in such matters to look it over for me. It did not take him too long to spot the deliberate mistake. Come; gather round, you must look close."

With a dramatic flourish, Harry produced from his dressing gown pocket a large ebony handled magnifying glass, with an engraved silver collar. He passed the glass to William, "Identification of the particular forged notes will not be difficult as I have been told how to do it. Whoever is the forger, he is brilliant. He is also vain. Vanity always seeks recognition. He has signed his work. Look carefully at the back of the note, down in the bottom right hand corner, where artists usually sign their work. See it, there, hidden amongst the fancy work. He has worked in the initials, WR inside a C. It would not be time wasted to check to see if the Keeble employs anyone with any combination of the initials W R C. Whoever he is, to pass so many notes through the Keeble, he or she, must have a connection to a present member of staff. "

It only took three days before William had collected ten forged notes. While he ate his breakfast with Harry and Tristan, William excitedly gave his report. He told them that he found all the forged notes in the till floats Ms. Andrews had prepared for the next shift in Charles's Bar. Harry also had good news. "Well done William, together we make progress. My colleague has confirmed he can siphon off all the money in Prescott's current and savings accounts, provided he can get undisturbed access to his blue tooth card reader for five minutes. He says it is to do with codes, pin numbers, connected with some other things known only to top rate computer geeks like him. Five minutes will be all he needs with the machine, although to complete the job, he will need to put in hours of work on his high-powered computer. He tells me that he looks forward to a new challenge."

Tristan asked, "How do we get his card reader out of his poacher's pocket. He never takes his coat off when he is on duty. You must remember Prescott is a master conjuror. He has to take his card reader home with him each night, to anchor it to his telephone connection so that his bank can draw down the money he has taken with it."

Harry rocked back in his chair, with his eyes closed for a minute or two, before he shouted, "Bloody Mary." Both William and Tristan looked shocked. "Swearing won't help us," Tristan grumbled. Harry laughed, "No, but it might, if a big enough Bloody Mary is thrown over his white barman's jacket. It will cause sufficient diversion for one of my friends in the Magic Circle to relieve him of the 'Blue Tooth' thing then pass it to our computer expert for the five minutes he needs. Tristan, you must be the one to throw two Bloody Marys over him. I will ask for them in one of the Keeble's other bars, however you must pay for them. "Me," Tristan said, "I'm not allowed in the Keeble. Prescott would recognise me the instant I stepped into his bar. He would not serve me any drink; let alone a Cocktail, unless it had poison in it."

"Exactly so boyo, exactly so," Harry agreed. "Two Bloody Marys will be far better than two pints of after the match chucking beer. When he sees you, he will call for the heavy brigade, the hotel's security force. You will accuse Prescott that the drink is short on Vodka, in addition to short-changing your friend, who will be me. That is why you will carry both Bloody Marys. Before the heavies arrive, you will sauce Prescott in the kafuffle, however you must try to make it look as though it was an accident. If you get it right, you might only get ejected, not arrested."

"By golly Harry, I am up for that," Tristan said, "I have lolled about in the castle for too long. To face up to Prescott will put me in the lists at last."

At Harry's request, William had brought copies of the Hotel brochure, tariffs, menus from their several restaurants, drinks lists, promotional material of all types, that included wedding brochures, festival brochures and notice of future events. They were all high quality beautifully presented works of the engravers art, with a distinctive house style.

Tristan asked, "Harry, why have you asked William to collect these bits of bumph that the Keeble uses to sell us things that we cannot afford? He was genuinely interested because he knew Harry would have a purpose, it would not be just for idle curiosity. Harry's enigmatic reply raised Tristan's curiosity, "Know the enemy boyo, Know the enemy; a maxim for war even better than the eponymous gun."

Chapter 21

The next morning, when Tristan arrived at Retreads, William Erskin Powell had spread the Keeble's promotional material that Harry had said would help them 'Know the enemy' over the big table on which Retreads guests ate their meals.

After a moment or two, spent in close examination of each item with the magnifying glass, he let out a war whoop to match any Indian brave at Custer's last stand. Stan scratched his belly laughing. Harry capered a little a jig. Tristan caught the mood, "What's going on here? Calm down Harry or you will have a heart attack. Have you daft lot won a free dinner at the Keeble, or what?"

Harry sank down in his usual cushioned chair, one that had arms, brushed a tear of laughter from his eye, before he declaimed, "Ecclesiastes; 'Vanity of vanity, all is vanity'. I told you the forger was vain, well so he is. Because of his sin, we know who he is. Every one of those Keeble publications has his initials hidden somewhere. To find them is a bit like that eighties puzzle book that was so popular, 'Where's Wally'. WRC, the initials on the forged notes, are the conceit of Walter Ronald Chambers. Pretending to be a doting father, who wanted special place cards for his daughter's wedding breakfast, I made a quick call to the Hotel functions manager. She told me Mr, R W Cambers, the chief graphic designer for the whole of the Keeble group of hotels would be happy to help. Feel the paper on which he has printed this wedding reception price list. Does it not have the feel of a twenty-pound note? You see, he even gets the Keeble to buy the paper that he uses to print his forged notes. He is greedy, he wants it all for nothing; rent, electricity, heat, paper, ink, all free for his private mini-mint.

On top form Harry continued, "The espionage phase is complete. The ladies observation proved that Prescott is still a thief. William's penetration implicated the dreadful Ms. Andrews. Examination of the Keeble Hotel's stationary gave us the facts. The forger is Walter Ronald Chambers. We are ready for action; to collect evidence, admissible to the courts, photographs of the printing press, a sample of an engraved plate and paper, and if possible the device they use to age the forged notes. I hope that you may find some part printed forged notes. However, before we search for the hidden mint, we must stage the fracas in Prescott's bar. We must get our hands on his card-reading machine. I propose that we do it tonight, after we have fed our guests, however not a word about this to Lady Margaret.

Tristan, you will pick me up at about nine o'clock, after you have called on Mr. Veasey to hire for me the same dinner jacket that I wore for the splendid dinner at Erskin House. Even my funeral suit is now so shiny that it would not pass muster for a gentleman about town who might call at a five star hotel for a late night snifter."

Stan grunted, "I am coming too, in case the security boys get a bit heavy handed. I shall wear a clean white shirt; it should be sufficient in these run down days where smart casual merges with punk Vivienne Westwood. Anyway, no doorman has ever tried to stop me. The only things that stop me are the turn styles at football matches. When I go to watch QPR, the turnkeys have to open the side gate to let me pass. After I break into my piggy bank, I will get to the Keeble early. Tristan, can you arrange for a house sitter for the evening; I want to bring Antonin with me, so that we can talk chef talk."

That evening, just after ten o'clock, after they arrived at the Keeble by taxi, Tristan and Harry passed the top hated, frock-coated doorman, to walk up the few steps of the front entrance. They sat at one of the low tables in the lounge area, outside the entrance to the bar where Charles Lucas Prescott had worked for so many years that the Hotel had changed its name from the 'Portman Bar' to 'Charles's Bar'.

Harry ordered two 'Bloody Mary' cocktails from the lounge waiter. Declining the waiter's suggestion that he run a tab, Tristan paid cash for the drinks.

The hired dinner jacket that Harry wore with Tristan's white silk scarf round his neck, together with the silk top hat, grey cotton gloves and Tristan's silver-headed black cane he carried, achieved his purpose. It made him look faintly ridiculous; no one noticed Tristan.

As soon as the waiter had taken their order, he went to get the drinks from Charles's Bar. Harry followed, but came back well before the drinks arrived.

"No need to worry" he said, "Both the conjuror and our computer expert are in place, sat together, with a lap-top computer, like businessmen up from Bradford. Stan and Antonin are inside the door, near to the bar. Stan's shirt maker must order his bolts of cotton from a sail maker."

When the drinks arrived, Prescott had decorated them with mint, borage, lemon and fruit. Harry frowned, "Dump the garbage. We do not want the tomato juice diluted. When they had divested the two drinks of ice and garnish, they looked as though each had had a drink taken from them. Harry sighed, "May your Good Lord forgive us. For a few minutes, we must wait for my computer man to pay his bill by card. Because the men are strangers in his bar, with a bill for only two drinks, I hope that Prescott will use his personal card reader to take payment, not

284

the Keeble machine. However, if Prescott does use the Hotel's black blue tooth card reader, our master of magic will have to use our diversion to pick Prescott's poachers pocket. He has confirmed that he can exchange it with the card reader we borrowed from the restaurant owned by Mary's sister; the blue one that Mary is sure is of the same make that Prescott uses to feed his pension fund. He is also sure that he can swap them back, after our computer hacker has what he needs. He says it will take him no more than three or four minutes, at the most, to use a USB cable to dump all the codes and ciphers he needs from Prescott's ATM to his laptop. The conjuror chap is tops, he takes my wristwatch off me every time we meet, without my knowledge, even though it has a leather strap, and I expect him to try to take it."

"Our signal to move is Antonin going to the bar. He will do so when Prescott offers either ATM card reader to my computer man, to enter his pin number. To distract Prescott, you must carry both drinks into the bar, and call out that he has short measured you. It should be enough."

The two men did not have long to wait before Harry saw Antonin walk up to the bar. He stood up to say quietly, "Beginners please, curtain up, come on Boyo, that's our signal." Tristan felt nervous; nevertheless, he picked up both drinks and followed. The excitement prompted a full word-perfect script when he sauntered over the threshold into Charles Lucas Prescott's domain. He stopped, just inside the open door. In a very theatrical George Sanders laidback voice, he called out for all in the bar to hear, "Barman, there is no bloody vodka in these Bloody Marys. As usual, you have short measured the drinks as all here can see. They are only tomato juice, to which you have added extra Worcester sauce to mask the absence of vodka. Prescott, I can tell that you still swindle the punters, just as you did all those years ago when P and O gave you the old heave ho for the same trick."

For once, Tristan could see that the gods favoured him. At first Prescott froze, before he turned, without recovering the card reader from the computer expert, to run back to the bar to summon the security guards with the hidden panic button. He made a serious mistake with his next move.

Charles Lucas Prescott lunged across the front of the bar, intent on doing Tristan some serious damage before the security guards arrived. Through clenched teeth, he roared like a wounded bear. He did not see Stan shoot out his left foot over which he tripped. Prescott fell heavily into Tristan's chest. Tristan had no difficulty to make it look like an accident that all the tomato juice from both glasses spilt over Prescott. The juice near covered the front of his clean white barman's jacket as well as his starched shirtfront before it ran down over the crutch of his black trousers.

The Security guards were on the scene within a minute. They did not recognize Tristan. Faced with a room full of excited people, as well as what appeared to be a body on the floor, oozing life, they did not know what to do. Stan, who had pinned down Prescott, with his size fourteen boot on his chest, relished his centre stage moment. With his massive frame unaffected by the body that struggled under his boot, he grinned at the security guards, "Seems your chap has run amok, I don't know why, he suddenly started to roar through his clenched teeth. He charged across the bar, like a wart hog with its tail on fire. I am sure that intended to inflict serious bodily harm to this poor chap here. I think you should send for the men in white coats and suggest they bring with them a straightjacket. Just listen; he has gone berserk, raving mad. I dare not take my foot off him. He might give us all rabies."

The guards were further confused when Harry's computer expert came over to ask a simple question, "Will you please take charge of this ATM thing? I have entered the amount for our two drinks with my pin number to pay my bill. I don't need a receipt. We must leave now, I am afraid that the violence of the incident has upset my colleague. By the way, I pressed the alarm button when he made his attack on this poor chap here. I used to work in hotels; it didn't take more than a moment to find it."

A security guard, obviously the senior one present, would have agreed to anything. "Alright Sir, thank you sir, I will look after it. I am sorry that you have been embarrassed. We will take care of him now. This has never happened before. I don't understand it. He has worked here for years."

He addressed his next remark to Stan." I think we can handle him now sir, thank you for, er, holding him, I think that you may safely let him go." Stan reluctantly removed his foot.

Tristan had not driven Prescott insane by his appearance in the bar, but his verbal assault had made him so angry, it made no difference. Once on his feet, he struggled so violently to get at Tristan that it took two guards to restrain him. A third guard who moved to shield Tristan from Prescott took the spray of Prescott's saliva. The senior guard, who found it difficult to cope, spoke directly to Tristan, "Please Sir, perhaps you could leave the bar to sit in the lounge. It seems that your presence here is not doing poor old Prescott any good at all."

Harry took Tristan's arm before he said, "Thank you officer, it is late; we will go home, I think that will be best, it has all been most regrettable." The guard replied, "Right you are sir, thank you for being so patient, we do apologize."

It had gone past midnight when Tristan, Harry and Stan came safely back from the fracas in Charles's bar to Retreads kitchen. Harry, who looked all in, had to ask them not to laugh or talk so loud, because next door, in the hall, eleven souls were asleep, or trying to sleep.

Stan kept shooting out his left foot muttering, "I'm normally a right foot, but Vinnie Jones could not have done it more good."

The events of the evening had Tristan fired up, "Harry I don't know where I got my script from, it just came into my head, but Stan showed hidden thespian talent. His masterly trip was Premier League, poetry of motion as was his epic verbal performance. I am sure it gave the computer man plenty of time to get all the data he needs to draw down on Prescott's bank account. We were lucky; Prescott's violent reaction meant that the conjuror did not need to use his pickpocket talent to switch the ATM devices. All in all, we did a good job."

While Tristan celebrated, Harry thought. After a short pause he admitted, "Well yes, you all did well, however we will have to move quickly. Because Stan had Prescott pinned to the floor like a specimen beetle, my man could not get his personal blue tooth card reader back into his poachers pocket. He had to give it to the security guard. By now, Prescott will have convinced the security guards that Tristan Edwards, had deliberately set him up, in revenge for his part in getting him sacked from the hotel. However, he will be worried that the senior security guard might have noticed that the card reader, handed to him by the co-operative guest, is different from those used by the hotel. Even so, management will not act straight away. The hotel's head of security will not be in until morning. The 'Investor's in People' codes of practice will require the Human Resource Manager to hold a formal enquiry before they initiate any disciplinary procedure. It may, or may not, take days. When the security guards return his blue coloured blue tooth device, Prescott will surely realise that we have rumbled him. When he does, he will act quickly to move all the money from his bank account that calls down his blue tooth ATM takings, to another bank. He will also tell Chambers to move his private mint. You will have to find the evidence of forgery tomorrow night, by which I mean tonight, as it has already passed midnight, however you must count me out of that one. I have used up my ration of adrenalin for this week. It's up to you Tristan." "And me," Stan butted in, "Tristan needs my left foot, also my right arm. He has not eaten enough of my good Polish food for me to let him out on his own. That Antonin, with his nouvelle French nonsense has reduced him to a shadow not worth boxing. I can walk unchallenged passed security into the

Keeble catacombs any time of the day or night. I shall be invisible, because I shall wear my full chef's fig, white coat with piped edges, black stud buttons, blue kerchief, gold medallion on my red ribbon, my very best toque, fancy cheque trousers and white leather clogs. Hotels like the Keeble go through so many chefs that they don't take them on salary, only weekly pay, or casual. Tristan can be my commis to carry my special chef's bag. In my shadow he too will be invisible."

"Good, that is all settled then isn't it?" Tristan mimicked Lady Margaret's favourite closure, before he announced, "I am off to find a taxi to take me back to Erskin House, where I am sure Antonin will be waiting to recount his side of the story. I had to ask Jenny to house sit until Antonin got back, so no doubt I will have to answer to Lady Margaret in the morning."

Stan yawned, "Harry, can I stay here tonight, I am on early tomorrow. In return for a good bed, I will bring you a cup of hot sweet tea before I go to work."

Tristan had not been wrong; just before nine the following morning he heard the front door open, followed by a more than usual sharp clip of high heels as they crossed the marble floor on the way to his pantry. Without a chance for Tristan to greet her, Lady Margaret used his proper names for the first time since his interview.

"Mr. Tristan Edward, what have you been up to? I only have half the story from Jenny, who had it from Antonin. How could you leave me out of your escapade last night?"

Tristan played the pompous butler, "Would madam care to take tea?"

"Don't you Madam me you rascal; please ask Antonin for coffee, with cinnamon toast. I am so cross that I have not had breakfast."

With a quick mood change, Lady Margaret graced Tristan with one of her special smiles that she used to seek a favour. She also dropped her sharp tone, to plead with a little girl voice, "Sorry to scold; now pretty-please, Sam must tell Midge everything that happened."

Because they had been successful, Tristan found it easy to recount the story, although it took longer to tell than it did to happen. There were many interruptions from Lady Margaret, aided by Jenny, who arrived only minutes after Lady Margaret. Jenny's questions were all about William. "Did you see him, had he been part of it, had he been in any danger?"

Tristan explained Harry's fears that Prescott may realise that they knew about his credit and debit card thefts, which would surely mean that he would try to change his bank account, before Harry's computer hacker could siphon off his funds.

He added, "Another problem we have, is that Prescott will alert Chambers to what we have found out. That means that Stan and I will have to go in tonight, to find evidence of the forgers' den, before Chambers moves it from the Keeble. If we find it, we must take away with us any material evidence of forgery and take photographs of the equipment that is too heavy for us to move. Even Stan will not be able to move a printing press. Magnetic cards operate all the door locks in the hotel. All that we need to gain entry to the Keeble's print room is an upgraded guest card that will clone a top-level security pass card. I rang Harry first this morning. He has his expert computer hacker working on it. He has agreed to book in to the Keeble, where they will issue him with a bedroom key-card that looks like a large credit card. He will use William's limited pass card, which gives entry to many, although not all areas, and by hacking into the hotels computer, he will clone both his and William's key card to be a master key-card to all doors. The clever bit is that he has assured Harry that he can frig the card to open all doors, so that it will not send a signal to the security control room. Although the hotel security system is a few years old, the control room can tell how many people are in any room in the building, at any time. Because our cloned pass-key won't send any message to the control room, the security guards will not know that we are in the building."

To cut off any further interruption from the ladies, Tristan issued a firm injunction. "Ladies, before you ask, the answer is no. You cannot come with us. You would give the game away. Whatever disguises you tried, even the most-clueless security guard would detect your fragrance, deportment and demeanour as quite out of the ordinary in the subterranean working corridors of a grand hotel. We would all be immediately escorted, if not ejected, from the building."

"Sam," Lady Margaret said with mocking haughty asperity, "I am surprised that you even gave it a thought. Of course, we will not come with you; we will already be upstairs, ready to cause a diversion. We shall keep the security guards fully occupied, while you carry out your covert operation. Well then, that is all settled then, isn't it?"

Tristan objected, "Regrettably, you lady detectives will not be able to cause a diversion because all the bars and restaurants will be closed. We will not go in until half past two in the morning, the hour when security will be most lax. The guards will have completed their first night patrols, after which they will probably sleep in turns."

Lady Margaret's head stretched out on her neck further than Tristan had ever seen it go before, "Don't talk such nonsense Sam, an attack to be successful must always have more than one front. Jenny and I will book into the Keeble Hotel, under assumed names, with a Yorkshire address. We shall pretend to be in town to shop, before going to a West End show. Mary will book in an hour later, so that the hotel staff will not connect her with us. Mary will be our non-sleeping sleeper. Exactly five minutes before you enter the staff entrance, a burglar will disturb Jenny who will scream blue murder. When asked what happened she will swear that she screamed because she woke to find a man in her room. She will add, tearfully, that her scream made the man run off."

"Oooh super," Jenny said, her cheeks flushed, "William can be the burglar. He can run amok down the corridor, shouting fire and make enough noise, to bring out all the people in other bedrooms into the corridor."

Tristan had to agree with Lady Margaret's plan; it made good sense, moreover the ladies would not have to take any risk.

Tristan took his chefs whites to Retreads, where he had arranged to meet with Stan before they set out on their search for evidence of the forger's business; the printing press, the machine that aged the forged notes, the special inks and paper and hopefully some forged notes. The ladies had already booked into the Keeble. They had called on their mobile phones, to confirm that they were 'On station'.

William had assured Tristan that he would have no difficulty in leaving his desk at the appointed time, as it fitted in with his usual half hour break. He agreed to use the stairs to reach the floor where Lady Margaret and Jenny had adjacent rooms and there to create as much mayhem as possible for two or three minutes only. Job done he would return to his desk to carry on his work as normal.

He would tell Ms. Andrews, if she asked where he had been, that he had gone to the canteens dispense machine, to buy a coke, having made sure to have an unopened can to show her.

Harry's computer expert had delivered the cloned passkey to Retreads, with an assurance that he had tested it and that the system codes for the master keys would not change while they were in the building.

His other news even better news excited them all, as he confirmed that he had cleared Prescott's bank account, down to seven pounds ten pence only, which meant that the Treasury would be more than five hundred thousand pounds better off.

He had however left a warning with Harry that he had only been able to provide a passkey for genuine Keeble doors and that any forgers den would probably be booby-trapped.

Although Harry could not take part he insisted that Tristan and Stan should not use taxis, but that Drummond should use a hired people carrier, big enough to allow Stan to get in or out, quickly; 'if needs be'. Drummond dropped off Tristan and Stan, who both wore their chef's whites, at the staff entrance to the Keeble Hotel at exactly at 2.35 a.m. The security guard in the small room inside the entrance was wide-awake, as he spoke excitedly into a telephone.

When Sam passed by the counter-window, the guard put his hand over the phone mouthpiece, to call to him, "Chef, watch out for some lunatic who has just tried to rob some young lass on the tenth floor. There's hell up. He has set off fire alarms and a foam fire extinguisher to cause a ruckus. Folk are out of their rooms, all over the place, two old biddies are already down in the lobby, each in nothing but their nightie. They are screaming that the house is on fire. If you see any suspicious young lad, grab him; bring him here. You look big enough to stop a tank not just a sneak thief."

The security guard went on talking to the person on the other end of the phone. "Good old Midge that gives us good covering fire,"

Tristan unconsciously had used her nickname, something he found difficult to do when face-to-face with her. "Where did William say that the Graphic design offices were?" Despite the late hour, even after he had worked a long day in a hot kitchen, Stan fully alert, coolly answered, "Two floors down, lower basement, third door on the left, half-way along the corridor from the lift. We don't do lifts, as that might send a signal to the security office that somebody is moving about. They might want to come to take a look-see; no one works nights down here."

Tristan sounded a tad concerned, "Trouble is they have left every second light on in the corridors. The security cameras will show random shots. We must hope the guards are not watching

293

the television screens but are out of their office on the tenth floor. The quicker we are out of the corridors into the Graphics department the better."

The cloned master-key card worked perfectly. Seconds after entering the corridor, they were on the inside of the door marked 'Graphic Design', where they ran into their first unexpected problem.

The light switch inside the door did not switch on the room lights. "Damn," Tristan allowed himself the mild profanity, though many more full expletives could have followed. "They must switch them off from a central control room to save electricity, now what do we do?"

Stan grabbed the bag that Tristan had carried for him. He took out and switched on a powerful torch, a black square thing with a lens as big as a car headlight. He said, "Angol, I told you that you needed me on this job. I also brought a torch for you to use," he laughed when he handed Tristan a pocket pen sized torch. The wide beam from Stan's torch showed that they were in what appeared to be part print shop, part open plan office, part photographic studio.

Stan opened out the collapsible case from which he had taken the torch. It turned out to be a full size cricket bag, big enough to carry kit for a batsman, to include bats, pads helmet, stumps, and towels. Seemingly fearless, Stan chattered on, "I occasionally play for the Polish club. They let me bat at number five, if I let them use two of my sweaters for the side screens. Na then, where is the forger's den? Not in this room, it must be somewhere, there must be another door."

Stan walked over to a row of six tall steel filing cabinets set against the wall facing the door where they had come in. "Here it is," he said, "Let me see how it works. Here hold my torch Tristan, while I have a look. Yes, here we are, they are piano hinged between the third and fourth cabinet, top to bottom, right down the middle, like I play my golf."

When Stan pulled on one of the cabinet handles, three cabinets swung away from the wall to reveal a solid wooden door. Tristan's clenched fists showed his frustration. Unlike Stan, he could not relax. When he tried to open the door he swore, "Bugger, it has an ordinary mortise lock, and it is locked." In an anxious voice he asked, "I don't suppose that you can break the door down can you Stan, it looks very solid to me?"

Stan said, "No need to swear Tristan, what would Harry or Lady M say. Yes, I can break it down, but don't worry, remember what I told you, they are careless. They must have been running this racket since they printed ten-shilling notes. Ah! Here is the key, on top of the cabinet, where else would it be?"

Inside a smaller room, after they closed the inner door behind them, they found all the evidence of forgery they needed to take to the police, even some uncut sheets of twenty-pound notes, printed on one side only.

They did not find or notice the silent alarm that had activated the moment that they opened the hidden door. Stan unhurriedly packed paper and ink samples into his cricket-bag, while Tristan took flash photographs of equipment.

When the wooden door opened, Stan turned to Tristan, to say quietly, calmly, "Well, this really might be a bit of a foot in a wasp nest, but not to worry."

Their immediate concern was that the man who had opened the door was clearly not a security guard. He was a small thin boned man, with sleek black hair, parted at the side, wearing a quilted collar black silk brocade dressing gown, silk pyjamas and Mandarin slippers.

The gun held in his right hand enhanced his contrived elegance. He waved the gun, like a slow pendulum arcing between Tristan and Stan, as he moved to a concealed switch to switch on the room lights.

In a cold voice, with the intonation of an old-fashioned head master who had caught the usual miscreants breaking the school rules, he said, "You, the barrel of lard, put the bag down, move away from it to sit down at that desk, the big desk there. Keep your hands on top of the desk, where I can see them. You, the skinny KP, sit on the chair behind him, with your hands on your rug. My colleagues will be here within minutes; we have previously had an unfortunate experience similar to this. They will take you away. You won't have to wait long."

Tristan did not know whether his cold sweat might be caused by fear, excitement, or anger at the man who thought his hair a wig. He had no doubt that the man with the gun was WRC, Walter Ronald Chambers. However, he managed to speak calmly, "Why bother Chambers, we phoned the police when we found the door to your forgers den. We have worked with them ever since your chum Prescott had me sacked. They will be here within minutes. You are a busted."

Tristan's ploy did not work; Chambers remained cool. "Mobile phones don't work down here. You read too many trashy novels, or watch too many black and white cops and robber films on the afternoon Telly If the police knew about our little money-maker, they would be here in force, not a couple of bungling amateurs. I suggest that you sit quietly, to reflect on your foolish ways. I keep killers on contract; you may be sure of that. You see, like good scouts, we are always prepared. In our lucrative cash rich line of business, we have to be prepared to deal, or not to deal, with people who try a hostile takeover. We have a plan for all eventualities. With the ready cash we have to hand, the contract assassin is cheap. Do not flatter yourself that you were first to find out about our little side-line. You will not be the first we have added to the police missing persons register."

The more that Chambers talked, the more Tristan's confidence returned. He could see that Stan, still sat at the steel desk, had moved his huge arm and hands to span the desktop. He had already curled his fingers under its edge. Desperate to keep Chambers attention and sure that he would not risk using the gun in the print room, without a glance at Chambers, Tristan slowly stood up, keeping his hands on his head. He walked to stand beside the device that he deduced the forgers used to age the newly printed forgeries.

It looked like a miniature tumble dryer with a system of lightly waxed cloth and leather belts. He said in a voice he did not recognize," I am impressed with the trick of artificially aging the newly printed notes, very clever that; was it your idea?"

The vain conceited Walter Ronald Chambers did not reply. He took the full force of the steel desk with its drawers full of files. It had flown for more than two meters, to knock him over. As it came to rest, it pinned his body to the floor. It did not worry Tristan when he saw blood come from the unconscious baldhead. Stan punched the air before he drew in a huge breath, to shouted "300 Kilo snatch, my best event. Get his gun Tristan; we have stayed too long in this catacomb, he may have been right, others may come as he said."

Tristan did pick up the gun; he also could not resist a sweet revenge. He picked up Chambers wig, which he wrapped round the gun, before he stuffed both into his pocket. Stan put the device that aged the newly printed notes into his bag with the sheets of uncut single sided forged twenty-pound notes as well as some engraved plates he thought might be to do with the forgeries. Together, they made a dash for the stairs.

On the second flight, they met Charles Lucas Prescott, on his way down, also armed with a pistol. Stan dropped the bag, felled Prescott with a single hammer blow to the top of his head. He picked up the unconscious body by the back of his collar. He shouting to Tristan, "Come on lad, grab the bag, I know what to do with this fellow." Stan dumped the still unconscious Prescott in the security guard's hut.

"Got your thief mate, he put up a struggle but banged his head on my fist. Send for an ambulance, get security down to graphics, there a chap there who needs a bit of help with a weighty problem."

Both men tried to walk calmly away from the Keeble staff entrance. However, they were too excited. One glance at each other broke their resolve. They set off in a hell for leather dash to get away from any other 'friends' of Walter Ronald Chambers, or his contract assassins, who Chambers had bragged were already on their way to add them to the police register of missing persons.

Drummond flicked the lights of the people carrier to attract their attention. Once inside the vehicle, an out of breath Tristan managed to gasp, "Change of plan, Mr. Drummond, we don't go to Retreads yet. First, straight to Islington Police Station please. I want to repay a debt to a constable Tom Warwick and a Sergeant Robbins."

Chapter 22

At ten o'clock on the morning after his night raid with Stan on the forgers den, the telephone at Tristan's bedside rang to wake him from a short deep sleep.

"Sorry boyo, Harry, never could sleep a wink after six, Evans here. I dare not let you have any more beauty sleep. I am already here, downstairs with Stan. I hope that you don't mind, I have persuaded Antonin to slather together crispy streaky bacon sandwiches, buttered and dipped, for us to dribble down our chins. Midge rang while you still slumbered to say the lady heroines would be here at eleven o'clock. They want to give and receive a full report. Stan has already told me a little about your side of the story. You had better have a scented bath and use lots of aftershave before you come down. You must smell like a hob ferret with all the adrenalin you pumped into your system last night. Sorry Tristan, I forget my manners; Good morning."

When the ladies joined Harry, Tristan, Stan, and Antonin, they were too many to meet in Tristan's pantry. In the library, Harry sat opposite Lady Margaret in the twin to her high backed regency chair. Jenny curled at her feet. Mary, who even Harry could not persuade to sit, stood sentinel behind her mistress.

Stan filled a two-seat sofa. The arrangement left Tristan and Antonin uncomfortable on rigid hall chairs. It seemed proper that they should all defer to Harry, who assumed the role of rapporteur, although he had dressed in his shiny blue suit, a woollen check shirt, a knitted tie, leather slippers, but no socks.

Even for Harry, he looked more than usually a shade the wrong side of well-worn when he started the proceedings, "We must hear first from the Ladies. I think that we all want to know, all that there is to know, about their diversionary tactics. Midge, perhaps you will start, if you will be so kind?"

"It was wonderful" Lady Margaret began, even more vibrant than usual. "With best military discipline, Mary, Jenny and me had synchronised our watches with Sam and Stan before we booked into our rooms at the Keeble. At exactly two thirty in the morning, as planned, Jenny started to scream. A fair ground house of horrors could not have sounded more dreadful."

Jenny, who wriggled with excitement, had to interrupt. "I opened my bedroom door before I started to scream. When I stopped screaming, I shouted, at the top of my voice, 'Stop thief, stop thief'. William acted his part wonderfully. He knew all about the cameras in the corridors, so when he left his desk he took with him a small case in which he had hidden a blackout sheet my mother found in the attic. We had cut it into a circle with a hole in the middle for his head and two holes for his arms. I sewed on a rain hood cut from my old school Mac to cover his head and he wore a scarf so that only his eyes were visible. He used the stairs to reach the tenth floor just before half past two by which time he had put on the hooded cape. When I screamed, he dashed out of the staircase lobby to run along the corridor. He banged at every door, making a terrific row. I saw him. He set off one of those fire extinguisher things before he disappeared through an emergency exit. He behaved better than Bond; he was the amalgam of Zorro, the Scarlet Pimpernel and D'Artagnan."

Midge used her notepad to admonish Jenny with a tap on her head, before she continued. "To pick up where I left off; before you could say 'Let the dogs loose' the corridor became a confusion of bleary eyed security men who ran amuck, like a herd of bullocks spooked by a swarm of gad fly. They collided with the guests who had come out of their rooms to ask if there had been a fire, a terrorist raid, or had war broken out. Of course, most of those who had left their room had not brought their silly card type door key with them.

The doors automatically shut behind them to lock them out. Several guests had forgotten their room number, so it took a long time before the security people could restore order and let everyone back into their correct rooms. When they tried to question Jenny, I drew myself up to my full five foot four. I put on my court voice to insist that they leave my niece alone, because the sweet young thing would undoubtedly be in shock. I told a little fib that we would answer their questions in the morning. I assured them that after a cup of sweet tea, my niece would go back to bed, to sleep late into the morning."

Lady Margaret, who knew how to tell a good story paused, to look at each of the party in turn, before she continued, "That phase of our strategy had been carried out as we had planned. However, Mary's second front offensive achieved an even longer diversion. As she had booked in separately, her idea, the Keeble allocated her a room on the ninth floor. When she was sure that things on the tenth floor had quietened down, she rang reception from the house phone in her room. Mary acted the drama queen, playing an opera diva, with full on histrionics. She screamed that a masked man wearing a cloak had entered her room to rob or to rape. It had to be a very big fib, because we had planned to rely on Uncle Jo Stalin's dictum that the bigger the lie the more likely people are to believe it. The chaos started again. Jenny's screams, William's crash attack, and Mary's histrionics, added together, achieved what we had planned to do. The security guards focused their attention upstairs for more than an hour. Now, Sam, did our diversionary tactics give you time to do what you planned to do in the basement?"

When Tristan stood up from the uncomfortable chair to give his account he felt proud of his part in the night adventure with Stan, but he knew that he had taken the lesser part.

He rested his hand on the back of the chair for support. He spoke slowly, as though recounting some half-forgotten dream.

He described how, wearing chefs clothing and walking in Stan's shadow, he had passed by the security guard un-noticed. He told them how the cloned master key card had worked to open the door to the graphic design department, but that a solid wooden door, with a mortise lock had temporarily held them up.

He explained how Stan had found the key, because the forgers were confident and careless. Stan brushed aside Tristan's tribute to his efforts, "Get on with it Angol". Urged on, Tristan gave a good account of how they had collected sufficient evidence for the police to prosecute Chambers for forgery.

Tristan had deliberately saved the best of his account to the last. Except for a slight exaggeration of the distance that Sam hurled the desk to pin Chambers to the floor, and changing their 'dash to escape' to a 'well- ordered withdrawal', he did not exaggerate the truth. His voice changed to become high with excitement.

"We had just about gathered sufficient evidence when Walter Ronald Chambers surprised us. He came quietly through the wooden door, dressed like a repertory matinee idol of long ago. He had an automatic heavy pistol in his right hand. He calmly told us to sit down to wait until his colleagues arrived. He smirked; he bragged that his cash rich business could easily afford to employ the best of the bad and that he had already called in his contract assassin to take us away for disposal. The smug smarmy horrible man almost crowed when he said that it would be a routine job for them, because he had previously used the same gang to get rid of others who had tried to interfere with his business. I admit that he had me truly frightened; my knees shook, my hands trembled. Only anger helped me to control my bodily functions. I was angry because Chambers had assumed that my hair was a wig."

"I took a chance to glance at Stan, who sat calmly at the steel desk. The slow wink from his left eye took away my fear. I knew immediately that I had no need to be afraid. Stanislause Klaginskaieski, he who we call Stan Kay, is a true Olympian. He saved my life by winning the gold medal in a new weight lifting event. From a sitting position, he threw the heavy steel desk, full of files, the clear twelve feet between him and Chambers. His super heavyweight lift flattened the jerk. It allowed me to pick up the gun. It also knocked off Chambers wig. I am ashamed to say I wrapped it round the gun, which I stuffed into my pocket. The job done, we made a well-ordered withdrawal. Stan took with him the device that they used to age their newly forged notes. We also took some part printed twenty-pound notes that we thought might be proof positive. On our way up the two flights of stairs, we met with Prescott, on his way down, also armed with a gun. To even things out, Stan flattened him. We dumped his still unconscious body in the security guard's hut and told the guard that someone should go and check the lower basement to help a chap suffering from depression. We left the Keeble with good conscience. Mr. Drummond took us straight to the police station where we handed in the evidence and the gun. As good citizens, we told them where we had found it, but do you know, in the excitement, I forgot to hand in the wig."

After several cheers and much relieved laughter, Tristan resumed his seat. Lady Margaret asked what the police had to say when they had taken the evidence to the police station. Tristan gave a shy grin, "The Inspector dressed me down good and proper for not handing the case over to them earlier. I did not mind the telling off, because of what the police rang to tell me, not long after Harry had interrupted my beauty sleep."

It thrilled Tristan that he could pass on the news that the police had in custody both the felon Charles Lucas Prescott and the

303

conceited counterfeiter Walter Ronald Chambers and that they had also arrested, although not yet charged, several others, including the corrupt old trot box Ms. Andrews.

Tristan could hardly contain his excitement when he went on to say, "The best bit of news is that when the police searched Prescott's house, during the early hours, they recovered the blue tooth ATM card reader from where he had it connected to his telephone line. The Detective Inspector told me not to be too disappointed, but it appeared that something, or someone, had rumbled his card reader swindle. Only one day before they raided his house, he had managed to spirit away over half a million pounds, to leave only a few pounds in any of his known accounts. Harry you had it banged to rights, the Inspector told me that it was unlikely that the Asset Recovery Agency would ever get the money back."

Harry responded in full Welsh baritone singsong. "Dieu, that is good news, good news indeed. Tristan, what you did last night I rate a quest worthy of a knight of King Arthur's court at Camelot. With Stan, you penetrated the dungeons of Keeble Castle; together you slew the dragon greed. You have earned your spurs. You are a true errant Knight, tested in battle. Last night 'Right' conquered 'Might'. You have a worthy tale to tell when you meet again with your friends in the north. Last night Stan composed a symphony in two flats; the corrupt Prescott flat out, Chambers flat as a silhouette. Together you won the Triple Crown and the Grand Slam, both doubled in spades, if that does not mix too many metaphors."

He went on to say, "Not that you could have done it without the ladies mind or that young tearaway William, whom Jenny seems to think, is a reincarnation of Tyrone Power."

Lady Margaret responded, "Thank you kind sir. We also have good news, I kicked up such a fuss this morning that the hotel manager, a real smooth talker, would not let us pay our bill.

Better than that, we got clean away before their head of security could ask Jenny any questions."

Jenny had her own good news, "William will not go back to that horrid job. He has asked me to meet his parents this evening, before we go to a little Italian restaurant he knows in Chelsea."

★★*★*★*★*★*★*★*★*★*★*★*★*★*★*★*★*★*★*

With Charles Lucas Prescott dealt with, Edna Spitewinter, the woman he had forced from her post as 'Housekeeper', at Erskin House. 'Evil Edna', as he had come to think of her, came foremost in his thoughts.

She had said that the Major would sack him and re-instate her as housekeeper. She had promised to use her friend to wreak a savage revenge on him. Friends who would cut him, break his legs or stretch his neck, dependent only on the score she would offer them.

Acting on Harry's advice, Tristan had spoken separately to the morning cleaners. He asked them to mention to Mrs. Spitewinter, 'Should she ever call,' that he would like a word with her about an idea he had in mind. With little hope of success, he had asked each woman not to mention his request to the other. So far, he had not heard from either woman, or from 'Evil Edna'.

To honour the promise he had made to himself, before the recent events, Tristan went to visit the Brassingtons at the Grassington Guest House. He chose to turn up, unannounced, during the afternoon of Sunday next. He took flowers, as well as Fortnum and Mason chocolates, for Elizabeth.

As expected she first blushed, then kissed him, before she scolded him, "You, shouldn't have." Equally, in tune with the occasion, when he accepted a bottle of single malt whisky John Brassington said, "By gum Tristan, you are a bit of a lad you are. Penniless one minute, then next minute you throw your money about like a drunken sailor."

Tristan told them that he felt secure in his well-paid job that had rather more to it than the advertised post of 'Gentleman's gentleman'. He also told them of the pride he felt, that, as he had recently been a vagrant, he was able to help Harry Evans at 'Retreads', a shelter for homeless but often worthy men. Men passed the age where employers became blind to their experience and reliability.

The Brassingtons were almost speechless with excitement when he showed them the cuttings from the Sunday papers that identified him as 'The mystery escort' of 'Midge', The Honourable Lady Margaret Elizabeth Bowes-Litton, neé The Honourable Lady Margaret Elizabeth de-Vere Erskin Tempest-Powell, celebrity debutante of the late fifties.

They were almost in awe when he told them about Charles Lucas Prescott and how he had brought him to justice, not only for cheating the customers and hotel, but also as part of a gang of bank note counterfeiters.

When he finally left the Grassington, with sincere invitations to keep in touch, Tristan's spirits were as high as he could remember. When he walked out of Brompton Road, on his way to Cromwell Road, to have a better chance to waive down a taxi, he passed Riejik's Café. Sight of the Café brought back dark memories about the low points in his efforts to find a worthwhile quest. He also had solemn thoughts about how much he owed to the brothers Branwell and Harry Evans. It saddened him that he could never hope to repay them.

After the success of supper parties, rather than formal dinners, Lady Margaret agreed to Jenny's idea to hold a 'Game and Games Party' for twenty guests, ten ladies, ten gentlemen. Lady Margaret asked Antonin to arrange the dinner, centred on both furred and feathered game. With Jenny in charge of the games, 'Political Charades', 'Defective Detective', 'Rhyming Slang Limericks' a beetle drive and 'Scabby Queen' with forfeits, it left Tristan with little to do. It amused him to hear Jenny call Lady Margaret 'Midge', a sign that she had been completely accepted. Even Mary, her confidant companion, still called her 'My Lady'.

It made Tristan wonder if Jenny had reminded Lady Margaret about her Grandfather. A feint shadow crossed Tristan's mind when Jenny let slip that a male gossip columnist who worked for one of the broadsheets would be a guest at the party. Tristan had always agreed with Harry Evans's concern that it might become impossible to keep the Old Sloan Parties discrete.

He felt sure that a gossip columnist, however up market, at any Old Slone event, would inevitably lead to leaks to the 'red-top' newspapers, and their links with the paparazzi would lead to trouble. When he taxed Lady Margaret with his concerns, she just chirruped "Oh Sam you are such an Eeyore," her family's pet term for a party pooper.

However as he felt sure that any scandal would be a threat to his job security, he could not treat the matter lightly. He knew that the dreadful woman Spitewinter would read the gossip columns, make the connection to Erskin House and inform the Major, exaggerating the facts.

The success of the Game and Games party genuinely surprised Tristan. Antonin had done wonders; he persuaded Lady M, as he called her, to add a soup course. For the dinner, he sent up a classic terrine of grouse with Cumberland sauce, followed by Scottish game broth.

For the main course, he served a choice of roast saddle of hare larded with wild boar bacon or pheasant in two sauces. Antonin allowed himself to express his wicked sense of Gallic humour; for dessert, he made 'Beignet's Ecosse, with caramel chocolate sauce'.

He swore Tristan to secrecy before answering his question, "What are these Scottish desserts, the Beignets Ecosse?" "I often makes em, dead easy they are; I deepfreeze lots of 'Mars Bars', before I crack off the chocolate and caramel. I roll out the squidgy middle stuff, on a dusting of icing sugar. I cut out discs the size of a ginger nut biscuit. As with all my beignets, I deep-fry them in tempura batter. The sauce is just the cracked off caramel and chocolate, warmed through with a splash of Drambuie."

Tristan laughed, as Antonin went on "They will love them; they always do, however they would die of embarrassment if they knew that they had enjoyed a Sauchiehall Street supper. As Romeo's Juliet almost said, 'By any other name they would taste as sweet."

During the pre-dinner drinks, while he attended table, Tristan became aware of a frisson, a fierce attraction that sparked between a wiry, hard faced man with short-cropped hair and a simply gorgeous tall slender woman. Her skin reminded him of the colour of luxury coffee cream; He thought her high cheekbones had been touched with a tint of Welsh gold. He noticed that Lady Margaret took particular care to introduce the couple before she sat them opposite to each other at the dinner table.

Tristan thought the man to be about sixty, although very fit, with an assured easy presence. However, he suspected his strong northern vowels were deliberate. Tristan felt he aught to recognise him, although he could not remember from where.

The woman, who stood a little taller than the man was clearly a few years younger. She simply radiated sex appeal, but a shell of exquisite style protected her from any hint of vulgarity. Tristan doubted that she qualified with the Sloan's Reunited born before rule. He thought her not just good-looking, but stunningly attractive; beautiful, by far the best dressed of all the women guests.

After he and Mary had cleared the dining table, Tristan made sure everyone had drinks before he joined Antonin in the Kitchen for a short break. He left Jenny organizing the games. By offering wages at 'double time, cash in hand', Tristan had cajoled both the morning cleaners to help with the washing up. The sour look they both gave him convinced him that they had talked to each other about his request to pass on a message to Edna Spitewinter, their previous boss.

Because he had not heard from Spitewinter, he had to assume that both women were in league with her. It worried him.

Even down stairs in the kitchen, with Antonin, Tristan could hear the guests' laughter; the years slipped from their shoulders as they joined in games that they had not played since their youth. Antonin gave a classic Frenchman's shrug, "Listen to the wrinklies; they are just like big kids."

"Well thank God for that," Tristan countered, "I don't think that today's youngsters could be persuaded to join in the games that we played in our courting days. Listen to them and be happy. I wish that I had forgotten to grow up."

After his short rest, Tristan went back to check on proceedings. He found the couple he had noticed who 'sparked' off each other, standing very close together, just outside the ballroom door where Jenny had charge of the games. As they moved quickly apart, the lady gave a deep throaty laugh.

"We are the crooks in the defective detective game. The lovely girl Jenny sent us out of the room, after she gave the other guests a card with twenty questions about each of us. They have to fill in the answers. For me, colour of hair, eyes, what clothes I am wearing, shoes, heels stiletto or flat, jewellery etcetera. For the man whether he had a parting in his hair, left right or centre, things like that. The one with the most correct answers gets a prize. It is not fair; we do not get a chance to win the prize. I don't know why Midge picked us."

The hard faced man, whose face had softened, smiled at Tristan when he said, aside, "I think I have won first prize and gone to heaven." His moment in paradise did not last. Jenny opened the door to call them both back into the room.

Tristan heard gentle laughter again when the players recognised how unobservant they had been, defective in both observation as well as recall, all of them utterly defective detectives.

The evening closed, in the same way that it had after the trial run and all subsequent Old Sloan events. All the guests left only after many good wishes, calls for more parties, and by the exchange of cards with their email address and telephone numbers.

Many told him that they had not laughed so much for years. Tristan noticed that the two 'Crooks' of the defective detective game held hands for a long time after the formal hand shake. When their hands did part, their eyes held contact for much longer than custom demanded. William, Erskin-Powell arrived to take Jenny away before Drummond came to collect Lady Margaret and Mary.

Tristan took the opportunity to ask Lady Margaret who the couple were that she had chosen to be the crooks in the defective detective game. Lady Margaret laughed with delight "Wicked aren't I. You will just have to wait until Monday when I will come in for a full debrief. Good night Sam, goodnight Antonin; put on your thinking caps, not your nightcaps. I want your ideas for next year's parties."

Prompt, at eleven o'clock on the Monday morning that followed the party, having called Tristan, Antonin, and Jenny into the library, Lady Margaret opened the debrief with a demand.

"First item on my agenda; Antonin, I want the recipe for those delicious 'Beignet's Ecosse' I think you called them." Antonin, who wanted to draw them all into a fools circle, raised his shoulders, shook his head, overstated his French accent, to say, "Pas possible, Lady M, we chef's must have our secrets, besides you really don't want to know."

Lady Margaret, who had not realised that Antonin teased her, said, rather forcibly, "Antonin, you have made me more anxious to have it. I must have it."

"They were scrummy super," Jenny said, "Oh, do tell, please." Antonin, who had been determined to tell them, even if they had not asked, shrugged one of his better-exaggerated Gallic shrugs. With his audience exactly where he wanted them, he whispered, "Well, you must keep it a close secret. You must tell no one what I have told you. You see, according to those epicene epicure food critics who scribble for the Sunday supplements, my Beignets Ecosse were the most reviled dish of our day; 'Deep Fried Mars Bars'.

"Oh golly, how awful," came instinctively from Jenny. Antonin laughed, "It's the way I cook em. You English will eat any dish given a French name."

"Well I still think they were wonderful," Lady Margaret enthused, "Everyone said how good they were. It proves what I said to Sam about a dinner party held at home, it beats anything the celebrity chefs can do in their overrated, overpriced, restaurants, where everything one says is overheard because they will not play gentle background music until there are enough people, all talking at once, to make it impossible to have a conversation. I did say that didn't I Sam, when we first decided to start Old Sloanes Re-united?"

Tristan replied with polite resignation, "Yes Ma-am, you did, you did say something like that, although I don't recall my involvement with the idea that Old Sloanes should be reunited, or for a debutants reprise, or is it the Royal 'We' that you use this morning."

"Hush Sam," Lady Margaret said, "You should take credit whenever it is due. However, enough of gourmet gossip, we must take note of serious business. Did you all see the brief bit in the gossip column this morning? It will make all of the ex-debs, also the later Old Sloanes of London and the Home Counties, wonder where the secret Mayfair reunions take place. I thought Andrew did it very well. It will assure us of a waiting list for years."

Tristan mumbled, "Very probably will ma-am, nevertheless you must be very careful. Interest in the good things in life often breeds jealousy. All the redtop gossip columnists will have picked up the scent already. Their aim will not be to inform or amuse, it will be to create exaggerated prurient interest. There may be a backlash, if not a whiplash."

311

The expected "Eeyore," came from Lady Margaret before she asked. "About future events, any ideas from you men, or do we two girls have it all to do?"

Only when, Lady Margaret asked whether anyone had any questions did Tristan have the opportunity to ask, "Who were the couple who you picked as the 'crooks' in the defective detective game." Lady Margaret put her index finger to her lips, "Be patient Sam, it really is a state secret."

Later, when Antonin and Jenny had left, she swore Tristan to secrecy. "Isn't it wonderful, I knew they would click? He is the Right Honourable Ralf Ratcliff PC MP, Minister for Industrial Reconstruction and Development. The Government has finally realised that we have to take back our industry from the Far East. They have appointed him, an ex-union general secretary, as a Secretary of State at Cabinet level. His constituency is somewhere unknown in the North, beyond England's protective coast-to-coast seal of Yorkshire and Lancashire. She is Lady Elizabeth Francis Slessinger; a very right wing lady. The Conservatives have appointed her to the House of Lords. Her Mother, a high borne Ethiopian, worked in the British Embassy in Addis Ababa. Her boss, our Ambassador, a sensible chap, wooed and won her. It could not be more fun. The Minister's wife died many years ago. She has never married; on the contrary, she has a string of men who have followed her for years. She really is a goer you know. The Party Leader moved her to the Lords from some high-level post in Conservative Central Office. I have this on the best authority; on her first day in the House of Lords, as she walked to her office, she overheard two young women political researches say, "Here she comes, 'Lizzie long legs'. When she passed them, she reduced them to ashes. She responded, "Lady Lizzie Long Legs preferred."

The Minister has already rung me to beg that I invite them both again; he wishes to continue their discussion about the removal of the trade embargo on Chinese cotton wear."

During the evening that followed the debrief, it did not surprise Tristan when he receive a call from Lady Margaret about the Minister and the Lady Member of the House of Lords.

"Sam, guess what, the Minister has just rung to ask if he might bring the Dusky Dame to Erskin House, for private talks, while they take afternoon tea. He says he needs somewhere discrete to meet, because of their divergent political prominence. He told me that they would both consider it difficult if lobby correspondents were to see them together. Will that be alright with you?"

"Of course Ma'am," Tristan replied, "It will be a pleasure. She is a bit spectacular is she not? I am sure that the removal of the embargo on Chinese cotton wear must be handled with absolute discretion."

"Sam, don't be naughty." Lady Margaret chuckled, "He will ring you direct to book the days when they would like to take tea. Charge what they charge at Claridge's, I am sure that he will pay cash and tip well."

Even with the added interest of the usually twice a week visit by the Minister with the Lady member of the Lords, Tristan's fears that a scandal might affect his future faded. The first party of the New Year had been a relatively quiet affair, a 'Burns Night Supper', with a twist. Although each man read or recited a Burns poem, as normal, each lady followed with a Shakespeare sonnet.

Both before and after the readings the guests voted for their favourite, the English or the Scottish Bard. The swing in votes to Burns surprised everybody. Antonin had provided a buffet supper of Elizabethan and Jacobean dishes with haggis the centrepiece. Jenny arranged for a piper to support the men; for the ladies she had engaged a quartet of Elizabethan music enthusiasts who played music composed or arranged for the lute, viol, hautboy and a harpsichord.

'The Flappers and Lounge Lizards dance,' brought the first report in the press about Old Sloans Re-united that alarmed Tristan. The very slim Jenny has suggested the Flappers Dance, to bring a politically correct balance to the attractions of the 'Monte Carlo and Bust' party. It had been the best party to date. For flapper music to dance to, Jenny's friend, William Erskin Powell used an old red and cream 'Dansette' record player to play his Grandfather's collection of vinyl records of Jack Hilton, Ambrose, Len Stone and the singer Al Bowly.

With William's help, Jenny had decorated the ballroom with art nouveaux lights, together with huge blown up copies of photographs taken from Lady Margaret's album of pictures of her parents, with their friends, at parties at the Café de Paris, Claridge's and Café Royal as well as pictures taken on the Union Castle Boats, during trips to South Africa.

Tristan had fitted himself out with a white cocktail barman's coat from Mr Veasey of 'Rose, for Second Hand Clothes'. Jenny had prevailed upon him to produce a range of cocktails popular in the twenties. Tristan had complained, "I have forgotten the ingredients of all the cocktails I ever knew, I would not know a 'Screwdriver' from a 'Gimlet,' or a 'White Russian' from a 'Moscow Mule'". Antonin interrupted, "Why should that bother you, just bluff, as all cocktail barmen do. No one who asks for anything more complicated than a Bloody Mary will have a clue of what is in it, or how to make it. If anyone challenges you, he or she will only be a show off. Tell whoever it is that yours is the original recipe from Victor's bar in the Antilles. It always wins the argument."

The newspaper article that concerned Tristan had been written, as a tease, by Andrew the broadsheet gossip columnist that Lady Margaret had invited to the Game and Games party, and the 'Flappers' dance. The headline, 'Midge the Match Maker' an alliterative style usually more favoured by the redtops, caught his eye. Under the 20-point headline, the article simply stated,

314

'Lady Margaret Elizabeth Bowes-Litton, the hostess known as 'Midge' to her old friends from her debutant days, regularly holds a politically neutral salon at a secret location in Mayfair. Her genteel parties for the gentry, and parties of different persuasions, have engaged a leading Tory Peer and an industrious Labour Minister. He clearly wishes her to cross over to become his leading lady, while she wants him to be her commons rat.'

As soon as he had calmed down after he had read the article, Tristan took the unusual step of ringing Lady Margaret, his vicarious boss.

"Hello Sam, I thought that you might ring this morning, I am pleased to learn that you have your finger on the media pulse. It is Andrew's piece in the celebrity spy column that you are ringing me about, is it not?"

Tristan replied, "Yes ma-am, I am concerned about the red-tops, The Sun, The Mirror, Express and the Mail and the News of the World. Their reporters will know who the couple are in one second from the heavyweight clues your friend Andrew has given them. Even 'Hello' and 'Today' will get it before the week is out. Perhaps we should cancel our next few parties, maybe lie low for a bit."

Lady Margaret would have none of it, "Nonsense, I will not have our fun spoiled by the tittle tattle press. Perhaps I will have a word with Andrew to ask him to leave the lovers alone. They really are suited to each other. I will not invite him to the 'Bacchanal', so please do not worry my dear old Eeyore."

Tristan almost choked, "What! What bacchanal is that for goodness sake?" Lady Margaret laughed, "Oh didn't Jenny tell you, we are to have a fancy dress party early in March, 'Carry on Cleo.'"

Chapter 23

Although Jenny's arrangements for the 'Carry on Cleo Bacchanal' impressed Tristan, his anxiety that it might provide Edna Spitewinter with an opportunity to bring him down meant that her preparations gave him no pleasure.

He worried; he doubted whether he would have the will to recover, as he had done with the Retread's help, after several events beyond his control had left him without any visible means of support, and with a bench on the Thames Embankment his only comfort. It seemed to him that once again, events had conspired against him.

He felt that if he did lose his job, he would have failed Harry's trust, He would not be able to go back to Retreads.

He also felt that despite Stan and his success in bringing the forgers to the attention of the law, he would not dare to turn up, destitute, at the planned reunion of the Grey Haired Knights.

To set the scene for the party, with the help of William Erskin Powell, Jenny had mounted old posters around the ballroom that had advertised the films Gladiator and Spartacus.

From the hall balcony, they had hung a three-meter by two-meter copy of the more famous poster from the film 'Carry on Cleo', the famous portrayal of Amanda Barry, starring as Cleopatra bathing in ass's milk. In the ballroom, they had replaced all the formal furniture with cushions and long low tables.

Deeming vinyl records played on the old 'Dansette' record player used for the Flappers ball inadequate, Lady Margaret had asked William to use the Major's modern powerful hi-fi system. William had willingly burnt a CD with a compilation of music including the Bacchanal, from Saint-Saëns's 'Samson and Delilah', Verdi's Aïda, Richard Strauss's 'Salome', interspersed with extracts from the sound tracks of the films 'Gladiator' and 'Spartacus'. A young friend of Jenny's, a student at Goldsmiths, agreed to play the harp. In return for a small bribe, he had consented to wear a short toga and sandals, with leather thongs criss-crossed around his calves. In turn, he had volunteered his petite girl friend to hide inside one of two papier-mâché vases hired from 'Palmbrokers'. The Ali Baba sized vases had peepholes at eye level but no base. They were old pantomime props that enabled actors to change stage positions unseen.

On the day of the bacchanal, Tristan's anxiety increased when Harry Evans rang him, early in the day, to read out a small but disturbing item from one of the redtop newspaper's political gossip column. He added that other newspapers also had the story.

'Whips are questioning their hard working Minister about his party habits, and his union ambitions. His party chums are talking about a cross over liaison with a leading lady from the wrong side of the other place.'

When he had finished reading, Harry had warned, "Tristan take care; the editors have let slip the mongrels of scandal. They have the scent. They will find your covert, even in deepest Mayfair. They will run you to earth. He added softly, "Perhaps I worry too much, so I wish you well with your night of revelry. Please give that sweet Lady Margaret my best regards. Do not mention the press item; there is no need to pass on my worries to her. I doubt that even the Paparazzi will fasten onto Erskin House tonight, unless that Spitewinter woman is involved." Harry's mention of the Spitewinter woman churned Tristan's stomach.

Antonin had created a buffet with roast suckling pig, roast goose, morsels of lamb braised with honey, rosemary and sage. He had also roasted several dozen quail that he labelled roast dormouse. He supplemented these dishes with silver salvers mounded with flat bread, fresh figs, grapes black, grapes green, dates, pomegranates, apricots, and peaches arranged together with other exotic fruits that Tristan could not name.

He also had ready, to send up from his underground kitchen, the finest array of fruit ices Tristan had ever seen. Lady Margaret insisted that Tristan must decant the wine from the bottles into amphora shaped vessels she had bought from a Chelsea flower shop. To Tristan's relief, although rough fired clay on the outside, the potters had glazed the inside of the vase.

After he had put up a noble, nevertheless impossible defence, against, 'We Girls', a term Lady Margaret used for the combined force of Mary, Jenny and herself, Tristan finally succumbed.

He dressed as a Roman slave in an outfit Jenny had hired from 'Angels'. The guests, some of whom Tristan recognised from earlier parties, mixed easily with those new to Old Sloane's Reunited. Under Jenny's direction they were all soon in the party mood. She had split them into teams to play Roman dice games, a Roman form of marbles that used marble not coloured glass balls, and chariot racing.

For the chariot racing, Lady Margaret had been to Hamleys to buy a horse racing game. To each of the six horses Jenny had attached a cut out paper chariot and charioteer and numbered them one to six. The guests who wanted to play had to bid to buy one of the six horses in an auction run by an Old Sloan who had been Chairman of Crockfords. All the money raised at auction went to the Retreads' charity, but Lady Margaret gave appropriate Roman themed prizes to the charioteer who won.

All the guests had come in Roman or Egyptian dress, some hired from theatrical costume agencies, some from fancy dress shops. The few homemade costumes were amongst the best.

Most of the men had opted for simulated full togas, because they could wear them over casual sports clothes. A few, presumptuously, wore a laurel wreath; the insignia of an Emperor or of a Caesar, others carried a staff. Most of the older men wore purple togas, as they thought it befitted their senior status.

The Ladies had used the opportunity to dress in splendour, some in minimal sensuous splendour. Lady Margaret opted for style over historical accuracy. She looked charming in a simple white full-length brushed cotton dress, tied at the waist with a gold braid. A wide heavy collar of gold rectangular beads accentuated her slender neck. She completed her costume with a replica of Nefertiti's famous headdress.

The two protagonists of the gossip columns did not arrive together; the Secretary of State came a little late, the Lady Elizabeth even later. From where William operated the Major's hi-fi, system he saw Lady Slessinger arrive and hand her full-length fur cape to Mary. Determined that she should have the grand entrance her appearance deserved, he cued in Gounod's 'Entrance of the Queen of Sheba'. She ignored the anachronism of more than a thousand years to make a regal entrance. Conversation stopped; after a pause, applause followed. Lady Slessinger did not acknowledge the welcome; she went straight to the Minister, her afternoon tea partner.

After a very brief head-to-head whispered conversation, they left the ballroom on their way to Tristan's pantry. Tristan, who had seen the exchange, quickly joined them to ask, "Is there anything that I can do. You seem to be concerned."

Clearly worried, Lady Elizabeth, replied, "Oh Sam, good of you to ask. I do not know for sure, however when I got out of the car, outside at the front door, someone may have taken my photograph. Because of the flash, I could not see anyone. Perhaps I imagined it. Oh dear, I don't know what to do."

"Bloody hell, I hope not," the Minister responded sharply, but as he could see that Lady Slessinger appeared to be concerned, he spoke softly in his deliberate broad northern accent, to make light of the incident.

"Nay lass, dunna worry, were in now, here we'll stay. I Julius Spartacus Romulus Nero Caesar, best dresser of a salad since Culpepper, will send out the Praetorian Guard, to throw into the Lions Corner House any plebeians, who may lurk out there. Come on lass; we will go back in. Sam has a good line in Carthaginian bootleg on offer."

He took his Lady straight to Lady Margaret. That done, he came back to Tristan to ask, "Sam, please check out this flash business. Neither of us wants to make our association, I mean friendship, oh, sorry Sam, you must have guessed. Yes, we are what the moderns call an item, but we are old fashioned. For various reasons we don't want to announce our engagement just yet."

Tristan pointed to his toga, bare legs and sandals, "I can't go out dressed like this, not into the mean streets of Mayfair, not without a vest on. However, my friend Jack Drummond is in the kitchen, he drives Lady Margaret on these party nights. He is security trained, I will ask him to have a good look round."

It only took Tristan a moment to find Jack in Antonin's kitchen. After he told him of the Minister's worries that the paparazzi may be harassing Lady Elizabeth, he asked him to go quietly out of the back door, in order to reach a point from where, un-noticed, he could see whether there were any photographers around the front door.

"I can't do it Jack, I have work to do upstairs. Ten minutes should give you plenty of time to see if we are under surveillance, under siege, or if our gutter is free of the press."

Already on his way out, Jack called back over his shoulder, "Right oh Slavious."

Upstairs, Tristan nodded to the Minister to indicate that the he had arranged for the necessary recognisance. Less than ten minutes later, all Tristan's worries were justified. When Jack came to the ballroom door Tristan could see that he wanted to talk.

320

He gave no casual wave, nor did he give the hoped for thumbs up sign to indicate the all clear. In the pantry, Jack said "Sorry Tristan, bad news. There is only one cameraman out front at the present; however, I am afraid that is not the full report. On my way out, three chattering women blocked the corridor to the back door. Two were the women who wash up for you. From your description, the other woman was the housekeeper who used to work here. They moved when I muttered, 'I need some fags'. When I past them, I heard one of the women say. 'Yes they are both here. She looks a right tart; he looks old enough to be her dad.' I could have smacked her."

As he had failed to deal with the Spitewinter woman Tristan felt angry with himself. His reply was terse, "Damn and double drat, that is not what I wanted to hear. The paparazzi will cluster thicker than twitchers round a roosting dodo. The redtop gossip columns will have to go 'Broad Sheet' to fit the page.

Clear thought is what we need. I shall ring Harry to ask him to come here with Stan. We need to field the full first team. I admire the lovebirds. I also enjoy my job. The Major is due home from South Africa next month. If he finds out that on my watch I have allowed scandalous behaviour in his home, he will sack me. I shall have no home. I will be back on the streets.

Tristan spoke softly into the phone in his pantry, "Harry, are you still up?" When Harry replied, "Yes boyo, I am always up to something, until someone finds out what, before they tell me to stop. What up is it that you call me about, when you should be looking after the revellers?"

"Sorry to disturb you at this late hour" Tristan said, "But I have a problem. That Spitewinter poisoned chalice of bile has put a terrier into our bolt. Any minute, I expect the hounds to sound at the entrance."

Harry Evans's acute mind had already started to plan what he might do. He told Tristan not to take any decisions until he arrived. He said that he would come over, by taxi, and use the back

321

door. His final comment failed to lift Tristan's spirits, "Keep the guests busy, they have no need to know. I look forward to seeing you in your nightie"

Jenny had the party fully engaged with the Roman games. The Minister and his Lady were relaxed, although they did not join in the games, they lay on cushions, deep in serous conversation, occasionally picking at the exotic food.

Half an hour after calling for Harry's help, Tristan saw him in his pantry and went to join him. Harry gave him a cheery greeting, "Are you licensed for those knees boyo. Good effort, but not quite Edward Poynter's 'Faithful unto death', is it."

Tristan, ignored the insults, "Good of you to come Harry, I don't know what to do for the best. The 'Whip Lash' scandal of the early nineties, and the earlier Profumo affair at Clivedon that rocked Macmillan's Government, come to mind. Scandal at Erskin House with leading members of both houses of parliament involved will not bring down the government, but I shall lose my job when the Major is told."

Harry, with a smile full of reassurance said, "Don't worry; with my brain, your local knowledge and Stan's strength, we will find a way out of the brambles. By the way, I spoke to Stan on the phone; he is already in the kitchen with Antonin."

"Harry Evans, how wonderful to see you," Lady Margaret had come to look for Tristan. "What is it that Sam does not have to worry about?"

Tristan replied before Harry could, "Well ma'am, we think, no I am afraid we know that the redtop press have been told about tonight's party. It follows that the paparazzi are likely to be here, in force. I believe 'Door stepping' is what the press call it. I am sorry Ma'am a photographer has already upset the lovebirds. The Minister has told me that they don't yet wish to announce their engagement." Lady Margaret trilled, "Engagement, how wonderful, I knew they were right for each other, but how do you propose to disengage from the enemy at our door?"

Tristan replied, "Well frankly ma'am, I am stumped. All I can come up with is to carry on normally, pretending that we do not know why they have laid siege to our citadel. I have asked Harry to come over because he is the wisest man in Christendom. Stan is already here, in the kitchen to give strength when needed."

Lady Margaret, who seemed unruffled by the news said, "Sam, please get Harry a drink. She turned to Harry, "Come, you must join the party. I shall introduce you to Lady Slessinger." At first Harry would have none of it, "No, no, Midge, no indeed, you don't want an old man like me in there, besides I am not in fancy dress."

Tristan laughed for the first time that evening, "Harry don't be unrealistic. No one will notice that you are not in fancy dress. You always look like an old-testament prophet, even if your py-jamas show under your trouser turn-ups." After he looked down at his slippers, Harry gave a sheepish grin, "Oh Dieu, so they are, I must have been ready for bed when you called. Perhaps you are right, no one will notice. I will risk ridicule because five minutes recognisance is worth two hours of battle. Harry took Midge's arm, "Ma'am since you are Nefertiti, I shall be your Akhenaten. I will be delighted if you will introduce me to the Queen of the Nile. Is it Shakespeare's Anthony, or Shaw's Caesar who escorts her tonight? Whoever he is, I would also like to meet him."

To give Edna Spitewinter the least possible chance of embarrassing the guests, Tristan went down to the kitchen where he paid her friends, the morning cleaners, the cash in hand double pay they had demanded.

He told them to go home, even though they had not finished. Sure that they were in league with Spitewinter, he escorted them from the premises, via the back door.

After a midnight sortie, Jack Drummond reported to Tristan that a crowd of at least ten men with cameras had gathered close to the front door. He said that some even had small stepladders to gain advantage and that he had noticed two women with tape recorders. He further dampened Tristan's spirits when he confirmed that there were two men, at the back door, each with a camera.

Harry had established a war cabinet in Tristan's pantry where they decided they would call an end to the party at about half-past one, with all the guests, except for the Minister and Lady Slessinger, marshalled to leave together. The two who attract media attention had agreed to stay the night, in two of the guest bedrooms. Lady Margaret, claimed the Chinese Room, so that she could also stay the night.

To break the siege by duping the press, Harry persuaded Mary and Jenny's boyfriend William to act as the lovebirds, and make a dash to get away from Erskin House without giving the press a photo opportunity.

Jack Drummond agreed to drive the Daimler to the front door, at one a.m. precisely, ready for Tristan to open the back door of the car, so that Mary, hand in hand with William, could run to the car with their heads and shoulders covered with a blanket. They agreed that, even if the ploy did not work, it would at least allow Mary to bring day clothes for Lady Margaret in the morning.

The deception worked. Jack Drummond drew the Daimler Majestic Major up against pavement, close to the front door. Tristan came down the steps first, to open the car door. Jack pipped the car horn. A moment later, two blanket-covered figures were in the back of the car.

Tristan slammed the door shut; Drummond drove the Daimler away, at speed. The press had little or no chance. Although they had flashed their cameras, and shouted banal questions, most of them slowly drifted away when they realised that they did not have the pictures, or the statements they wanted to sell to the prurient press.

At half past one in the morning, shortly after Lady Margaret had presented the prizes, Harry took the microphone that William, had plugged into the hi-fi system.

"Ladies and Gentleman," he declaimed, "You do not need to know who I am. For reasons of national security, I hope that you will not ask, however please take notice, for I speak with authority. Tonight, you may have imagined that great Caesar brought the Queen of the Nile to your party. It was merely a sorcerer's trick, a figment of your imagination, perhaps an hallucination induced by the wine that flowed freely from the amphora. On your Old Sloanes honour, I ask that you pledge to deny that they were here. When you leave, you may hear the siren voices of the vulgar press who will offer bribes. Pass them by. Talk happily with each other. Ignore them. Only if you keep your pledge, can we meet again for more revels. It will be best for you protection if you all leave together, as a disciplined troop, to march the short way to Claridge's, where I have arranged for a fleet of Taxis to take you to your homes. This will give me time to issue the necessary 'D' notices."

When Harry got back to the pantry, he breathed out a great sigh before he said, "May the good Lord forgive my porky pies. If he wills it, they will all believe that I am Special Branch, MI5, MI6, and the couples personal ex SAS bodyguard, all fused together and disguised as the profit Methuselah. Tonight, grouped together, not to let the side down, they will keep the secret. From tomorrow, they will dine out on the excitement for weeks. "Tristan, a man relieved, called out, "Brilliant Harry, you are a genius; I knew you would find a way."

"Don't count your chickens yet, I have a bad feeling in my bunion," Harry replied, "After we have marched out the guests, we must take what rest we can. I want you all down ready for one of Antonin's full English breakfasts by eight o'clock, sharp."

With Lady Margaret, Jenny and Tristan busy fetching coats, scarves, handbags, forgotten spectacles and gloves, Harry had the guests formed up in the hall, in ranks, like a squad of Chelsea pensioners, First World War regulation, four deep, with a nursing auxiliary attached. Tristan unbolted both front doors. Harry called out parade style, "On my order, I want an orderly march straight to Claridge's. Mind the steps."

The guests took it all as a great game. On Harry's order "Quick march," Stan opened the left hand side of the door while Antonin opened the right hand side. The guests, led by Jenny, swept out, in ragged ranks of four. Tristan saw just one or two camera flashes before the doors closed behind the troop.

He smiled when he heard some of the wags start to sing a favourite farewell song of their youth, 'Show me the way to go home, I'm tired and I want to go bed'. "Well, that's a good job well done." Tristan said to himself, after he had congratulated everybody.

Minutes later the phone rang. Before he had time to say Major Erskin Powell's residence, his stomach churned again.

The Spitewinter woman's voice caused it, "I told you that you were a clever dick, but not clever enough to best me. The Major will sack you for this. He will be sure to give me back my job. The papers will be full of it tomorrow, and all of next week. They will describe Erskin House, the Major's house, as no more than a cheap knocking shop. Your little plan did not work. After you paid off my loyal friends Barbara and Caroline, Barbara came back to the house to watch your pathetic performance. Barbara is small. She used one of the Ali Baba vases to observe. Your silly trick backfired on you. She watched your ridiculous efforts to fool the press. She has only just come out. I have given the full story to my friends in the newspaper business. Just in time for the scandal pages in the late editions of the big hitters. They are paying me good money. Cretin, I told you that you were nothing but a bow tied ponce. The papers will rate you as a pimp for the tart you have shacked up with the kerb crawler, not just tonight, but for all those cosy afternoon short lets. The Major will know all the lurid details tomorrow. He reads the papers on the internet."

Chapter 24

On the morning after the 'Carry on Cleo' bacchanal, Tristan felt that whatever happened, it would come to no good.

The only people still in fancy dress were the Secretary of State and Lady Slessinger.

Neither seemed the slightest embarrassed. Both enjoyed the breakfast prepared by Antonin, however after breakfast, Lady Margaret took Lady Slessinger upstairs to gossip, leaving Harry, Tristan, and Stan, with the Secretary of State to deal with matters, as they stood.

In his effected blunt northern manner, the minister asked for help. "Na then lads, what can we do to sort out this mess? Lizzie and I want to get out of here and we don't want the press to take photographs. Tristan tells me that the press have sent in reinforcements. I would be happy to make a formal announcement of our engagement on the steps this morning, although I don't think it would be fair on Lizzie, not dressed as we are. The press would make sordid assumptions about our sleepover. Anyway, the ring is still at Asprey's. They are re-sizing it, not the diamond, the ring bit. Has anyone any idea of how we can do an early morning flit, un-noticed. I'm beggared if I have a solution."

Harry had refused the offer of a bed. He chose to sleep in one of the armchairs in the library, with his feet on the pouffe. However, he felt rested, bright and cheerful when he told them that he had a plan. His declaration assured him of their full attention; he did not disappoint them.

"Throughout my long life, I have learned that when faced with a problem, the answer can be found in history or literature. When I woke this morning, I observed that both applied. The solution to our problem stared at me from the floor."

Puzzled, Tristan asked, "What was it that stared at you from the floor?" Harry almost shouted, "Why the carpet boyo, the Persian carpet."

"What is it, a magic carpet that will fly them out of Erskin House, at night, from an upstairs window?" Tristan asked. "No you man of little classical education. Don't you see Stan can play the part of Appollodorus to smuggle Cleopatra past the press, rolled up in that elegant silk carpet, the one on the floor in the library."

"Good Lord, there's a thing," the Minister said, caught up with Harry's enthusiasm. "You mean, as I saw it in Shaw's, Caesar and Cleopatra when we did it at school. Good idea, but what about me, how do I get out?"

Harry had his idea ready, "I've thought about that too, you are not one of the obese of this land. I am sure that, knees bent, you will fit into that rather grand monk's chest in the hall, the one just inside the door. Stan, our human forklift, will carry you out, tucked under one arm, with no more effort than I would use to carry a rolled up newspaper. That will deceive all who watch. Even the paparazzi will assume that the chest is empty

"Good Lord there's another thing," the minister said. Harry went on to explain the rest of his remarkable plan. "We are in luck; it is Sunday, the Good Lord's special day. I have already been on the phone to our friend Mr. Bentley of 'Beeswax and Tung-oil'. He has promised to bring his large van round feigning to collect some furniture that needs attention, together with a few paintings that need to be re-stretched."

Harry's idea excited Lady Slessinger, who had come down from her room, with Lady Margaret, to find out if the men had a plan. "You don't mean Figgy Bentley do you?" she asked, "He is an old friend of mine. If you do, that is good enough for me. I'm game if you are Ralf."

Clearly happy to continue with his plan, Harry asked, "How many are there in the paparazzi pack outside?" Jenny, who had come back to "Enjoy the fun", as she put it, reported, "I reckon I saw about thirty, however I am afraid that the wicked witch Spitewinter, followed by her two coven crones circle the press pack on their broomsticks. By the way, there is a police car, parked up, further along the crescent, and two beat policemen who watch from the other side."

After Tristan found some cushions to put in the bottom of the monk's chest, the Right Honourable the Secretary of State for Industry and Reconstruction tried it for size.

He assured his anxious partner that he would be quite comfortable, that he could breathe easily. He made them all laugh when he promised not to smoke.

Stan came beaming into the hall clutching a long piece of canvas fire hose he had cut from the reel that hung by the back door. With a sheepish grin he said, "Sorry boss, needs must, I could not find any rope. This will be more comfortable. If I loop it round the chest, take both ends across my back, over my right shoulder, I can carry his lordship to the van, no problem. If I hold the two ends in my left hand, close against my much bigger chest, it will leave my right arm free to steady the load."

"Brilliant, Stan," Tristan patted him on his massive shoulder, "If you get this right, I will give you a chocolate gold medal to make up for the medal you missed when you opted for the free West rather than to stay behind the curtain with the Reds."

With Stan's help, Tristan brought the Persian carpet from the library to the hall, for a rehearsal. With little fuss, Lady Slessinger rolled herself inside the carpet. Stan lifted the precious bundle, as easily as he would pick up an eiderdown. Harry's calm voice settled everyone, "All we need is our friend Figgy Bentley, with his van and we will be under starters orders. We must be on our guard, I am sure that the spiteful Spitewinter, first of the three sisters, will try to put her broomstick into the spokes of our well-oiled wheels. Before Stan carries out the valuable consignments we can put up a smoke screen if we take some other antique bits and pieces to the van."

Harry grinned, "Oh, sorry Ralf, no offence meant." When Jenny called out, "The van is here," Lady Slessinger giggled; the Minister blew out a long breath before he said, "This is a new sort of cabinet for me. I hope that it is more solid then the one I sit in at number 10."

Mr. Bentley, dressed in a traditional brown smock coat of the removal trade rang the front door bell to the accompaniment of several camera flashes. He came up trumps. He had a quick mind quick enough to create his own script. "Do you mind chaps; I have a job to do. Sunday is the only time I can park to load up. I have to work, even if you don't. Please keep to one side of the door, clear of the steps."

With Mr. Bentley inside, Harry had explained the situation, as well as his plan. Figgy added his own ideas. He first went to greet Lady Slessinger, before he said.

"That big picture of Cleo in the bath, it is large enough to make a perfect screen if Tristan helps me to carry it out to obscure Stan from the cameras, when he carries the Minister out in the chest. It will hide even Stan's great bulk."

"Good man, great idea," beamed Harry, obviously well pleased with the way things progressed. However, he added, "Please make sure that the back of the picture is facing the press. We do not want them to get over excited."

It did not take long for Figgy, helped by Stan, to take a few small antique pieces of furniture to the van and stow them safely. Back in the hall Figgy asked, "Ready Minister?"

Lady Slessinger gave the Minister a kiss before she closed the chest lid. Stan looped the hose round the chest, bent at the knees, took both ends of the hose across his back over his shoulder, before he called softly, "Door." He straightened to full height, pulled the hose ends down across his massive chest until the monk's chest, with its human cargo, came to waist height. Once steady, he walked calmly to the door where Tristan waited with Mr. Bentley, ready to carry the large framed poster to screen him from the cameras.

Within seconds, both the chest and poster were in the van. The press had been unable to take a single useful photograph. Not even out of breath, Stan slipped the hose free, before he walked back up the steps into the house. Lady Margaret said, "Now for the easy bit, Lizzie, if you would not mind." With practised ease, Lady Slessinger rolled herself into the carpet. Figgy Bentley took over as foreman. "Right, that's the lot. Tristan, I will get ready to drive off, just as soon as you close the van doors. Give them a hefty clout so I will be sure that Cleopatra is in, secure, with the doors closed."

When Stan lifted the carpet bundle Harry said, "Be gentle with her, she is a bit special this Queen of the Nile."

They waited to make sure Figgy was in the driver's seat and had started the engine, ready for the Tristan's signal to move off. Stan carried the precious bundle in the crook of his arms to walk the short distance to the van. Tristan followed ready to close the van doors and give Mr. Bentley the signal to move off.

When Harry closed the doors to Erskin House behind them, he sighed with relief. He went straight to the window that overlooked Lee's Crescent to watch the final act in which Stan would safely deliver Cleopatra to the waiting Caesar.

However, his final act did not play out according to his plan. It did not play as Shakespeare wrote it, nor did it play to Shaw's romantic script. Historical re-enactment broke down into modern farce.

Mrs. Spitewinter, the evil Edna, had guessed that Stan was using the carpet to smuggle out Lady Slessinger. She broke through the few remaining photographers and knocked Tristan out of her way. She pulled one of the policemen with her screaming, "The carpet is full of drugs. The one that followed the big ape is the drug baron; arrest him."

The other two harpies were shouting, "It's true, it's true, he's a right bastard he is. They were all stoned last night, we saw them." Both policemen, conscious that the press wanted a story, were in a fix, not knowing quite what to do. Spitewinter screamed again, "Arrest him you fools, before he smuggles the stuff away in the carpet."

Spitewinter had a wicked device fitted over the four fingers of each hand. At the back of the hand they appeared innocent, just a ring on each finger. Viewed palm up, each connected ring had a fishhook sharp point that curved inwards like a cat's claw. Like a cat, she sprang to claw at the carpet. When she failed to make any impression, she attacked Stan's face, ripping deep bleeding scratches across his forehead, down the side of his face, as far as his throat. Stan batted her away with his one free arm. Nevertheless, it upset his balance. When he turned to go back up the steps into the house, he tripped. However, he managed to set down his precious bundle gently enough. Spitewinter, with one foot on the edge of the carpet, used both clawed hands to make it unroll down the shallow steps into Lee's Crescent. It left a startled Cleopatra exposed, not to Caesar, but to the unsympathetic cameras.

Farce escalated into pandemonium, which degenerated into chaos. The paparazzi fought each other for the best angle with the inevitable climax of a Greek not Roman tragedy. Tristan, blazing mad that Spitewinter had frustrated him, thought that he must be hallucinating when he caught a glimpse of the strange old eccentric with the stitch brimmed hat. The man who he thought had sought him out previously; once in Scagill, once on the embankment, again when sight of him caused him to trip over the sign that led him to Rose for Second Hand Clothes. He still wore the wide stitch brimmed hat, straggly white beard under a droopy moustache, although his gait did not seem real.

Wraith like, he passed though the brawl, but it seemed that he did not touch anyone, or that anyone, other than himself, was conscious of him. It appeared to Tristan, that although the old man must have been too far away to touch Spitewinter, even with his outstretched arm extended by his thin black walking stick, but something hit her with such force, that she went, off balance, backwards down the shallow steps to fall against the side of Mr. Bentley's 'Beeswax and Tung Oil' van. Both her hands slapped hard against its side. Mr. Bentley, thinking this to be Tristan's signal, let in the clutch to speed away.

It had to happen. The law of unforeseen consequences combined with the laws of nature. The frictional resistance and mass of the unsecured monk's chest, even with the minister inside it, did not equal the force of the van's acceleration. The chest fell off the back of the van into Lee's Crescent. The lid flew open to reveal a very irritate Minister of the Crown, dressed in a purple toga. The Minister became the new focus of all the cameras.

Harry came out to help injured Stan. The Secretary of State pushed through the frenzied press pack to aid Lady Slessinger back up the steps into the house. Tristan called out to Harry, "Get an ambulance for Stan; I want a word with the Police." When he returned, he told everyone that the police had sent the three women away, handcuffed, in a riot van. He added that the police would take a statement from Stan, after the hospital had patched him up. "I have told the press that an announcement will be made on the steps of Erskin House, after we have had time for a cup of tea."

Rather tentatively, he asked, "I hope that is alright with you Minister?" Lady Margaret with Mary, who had come with day clothes for her mistress, had taken Lady Slessinger to the bedroom she had occupied during the previous night to restore the damage to her hairdo, make-up and costume.

Harry took the Secretary of State into the library, where they were alone. Harry said, in a voice earnest enough to convince a sceptic that all publicity is good, "Look you boyo, this morning has been a right shambles, nevertheless you can both come out of it well, if you appeal to the romantic that is in us all. You mentioned earlier that, but for the lack of a ring, and your fancy dress, you might have been prepared to announce your engagement on the steps. Well, why not, you both look wonderful, the sun is shining; the steps to the door of Erskin House make an appropriate setting. Go out there with your lovely fiancée. Announce to the press that you love each other and are to be married. Use the press to tell the whole world that true love can cross the irrational divide of political persuasion. The editors will crucify you if you try to fob them off, however if you play the part with confidence, they will claim it was 'them what done it', while they shed tears of joy at their circulation increase."

A week after the Bacchanal, the three friends were crowded into Harry's room at Retreads, reading the Sunday papers. The papers had front-page photographs of the 'Happy Couple' in front of the beautiful double door in Lee's Crescent, Mayfair.

Both the Minister and his fiancée had recognised the wisdom of Harry's advice. Every editor had chosen only the best, the most dignified pictures they had bought from the paparazzi. All the papers had spread their romance over many pages. Lady Slessinger looked radiant, in all the pictures. The Secretary of State, standing one discrete step above his fiancée, to balance the arrangement, had the air of a true statesman.

The photographs of Stan made him look like a monster Pudsey Bear with bandages around his forehead, across one eye, down both cheeks to finish all round his throat, yet despite his injuries, he had an easy smile.

Only the 'Guardian' referred to him as Appollodorus.

On top form, Harry wore his expansive smile, when he picked up the 'Sunday Express'. "I must read this one again, the one that talks about the vile woman who tried to wreck a real romance."

Stan had a broad non-vindictive grin, "It says here, in the 'Mirror', that Spitewinter could get a couple of years, at least, for G.B.H."

Because Tristan had not spoken for a while, Stan asked, "What is the matter with you Angol. We all done good, but all morning you have had on a face as long as a runner bean long passed its sell by date. Come on, out with it."

Tristan heaved a sigh, fit for a jilted TV soap heroine before he said, in a flat voice, "Lady Margaret called me earlier this morning. The Major has come home, weeks early. He has asked to see me this afternoon, at four o'clock, so that will be that. I shall be back on that seat in Victoria Embankment Gardens, a down and this time permanently out vagrant, ready to share cold day old chips with my peers. Harry, it's what I used to call a double bugger day. I have not had one of those since the day that you took me into Retreads."

"Don't be too down boyo;" Harry smiled a sort of distant smile of recognition, "I am sure that Retreads will fit you up with a job, should things go against you. I hardly think that Midge will let you down. After all, the idea came from her, not you. You have only done your duty, as you saw fit." Tristan said, "Fit, I think he will have a fit. He is very 'Old School' you know."

"That's as may be Tristan," Harry said, "But old school' has always been an honourable school."

At four o'clock prompt, Tristan waited in his pantry for the Major's summons. To his delight, Lady Margaret, not the Major, called him into the Library. Unusually, she did not ask him to sit down or call him Sam. She spoke formally, "Good afternoon Mr. Edward. The Major will be through in a minute or two. He has just had a couple of hours rest after his long flight, plus the inevitable delay at Heathrow. Drummond picked him up, so I have not seen him yet. Tristan thought her coldness not a good omen. His poor spirit did not recover, even when Lady Margaret went on in a more familiar tone, "I wonder if the Major has seen today's Sunday Papers. I was disappointed that Old Sloanes did not get a mention. After all we brought them together."

Tristan replied, very formally, "Yes indeed you did, Lady Margaret." Tristan put a heavy stress on the word 'You', "Although I'm sure that neither of them were Sloanes. He came from trade unions and industry. Lady Slessinger is a career girl, a high flyer, far too young for your membership rules."

The revolving bookcase spun so fast that it projected rather than let the Major into the room. Immediately, like an un-caged lion he roared, "What in the name of all that is holy have you two rascals been up to. My house used as a bordello, my name traduced by the gutter press. Worst of all, you have harboured a damned socialist. What do you have to say to that eh? What do you have to say to that? Midge, I cannot believe you acted alone. This fellow here must have put you up to it. Am I right, eh, am I right? Or, have I got it wrong, did this chit of a girl here lure you from your duty sir, your duty eh?"

Tristan stood, as implacable as a terracotta soldier to say, "Sir, I am conscious that I have embarrassed you with unwelcome publicity and cannot therefore continue in your employment. I have already prepared a formal resignation letter that tomorrow I will deliver to your cousin Mr. Erskin-Powell. I shall have cleared my rooms before tonight. "

The Major turned away to face the bookcase. Tristan thought that he appeared to shake with rage. When Tristan looked towards Lady Margaret, she had curled up in the chair that she graced so well, her face turned away. To Tristan's surprise, he saw her laughing. When she turned again to look at him, "Oh Sam," was all she said.

The Major spun round, "Nonsense," he bellowed, "I will have none of it. I came home early, however obviously not early enough.

I seem to have missed all the fun. The last few months has cost me a small fortune in telephone calls. Midge has kept me informed; on a day-to-day basis don't you know, of your old-fashioned enterprise. However, there will have to be changes. We must be more organised. Erskin House will be the first new club of any style in London for a century. A new 'Pickwick Club'; we will call it Sam's, no not Sam's that sounds like a jazz joint or a betting shop. Weller's I think would be the thing. What do you say to that eh, what do you say to that? My wilful cousin Midge, together with you Sam, will both be directors, each with twenty-four percent of the shares, issued at a pound each; I shall be Chairman with fifty-two. We shall make that Secretary of State fellow, with his bride, honorary members. That will pull in people of all political persuasion; political correctness will be black balled. I will not allow any Nationalists, be they Scots, Welsh, Irish or English. It will be a Great British club. Our Annual Dinner will be held on Empire Day, the 24 May."

When the Major paused, Tristan realised that the phone in his pantry had been ringing for a very long time. Tristan knew that he was not in trouble when the Major suggested, "Perhaps you had better answer that Sam. Get rid of whoever it is, we three have much to talk about."

When Tristan walked quickly to the phone, only a few paces away across the hall, he felt a deep dread of the shrill monotonous beat of the demanding call. For some reason he knew it was the harbinger of bad news.

"Tristan, Stan here. I don't know how to say this any other way it's such awful news. Please come, we need you. Harry is dead."

****

The Reverend Branwell Evans had conducted both the church funeral service, as well as the committal at the crematorium for his beloved elder brother Harry.

After he had waited for the Vicar to talk with many of Harry's friends, Jack Drummond drove Branwell and Tristan, in the Mulliner Bentley, to Retreads where Antonin had prepared a buffet funeral tea.

He set them down by the larger of Retreads two doors, open because of the number of people expected to follow on from the funeral services.

When Tristan got out of the car, the sight of the a bearded eccentric, on the other side of the road, wearing a wide stitch brimmed hat that made him unmissable in any crowd, in any city, made the hair on the back of his neck rise; his skin prickled. Tristan was not sure that he was the same man who suggested that he go to evensong in Scagill where he had met Branwell. He was not the same as the fellow who had offered him cold chips in the Victoria Embankment Gardens, the amiable vagrant who had told him he would not make a fortune, but that his luck would change at the turn of the tide.

He certainly looked different, in many ways, to the curiosity that had later made him trip over the A frame that advertised Rose for Second Hand Clothes. He was different again to the figure he thought he saw during the brawl outside Erskin House. Although all were clearly different, Tristan felt a strange reality that they were connected to a force that had influenced all that had happened to him since he took a vow to put aside old age, to seek a worthwhile quest.

It had appeared again, with his thin black walking stick pointed straight at him, while it gave a gentle smile and a wave of recognition with the other hand. Before he could respond, a London bendy bus went passed to obscure Tristan's view across the road. Agitated, he asked Branwell Evans to excuse him. By taking risks to dodge the traffic, it only took Tristan a moment to cross the road. It did not surprise him that he found no trace of the curious eccentric, however it further saddened Tristan's already miserable day.

When all of the many mourners, who represented all stations in life, had left Retreads, the Reverend Branwell Evans asked Tristan to sit with him in what had been Harry's small office in the balcony of the old non-conformist chapel. Tristan spoke first.

"Vicar, who was Harry, he never talked about the past, or what he did before he came to Retreads? I asked him many times, I even threatened him with bright lights and the truth drug. He never answered. I always found that I had to answer his question."

Branwell Evans thought for a long time before he answered. "You will have noticed that during my short eulogy in St. Martins in the Fields, a church full to standing this morning, I did not talk about his early life. I only spoke about his work here at Retreads. I know that is what he would have wanted. Harry became an ordained priest when very young. After a few years, as a curate in Swansea, he served nearly all his formal ministry as a chaplain in the Royal Navy. He won an MC in Korea, though he never mentioned it. When he left the Navy, he worked in a Cheshire Home, where he found his dog collar a handicap when he worked with people who had lost their way. He remained an ordained priest until his death. He never lost his faith; he just chose to do God's work in his own way."

After a long silence Branwell spoke again, "Tristan, do you remember that day, not so long ago, when we first met in Scagill's parish church, that day when you saw God's kaleidoscope. It was a sign of God's purpose I am sure. Random floating dust that he knows will settle in good time. Perhaps he arranged it that you would settle here, at Retreads, to take the place of my dear brother."

Tristan protested, "I can't take his place, no one can, Harry was unique, I do not have the support of his deep religious conviction, nor his many gifts." Branwell said, "Perhaps not, it maybe that you cannot take his place. You can follow in his ways, because of all that he has taught you. I am sure that you have

339

true faith in God, as you understand him. Faith transcends all religious dogma. You can take on Retreads, able to carry on Harry's idea, but in your way. You have already achieved great things here. Lady Margaret has agreed to join the Board of Trustees. They want you to do it, Stan needs you to do it, the present guests and the Retread old boys expect you to do it."

Tristan recognised his true quest. He became Master of Retreads.

The End.

www.ingramcontent.com/pod-product-compliance
Lightning Source LLC
Chambersburg PA
CBHW062019170626
46813CB00001B/217